THE OVERTIME KISS

LAUREN BLAKELY

COPYRIGHT

Copyright © 2025 by Lauren Blakely
  LaurenBlakely.com
  Cover Design by © Qamber Designs & Media

ABOUT THE BOOK

Just what every bride dreams of—running straight from her cheating fiancé into the arms of a hot hockey star... and then getting hired as his kids' nanny.

Tyler Falcon is protective, flirtatious...and frustratingly responsible. We *almost* did something reckless when he found me alone in my wedding dress, and I blurted out all the things I'd never truly experienced.

Now, the sexy single dad is saving me again with a job I desperately need—and a promise to never mention The Night of 1001 Confessions.

I live in his house. Take care of his kids. Pretend I don't notice his heated gaze lingering on me after they fall asleep.

Until one night, the tension snaps.

Now we have a deal. Five lessons in seduction. No strings attached.

But he's not just good in bed. He spoils me with thoughtful gifts and supports my dreams. For the first time, I feel like I belong.

Except...this was never meant to last. I'm his

employee. He has kids to protect. And neither of us can afford to make a mistake.

The more nights we spend tangled up together though, the harder it is to pretend it's just physical. Because I'm not only falling for my boss—I'm falling for the man whose kids have stolen my heart.

Tropes: Jilted Bride, single dad/nanny, she's his daughter's skating coach, lessons in seduction, oops we almost banged before he hired me, confession of all secrets, love notes, forced proximity, major found family vibes

DID YOU KNOW?

To be the first to find out when all of my upcoming books go live click here!

PRO TIP: Add lauren@laurenblakely.com to your contacts before signing up to make sure the emails go to your inbox!

Did you know this book is also available in audio and paperback on all major retailers? Go to my website for links!

For content warnings for this title, go to my site or email me laurenblakelybooks@gmail.com.

THE OVERTIME KISS

By Lauren Blakely
Love and Hockey #5

1
———

I HEAR WEDDING BELLS AND VOICEMAILS

Sabrina

This wasn't the ceremony we'd rehearsed, but sometimes a bride has to improvise.

I gather the billowing tulle of my dress so it won't slow my hustle toward the Grand Ballroom of The Luxe Hotel in Lucky Falls. I only stop at the end of the hall to swallow my bridal rage and fasten on a smile while I'm still out of sight.

A glance around the corner shows the poised and polished wedding planner outside the ballroom door with her headset and tablet, directing the preparations like air traffic control.

Tessa is such a consummate professional that I almost feel bad for enlisting her unwitting help in this dastardly measure I'm about to take.

Almost.

Because sometimes revenge is best cooked up in the heat of the moment.

"Psst, Tessa," I whisper around the corner.

She snaps her blue gaze my way and blinks in surprise. Still, her blonde, news-anchor bob barely moves, and she adjusts quickly, abandoning her post to join me in the more private hallway.

"Sabrina, is everything okay?" she asks quietly. "You're supposed to be waiting in the—"

"The bridal suite. I know." I give my best *I can't wait to get hitched* face. "But I have a surprise for Chad. I didn't think I'd be able to find it, but I tracked it down at the last minute." I point to her iPad. "Can you cue up the MP3 I just sent you? It's the first voicemail Chad ever left me when he asked me out six years ago. And I know it would make him so, so happy to hear it today," I say, setting a hand on my heart and leaning in on the hearts and flowers.

"That's sweet. But are you sure you want to change things up now?"

"Positive." I don't want the first arrivals for the wedding that my mother planned—from the cloying all-white flower motif to the interchangeable cast of atten-dees plucked from the country club brochure—to spot the bride in the tiara and ball gown. I don't want any witnesses. "But don't tell a soul. It's a surprise."

Please don't ask any questions. Please don't play the file first.

If she does, I have a backup plan. I'll keep my phone tucked inside my white lace bra, ready, if necessary, to hit play on the, well, let's call it the new bridal march.

Tessa scans her iPad, spots my email, and nods. "Here it is. There's not much time for changes." Her crisp tone worries me for a moment, but then she adds, "But this is so nostalgic, delightfully so. How can I resist?"

"That's us." Romantic nostalgia is the theme my mother chose for the wine country wedding with its throwback vibe and my old-fashioned dress. And since Mom's nostalgia is paying Tessa's bills...

"I'll have it cued up and ready to go," she says.

"Right after Madison reaches the front." Somehow, I say the maid of honor's name without the sharp edge of anger cutting through my carefully composed calm. "And as soon as I take the first step down the aisle."

Timing is everything.

"Got it." Tessa gamely rolls with the change, and...fine, I do feel bad that she'll be collateral damage.

But then I mentally replay the misdirected voice message I received about an hour ago. The one that sent me through the five stages of romance grief in sixty minutes. I've reached a sixth stage now—getting even.

"You're the best. I'll leave you a five-star review." I scurry away, holding onto my tiara to keep it in place. It's the only thing I actually picked for this wedding, and I love it in all its sparkly outlandishness.

Ten minutes later, I stand at the French doors to the grand ballroom. My heart gallops, but my nerves are steel, conditioned by years of cutthroat ice-skating competitions.

My friends in attendance don't know the plan either. It's easier to keep it a surprise if I only trust myself with the scheme.

I square my shoulders, lift my chin, and smile without showing any teeth. I'm next to my father, ready to walk down the aisle and tell the world how I really feel about Chad Huntington.

The groom waits under a crystal chandelier in front of two hundred and fifty guests, with his perfectly coiffed blond hair, his perfectly fitting tux, his perfectly ordained life with this perfect wedding to the daughter of his father's business partner—a merger of a marriage here in the same town where my dad's business began.

The maid of dubious honor arrives in front of the rows of chairs, and the music on the ballroom's sound system fades out, ready for "Pachelbel's Canon" to start. Instead, the crackle of a voicemail booms.

"Hey, hey, Furby." Chad's singsong coo addresses the orange kitten I've been fostering for a San Francisco rescue. "Guess what today is?"

I'd been pulling on my sheer, white stockings when I first heard the message. Earlier, Chad had called to make sure my uncle Jay knew to go to the grand ballroom, not the band ballroom. I hadn't picked up in time, and the call went to voicemail. Chad didn't realize he hadn't hung up properly before he started serenading the three-pound orange cutie about our wedding.

I'd let the message play as I slipped on one satin shoe because how adorable was that? We'd laugh about it later.

Well, one of us would.

"Guess who's coming over?" Over the speakers, Chad croons another line of the kitten song.

"What the hell is going on?" my father whispers, low in my ear.

I give Dad one of the polished smiles I've been throwing to spectators for years. The one he expects from me. "Just a sweet little something for my groom."

At the front of the ballroom, Chad cocks his head, his gelled hair unmoving, his eyes wary as I glide up the aisle.

Please, universe, let me pull this off like a triple lutz in competition.

The song plays on. "She'll be here in a few. Because

Madison has something to do. She's bringing me a secret wedding gift. The one that'll give my spirits a lift."

My father's jaw ticks. "Sabrina Snow," he hisses to me. Me! He doesn't yell it to Chad, like he should.

But even as the familiar click of Tessa's shoes sound behind me—she's probably rushing somewhere at the speed of sound to hit end on the song that isn't romantically nostalgic at all—we've already reached the good stuff. The prestige, as they call it in a magic show.

Tessa must succeed since Chad's voice stops carrying over the sound system.

But a good performer doesn't let a thing get her down.

I stop halfway up the aisle, letting the weight of Chad's words so far settle over the entire ballroom full of guests with their jaws agape. My father stiffens beside me, his grip tightening on my arm. All eyes are on me now.

I reach into my bra, tugging out my phone like the plot twist of the century. The crowd gasps as I hit play, letting all the guests take in the grand finale of the groom's impromptu kitty serenade. "She's gonna come through, with that BJ courage I need to say...I do." There's a chuckle, then Chad speaks the last words. "And then I'll get my bonus in six months. How smart am I, kitty boy?"

Furby meows angrily, and I swear in feline he's saying, *You're a dumbass. The red light's on, recording this session.*

"Ladies and gentlemen," I announce, loud and clear, "I'd like to thank Chad Huntington for sharing his musical talents with all of us today. I hope you enjoy the seasonal salad and seared halibut. I hear it pairs great with a cheater's wedding that didn't happen."

With that, I turn on my heel and march right out the French doors, leaving two hundred and fifty guests, my whole family, a backstabbing maid of honor, and a cheating groom and his bonus in the dust.

* * *

With tears of rage and hurt stinging at the back of my eyes, I'm halfway to the nearest exit, ready to bolt to who knows where, when my father catches up to me.

My heart is galloping, but he's barely even breathing hard as he issues an edict in his commanding tone: "Sabrina Snow. Do not even think about leaving."

He says it like I'm a thief trying to slip out of one of his fancy ski stores wearing the high-end gear with the tags still on.

With my cartoonish dress suddenly feeling far too constricting, I turn to him and lift my chin. "It's a little hard for me to stay," I say, hating that my voice is full of potholes. My father won't want to hear any of my emotions. He's never been interested in them.

With a dismissive grunt, he reaches into the inside pocket of his tuxedo and hands me a tissue, like *problem solved*. "Straighten up and let's get back in there. Time to apologize."

My head spins. My world tilts on its axis. Did he really just say that? "I'm supposed to apologize for my groom cheating on me an hour before the wedding? With the maid of honor, no less? She's not even a friend of mine! Madison's your marketing manager—and you asked me to have her as the maid of honor."

"She's the VP," he says, correcting me, since that matters. But to him it does—everything must be precise. "And yes, that's what you should do, because that ridiculous stunt you pulled was unacceptable."

"Are you ill, dear?" my mother asks as she arrives—trim, sleek, and impossibly stylish in her off-white sheath dress. Of course, she would wear the same color as the bride. "It's not even a taboo anymore," she told me when she showed me the dress her personal stylist had selected for her because it matched her skin tone. "It's totally acceptable for the mother of the bride to wear cream."

Sure, Mom.

I swallow another rebel sob. I can't believe they're siding with him. Him—the guy I've been faithful to since college. The guy my dad set me up with. The guy I've been on again and off again with for six years. But I've always been faithful to him, even when we were off.

That guy is walking toward me now, shaking his head, tutting like I'm a naughty child.

"Sabrina, honey pie, what's come over you?" Chad asks with so much faux concern I'm pretty sure I'm living in a multiverse.

"What came over me?" I spit out, my voice hitting the ceiling of this hotel. No, it's hitting the stars above us. "I won't ask what *you* came over, since that's abundantly clear now."

My mother gasps, then whispers, "Language."

I don't point out there's no language in my statement. Not to my pearl-clutching mom, who fingers the little white balls on her necklace as if it's choking her.

Chad sets a gentle hand on my shoulder. I recoil, but he tries again, rubbing me soothingly like all I need to do is calm down. "There, there. If you were getting cold feet, you didn't need to make up something like that. We could have just talked through it as healthy couples do."

What kind of world am I living in? My eyes pop as I

shake off his slithery hand. "Make it up? You left a voice-mail about another woman on our wedding day!"

Chad rolls his eyes in that gentle, caring way again. "No one leaves voicemails anymore."

That's how he's defending his infidelity? Like the anachronism of voicemail proves his innocence? "That was literally *you* singing to *my* foster kitten on my phone." I wave the device in front of his face. It's teeming with text message notifications, but who cares?

"I just explained the whole thing to your dad. Technology is amazing, isn't it? I'm impressed you could pull off something so advanced," Chad says with the smuggest smile I've ever seen.

Right. I spent late nights stitching together audio clips of his voice to frame him. Because that's the kind of hobby soon-to-be brides take up between dress fittings and cake tastings. "Gaslight much?"

Chad patronizes me again. "But honey pie, we really should've just talked before you did something like that. I know you can be prone to, well, perfectionism," he says, twisting everything I've shared with him, like the lists I kept as a kid in notebook upon notebook. "And if you didn't think I was good enough for you, we could have discussed your 'perfectionist' concerns before all the guests showed up."

"That's not what happened," I seethe, but I feel like I'm fighting a losing battle with them.

My mother's face pales, contrasting with the velvet rose shade of her Chanel lipstick. She waves a hand in front of her face, like she must locate her smelling salts immediately. "Do you realize what you've done, Sabrina? I had to skip my hair appointment this morning to help with last-minute arrangements, and now you're blowing up the wedding in front of everyone. I'll never be able to show my face at Pilates again."

Oh no, not the Pilates moms.

Chad gives her a comforting smile. "It'll be okay, Mrs. Snow. I'll fix everything. You know how Sabrina can get when things feel...overwhelming," he says, and I want to wring his neck so hard, especially when he turns back to me, using the same saccharine tone. "If you want to get back in there right now, I will happily take you as my bride, and we don't have to speak of this ever again."

Who even is this man? How can he lie this fearlessly? "Maybe you didn't get the memo, but...*you just cheated on me.*"

"No," he says, like he's coaxing a toy from a Border Collie. "I didn't. And you really need to drop this routine."

I jam my hands into my hair, not caring if I'm messing up my perfect hairstyle. Not even caring that I've knocked the tiara askew as I shout, "You got a blow job from Madison!"

My father glares at me, his voice steel. "Your mother said no language." He points an angry finger in the direction of the grand ballroom. "Are you going to get back in there like a reasonable adult? Or are you going to keep embarrassing all of us with this...this...performance?"

For a few seconds, guilt pricks at me and I wonder if I should have just left a note for the groom. Informed the wedding planner. Walked away quietly. But the fact that I didn't even consider those options speaks volumes. "I wanted you to know the truth," I say, holding my ground.

My father steps an inch closer. "The truth? Like that time you said you were too sick to compete in Junior Nationals, but did you really throw up? Or did you toss a can of soup into the toilet bowl and clutch your stomach dramatically?"

Shock reverberates through me. How could he think that? "I had the flu," I choke out. "I could barely eat."

"Or maybe you were just afraid to lose. Just like you're afraid to walk down the aisle today, so you invent this fake song that only exists on *your* phone."

My tears burst forth, unstoppable now. They are geysers. I'm replenishing all of the earth's dry lakes and waterbeds with my pain. It's not the cheating or even losing Chad that cuts deep. It's realizing, once again, that my parents are more concerned with appearances than with me.

"Do you not understand what happened?" I say, my voice wobbly. "Chad's only marrying me for the bonus you'll pay him when he hits five years with your company in a few months!"

My father shuts his eyes, his jaw ticking, then opens them, his stony face unreadable, his gaze as hard as onyx. "Listen to yourself, Sabrina," he says in the quietest voice possible—one that slithers into my ear. "This is a ridiculous tale. When a man cheats, he simply goes to a goddamn hotel room to fuck another woman."

My mother clings to his arm like she's fainting. "Horrible," she mutters.

"His language? No kidding," I say.

"No, the details about cheating. I can't bear to hear them," my mom says with a dramatic sniffle as she fumbles through her bag for her signature lavender sachet for stress relief.

My father intervenes, dipping his hand in and finding it for her. "There, dear," he says gently.

"Thank you, David," she says, bringing it to her nose.

As she inhales, my father turns his full fury on me again. "Singing to a rescue kitten? Really, Sabrina? Is that the best you can do? It's such an obvious lie. Also, the song rhymed. Clearly *you* made it up. You were always the creative one. Chad's not a rhymer."

My jaw drops. "My groom can't rhyme? No one uses voicemail? Those are your arguments?"

"Those are just facts," Chad says, chiming in like I care about his opinion now.

I wheel on him. "You have a deep misunderstanding of facts."

"And you have a deep misunderstanding of what it means to be an adult," my father cuts in. "You're twenty-six. But you don't want to grow up and get a real job."

"I'm a skating coach," I say.

My father rolls his eyes. "That's not a real job. And to think, I've tried to give you work with my company, and this is how you repay me?"

Fine, since my role in the chorus at an ice-skating show ended recently, I've been doing some accounting for my dad's company while I build out my coaching business. But they offered me the job.

Still, I can't believe they're blaming me for the cheating. Except, of course, I kind of can. "You really think this is my fault?" I manage to ask through the hurt and the shame.

My father crosses his arms. "Yes. This is unprofessional. This is unbecoming. This is uncouth. And I am cutting you off from the family business...unless..."

I'm reeling, backed against the wall. Not only did I get cheated on, not only did I get dumped, but I've also just been fired by my own family on my wedding day.

But it's the insults that hurt the most.

Still, I lock onto that last word. I'm not sure I want to know what's behind door number three, but I peer anyway. "Unless what?"

My father nods to Chad.

My former groom takes the baton, giving me one last sad look as he offers me his hand. "Unless you want to pretend this never happened."

I look at his hand, imagining him touching Madison with that hand less than an hour ago as she got down on her knees. Then, him zipping up and having a good laugh at my expense, figuring I'd never find out.

But Furby was right—Chad's a dumbass and the only thing worse than a dumbass is a cheating dumbass.

"You must really want your bonus," I say to him.

Something flashes in Chad's eyes—anger. Then he drags a hand through his perfectly gelled hair, a tell I've seen a hundred times before when he plays poker with the guys. When he tries to bluff with a five of hearts.

"If you need an hour to think about it, I'm sure we can work something out with the hotel," he says, grasping at straws.

My father bites out: "This is your last warning. I didn't build this family business just to let you disgrace it in front of everyone. You'll apologize, or you'll be out of work, out of a place to live, and out of our lives."

They're all staring at me like I'm the villain. Not Chad. Not Madison. But me.

The bride who ruined everything by telling the truth.

Maybe this is my fault for pulling a stunt. But deep down, I know that even if I'd pulled my father aside and talked to him privately, he'd never have believed me.

Maybe that's why I made a production of it. Sometimes you have to be loud to get people to hear you. Even then, they don't. I never realized how alone I could feel when surrounded by people who are supposed to love me.

I look at my mother with her lavender sachet security blanket, at my father with his cold, unflinching eyes, at Chad dragging his hand through his hair like the ruthless liar he is.

My *stunt* is the kind of "behavior" that would have gone on my list of what not to do again growing up. But I'm not that kid anymore. I've come too far and worked too hard to claim what I deserve—respect from myself and others. And I deserve better than a lying groom, a gaslighting father, and a mother more worried about Pilates moms than me.

I look down at the bouquet in my hand. I barely realized I was holding it this whole time. As I head to the door, I toss it over my shoulder. "Enjoy the halibut."

"Where are you going? You didn't drive yourself here," Chad says, like I'm the idiot.

I lift my hand, waggling my phone. "Oh no, whatever will I do?"

I push open the door and take off, running in heels. I'm an athlete, and all those early morning miles I logged as a kid pay off now. I'm gone before anyone can even think about catching me. I could call one of my friends here today, like Leighton or Isla, but there's not enough time.

I quickly order a Lyft to—think fast. I know! There's an ice-skating rink nearby in Cozy Valley. I plug in the name as I sprint across the hotel grounds in this tulle-and-lace abomination, heading straight for the street. My getaway driver pulls up just as I check the app. Yup.

A black Prius, and the license plate checks out.

I slide in, breathless. "Hi, Rhonda. Can you help a girl out? I need to get out of town *fast*."

"You want me to step on it? Just say the word."

"Step on it." Holy shit, that was fun to say.

The grandmotherly woman with a wicked smile eyes me up and down in the rearview mirror, then flashes a *partner in crime* smile. "I've been waiting my whole life for this chance."

She peels away like it's a stunt.

But it's not. It's me taking my life back.

2

I TOLD YOU SO

Tyler

Ah, there's nothing quite like a night off from the kids. Don't get me wrong—I love those two little stinkers more than I love playing hockey. But an evening without a request for mac and cheese? Without complaints about who got more or whose turn it is to do the dishes? I'll happily take it.

It's been so long since I've had a free night that I'm barely even sure what to do with my time. After finishing dinner with my agent at a restaurant here in Cozy Valley —a productive meeting where we agreed to focus on making the next season better, both on the ice and with sponsorships—I head to the hotel bar. I'm staying overnight in this small town about forty minutes outside San Francisco since I'm playing golf tomorrow morning in a local tournament some friends here roped me into joining. But until then, no one needs me.

When I catch sight of the baseball game on the big

screen, I know this is exactly what a perfect night off looks like. The bar has a warm, relaxed vibe, with wood-paneled walls, a long, polished counter, and a vintage record player playing a pop tune I won't admit to my teammates that I know by heart. A row of wooden stools lines the bar, and there's a faint hum of chatter from a handful of patrons. A woodcut sign boasts brews crafted locally.

I grab a seat and say hello to the bartender, a weathered old dude in a vintage concert T-shirt whose name tag reads Ike. Fitting.

He slaps down a coaster and asks, "What'll it be?"

"Whatever you've got on tap," I say, since I'm not picky, and I bet he thrives on being trusted to pick a beer.

With a quick nod, he says, "You look like a lager type."

"Works for me." I settle in, letting the pressure of the past season—a tough one with a new team—melt away as I focus on the game on TV and the cold glass of beer Ike brings me. Only, the game isn't exactly relaxing. By the second inning, it's clear the umpire needs to be tossed out.

"Are you kidding me? That was such a strike," I mutter.

"Nope. It dipped by the outside corner, Tyler. Hanging curve that hung too long," a confident, feminine voice says —someone who clearly knows me.

I turn toward the sound, and my brain fractures for a second. It's like running into your doctor in the cereal aisle—that is, if you have a wildly inappropriate crush on your gorgeous, sassy doctor.

Or your ten-year-old's ice-skating coach, who's incomprehensibly here in a small-town hotel bar instead of the city where I see her every week, but who's counting?

Sabrina Snow flops down onto the seat next to mine in

a cloud of white poof, wearing a lopsided tiara. But she doesn't look like the polished, pink-cheeked, ponytailed woman who teaches Luna how to execute toe loops. With her wind-whipped blonde hair, tiara askew, and a wedding dress that seems completely out of character, Sabrina looks like she's seen better days. Especially since she's kicking a foot back and forth—and I can't help but notice she's wearing mismatched shower slides—one pink, one orange.

"Sabrina?" She's the last person I expected to run into tonight—especially like this.

"That's me," she says dryly. Too dryly. She laughs, but it sounds forced. "Fancy meeting you here."

"Sure is." Running into this woman on her wedding day is a wild card. Call it a gut feeling—or that forced laugh—but I'm not sure the groom is around.

"How's Luna? What's she up to since I saw you all the other day? Are you having a fun little family getaway?" she asks, but her voice is full of manufactured cheer.

I shake my head. "Nope. The kids are with my mom and her husband." I catch myself before I ask, *And you?* Read the room and all.

But with hope that honestly shames me, I dip my gaze to her left hand. That massive rock that's been mocking me since I met her still shines brightly, but her smile does not. Maybe she hasn't removed the ring yet, but I've got a sense the bling's on a goodbye tour.

That's not something I should celebrate. But whether her single status is self-induced or not, I offer what I can. "Let me buy you a drink."

She sighs with the weight of the world in that one breath. "I guess it's obvious I need it."

I don't say, *Yeah, it seems like your wedding day went side-*

ways, or, *What the hell happened?* She'll tell me when she's ready. "You are in a bar, so I figured you might want one—context clues and all."

She gives me the smallest smile. Glancing at her skirt, she gathers some material in her hands, then flicks it dismissively. "I was heading for the local rink, but it was closed. So yeah, it's a tequila kind of day now."

Her vibe is more of a jilted bride than a runaway one, but I've seen enough movies to know the two usually go hand in hand.

I raise a hand to flag down Ike again, but before I can say *a shot of your best tequila,* Sabrina interjects. "I'm going to need a double." Her voice is steady, though her expression, somewhere between dazed and exhausted, hints that she's already been floored.

I turn to her, skeptical. "Are you sure?"

The glare she shoots me could freeze the sun. I haven't seen anything that potent since Luna caught Parker eating the last slice of pizza. "I'm wearing mismatched shoes the Lyft driver gave me, I've been disowned by my family, and when I called out the guy I caught scheduling a blow job from the maid of honor an hour before we're supposed to say 'I do,' he tried to convince me that I was actually trying to frame him as a cheater."

I swallow my shock as she barrels on about the next level shitshow that had become her day.

"The only thing that went right today? On the ride up here from the wedding venue, I called my cat-sitter, and she agreed to take Furby, the rescue kitten I was fostering, to her place. At least Furby will be away from Chad." She stops for a breath. There's nothing funny about this but... *of course* his name is Chad. "But what if he took Furby?"

"Then we'll have to kill Chad." I grin, and to my surprise, so does she.

"Thank you. You get me." She blows out a breath. "Anyway, she picked up Furby and now I'm thinking of renaming my ex 'Fuck Chad.' What do you think?"

I'm thinking, *How is it possible to be more attracted to her now than I was before?*

Instead of voicing that thought, I turn to the man behind the bar. "I'll take two double shots of tequila, Ike."

He smirks. "Coming right up."

As he heads to the shelf of bottles, Sabrina shoots me a curious, but worried, look. "Am I ruining your night? Is there a date about to join you? Because I can leave—"

I cut that notion off at the knees. There is no place on Earth I need to be besides right here, right now. "I'm alone. We're all good."

"Me too," she says, then winces. "Obviously."

In the pause while the bartender pours, Sabrina rolls her lips together as if fighting off emotions. When she sighs, her shoulders sag a little.

"Do you want to talk about what happened?" I ask, both gentle and straightforward. Her day has been the worst—no question. And my goal has become to help her survive this terrible night. "Or do you want to watch the game and debate the awfulness of the umpires?"

Her lips, wiped free of lipstick, twitch in a weak smile. "Tempting. I have a lot to say about the state of officiating. But I'm starving."

"I hear the burgers are good. Interested?"

I'm interested in erasing the memory of Chad from her mind. I have been for a long time and haven't done a damn thing about it. Now, she's in a vulnerable spot and the last thing she needs is some asshole trying to make a move. Even if every nerve in my body is screaming that I want to.

"Nachos," Sabrina says without hesitation. "With cheese. And guacamole. And jalapeños. But no meat." She pauses, then adds, in a devilish whisper, "My mother would faint if she saw me eating nachos tonight. She thinks finger food is gauche." Mischief flickers in her eyes. "But I'm not living by her rules anymore."

I lean back, watching her, understanding more than she's saying. From the way she says that—defiant, proud—there's a story there, and I want to hear all of it. For now though, I'm just here for the ride. "Then it's a good night to order extra guac."

Sabrina smiles. "Let's do it."

It's the *let's* that does it for me. I'm suddenly in on this *fuck it* moment with her, like the night belongs to only us.

When Ike returns with our shots, I order the nachos. Once he takes off, I lift my shot glass the jilted bride's way and say, "To the end of the Fuck Chad era. I don't know a thing about him, but he clearly didn't deserve you."

She raises her glass, clinks it against mine, then knocks some of the tequila back as I do the same. A moment later, her face scrunches. "Oh my god, who let me order a double? This tastes like gasoline and regret." She coughs, fanning her mouth dramatically as she sets the mostly full glass down.

"Have you ever had a tequila shot before?"

"No! I'm a bubbly kind of girl. A white wine fanatic. Why the hell did I order tequila?"

"Probably because of the mismatched slides?"

"They were the only thing Rhonda had—she was my Lyft driver—and they seemed a fair trade for my white satin pumps. Don't ask why her slides don't match."

Ah hell. I can't resist. "Why don't they match?"

"I don't know." She's laughing now, soft and genuine. It makes my chest ache in a way I don't want to think about. "I told you not to ask."

"For the record, I tried to save you from the double shot," I remind her.

She narrows her crystal blue eyes. "No. You said, *are you sure?*"

Damn. Good memory. Still. "I feel like that falls under the tried-to-stop-you umbrella."

Those eyes turn to slits. "This is not a good moment to say, 'I told you so.'"

"You started the I-told-you-so-ing."

"Don't cross me today, buddy." But she's smiling, and so am I.

"Fine." I drop the teasing, even though she's so damn cute when she's smiling. "Let's get you something else. But whether you're a bubbly aficionado or not, no champagne, all right?"

"Fair enough," she says, still hoarse from the scorched earth the tequila left behind. "Let's go with something that won't leave me gasping for air or weighed down with even more regret."

I give her a sympathetic smile. I understand regret—and that the best move is to get the fuck past it. "What's the least wedding-appropriate drink you can think of?" I ask, eyeing her dress and tiara. "I'm guessing keg beer or a Jell-O shot. Want one of those?"

She wrinkles what is probably the cutest nose I've ever seen and shakes her head. "You're really leaning into the trashy theme here."

"Just trying to cause some good trouble," I say innocently.

That seems to spark her interest, and she raises a curious eyebrow. "Are you a troublemaker, Tyler?"

"Maybe I was. Back in the day," I say.

Her lips shift in amusement. "Think you've still got it in you?"

"Those are fighting words." I drum my fingers on the counter. "How about trouble in the form of a spicy margarita? Can you handle the heat?"

Her smile falters for just a second, as if I'd asked about more than a drink. "I don't even know."

Her blue eyes flicker with something deeper—with uncertainty, maybe, or a vulnerability she's trying to hide. Or possibly...interest. Since for a moment her gaze lingers on me, roams over me, like she's trying to figure something out.

Like what she wants me to do to her tonight?

What the fuck?

That is not a thought I should be entertaining. Too bad my lust-struck mind is already running away with the image, imagining what could have been if she wasn't wearing that damn ring. *Not today, brain. Stand down.*

"Let's find out," I say, as I resume the role of runaway-bride wingman. I change her order, and when the bartender returns with the margarita, we toast again, her with her cocktail, me with my lager, which—as Ike promised—is incredibly good.

"To the opposite of today."

"The opposite," she echoes, her gaze...curious. But I don't want to read into it even though I want to read everything into it. I have ever since I first laid eyes on her last fall when she stepped onto the ice at the Sea Dogs arena during intermission in one of our games. She performed a routine that captivated the crowd and, well, me. I watched it from the tunnel, even though I was supposed to be in the locker room. But Sabrina was impossible to look away from. She's impossible to look away from, too, when she coaches my kid.

She's always worn that ring though. So I've kept all my secret wishes locked up tight. I still need to since she's barely single. And I'm not the kind of guy who'd take advantage of a woman when she's vulnerable.

"All right." I lean toward her, waving off the ball game playing on the big screen. "Want to talk about what went down? I've already stopped caring about the baseball game."

"Me too," she says, then takes a cautious sip of her drink before nodding her approval of it. "If you're wondering how the wedding went south, it was kind of my fault."

I raise an eyebrow, bracing myself for her story as I lift my beer to finish it off. "How so?"

She sets the glass down and twirls it absently, her lips curving into a mischievous smile. "See, I caught my groom singing to the foster cat about how he was going to get a blow job from the maid of honor. And I thought, why not play the voicemail for everyone to start the ceremony?"

My beer freezes halfway to my mouth. "You didn't."

"Oh, I did." She's grinning now, a mix of pride and mischief lighting her face. "I had the wedding planner cue it up on the sound system, unbeknownst to her, and play it for all two hundred and fifty guests. You should have seen the worry in Chad's eyes when his own voice started echoing through the venue."

For a second, I can't do anything but laugh—this low, disbelieving sound that rumbles out of my chest. I've had my share of wild nights, but nothing quite like this. And nothing with someone like Sabrina—gutsy, raw, and somehow still magnetic. "You're telling me you broadcast the evidence of his infidelity to everyone?"

Her answering smile is deliciously satisfied. I almost applaud.

"I sure did," she says.

Then, fuck it. This woman deserves some applause for standing up for herself today. I slow clap for her—nice and deliberate, like she just nailed the long program at the Olympics.

She waves a hand as if to say *stop, stop*. But with real concern in her voice, she asks, "You don't think I'm horribly selfish?"

"Not in the least. Why would you even think that?"

"Because that's what my parents said. But the thing is— it wasn't just revenge, my playing the message. It was karma. Chad deserved every single eye on him after what he did. He'd walked down the aisle lying to me and everyone in there who showed up for us. I was just shining a light on it."

I lock my gaze with hers, making sure she sees my eyes, knows how serious I am. "Some things call for public sharing *and* public shaming. Cheating at any point but especially on your wedding day? Top of the list, Sabrina. Top of the fucking list."

Sabrina's face lights up, and I can't help but think— this woman is a fucking legend.

"Thanks, Tyler. I needed to hear that," she says, her tone sweet and genuine and making my chest feel far too tight.

I ignore the sensation as I say, "And I think you need to hear this too: I believe you've earned a gold medal in being a total badass."

"I accept," she says, then dips her head, pretending to receive said prize. I mime putting it over her neck.

And wouldn't you know? My fingers graze her soft blonde strands. Her breath hitches as I touch her, and in a heartbeat, she raises her face. Her tongue darts over her bottom lip, then she sets a hand on her chest, where the medal would be. "How does it look?"

That tightness in my chest amplifies, turns hotter as I hold her gaze, unable to resist saying, "Very pretty."

The silence extends for several beats, like a note held long on a guitar.

But then it's broken when the bartender slides the plate of nachos between us, the cheese still bubbling and jalapeños gleaming under the bar lights. "The best in Cozy Valley," he says.

"Thanks, Ike," I say, refocusing on the task at hand—wingmanning. Not flirting. I gesture to the towering snack, thinking back to the comment she made before we ordered it. "Your mother would be scandalized."

Sabrina grins, not missing a beat. "Good. I'm aiming for maximum scandal tonight. She'd faint at the sight of me eating finger food in my wedding dress. Especially since she nixed my chocolate chip cookie idea for the wedding."

This woman. It's hard to keep up with her, but I am here for the keeping up. "Explain."

"I'd thought it would be nice to have an array of desserts at the reception—cake, ice cream cake, and chocolate chip cookies. The kind that my friend Mabel makes. They're perfection. But that was too *scandalous*." She shudders, imitating her mom, I suspect.

"We need to get you cookies soon too."

Her eyes sparkle. "Yes! Let's be scandalous," she whispers, almost salaciously.

I could think of many scandalous things to do, but instead I shovel a chip, load it with guac, and offer it to her. "Be scandalous, Sabrina."

She takes it and crunches down, then moans in pleasure. "Second-best thing to happen today," she says, after she finishes the bite.

"What's the first? The cat-sitter saving the day?"

She pffts. Pauses. Then nods toward me, that vulnerable look flashing across her irises once more. "No. The company."

I shouldn't. Really, I shouldn't.

But I pull my stool closer to the bar and settle in next to my daughter's suddenly single skating coach.

What started as a simple night off has turned into something unforgettable.

3

THE NIGHT OF A THOUSAND CONFESSIONS

Sabrina

A few hours and a couple margaritas later, my sides ache from laughing harder than I have in months. The bar is warm and cozy, like the town's name promises. The low hum of conversations and clinking glasses blends with a clever playlist that gives a comfort vibe with modern tunes.

The best part, though, is this big, sturdy man with the dark wavy hair, the trim beard that has me thinking all sorts of beard-y thoughts, and the devastating hazel eyes that sparkle with amusement as I tell him all about my wedding that wasn't.

"I swear," I say, trying to catch my breath, "I really tried to convince them that I should walk down the aisle to Amelia Stone's 'Only You.' It was always one of my favorite songs to skate to. Plus, it's romantic."

Tyler raises a skeptical brow, leaning back in the stool with an easy confidence. He does everything with an easy confidence, and I totally get why Sea Dogs fans sing "Daddy's Home" when he hits the ice. This big, muscly man who looms menacingly over opponents also exudes a whole 'I've got this' vibe with his friends and teammates. The combo is hot—he's deadly and you want him in your corner. And, it seems tonight, he's in mine as he says, "Even for you, walking down the aisle to a pop song is bold."

"It's bold, but true. Scout's honor." I laugh, but there's a warmth in his teasing that makes my chest flutter. He already knows me, or at least it feels like he does. Is that just from the skating lessons with Luna? I mostly interact with her—and I've never really noticed him as anything other than a parent since I was engaged.

Was.

I glance at the diamond solitaire on my finger. It looks like it belongs to someone else. I blink away from it and meet Tyler's gaze again. He's watching me intently, his focus entirely on me, as if I'm the only person in the room. A part of me wonders if I should let myself feel this so soon after walking away from everything I thought I wanted. But I rarely felt this kind of focus from Chad, and I like being in Tyler's spotlight. Especially since it always seemed like Chad's attention was elsewhere. Turns out it was.

Tyler's brow arches higher, bringing me back to the conversation. "I call bullshit. You weren't a Girl Scout."

"How are you so certain I wasn't a Girl Scout?"

"Girl Scouts follow the rules. You don't."

I tilt my head, bobbing a shoulder. "I'll take that as a compliment. But I was a Girl Scout."

"It is a compliment," he says, his captivating eyes never leaving mine. For a moment, I can't remember why I felt like the unhappiest girl in the world today. Between the margaritas coursing through my veins and the way Tyler can't seem to take his eyes off me, I'm the happiest.

"Okay, fine," I admit, "but I had this whole list I shared with them of the five reasons why it was a good song."

"Five, not six?" he asks, a playful smirk shifting his lips. *What would they feel like sweeping over mine?*

I force the thought away. I almost said *I do* today. I shouldn't think about kissing someone else—someone else with firm lush lips, a strong jaw, and a slightly crooked nose, like he's logged a few fights on the ice.

I reroute my wandering thoughts back to...the list. "Yes! Five reasons," I exclaim, then rattle them off—it's romantic, unconventional, fun to dance to, more interesting to listen to than the same old tune, and it makes you feel good.

Tyler laughs even harder, the sound deep and warm. "Sabrina Snow, you are something else."

There's admiration in his voice, but something deeper, too—something that feels a little like desire. It's foreign and thrilling, a spark I haven't felt in a long time. Or...ever? I flash back over my life and times with Chad, and nope, I'm pretty sure I haven't felt this way before.

Like the world is spinning with potential and not the dread of someone else's expectations. I lift my glass and take another sip, thinking of the details, all the endless details that had to be so perfect for my family. "I wanted to test them—my mom, Chad. Push the boundaries of what I could get away with, considering I was getting away with very little for that wedding. God, it wasn't even my wedding. It was my mom's," I say as the reality of what went down today slams into me.

"And now you're free of it," he says firmly. "Because you had the guts to walk away."

Tyler tells it like it is—straightforward and real—and somehow, that makes me feel more valued and appreciated in a few short hours than Chad and my parents ever did.

I drain the margarita, and as I set the glass down, the weight of the day starts to lift off me. More wedding day truths bubble to the surface. "And, to be fair, I did get my two wishes—no doves and to wear a tiara."

"Doves?" he repeats, his brow furrowing. "Please tell me those were never actually planned."

"I put my foot down on that one. My mother wanted to release them after the ceremony, but most doves can't survive in the wild. They're just for show, and it's terrible for the animals. I told her no."

"My daughter would love that answer." Tyler's fond smile says he's so smitten with her. "She's obsessed with learning about animals, so I've picked up a thing or two."

"That's sweet," I say, enjoying the way he talks about Luna. He's always listening to her wishes at her lessons. That's not something a lot of parents do. Mine hardly ever did. They wanted more drills, more exercise, more time. "She asks me so many questions about my foster kittens when we're skating."

"She loves hearing about them almost as much as she loves practicing her twizzles," he says. Then he nods to the tiara. "So that's all you, then? The bling?"

I can't tell if he thinks the tiara is silly, like Chad did, or if he's asking sincerely. But then I decide he's not the type of guy who'd think a tiara is ridiculous.

I touch the crown absently, the rhinestones cool under

my fingers. "It's not about being a princess or anything. I just like sparkly things."

"No surprise there," he teases.

I swat his thigh, laughing, and then freeze. My hand lingers for a second, resting against the solid, denim-clad muscle beneath it. The heat of him radiates through the fabric. The strength of him makes my mind wander, and my pulse takes off. "I'm sorry I hit your thigh."

But I'm not really sorry. Mostly I want to touch him again. The intensity of my desire is surprising. And not unwelcome.

"I noticed," he says, his grin widening as I remove my hand.

"And...it's rock hard," I say, louder than I should have.

"Thank you," he replies, the corner of his mouth twitching in amusement.

I clear my throat, recovering quickly. "Hockey players. Strong thighs. Comes with the territory."

"It does," he agrees, his gaze skimming me briefly. There's a flicker of something in his eyes—interest, maybe even desire too. "But figure skaters are no strangers to hard work either."

"We'll have to have a skills competition sometime," I say.

"That so? You want to take shots on goal while I—"

"Do the camel spin," I say impulsively, the image of him doing the pretty spin in hockey gear delighting me.

"You're on, Snow," he says, then offers a hand for shaking.

I take it. Is it wrong that I'm a little turned on by how much better his handshake is than Fuck Chad's? Well, if it's wrong, I don't want to be right.

"It's a deal, Falcon," I say.

He lets go of my hand, then clears his throat. Those haunting hazel eyes linger on me, like he's working through not what to say next but whether or not to say it. "For what it's worth, you wear a tiara very well," he says, a hint of something more in his tone.

The compliment is thrilling. Temptingly so. My chest heats, and I wonder if he feels this connection too.

"Thank you," I say, warmth spreading through me, my limbs loose and melty, my inhibitions dropping. Was I ready to pledge my love to Chad today? Of course I was. Did I have some doubts in the back of my mind? Maybe. Have I been taught by my parents to ignore my doubts, ignore my feelings, ignore everything except the attainment of success? Yes.

Except...I don't want to ignore the way I feel right now with this sexy, smoldering man I'd never flirt with at work. But we're not at work. His kids aren't around, and I'm unexpectedly single.

And very interested in this hot single dad—his clever mouth, and soulful eyes, his big hands. What would those hands feel like coasting over my body? How would his beard feel whisking across my face, my belly, my legs?

I clench my thighs, and the questions keep coming. How would I feel if a man like him showed me...everything I've been missing in bed? Because I have definitely been missing, well, everything.

The margarita whispers that it's a good idea to see if he'd like to go to my room. Then I remember I don't have a room. After finding the rink closed, I spotted a roadside sign for a hotel and asked Rhonda to take me here. Rhonda dropped me off, giving me her card and insisting I call if I need anything, but the front desk said they were fresh out of rooms.

So, I marched into the bar, no idea what to do next.

A yawn overtakes me as the events of the day catch up all at once. "I think I need to crash," I admit reluctantly. I don't want this night to end, but I'm exhausted, and a little buzzed. Maybe more than a little. And now I need to find a place to sleep too. "Today's been...a lot."

"Of course it has," he agrees, standing as I do, steadying me with a warm, sure hand. His strong touch sends a shiver down my spine. "Do you need a ride somewhere?"

"I don't even know where I'm staying tonight. I don't want to go back to Chad's place, and the hotel is booked. I guess I could go to a friend's house." There's Leighton, and I could call her in a heartbeat. I could ring my friend Isla too. Both phoned me when I was in the Lyft, and I called them back on FaceTime together, telling them what happened after I left the ballroom. They cheered me on after the fact, which I appreciated. Rhonda cheered, too, as she drove.

"You're not going to a friend's house," Tyler says firmly, and I like the certainty in his answer. Even better is when he says, "Come with me."

His words linger between us, full of possibility. There's a vulnerability in his gaze, like he's taking a chance, too, as he asks for the bill and quickly settles up. We say good-night to Ike, then leave together, heading toward the elevator, our shoulders brushing slightly.

Chills erupt down my spine. I can't help but think this man might be everything this runaway bride needs.

And what does a bride need most on her wedding night? A real good time.

As the elevator rises, I picture Tyler unzipping my ridiculous house-of-a-dress, sliding the silly straps off my shoulders, and shimmying this ludicrous lace down my body.

Then hissing in a hot, lusty breath when he looks at me.

When he touches me.

When he tastes me.

The desire for him wallops me—powerful, primal, and almost out of nowhere. But really, it's been building all night. The way he listens, the easy vibe he gives off, his utter capableness. It's hot when a man gets shit done.

With his hand on my back and his room in our crosshairs, Tyler seems like a man who can finish all sorts of jobs.

As the elevator dings on the fifth floor, I whip my head toward him. "Chad was like a St. Bernard."

He blinks. "Excuse me?"

We step off the elevator and the words flow. "In bed. He was like that in bed."

He shoots me a curious look, like he's dying to say more but feels like he shouldn't.

But I want to tell him. And tequila—it might burn, but mixed in Margaritaville? It loosens my lips all the way up. "He's the only man I've been with. He was my first, and I was faithful. But he went down on me like a St. Bernard," I say as we walk along the hall.

Tyler parts his lips to speak, but it seems I've stunned him.

Good. I have no problem elaborating. "Sloppy. Abysmal. Like a dog."

He swallows hard. "I...put two and two together."

But I'm like a traveler on a plane that's going down. And I can't stop airing all my secrets. The things I've never even said to my best friends. Because who wants to admit the truth of their tragic sex lives? "It was so bad I didn't even fake it," I say, unable to stop telling him tales from *Bad Sex and Other Catastrophes*. "Instead, I just told him it wasn't my thing—him going down on me—so he'd stop licking me like a slobbery dog. But...I think it could be my thing. I wanted it to be my thing. Just not from him."

Tyler scrubs a big hand along his jaw, clearly unsure how to handle me right now.

But I'm undeterred. "And then," I barrel on, like the plane is nose-diving into a field and I've got to let out all these terrible truths, "he said it was fine I didn't want him to go down on me because he didn't like it when someone went down on him. He claimed he didn't like blow jobs. So, it felt fair, he said." I roll my eyes. "But, in reality, he was getting them from Madison. She's my dad's VP of Marketing, by the way. My dad insisted she be the maid of honor. She's not even a friend."

"I don't know which of those things is worse," Tyler mutters, then waves his room key over the lock, the door clicking open as he pushes it wide for me. He steps aside, holding the door, then tilts his head with a half-smile. "And it's a shame there's not a card that says 'I'm sorry to hear about your St. Bernard ex.' But trust me, I am."

There's a flicker of something deeper in his eyes. Curiosity? Interest? Definitely not judgment.

"Why are you sorry to hear that?" I ask, because my mouth can't stop moving tonight.

He hesitates, his jaw set hard, like he's debating what to say as I step inside. "Because I bet you'd enjoy it done properly."

I'm ignited. A fire burns brightly inside me, flames reaching high. "I bet I would too."

My gaze swings to his hands. He's clenching them into

fists, like he's holding something back. Himself, maybe? Or is that just wishful thinking?

The door snicks shut behind us. "And the sex, Tyler," I say, stepping deeper into the room as he follows, "was just...the same. Over and over. Like hammering." I mime the motion. Then, for good measure, I switch to a jackrabbit gesture, pumping my hips as I turn around to meet his gaze. And I wonder what has come over me. But suddenly, everything is pouring out—details about a sex life I never really enjoyed. "He never mixed it up. Over the last year, he only wanted me on all fours, and I thought it was because it felt primal to him. But I think he wanted to pretend I was someone else."

Tyler seethes. "He didn't deserve to see you come."

Pleasure zips through me. Courage too. "He was like a woodpecker. Same motion over and over. I never came," I say, and wow, I don't usually confess everything to anyone. But I can't stop now. Everything is coming out tonight. "I didn't fake it either. I just told him it wasn't a big deal that I didn't come."

He growls. "It is a big deal. It's *the* deal."

My smile takes off, powered by the jet fuel of his passionate words. "I think I'd like it."

"Coming?" It's asked roughly. Carnally.

"Yes. I like it when I'm alone."

"Good. You fucking should."

"I do," I say, breathless and tingly all over. I ache every-where, a heavy throb that thrums in my cells, that beats like a low drum in my ears. "My solo time? I've enjoyed that. And I've spent a lot of it picturing all the things I want. So many things."

I look at Tyler—tall and broad with muscles for days —the kind of man who could toss me onto the bed and take me apart. And he's listening to my every word. "Know what I mean?" I ask breathily.

"I'm following you loud and clear," he rasps out.

He's standing near the king-size bed, and I'm mere feet away. That won't do.

I step closer. "Are you?"

He breathes out hard, swallows, closes his eyes for a few long seconds, then opens them with a nod. "Yeah."

One word, and it feels like permission.

I don't weigh the next thing. I jump headfirst. "And Tyler? I definitely think you could deliver them."

His eyes are locked on mine, his chest rising and falling in slow, measured breaths.

"And I'm ready," I say, fueled by spicy margarita bravado.

"Ready?"

"For you to take my real virginity."

Everything goes still in the room. I can hear the June crickets chirping outside the window, the low hum of a truck rolling by, a nightingale singing.

But Tyler says nothing. He just scrubs a hand along the back of his neck while I stand here, a livewire, every nerve firing, every molecule humming.

I'm electricity itself, crackling.

And he's still a statue.

Maybe I wasn't clear? What if I'm being too... euphemistic? Really, why should I be anything but crystal clear? "I'm a virgin to good sex. And I want good sex." Then, I give him my best come-hither pout—lips parted slightly, one shoulder bobbing coquettishly. Look at me go! I must radiate sex appeal right now. "I'm pretty sure you could do it right. I have this whole fantasy that starts with your beard."

His eyes flicker. His lips twitch. "That's awfully specific."

Heat shimmers between us. I step closer. "I keep thinking about how it'd feel. I keep wondering, too, about those arms," I say, my gaze drifting to his biceps, visible in his tight polo. "How you could pin me down. I wonder about your mouth. I think I'm obsessed with it."

He winces, then shakes his head.

Shoot. I've crossed a line with a student's dad. But then, maybe even against his better judgment, he asks, "How obsessed?"

My knees buckle. I'm hot everywhere. "I can't stop thinking about how you might kiss me." I take another step closer in my mismatched slides. "*Everywhere.*"

And I wait. This time, though, he doesn't make me suffer. He closes the distance between us, lifts a big hand, and cups my cheek.

I gasp.

Dear god, the feel of his hand on me. It's unreal. Warm and strong, everything I want. I lean into his touch, lit up from the electricity sparking between us.

He slides a thumb along my cheekbone, up and down, like he's memorizing me. Then, one more small step, and he dips his head closer.

I sway.

I'm falling closer to him when his lips dust across my forehead.

The gasp that escapes me is both carnal and innocent, like his kiss.

Then, he lets go, scoops me up, and lays me down on the bed.

Carefully, he removes each slide, even though I could

kick them off. He drops one more kiss to my forehead and says, "I'll be right back."

His footsteps grow quieter, the door clicks shut, and I squirm, relishing in all these delicious sensations zipping through my body.

I should take off this dress.

I should get ready for his return.

He's probably getting a condom.

He'll come back, fuck me senseless, and serve me breakfast in the morning.

I stretch like a cat as I picture the rest of the night.

Until the day floats before my eyes—a song, a fast ride in a car, a forbidden snack, a caring man.

And a very soft pillow for my tired mind.

4

GIVE OR TAKE THE BLOWTORCH

Sabrina

The funny thing about a dull throb is it still hurts like a motherfucker. Sunlight spills through the curtains—too bright, too soon, and like a hammer to my head. My dress is twisted around my waist, the delicate fabric going every which way, including down my chest.

Great. I'm flashing the top of my boobs at...I pause, listening. Nothing but silence.

Okay, so I'm flashing my boobs at myself. Wonderful. I grab the bodice and wiggle it back up when I remember —my tiara. I reach for it, but it's not tangled in my mess of hair or tossed onto a pillow. My French twist is askew too. I peer around, but the tiara's nowhere in sight.

I sigh, regret slamming over me, hard and sharp. The tiara was the only thing I truly wanted to keep from last night. It's probably on the floor somewhere, tangled up with my dignity.

My mouth tastes like mistakes as I push myself up, the rustle of this awful tulle dress filling the quiet room.

Too quiet.

Hmm. Where's Tyler? Did he stay? Did we...oh god, did I...?

The memory hits me like a slap.

The last thing I remember is Tyler kissing my forehead and saying he'd be right back. To get a condom, I thought. Or at least, I'd hoped. I was half-drunk, fully committed, and one hundred ten percent ready for the hot dad to make all my fantasies come true. And then... nothing. I conked out.

I groan, dropping back onto the bed, the tulle of the skirt rustling like a soundtrack to my humiliation. *He must've come back to find me passed out cold, mouth open, probably snoring, and still dressed like a fairy-tale disaster.*

Ugh. I didn't radiate sex appeal last night. I radiated Weird Barbie making rude sex eyes in a garish dress.

When I sit up, the dull throb in my head jeers *How do you like me now?* I wince but then spot a glass of water on the nightstand and a little silver dish with three ibuprofen in it. My throat tightens with unexpected emotion. It's such a thoughtful touch that I want to cry for reasons I can't even explain.

I down the pills with a gulp of water, grateful for small mercies. A neatly folded note sits beside the glass, but before I can reach for it, there's a knock at the door.

A flare of tension rushes through me. It has to be Tyler. I don't think we screwed last night, but did we...this morning? For a few seconds, my hormones dance a jig. *Oh, I hope he fucked me really good.* But when I glance down at the sea of lace and tulle—and feel my panties still firmly in place—I'm pretty sure nothing came off last night or this morning.

Damn shame.

I shuffle to the door, past his suitcase, bracing myself to face him and his understandable rejection of me. Peeking through the peephole, I see...room service? I crack the door open just enough to avoid inflicting my dragon breath on the unsuspecting server.

"Sorry, I didn't order room service," I mumble.

"Mr. Falcon did," the server says brightly. "He asked for it to be brought to you around ten a.m. and to be left outside the door if you didn't answer. But here you are."

He wheels the cart in and sets the tray on the desk. The spread is ridiculous: a bread basket with toast and scones, plus fruit, coffee, and condiments.

I try to muster some decorum, but the embarrassment is real. Do I tip him? With my own money? On Tyler's room?

"Uh, can I tip you with...Venmo?" I ask since that's all I've got.

The server shakes his head, smiling. "No need. Everything has been taken care of by Mr. Falcon. Please enjoy."

He slips out, leaving me alone in Tyler's room once again. My stomach growls. Apparently, eating is a good idea. I grab a piece of toast and take a bite, moaning softly. *Heaven.*

Thank you, Mr. Falcon.

As I devour another bite, something shiny catches my eye across the room. There it is—my tiara—sitting neatly on the small couch, placed atop a royal blue Sea Dogs hoodie. Setting down the toast, I pick up the tiara, then the hoodie, feeling warm all over when I spot what's beneath it: a pair of leggings, tags still attached. They're clearly from the hotel gift shop. Pretty damn close to my size.

The thoughtfulness of it all makes my chest ache. *Who does this? Nobody—not for me, at least. Not when I've actually needed it. And now here's Tyler, being...well, perfect.*

And what did I do? I threw myself at him.

Smooth move, Sabrina. I press my hands to my face, cringing as last night's greatest hits flood back: public oversharing, drunk rambling, and—oh, yes—confessing every single one of my sex fantasies to the hot dad of one of my students.

He'll probably fire me. Yup. I bet that's what the note's about. A polite, *thanks, but your services are no longer needed.* Of course, he'd do it nicely. While serving me breakfast.

With dread swirling in me, I grab the note from the nightstand and unfold it.

You deserve more than St. Bernards, sloppy kisses, and a guy who holds you back. You deserve someone who lets you shine. Glad you left him. Never second-guess that choice.

Just so you know, you conked out before I returned with your leggings. Figured you'd need something to wear today— you probably wouldn't want to wear that dress again. There's a hotel laundry bag for it, and I left toothpaste and a tooth-brush on the sink.

Keep that tiara, Sabrina. It's legend, like you.

I've got an early tee time, so I probably won't see you. I arranged for a late checkout so stay as long as you need.

Oh, and in case you're wondering, nothing happened last night. I promise. I slept on the couch.

—T

． ． ．

My throat tightens, and the dam breaks. This time, the tears are heavy, born of small acts of kindness rather than heartbreak. Despite the ache in my head, I feel... cared for. It's a new feeling, but one I don't dare get used to.

This isn't how my world works.

I shimmy out of the dress, take a quick shower, brush my teeth, and pull on the fresh clothes. I turn my chin to my shoulder and inhale the hoodie, sneaking a hit of Tyler Falcon. He smells like woodsmoke—a cabin in the forest, guiding me home after a long, snowy trek.

I almost, *almost*, want to stay and thank him in person.

Instead, I grab a fork, stab a few blueberries, savor the tang of the fruit, then take a bite of a buttery scone, hearing my therapist's voice telling me *it's okay to enjoy life's small pleasures, even if they aren't on your to-do list.*

It feels a tiny bit wrong to enjoy anything today after yesterday's disasters, but I've spent a long time learning how to savor little things. The race of my heart when I see a frozen lake, the taste of melting caramel, the warm sun on my shoulders when I'm outside in the garden in the summer. They all add up to *free time.* Something I was never encouraged to enjoy growing up.

I take one more bite, since that's all I truly want—this taste of free time, in a way—then leave the rest on the plate.

Before I go though—and I really should take off before he returns—I jot a note:

I can't thank you enough for being such a gentleman. Also, I love minty toothpaste, so thank you for that too. And everything.

-Sabrina

I place the note on top of his suitcase, then leave the room, ready to face the shambles that is my life when a notification pings on my phone for my next skating lesson with Luna Falcon. I gulp. The day after I was supposed to return from my honeymoon. Now it'll just be a random weekday—one where I have to see the man I threw myself at.

I guess I've officially entered my hot mess phase.

* * *

Rhonda comes to the rescue, as advertised. I'm overcome with gratitude when she pulls up outside the Cozy Valley Inn in her black Prius, pineapple-shaped air freshener dangling from the rearview mirror.

She leans across, shoves the passenger door open, and grins up at me. "Tell me everything."

Her white hair blends seamlessly with her pale complexion, and there's a grandmotherly vibe about her —if grandmothers wore purple sweatshirts featuring a cat riding a unicorn and brandishing a lightsaber. Below the graphic, it reads: *Here I Come to Save the Day.*

"Where do I even start?" I buckle my seatbelt and sigh. "Ever blowtorched your life and then woken up with a headache, no place to live, and the realization that you don't make enough money to pay rent?"

She flashes me a smile. "Honey, you just described half of America—give or take the blowtorch."

Her can-do spirit draws out a laugh I didn't know I had in me. "Well, let's just say I'm in the half with the blowtorch. I need to get my act together. Not only did I run away from a wedding where I was nearly gaslit into marrying a cheater, I was fired by my family and capped off the night by hitting on the hot dad of one of my skating students."

"Ooh, how hot?" she teases, pulling onto the winding road toward San Francisco. "Don't leave out a single thing."

I don't hold back. I describe Tyler in excruciatingly delicious detail—from his rugged beard to his full lips to those piercing eyes that just...undo me.

"I think you need to bang him," Rhonda declares matter-of-factly, "so I can live vicariously through you."

"Yeah?"

"Oh, yes. Please, for all of us. Ride that hot daddy and then tell me everything." She sighs happily as she switches lanes. "I wouldn't mind finding a sexy pool boy myself."

Her playful honesty is refreshing, but she quickly shifts gears. "Now, what's next? You need a plan."

"I do." I tell her about the foster kitten I need to pick up. "Are you okay with a kitten in the car?"

She scoffs, giving me a look that suggests I've said something absurd. "Did you see my shirt?"

"Scratch that. Of course you don't mind."

A few minutes later, we pull up to the cat-sitter's house in Sausalito, a few miles away from where I lived recently with Fuck Chad. I'll need to get my things from his place and have someone bring my things from the hotel in

Lucky Falls, but I'll figure that out later. For now, I retrieve a pink crate containing a tiny orange kitten who meows excitedly at the sight of me, as if saying, *I did good, didn't I?*

I scratch under his chin. "Yes, you did, little guy. Thank you for looking out for me."

When I'm back in Rhonda's car, with Furby tucked safely onto the backseat, she asks, "Where to next?"

I've already texted Isla and Leighton to see if they can meet me. Because what does a runaway bride need most? Her friends.

"High Kick Coffee." I give Rhonda directions to Leighton's favorite coffee shop. Of course, the owner happens to be Tyler's grandmother. But the man who left me a heartfelt note after I drunkenly threw myself at him won't be there today because he's golfing. I never thought I'd say this but thank god for little white balls. I'm not sure I could face Tyler yet, even though I've already decided I'll keep that note forever. Facing him at Luna's next skating lesson? That's future Sabrina's problem.

As we drive toward the coffee shop, I share more of my epic spiral with Rhonda, including my current state of homelessness. She listens, then dives right into problem solving. "I've got a friend who owns a vegetarian hot dog place called Garlic Crush. She's got a little micro-studio above it. She's been thinking of renting it as an Airbnb but hasn't listed it yet. I could ask her."

Rhonda's offer feels like a lifeline, but it's also a reminder of how far I've fallen. A hot dog place and garlic fumes aren't exactly my dream. But then again, when your life's a pile of ashes, you can't be picky about where you start rebuilding. Besides, I know exactly what rent looks like in San Francisco—way out of my league. But my business is here, and I need to be close to potential clients.

I force myself to smile. "I'd appreciate it if you could ask her."

"Count on it." Rhonda beams.

"Are you a fairy godmother?"

Rhonda shakes her head kindly. "Nah. I'm just someone in the right place at the right time to help."

When we reach the coffee shop, I ask how much for the ride.

"Free for you," she says with a smile.

"Rhonda, you need to make a living."

"Sabrina, I need to do nice things for other women too. This is how we help each other."

I smile, feeling warm and fuzzy. Women helping women. I like that. "Thank you."

She waves me off with a dismissive, "Don't worry about it."

But I'm crafty. Once I get out of the car, I find her on Venmo, send her a tip, and include a GIF of a rainbow-shooting cat.

Because sometimes, the smallest gestures can say the most.

* * *

"Shhh," I whisper to Furby as he meows from under the table I'm sharing with Leighton and Isla at High Kick Coffee.

But Furby isn't having it. He lets out another dramatic little mewl.

"Maybe meeting here wasn't the best idea," I admit, trying to hush the kitten in the pink crate beneath me. I'm not sure if he's annoyed. Mostly, he's just chatty.

"He's fine," Leighton says with a wave of her hand.

"Birdie doesn't mind animals, as long as they steer clear of her espresso machine." Birdie's the shop owner, and Leighton knows her well since she's her boyfriend's grandma. "Her exact words."

"That's fair," Isla says, thoughtfully brushing a strand of chestnut hair off the fair skin of her cheek and tucking it behind her ear. "Do you know how hard it is to get fur out of an espresso machine?"

I blink at her. "I don't, actually. Do you?"

"Very hard," she says with the confidence of someone who always has an answer. Well, she's not the city's best matchmaker for nothing. "But let's talk about your situation."

Leighton turns to me, she's all business. Fiercely independent, Leighton knows a thing or two about surviving in this city. "All right. I have some ideas for you while you figure out if the garlic lifestyle is for you. And the place I have in mind is pet-friendly."

"That's key," I say. Even though I'm only responsible for Furby for a few more weeks, I promised the rescue to give him a place to stay until he's ready to be adopted.

Isla doesn't miss a beat. She pulls out her iPad and begins tapping. "Let's start a project planner for you. We'll list options and figure out what makes the most sense."

Leighton nods to Isla and asks me, "How lucky are we to have the world's most organized person as a friend?"

"The luckiest," I reply, grinning.

Isla brightens, radiating Disney-princess energy. She could summon chipmunks to alphabetize a forest. "We're all the lucky ones," she says.

"We are," Leighton seconds then adds casually, "you can always stay with Miles and me."

I'm floored. Leighton's generous, of course. Caring and

supportive. But I'm not used to offers like that, even from friends. But it's very her, something I've learned since we met several months ago and became fast friends. She's a photographer and snapped photos for my new coaching business when I finished my run with Glacé earlier this year. I'd loved ice skating in the Cirque du Soleil-esque show during the months it was here in the city. There aren't that many professional opportunities for ice skaters, as my father reminds me far too much.

But I push him out of my mind and focus on Leighton. Before I can answer her, though, Josie, Everly, and Maeve sweep into the café, turning our little meeting into a full-blown girl-gang intervention. I quickly run down my current crisis for the new arrivals, and then the offers start flying.

"You can stay with Wes and me," Josie says cheerfully, readjusting her loose bun.

"Asher and I have space," Maeve adds, since my new artist friend is always happy to help.

"Same here for Max and me," Everly chimes in with her efficient spirit. "The only caveat is I'm not sure Athena's great with other cats."

I'm speechless. Truly, I didn't expect this. The outpouring of support from these women—women I've only grown close to since meeting last fall—hits me hard. I haven't had these types of friendships before. Not like this. Maybe because I've been so itinerant since graduating from college, bouncing from ice-skating show to ice-skating show, from cruise ships to occasional residencies. But now, settled into the city for the past several months, I've become part of this group of friends, and it's such a gift to be one of the circle.

At the same time, I feel terrible taking them up on

their offers. They're all cozily paired up with hockey play-ers, and I'm over-the-moon for them. But I'm not sure I'm ready to face all these happily-ever-afters when mine was torpedoed yesterday. It's like peeking into a world I don't quite belong to yet.

"I can't thank you all enough," I manage, swallowing the lump in my throat. "I'm honestly touched."

"I've been there," Leighton says sympathetically; she bounced around a lot last year, trying to make it on her own.

"Me too," Josie adds. She lost a place right after she moved to town.

Isla leans in with a gentle smile. "My place is always open as well. It's small—a studio. But the couch is excel-lent for napping, so it must be good for sleeping."

Maeve clears her throat. "Which is a bonus, you know. Not all couches can go the distance and be good for night sleeping."

"That's very true," Josie says thoughtfully. She's the curious one, I've learned quickly. "I wonder if anyone's ever done a study on that."

Even though I don't know exactly when the garlic place will be ready—or if it ever will—I do need some-place to stay immediately.

I turn to Isla, the only other single woman in the group. "I'd love to stay with you, Isla. You're the closest to the rink."

"Perfect." She beams. "My couch has been waiting for someone to break it in."

I laugh. Just one last thing. I lift my hand and wiggle the engagement ring still on my finger. It's not a tiny rock. "Now, where's the best place to sell this thing? I need the cash to keep my business afloat for a few months." I feel nefarious in the best of ways. But I'm the woman who marched down the aisle to a cheating voicemail, so it seems on brand.

"Let's add that to the planner." Isla is already typing, then hitting search. We pore over options and make an appointment for an hour later at a diamond merchant. No time like the present.

That afternoon, I ditch my ring for a cool five figures, field a call from Rhonda—her friend Starla is happy to rent her micro-studio to me this summer (emphasis on *micro*)—and then check in with my clients to let them know their regular lessons are back on if they want them. I might as well get back to work.

Later, I send Rhonda a thank-you gift: a brand-new cat sweatshirt, a nail salon gift certificate, and some of Birdie's toffee brownies.

At least this hot mess still knows how to get things done.

The next day, I pack up Furby and move into Starla's "micro-studio" above the garlic hot dog place. She might have been overselling it by calling it *micro*. It's more like a walk-in closet. There's not even a shower—just a sink and a toilet—but I can shower at the gym. I'm an athlete. I've been doing it my whole life. I retrieve my things from Fuck Chad's while he's not home, store them at Leighton's, and then spend the night with Furby on a futon that smells like the strongest spice.

At least it's mine for now, and that's what I need.

There's one more piece of unfinished business. I'll have to face Tyler Falcon again at Luna's skating lesson. And I'm not sure I'm ready to see the gentleman who kindly turned me down on my wedding night.

How do you face the man who left you ibuprofen and

a tiara after you came on to him like a dog comes onto a bone?

But I know this much—I absolutely have to grab a minute alone with the man I propositioned.

I just hope that when I do, I don't stink like garlic.

5

A GROWN-ASS ADULT AND HIS MANTRA

Tyler

Look, I'm not the kind of guy who throws a pile of clothes on the bed and debates what to wear. For anything. I don't call my sister or my mom on FaceTime, holding up one shirt after another and fielding opinions.

But today? Today, I'm fucking annoyed at the mountain of shirts and the number of options I've considered. I blow out a harsh breath, shake my head at my reflection in the mirror, and mutter, "Get it together, man."

Getting it together means closing my eyes, plunging a hand into the mountain of clothes, and grabbing the first shirt I touch. Doesn't matter what it is. With my eyes barely open, I tug it on. When I glance back at the mirror, I shake my head.

"Of course," I mutter.

The text on the gray T-shirt reads: Fun fact: I don't care. My sister gave it to me because she's nothing if not irreverent. It's a little rude, sure, but what can I do? I made a deal with myself.

With that decided, I try to shake off my irritation. I shouldn't be thinking this hard about what I look like in front of my daughter's skating coach. I've been taking Luna to the rink for years and to Sabrina's rink for the last five months. Since the second week of January, to be exact.

I'm just a dad taking his kid to a lesson during the off-season. That's all.

Except it's not. This is the first time I've seen Sabrina since her wedding night when she—let's just call it what it is—threw herself at me.

Translation: offered me my greatest fantasy.

In a cruel twist of fate, she was far too tipsy for me to do a damn thing about it. Didn't take much willpower to walk out of that room like I did, given those three margaritas she'd had.

But even though resisting her was the right thing to do, it was the hard thing to do as well. Watching over her? Taking care of her? Looking out for her? Easy.

Still, I have no idea how today is going to go. Or, honestly, if Sabrina still wants some of those things.

A man can dream.

But one thing is clear: things cannot get weird between us. Luna loves skating. She also loves Sabrina. She tried a few coaches when we moved here last summer and finally found someone she clicked with in the feisty, upbeat, bright, and enthusiastic Sabrina Snow, former competitive figure skater and performer turned coach. And nothing—not a thing—can mess that up. Which means I need to make sure Sabrina knows we are all good.

Even though I can't help but wonder if it'd be the worst thing in the world to ask her out. We're both adults.

We could be cool about it, right? Doesn't have to mess things up with the lessons.

Earth to Tyler—She's barely single.

Right, right. It's a bad idea for many reasons.

But, is it though?

I do my best to silence the devil on my shoulder as I leave my room and walk into the chaos of the living room of my home in Pacific Heights, the same neighborhood where most of my hockey teammates live. My son, Parker, is perched on the floor, building not just a Lego spaceship, not just a Lego space station, but an entire Lego space city. And he's doing it with none other than my teammate, Asher Callahan.

Parker and Luna's mom is pretty busy with med school —and I'm seriously proud of my ex-wife for pursuing her lifelong dream to become a doctor—so the kids are with me a lot of the time. Or their nanny, Agatha. Or my mom.

Today though? Agatha's off, and Parker asked Asher to come over and build, so my buddy showed up for my son. I fucking love my teammates.

"I bet I can finish it faster than you," Parker says, glancing at the star winger on our team.

"No way," Asher replies with a smirk.

"Way."

"Dude, we're building this together."

Parker huffs, then smiles like the little devil he sometimes is. "I was just kidding. I'm not that competitive. Like my dad and you."

I smile. "It's our job to be competitive."

Asher laughs, ruffling Parker's hair. "But right now, we're a team, little dude."

"I know," Parker says, then grabs a yellow piece, squinting as he studies where it goes.

They both turn toward me, and Asher's smirk deepens. "Wow. Did you just turn into a dad in a fun fact shirt or what?"

I give him a side-eye. "What's that supposed to mean?"

"It's charming, man. You're pulling it off. Own it."

I arch a skeptical brow, then pluck at the tee. "Should I —" Nope. Not going to second-guess. I made a deal with myself, and I stick to my deals. I've never once broken a New Year's resolution. Not going to break this either.

"Keep it on, man," Asher says, reading into my unfinished sentence anyway.

"Thanks, Asher."

"Anytime, man. Anytime."

"Dad, are you ready?" Luna calls from the kitchen. "I have to show Sabrina what I've been working on."

Luna bounces into the room, her brown hair pulled tight into a sleek ponytail, exactly the kind Sabrina wears to every lesson. Exactly the kind Luna fashions when my mom takes her to the rink, which she does every chance she gets, indulging Luna's love for figure skating. It makes my heart squeeze, the love this kid has for the ice.

"Let's do it," I say, waving goodbye to Parker and Asher, then trying to fight off the annoying nerves twisting in my stomach as we load into the car.

Seeing Sabrina again...I don't know what to expect, or what expectation I could even have. We haven't talked about all the things she said. All the tempting, sexy, sinful, inviting things that crossed those glossy pink lips. Not to mention all the things I wanted, and still do want to ask her, like, *Did you really mean it that you want me to take you apart with my tongue? Do you truly fantasize about me running my beard across your thighs? Are you thinking about me late at night?*

Like I fucking am about her.

But I push those down, focusing instead on Luna's grin and Parker's laughter back in the house. They're doing so well in San Francisco after we moved here nearly a year ago when Los Angeles traded me to no better place than where my family lives. Mom's here. My stepdad, my sister, my brother, and my grandma Birdie. Life is good. The only thing in my life that's not great? My stats. Last year was an okay year—not bad, but not great. And okay is never acceptable in hockey. I'm thirty-two, I've logged ten good years in the pros. A couple of them were great, but not last year. When the season starts again in a few months, I need to get back in the great zone. If I do that, I can play a few more years and make good money, put plenty aside, and be all set when it comes to taking care of the two loves of my life. Something my own dad never did for my siblings and me, considering he walked out the door with barely a word when I was ten. I never heard from him again. He died when I was fifteen, and I'm not even sure I cried when I heard the news. What would I have mourned? The loss of a ghost? That's what he'd become to me in those five years. *Absent*. A man who wasn't there for his family.

I won't be like him. Not a chance.

Which means...now is not the time for romance. My kids are young, still adjusting to a new city. I really should set aside any thoughts of asking Sabrina out for real. The timing is all wrong for so many reasons. There will be space for romance later. And, really, what am I even missing? It's not like I had a great, passionate romance with Elle that I'm longing to replace. My ex and I were friends before; we're still friends now. I'm not missing anything.

As I drive through the city toward the rink on the edge

of the Marina District, Luna's voice breaks into my thoughts. "Dad, did you watch the video I sent you last night?"

"Of course I did. Loved the moves and the song," I say.

"Me too." She beams. "I want to be able to do something like that. It's so fun."

She chatters on, her excitement contagious.

As we pull into the Sunnyside Rink parking lot where Sabrina hosts her lessons, I'm resolved. Time to face whatever awkwardness might come my way. Then to move on.

* * *

When Luna nails her axel with fierce determination, I jump to my feet and cheer. "That's how we do it!"

She glides over to me, her cheeks rosy, her smile so big it could light up the rink. "Did you see that?"

"Dude, I literally just shouted loud enough for the whole rink to hear," I say, though there aren't too many people here—just a few others involved in private lessons happening at the same time.

"I know!" She grins, leaning against the boards. "I just wanted to make double, double sure."

"You crushed it," I tell her. "Now get back out there and finish strong with Sabrina, okay?"

"I will!" She beams, flying back to the center of the ice to tackle some footwork. I watch her for a moment, pride swelling in my chest. She's so confident, so focused. But something's nagging at.me—Sabrina hasn't skated over to say hi, and that's not like her.

Shit. Maybe she feels bad. Maybe she thinks I'll fire her.

The thought twists in my gut. When the lesson ends, I pull Luna aside before Sabrina can bolt. "Why don't you play that arcade game you like for a few minutes?"

"I love Ms. Pac-Man," she says. She's been thrilled since we started coming here that the rink has a collection of vintage games.

I hand her some dollars that she'll turn into tokens, and once she takes off her skates, she dashes off, already excited.

I draw a deep breath, steeling myself for this conversation with Sabrina. I have no clue how it's going to go, but I need to clear the air.

But before I can so much as move, Sabrina skates over with a smile that stops me in my tracks. "Do you have a minute?" she asks, her voice light, but something in her eyes makes my chest tighten.

That smile, those sparkling blue eyes, the memory of her soft, warm skin when I kissed her forehead in the hotel room—they all flood back in an instant.

Maybe it's not such a bad idea to date my daughter's skating coach. With the way she looks at me, it feels like a damn good idea. I don't want to move on. I want to take her up on her offer—and take her out.

"Yeah," I manage to say, my voice low and gravelly, my skin hot.

Screw the timing. I'm not looking for love, but I can damn well handle dating, parenting, and playing hockey. I'm a grown-ass adult. I'll hunt for an opening as we talk, just like I hunt for opportunities on the ice in every damn game.

Sabrina swings open the gate and steps off the ice, grabbing a canvas bag with an illustration of a fox twirling in skates on it, and the caption: *Skate Like No One's Watch-*

ing, For Fox Sake. She reaches into it and pulls out her pink skate guards. Of course, they're pink. This detail delights me more than it should. With practiced ease, she slips them on and then motions toward the metal bleachers at the far side of the rink.

This is going to be good. My pulse kicks up. If she wants to sit down, that's a sign, right? As I gesture for her to go first, I quickly cycle through the best ways to ask her out. It's been a long time since I've done this. Too long.

Since Elle, I've barely dated. My few attempts were app-assisted and didn't go anywhere. This in-person stuff? I'm at least a decade out of practice. But winging it has always been my style. I'll make it work.

There is the tried-and-true direct approach: *Sabrina, I'd love to take you out this weekend.*

I could go with something more specifically tailored to her energy: *How would you feel about mini golf and the best cheese fries in the city tomorrow night?*

Then there's always the option of just leaning into her wishes and wants: *Want to see a baseball game and debate the umpires, then I can take you home and we can start working through your fantasies one by one? Because I'd really like to show you precisely how I'd like to devour you all night long.*

Yeah, all those sound good, and I'm going to have to roll the dice in the moment. I've got this.

We reach the end of the metal bleacher, and she sits first, setting the bag down on her lap. The soft buzz of the rink's air-conditioning hums around us, mixing with the occasional scrape of skates on the ice below. I lean back against the cold metal railing, trying to act casual, though my chest is tight with anticipation.

"First of all, I truly appreciate everything you did last

week," she says, her tone earnest, her hands twisted around the strap of the bag. "I wasn't really in a good place, obviously, and...you were kind of amazing."

That's a damn good start. "I'm glad we ran into each other," I say simply, though inside, every nerve in my body is taut.

She gives me a small, grateful smile. "Me too. Really glad it was you."

Hell yes. My brain starts playing her words from that night on a loop, like a greatest-hits album of everything I've ever wanted to hear.

I have this whole fantasy that starts with your beard. I keep thinking about how it'd feel. I keep wondering, too, about those arms. How you could pin me down. I wonder about your mouth. I can't stop thinking about how you might kiss me. Everywhere.

It was tequila-fueled honesty, but the memory of her voice, bold and fearless, is seared into my mind.

"Same here," I say, the words slipping out before I can stop them. My pulse quickens as we lean slightly closer, and *this is it. This is the moment.* But just as I open my mouth to ask her out, she speaks again, her voice softer now.

"And I want to say thank you," she says.

I pause, letting her finish. My mom would hand me my ass if I didn't listen to a woman. My grandmother too.

"You don't have to," I reply, shaking my head. "Truly, you don't."

"But I do." She's almost pleading now, her voice raw. "You were there for me when I was incredibly vulnerable. And, honestly, drunk," she adds, her cheeks flushing pinker. "I don't know if I would've gotten through that night without you to talk to, to...share things with." Her gaze flickers away to the ice, and to a woman setting up for another lesson, before coming back to mine. "I just feel really fortunate. So I wanted to get you something."

Like a real chance with you?

She reaches into her bag, her fingers brushing the edge of something inside. For one stupid second, I imagine it's something meaningful—an invitation, a gesture, a sign she's about to give me the green light.

Then she pulls out...a mug. She thrusts it at me with a little shrug, her smile both shy and teasing. "It's not much, but I was trying to make light of the situation."

I take it, turning the ceramic in my hands. There's an illustration of a St. Bernard on one side and the words: *"Sorry About Your St. Bernard Ex, But Here's to Better Dogs Ahead."*

A laugh bursts out of me before I can stop it. "This is..." Perfect. Funny. Completely Sabrina.

And maybe, a little promising? Hell, it feels like a good sign if she can make a joke about her sex confessions in the light of day.

She grins, her face lighting up like it did the first time I saw her smile at Luna. "You said it was a shame there wasn't a card for that, so I figured—why not a mug? Oh, and—" She reaches into her bag again and pulls out the Sea Dogs hoodie I left behind. "I washed it, air-dried it. Thought you might want this back too."

The second she hands it over, I know. This isn't the beginning of something—it's the end of the best fantasy I've ever had.

And just like that, my stomach sinks. She's not here to talk about taking me up on her offer. She's here to apologize and return my shit.

With reluctance, I take the hoodie, briefly toying with saying something like, *"You can keep it."*

But what'd be the point? I'd just be some parent of one of her students pushing my team's merchandise on her. Not cool.

"This is really thoughtful of you," I say, keeping my tone friendly. "Honestly, I love the mug. But I swear, you didn't have to do this."

She winces, frowning. "But I did," she insists. "You were a total gentleman, and I threw myself at you. You're the father of one of my students, and...I'm so embarrassed, Tyler," she says, her lip quivering briefly before she steels herself with a deep breath.

A fueling one, it seems, because she continues on, her voice stronger now. "I just want you to know it was the margaritas talking. The tequila, and...and all the emotional trauma of that day. I just...I feel awful, and I wanted to reassure you that I'd love to keep teaching Luna."

Her words hit like a slap shot to the chest. Any hope I had of a date? So far gone they're sailing out into the ocean. My shoulders sink, but I force a small, tight smile. "Sabrina, you're a fantastic teacher. My daughter adores you. You didn't make me feel uncomfortable at all." Then, I pause, girding myself to say the harder thing, but the damn necessary thing. "If we can just pretend that night never happened, everything will be fine."

Relief washes over her face, and she presses a hand to her chest. "Thank you," she breathes, her pink workout jacket hugging her frame in a way I shouldn't notice. Shouldn't like. Shouldn't fucking think about.

But my mind is whirling through what might have been. What I wanted to say.

I want to cross that line with you right now. I want to take you out, and take you home, and take your real virginity like you offered, and then do it the next night and the next, screw the consequences.

But clearly, it was all the tequila talking that evening, nothing more. She has no idea she handed me my greatest fantasy.

No idea.

That repeats in my head.

And really, isn't it best if she keeps having no idea? I glance toward the arcade in the rink where Luna's playing Ms. Pac-Man. Yep. *No idea* is my new mantra.

"We're all good," I say, my voice even and reassuring since that's what Sabrina needs right now. "You don't need to worry."

Her smile turns playful, her mischievous sparkle returning. "What happened?" she asks innocently, tilting her head.

I force a chuckle, scratching my jaw. "No idea what you're talking about."

She laughs softly, her relief palpable. "Thank you."

"My pleasure," I say, lying—bald-faced lying—but this is the way things have to be. Especially as Luna runs up to us, announcing she's nailed a high score.

I focus on Luna, on what matters. My kids. My career. That's it.

But dating? No thanks. Not anymore.

6

———

THE SUMMER I MELTED AND REGREW

Sabrina

I'm sweating buckets. No, seriously—enough to fill a literal bucket. They could mop the floors at the baseball stadium with my sweat. But no one will ever know because I can't let on that I'm a walking inferno inside this cougar costume, sprinting around the bases during the sixth inning of a sweltering baseball game.

I think that's second base up ahead. Hard to say with this furry head obscuring most of my vision. But I know what I'm supposed to do: slide butt-first into the base, then pop back up like I'm the most agile mascot to ever grace a diamond.

Here goes nothing—*wham!* My giant paw hits first, then my fluffy rear. I'm back up in a flash, waving to the crowd at the ballpark. I clown around some more, hamming it up with the grounds crew during a break between innings. I even pretend to help rake the field, but really, I just create a bigger mess.

Seems fitting for my life right now while I drip inside this suit.

Why is July so aggressively July-ish, even in San Francisco? Mark Twain lied when he said the coldest winter he ever spent was a summer in this city. Then again, we didn't have climate change back then, so I forgive him.

I can't afford to let my mind wander too much in here, but it drifts anyway—to Tyler. Clearing the air with him last month was harder than I'd expected. Facing him after blurting out every dirty dream I'd wanted him to fulfill— and then asking if we could just move on—was more awkward than I'd imagined. And as much as I've told myself it was for the best, I can't help but wonder some- times...what if?

What if we'd tried something? What if I'd let myself have one reckless, ridiculous moment? A fling, maybe. Or something more, though I can't picture what that would even look like.

But then I remember the state of my life: a micro- studio that barely fits a few books, no shower of my own, and a skating business still struggling to take off. Tyler deserves more than someone whose existence feels like it's held together with duct tape.

Still, it's hard not to regret it just a little. Especially when I think about how tempting he is. Just once wouldn't have hurt, right?

But there's no use dwelling on that—not when the crowd is calling, and I've got another few innings of sweating my way through the summer heat to go.

When "Take Me Out to the Ball Game" wraps up, I do a goofy, mascot-style dance on the pitcher's mound, earning cheers for the San Francisco Cougars. My time's up for this inning, so I grab a stray ball and toss it into the stands. A kid catches it, and the crowd roars. Then I hustle off the field before I melt completely.

The moment I hit the corridor, I rip off the furry head, panting an inhuman amount. Reese—the team's publicist —greets me with a smile and hands me a fan.

"You're almost done," she says sympathetically. "Sorry the costume isn't air-conditioned."

"It's great. I don't mind," I gasp between breaths, fanning my face as if that'll actually make a difference.

And honestly, I don't mind. Not really. Not when this job is part of the strange patchwork quilt that is my summer.

Yes, I sold my ring. I made five figures off it, but some of that went back into my skating business, the rest into savings. Shockingly, summer isn't exactly peak season for ice-skating. No shows, no cruise ship gigs. And getting work as a female athlete? Practically impossible. So here I am, cobbling together a living with odd jobs like this one.

I've auditioned for holiday shows and reached out to both local hockey teams to see if they need help with their ice crew, but hockey pre-season doesn't start again until late September. I even landed some freelance accounting work with a company that makes tiny homes. Since I live in a micro-studio, that feels fitting.

What I *haven't* done? Seen my parents. Talked to my parents. Visited my parents. I haven't seen Chad, either, though I've stalked him on social media, of course. He and Madison look disgustingly pleased with themselves, happily using the blenders, napkin rings, and pasta makers they kept. Seems they didn't mind receiving regifted items; I recognize a lot of them from the registry Mom set up for my wedding to Chad. They used them for their wedding, held the next week. I don't get it, but they deserve each other.

No doubt, Chad convinced my dad that Madison healed his broken heart and so will the bonus he'll earn too.

But there's good news. Furby, the kitten I fostered before and after the breakup, has been adopted, but I haven't taken in another. My situation feels too...unstable. My heart aches a little for that. Then a little more every time I trek to the nearby gym for a shower. Sometimes I even work at the gym, cleaning equipment at the end of the day to make a few more bucks.

It's not that I'm afraid of hard work—I'm used to it. It's just...things made more sense before. When I was performing as a skater, even if the gigs were patchy. Cruise ships, shows, and accounting for my parents was a bizarre but functional combo.

Now? It's all gone and I'm truly starting over, since I only launched my business as a coach several months ago.

When the game finally ends, I store the mascot costume in the equipment room, change in the ladies' room, and catch a bus home. I reek of sweat and garlic fries—a special kind of indignity.

I head back to the Garlic Palace, my new name for the micro-studio above the hot dog place, missing the soft companionship of a kitten and wishing, just once, that things would fall into place a little easier.

* * *

The summer isn't without bright spots. I see Tyler a few times—not intentionally, but not entirely by accident.

Luna is one of the few summer regulars, and Tyler still brings her to weekly skating lessons.

Tyler and I do as we promised. We act like nothing happened that night of my almost wedding. Like I didn't spill every dirty fantasy I ever had about him. He never brings it up, and I pretend I don't wake up sometimes, hot and bothered and alive just from the memory of his kiss on my forehead and the things I begged him to do to me.

Sometimes his nanny, Agatha, brings Luna to her lessons. Agatha is this sweet little old lady who I bet Rhonda would adore. She's lovely and seems homesick too—she chats about her family in Los Angeles and how much she's missed them since she moved here last summer. But mostly Tyler brings Luna himself. My pulse always seems to kick up the second I see him. I do my best to ignore it, and we exchange polite smiles.

We talk about hockey, his summer training program, or old figure-skating videos we send each other for Luna to watch, while she ties her skates or rushes off to play arcade games. During most lessons, Tyler sits casually in the bleachers, watching us. I'm keenly aware of his presence even as I focus on teaching. When the lessons end, sometimes we talk about neutral things, like how Luna's improving or the weather. It's maddening and strangely comforting all at once.

I'd like to think I'm over the Night of a 1000 Confessions. But then he'll flash me a crooked grin, and for one stupid second, I'll forget how to breathe.

But any comfort I'm feeling vanishes when I make the mistake of going to my parents' house to pick up boxes of old skating costumes. I take a deep, steadying breath as I get out of the car and walk the long circular driveway, then up the steps framed by columns to their enormous front door. They might as well have a butler in full livery ready to answer it.

Their stately home gleams white, and their lawns are immaculately trimmed, with hedges that could win competitions and roses that my mother grows—which absolutely *do* win competitions.

I'm a little surprised they would leave something as unsightly as boxes of my clothes on their front porch, but then again, they probably don't want to have anything to do with me. My dad, of course, has neatly stacked them there, as though to ensure I don't step inside.

He opens the door just as I'm hauling the last box to my car. He's crisp and cool in tailored slacks and a perfect Oxford shirt, like he's incapable of sweating despite another hot summer day.

"So you're still clinging to those costumes?" he asks, the question sharp enough to slice through bone.

I steady myself. I'm an adult. I shouldn't be affected by his criticisms. "I made most of them myself," I remind him. I taught myself how to sew my own costumes, tired of hearing, over and over again, how expensive skating was. As if my parents didn't have all the resources in the world to support me if they wanted. As if it was *my* fault that it was an expensive sport.

"I need them for my business," I reply, keeping my voice steady.

"Business. Right. I suppose they'll come in handy now since skating didn't work out for you."

"I made it to the Olympic trials," I say, my throat tightening. I hate the hurt and anger welling up inside me.

He shrugs. "Not the Olympics though. And trials don't get you sponsorships, do they?"

"It was six years ago," I point out. "I was in college. At least I finished college."

"Which you delayed finishing by taking a year off," Dad says, hitting where it hurts. It was hardly a year to fuck off. It was a year to get better. *Off the ice.* But he never saw it that way.

"I hope your accounting degree is working out nicely for you," he continues. "Perhaps we should've given you more opportunities to be in the Olympics. But then again, you've never been good at finishing things, have you? Do you even have the final accounting report for the last quarter you worked for me?"

Of course I do. I emailed it to him, but if he can't find it, I don't care.

I don't think about how my heart's caving in. I think of my therapist, Elena, and what she's taught me about standing up to my father when he lashes out. It's okay to walk away. It's okay not to answer him.

"Thank you for the boxes. I hope you have a great day," I lie calmly. I hope he has a shit-tastic day, but I won't let on.

Because part of standing up is walking away. And I just keep going.

That night, I fight the urge to spiral. When I was a teenager, I used to log the time I spent training. Now, if I'm not careful, I'll find myself listing, to the minute, the time I spend answering emails, shooting skating tutorials, and researching jobs. I call my friends, instead. Better to give attention to the people I care about, than obsess over whether I'm spending my time correctly.

Isla and Leighton meet me the next day for an escape room adventure. We work together to crack the code and bust free from a speakeasy with "one hundred thousand dollars" in fictional cash. We make it out in fifty-five minutes and feel like badasses.

August slinks in and out like a lazy cat while I fill my days with friends and odd jobs. Soon it's late summer, and whispers of autumn bring the promise of change.

The hockey teams start posting pre-season schedules. I submit my résumé for the ice crews and double down on my social media campaign, shooting and sharing skating videos and short tutorials. Leighton, ever the supportive friend, helps me optimize everything. Parents start emailing about group lessons, and a few even ask about private sessions.

It's been three months since I nearly walked down the aisle and said "I do" to a cheater. But I didn't. I said, "I don't," and I stood up for myself.

"Starting over isn't supposed to be easy," Isla tells me thoughtfully as she and Leighton take me out for dinner at Happy Cow, one of my favorite vegetarian restaurants in the city.

"Maybe that's not easy, but cake is," Leighton adds, cuing up the arrival of the waiter with a surprise: a three-month anniversary cake.

"You didn't," I protest, beaming, and secretly glad they did.

"Three months since the day you left your old life behind," Isla says, and I hug them both, feeling...healed.

On top of that, school is mercifully back in session, and with the new term comes a rush of extracurricular sign-ups. My inbox overflows with inquiries about skating classes in September, and for the first time in months, I feel a spark of hope.

Not just hope. Pride. I made it through the summer without falling apart.

No thanks to Mom, Dad, or Chad.

On a Friday in late September, I'm getting ready for a lesson with Luna when a text pops up.

> Tyler: We're on the road for a pre-season game, but my mom will bring Luna and Rowan's daughter, Mia, too. That okay?

> Sabrina: The more, the merrier!

I'd expected him to say Agatha would bring them. She usually does.

> Sabrina: How's Agatha? Is she visiting her family in Los Angeles?

> Tyler: She quit.

I stare at the screen, caught off guard. Agatha was as much a fixture in their lives as Luna's ponytails and Tyler's crooked grins. I can't imagine her walking away from them.

But, as this summer taught me, nothing stays the same forever.

7
____

GO FOR IT

Tyler

The Boston forward barrels down the ice, his stick cradling the puck, dead set on breaking the tie in this scoreless game. I'm right on his tail, close enough to feel his desperation, when he slips it across the zone to a teammate.

But Bishop—the other Sea Dogs defenseman on this line with me—reads the play perfectly, stepping in to block the shot on goal. The Boston winger panics and flings it back across the ice—straight to me.

Thanks for the gift.

The puck's mine now. I take off behind the net, scanning for an open teammate. My brother's cutting through the zone, stick ready. Perfect. But before I can make the pass, the forward slams into me with a crack that rattles my bones and pins me to the boards.

Pain flashes through me, sharp and electric. But this? This is the kind of hit I live for.

I throw an elbow, carving out just enough space to battle for the puck. No way am I letting him keep it. A shove here, a jab there, and I wrestle it free. With one sharp flick, I send the puck across the ice in a clean pass to my brother.

My glare cuts back to the Boston forward. It's a warning: don't try me again.

He will. They always do.

But I'm bigger and meaner, and I don't lose these battles. At six-five, I'm one of the tallest guys on the ice, built like a tank—an advantage every defenseman needs. And I play like one too. Rough. Hungry. Taking no prisoners. That's the mission this season—make it better than the last. I'm out to prove something.

With only five minutes left in the third period, I curve around the net, pick off a stray pass, and send it clean to Devon, who rockets down the ice. With a snap of his wrist, he sneaks the puck past the goalie's glove and into the net.

Yes!

Devon circles back to me, grinning as we slap gloves. It's only pre-season, but it feels damn good to start with a win.

Back in the locker room, Coach McBride paces, doling out post-game notes. "Nice work getting down the ice," he says to Ford Devon, who nods, clearly still buzzing. Then, with a rare smile, Coach turns to me, flipping me the puck. "Good job wearing them down out there. That's what we need."

I catch the game puck, a flicker of pride settling in my chest. This pre-season has been good. The real work? Keeping it up when the regular season starts next week.

As I tug off my jersey, my phone buzzes from inside the stall. Better check that. It's a clear reminder that real life is waiting for me the second the game ends. I grab it, scan the messages. Agatha gave notice a week ago, and my life since has been a whirlwind of pre-season games and nanny interviews. None of them have panned out. The first one didn't think she could handle a schedule as unpredictable as mine. The second wanted to bring her boyfriend along to my home, which was a hard no. And the third? She told me, with zero hesitation, that she'd "never been much of a kid person." Why she applied for the job, I'll never know.

Mom has stepped in to help, which has been great, because she's good with this stuff. Hell, she's good at everything—like raising three kids on her own while balancing a full-time career.

Today's message lights up my phone while I loosen the laces on my skates.

Mom: I have an idea.

Tyler: Yeah? What is it?

Mom: To solve your nanny problem.

Tyler: You're the best mom ever. But what is it?

Mom: I'm working through it right now.

Tyler: Don't you need to get to a skating lesson?

Mom: Of course. I'm here already. Thinking. Parker is right next to me, totally absorbed in reading that new Astronaut Explorer book, and my brain just won't stop working.

> Tyler: So what's the idea? Did the agency find someone?

> Mom: Agency of Mom.

I can't even imagine what she's up to. But she sold homes for most of her career before retiring, so she knows people—and dogs. She has four of them, so I'm betting she met a babysitter at the dog park. Or maybe a dog-sitter wanting to expand. After the trouble I've had finding someone, I wouldn't rule anything out.

What have I got to lose? Mom's been at every interview, vetting candidates and keeping me sane. She knows what I'm looking for—a kind, caring person who isn't on their phone all the time, and someone who's good with kids. It's that simple.

And besides, I trust her.

> Tyler: Go for it.

I set down the phone, hoping Mom's solution will solve the nanny problem stat. Especially since the season is nearly underway.

8

—————

YOU'RE HIRED

Sabrina

I'm skating backward in a circle, leading Luna and her friend Mia through a warmup drill, but my mind keeps wandering. Tyler's nanny problem isn't technically mine, but I can't help brainstorming. A few women I worked with at Glacé might be interested. Or maybe that sweet guy from my sewing club who graduated from cat-sitting to babysitting.

I'd like to help Tyler. After all, the man helped me out in a big way back in June. This would be a real chance to pay him back.

"Okay, you two!" I clap my hands. "Switch to one-foot glides. Remember, strong knee bend!"

The kids follow along. Luna nails it immediately—of course she does; she's a natural—while Mia sneaks a glance at her friend and tries harder. I skate up beside her.

"Arms out in front for balance, like you're holding a beach ball," I say.

Her face scrunches in determination, and this time, she glides farther before wobbling.

"Got it!" she says, grinning.

"That's right! You sure did!" I high-five her.

When the lesson wraps up, I skate with the girls toward the bleachers, where Tyler's mom is waiting. Lauren Falcon is warm, friendly, and a huge fan of Isla's dating advice podcast, which has given us plenty to bond over the few times I've seen her.

"Sabrina!" she calls, waving me over. "Do you have a moment?"

"Of course." I slide to the edge of the ice, adjusting my ponytail.

She sends the three kids off to the arcade, then turns to me with a focused look that's a little...intense. Tension curls inside me. Did I mess something up? Don't know what I did, but it's probably something. I spent my entire childhood in trouble for one thing or another. Writing down the things I needed to work on. The routines I had to improve. The jumps I wanted to nail. The choreography that had to be better.

I created a running list of things not to do again so I wouldn't get in trouble. Images of stacks of journals lining my bookshelves flash before me, but I blink them away. *This* is not *that*.

"I have to say, you're incredible with them. Luna and Mia adore you, and I can see why."

I relax, caught off guard but delighted. "Thank you. They're great kids. It's easy when they're so eager to learn."

Lauren nods, her smile shifting into something sharper. "They are. And I've been thinking—Tyler's struggling to find a new nanny for Luna and her brother,

Parker. I've been helping out, but I can't keep it up once hockey season starts."

"Of course. You've got your hands full with your own kids." And by "kids," I mean her four rescue Chihuahuas, whom she lovingly refers to as her children.

"I do. And Harvey and I want to travel. New York. London. I hear the new production of *Crash the Moon* is supposed to be amazing. Seeing musicals all over the world was always a goal of mine."

"You should absolutely do that," I say, still unsure where this is headed but willing to support her dream.

She nods again, her expression turning serious. "Watching you with the girls...you have a gift, Sabrina. You're patient, creative, and you actually seem to enjoy it," she says, and her praise makes me feel like a flower in the sun. I soak it up. "Would you consider a different but adjacent kind of role—something with a guarantee for several months?"

I furrow my brow. "What do you have in mind?"

"Tyler needs someone he can trust, and I can't think of anyone better. You'd have a garden apartment with a separate entrance, so you'd keep your independence. And Tyler's flexible with the hours—he knows how important your coaching is. So he'd work with you around your existing and future schedule at the rink."

Wait a minute. She's offering *me* the nanny job? "I've never nannied," I say slowly, still trying to process this curveball.

She waves a hand. "You're great with kids, you're reliable, and you clearly care. That's what matters. We're thinking the job would be for the hockey season for now, and then we'll see what we need for the summer. But we can pay for a full year. So, what do you think?"

I think I'd be less surprised if my father called to say he was proud of me. But also? Living on Tyler's property? Working for the man I begged to sleep with on what was supposed to be my wedding night?

My brain scrambles, conjuring awkward images of us bumping into each other in the kitchen, both trying not to remember how I threw myself at him, begging him to do un-St. Bernard-like things to me.

"That's...a lot to think about," I manage to say, my voice even despite the storm of awkwardness brewing inside me.

"He's completely on board," Lauren says, correctly reading my hesitation. "He told me to make it work if I found the right person. And Sabrina—you are the right person."

I've wandered into an alternate reality. And then Lauren says a number—a big number—that makes me question if I've stepped into *someone else's* life entirely.

I grab the boards for support. That's more than I've ever made. Enough to market my coaching business more. Add clinics. Connect with additional schools. Reach other kids who want to learn and grow in ice skating, the best sport there is. Enough to actually save money instead of constantly scraping by.

Plus, a steady job. A real place to live. No more juggling side gigs or showering at the gym. Maybe I could even afford to see my therapist, Elena, again. But could I really work so close to Tyler without melting into a puddle of lust? The man just exudes hot capableness in a beard and big body.

"I'll need some time to think about it," I say carefully, trying to erase thoughts of this woman's sexy son from my head.

Do not lust after her son in her presence.

"Of course." Her smile softens. "But I hope you'll say yes. You're exactly what Tyler and the kids need."

As she gathers the children, the weight of the decision presses on me. Turning this down would be a mistake. But living that close to Tyler might be asking for trouble.

Time. I need time.

Except...did I overthink Chad's cheating? Nope. I handed over the MP3 and marched down the aisle.

And I won't overthink this either. This is the opportunity I've been waiting for—and the money I need to finally make it on my own. I am strong. I can commit to this like I've committed to practice my entire life.

Just don't sleep with your boss.

How hard can it be?

I jam on my skate guards and catch up to her. "I'm in."

She beams. "Can you start next week?"

There's only one answer.

"Yes."

And honestly? No more garlic is reason enough.

9

———

THE MOM TRAP

Tyler

One minute, you're having a nice Sunday meal at your mom's house. Chicken and risotto, with sautéed green beans, the kind of dinner your stepdad gets way too excited about. You helped him make it while your mom boasted—understandably—about a new trick she taught her four rescue pups.

Group shake. It's so absurdly cute that you almost forget the chaos your family can bring to the table.

Almost.

The next minute, your fork is halfway to your mouth when your mom casually drops a bomb that makes you freeze.

"What did you just say?" I set my fork down, staring at her like she's lost her mind.

My little sister, Charlie, grins like a sweet, sassy devil. "She said she hired Sabrina as the nanny," she says, overly helpful, like I truly didn't hear Mom when actually I can't believe my ears.

At least Luna and Parker are in the other room, giggling over something the dogs are doing, since the kids already ate. Thank god. I don't need them to hear this.

I drag a hand down my face and meet my mom's gaze. "You hired Sabrina?" I sound as shocked as I feel. Because I am.

"Why wouldn't I hire her?" Mom asks it with the same casual air she'd use to say *is it sunny outside* then she sips her iced tea.

Across the table, my older brother, Miles, looks like he's choking back a laugh. His fist is pressed to his mouth, and his shoulders shake.

Harvey, my stepdad, catches on. "I have a feeling Miles might know why," he says, his tone full of unspoken amusement.

Miles schools his expression immediately. "Sabrina sounds like a great idea."

Traitor. If Leighton were here, she'd rein him in. But his girlfriend is off at a photo shoot. Though, come to think of it, she seems to enjoy trash-talking me too. Another reason they're perfect together.

Mom sets her tea down, straightening her shoulders like she's daring me to argue. "It is an excellent idea. She's fantastic with children. Luna already adores her, and we all know Sabrina well enough. We trust her. She's great at what she does."

I groan, dropping my forehead into my palm. "This is bad. This is so bad." Shit. Did I say that out loud? Now they'll all know.

Mom's eyes narrow into an inquisitive maternal stare. "Why is it bad?"

How do I even explain that blue balls are a real thing?

Not that I'm going to say that out loud. And it's more than that with Sabrina—I wanted to date her. I wanted to take her out and show her how a man treats a woman in and out of bed because, clearly, she'd had none of that from the world's worst ex.

And now I'm supposed to live with her? Every day? Irresistible Sabrina, who finds me completely resistible? "It's just...a lot of Sabrina," I mutter weakly.

With an eye roll, Charlie dramatically sets down her fork next to the special meatless risotto made for her and Luna. "Oh my god," she bursts out. "What he's trying to say is that he has a raging, unrequited crush on her." Her voice is sugar-sweet, but her grin is pure devilry. "It's cute, really. Big, tough hockey player brought to his knees by his daughter's skating coach."

I snap my gaze to my pink-haired sister. "Did I say that?"

"You didn't have to."

"I do not have a crush on her," I lie through my teeth.

"You do too," she says. I've never been able to fool her.

"Enough," I growl.

Mom's lips twitch. "Well, if you do have a crush on her, that's understandable. She's delightful. Beautiful. Caring."

She's so much more than that. She's fierce and strong. She speaks her mind and goes after what she wants. I met her last season when she performed at our arena one night, and yes, at first it was infatuation. As I got to know her during Luna's lessons, the more the crush intensified. Then, after her almost wedding night, the crush swelled into...feelings.

Fucking feelings.

I hate feelings.

Especially the way they crashed and burned when we agreed to never speak of that night again.

"It doesn't matter," I say, firmly shoving aside those pesky feelings. "I thought she was pretty. That's it. No big deal." If I don't shut this down, my family will never let it go.

Mom tilts her head thoughtfully. "Would you like me to fire her?"

"What? No!" It comes out sharp, and the room goes quiet for a second. I look around the table with the feeling I've just walked into a trap.

Harvey chimes in, deadpan, "Of course, if you can live with yourself for firing her when she's clearly grateful for the job and excellent for it, I think that's fine too."

"I mean, if it's going to be too hard for you, Tyler," Mom says, all calm practicality, "living with such a lovely, competent, capable woman. If you think you can't handle it..."

I groan again, scrubbing a hand down the back of my neck. "Family," I mutter.

Miles leans back in his chair, smirking. "Family is hard, little brother."

"You're telling me. And no, of course I don't want you to fire her." But that raises a question. I point a finger at Mom. "Why did you even hire her?"

She arches a brow, entirely unrepentant. "You told me to."

"I didn't tell you to hire Sabrina!"

"I believe your exact words were, 'Go for it.'"

"You didn't tell me that's what you were up to," I sputter.

"Of course I didn't." She is unperturbable. "Because I was helping you."

Damn it. She's right. I told her she could hire anyone. I just didn't think *anyone* would be the woman I can't stop thinking about.

* * *

Back at our house that night, I tuck my son into bed. After a flutter of his eyes and a long yawn, I set the space explorer book on Parker's nightstand and turn down the light. But instead of the usual muffled "Night, Dad," he lets out the world's longest sigh. That's not the kind of sigh you expect from an eight-year-old. It's an old-soul sigh.

"What's going on, buddy?" I ask, ruffling his hair.

He flips over in the darkness of his room, lit only by the glow-in-the-dark stickers of moons and stars he plastered to the ceiling.

"Agatha helped me with those," he says, pointing at the stickers.

I helped too, but I figure that's not worth mentioning right now. "I remember. We hauled up the ladder from the garage a few weeks ago."

"She helped me figure out where to put all of them."

"They look great," I say, admiring the constellations—or at least, I think some of them are constellations. I definitely don't know my astronomy. I squint at the configurations. "Is one of them the Big Dipper?"

Pretty sure the Big Dipper is supposed to look like a cup, and none of these shapes do, but that's okay.

Parker points to a shape right above him that looks a little more like a bowl. "It's right there."

"Cool. What other constellations do you have?" I ask, even though I don't think he really wants to talk about constellations. I think he just wants to talk.

He turns his face toward me slowly, his blue eyes giving me a curious look, his floppy hair falling over his forehead. He's pure Elle, especially with his love of science.

"The Big Dipper isn't a constellation, Dad."

Oh. "I didn't know that," I say, feeling a little chastised.

"People think it is," Parker says, then clucks his tongue. "Agatha knew the constellations."

And there it is. He misses her. "Yeah, she was good with all that stuff."

"The seven stars of the Big Dipper are actually part of Ursa Major. People call it the Great Bear. Do you know what the Big Dipper actually is?"

I give a small smile and shake my head. "I think we've already established the stars and skies aren't my strong suit, kid. Why don't you tell me?"

That earns me a smile from Parker who says, "It's called an aster..." He gets stuck on the term. "An aster—"

"An asteroid?" I supply, though I know that's not right.

"No! It's an asterism," he says, blowing out a triumphant but relieved breath, even as his tongue tangles on the unusual word.

"I have no idea what an asterism is."

"It's a bunch of stars within a constellation," he explains, then points at the ceiling and shows me how the cup—or the bowl—forms part of the Great Bear, which kind of looks more like a blob.

"And I learned something new today," I say.

He sighs again and is quiet for several seconds. "I wanted to put more stars on the ceiling," he says, like he had his whole heart set on it.

"What's stopping us? We can do it together."

"I don't know. I mean, I guess, if you want to."

"Of course I want to. Why wouldn't I?"

He flips over again, facing away. "But I don't know if the new nanny is going to want to."

I ruffle his hair once more. "I bet she'll be really happy to help put more stars on the ceiling."

"Maybe," he says, picking at the edge of his midnight-blue blanket, the color of the night sky.

I drop a kiss on his forehead. "We'll get more constellations up there. Asterisms too. I promise."

"Okay, Dad," he says, his eyes drifting closed.

"Maybe even asteroids," I add.

He laughs. "We'll see."

But as I leave, he sighs again, and my heart squeezes.

The thing they don't tell you about parenting? Your heart aches every time your kid's does.

* * *

If I thought my immediate family was bad, they're nothing compared to my hockey fam. Specifically, my single dad friends.

We're all at the gym on Fillmore Street early the next morning, squeezing in a workout on an off day. I've dropped Luna and Parker at school already, assuring Parker we'd be picking up star stickers this coming weekend. Even though he has to wait all week, he seemed happy enough about that. His sister, a busy bee and social butterfly, raced off into the building with a quick goodbye.

"Wait, let me get this straight," Rowan Bishop says, leaning against the pull-up bar with his signature scowl. "Later today, the woman you've been crushing on is actually going to be moving in with you?"

I pull down on the fly machine, my grip tightening with every word. "Yes."

Nearby, Corbin—the Golden State Foxes' forward and part-time shit stirrer—is on the leg press. His loud laugh echoes across our corner of the gym. "This is the woman you were brooding about when we played golf back in June?"

Fuuuck. The man has a steel-trap memory. I did say something that morning, but nothing specific. *Why does this guy remember everything I want to forget?*

"I wasn't brooding," I mutter. "I just mentioned I ran into someone at the hotel."

"That's true," Corbin says, grinning like he's about to bury me. "You also said nothing happened with her."

"Yes," I grit out, pulling the bar down harder.

"And that it was a shame nothing happened," he adds, as Rowan grabs a pair of heavy dumbbells.

"Yes," I say, sharper this time.

"You seem awfully...*taciturn*," Rowan cuts in. The guy loves his word-a-day app.

Corbin leans forward on the leg press, his grin widening. "Do you want to go back in time and repeat the day?"

"Just the part where I whipped your ass at golf," I shoot back.

Corbin laughs, not missing a beat or a rep. "Highly satisfying, huh? We'll circle back to that later. For now, I want to hear more about this 'foot-in-mouth' move you made by inviting the 'nothing happened' woman to be your nanny."

These guys.

"My mom did it," I snap, but it only makes them laugh harder.

"When in doubt, blame your mom." Rowan smirks as

he alternates arms with his hammer curls. "You can tell us," he says in a conspiratorial whisper. "You auditioning her as wife material?"

"Shut up. It's fine," I growl as I lower the bar again. My traps are going to be sick at this rate.

Corbin pauses mid leg press. "Someone's a little sensitive."

Yeah, because it's complicated, especially with Parker's worry, and the way he's clearly missing Agatha. The kid's life has been topsy-turvy the last couple years with the divorce, then the move. I have primary custody of the kids while Elle's busy with med school. The arrangement is more than fine by me. I want to be there for them every damn day I can, and Elle deserves the chance to go back to school. But I also have this season to think about and my own goddamn lust to keep in check.

So I ignore both my friends as I let go of the bar and cross over to the rack, grabbing a heavier set of dumbbells. Heavier than Rowan's. Starting a set of curls, I glance at my teammate. "And you still can't lift more than me."

That'll shut him up. Rowan is competitive as hell.

"One," he says, ignoring the bait, "we both know I can. Two, I know what you're trying to do." He tips his chin toward Corbin. "Don't you, Corb?"

"Sure do." Corbin moves to a bench press. The low thump of the gym's playlist mixes with the clinking of weights, but it does nothing to drown out Corbin's laugh.

"And?" I challenge.

"And it's hilarious how you think we're going to let this go," he says as he adjusts the weights.

I groan. These assholes.

Corbin pauses, his eyes lighting up. "Does this mean

we'll be seeing more of you in Cozy Valley? Our bocce ball and cornhole nights are good therapy?"

"I'm going to be fine." I am counting the days until our next night at The Gameyard. We get together at the Cozy Valley bar for dad time while the kids play Skee-Ball and Whac-A-Mole in the activity room. I need those nights badly. They...reset me. Not like I'd tell that to these fuckers.

"Fine?" Corbin echoes. "You're going to be fine?"

"Yes," I say, hoping it's true.

Corbin arches a brow and gives Rowan a look that says I am full of shit. "You want to place a bet on this?"

The idea piques Rowan's interest. "Hell yeah, I do. What's the wager?"

"How long he holds out," Corbin says with a sly grin.

I set down a weight to raise a hand. "Stop," I say completely serious this time. "We are not betting on a woman."

"Dude, of course we're not," Rowan says, mock-offended. "I'm not that kind of guy."

"I might be single, but I'm not an asshole," Corbin says, then adds with a glint in his evil eyes. "But I do bet on my idiot friends when they do highly mockable shit."

"Then why are you asking how long I'll hold out?" I ask, incredulous.

Corbin shrugs, feigning innocence. "I didn't mean how long before you and Sabrina fall into bed together. Obviously, that'll happen on the eve of never, because she has taste."

I flip him the bird before I pick up the weight again. "With friends like you..."

"You're lucky to have us," Rowan says with a smirk.

"Then what the hell are you talking about?" I ask as I move to shoulder presses.

"How long before you give in? You know..." Corbin says, moving his fist in an obscene gesture, already mocking my defeat.

I stare him down. "Are you really this immature?"

"Of course," he says without hesitation.

Rowan tips his chin toward me, deadpan. "Just accept defeat gracefully and start prepping excuses. It'll save you embarrassment later."

"It's a miracle you two are allowed to raise children," I say, with a heavy sigh to rival Parker's. "The maturity level in this gym is astounding."

"Hey," Corbin protests as he grabs a towel. "I'm not afraid to admit I have a healthy relationship with my hand. Maybe you should consider the same."

"I came here to work out," I growl. "Instead, you worked out my patience."

"You're welcome," Rowan says. "Also, good fucking luck living with temptation."

"One week," Corbin predicts as he lies down on the bench and positions himself under the bar.

Rowan shakes his head. "Two days. No way he lasts longer."

I roll my eyes. "How would you even prove such a thing?"

Corbin's smirk sharpens as he curls his palms around the weight. "Don't need proof. You'd consider it rude to lie to us. You're too competitive."

He asks Rowan to spot him. I curse under my breath, dropping to the mat for crunches. Tension ripples through my abs as I work them, trying to shake off the taunts. The crunches aren't helping. They just give me more time to think. About Parker and his new worries. About Luna and the way she loves to skate. About Sabrina, and how upbeat and fun and gorgeous she is.

Will I really be fine? Living under the same roof as Sabrina? It's not just temptation—it's her smile, her bright attitude, her everything. That's the real challenge.

I'll have to face it soon. After this workout, she'll be at my house, moving into my garden apartment.

Send help, I want to say. But never out loud, of course.

Later, we're leaving the gym and Ford strides in, floppy hair in his eyes, focus on his face before he pops out his earbuds. "Did I miss anything good?" the forward asks.

"We're betting on how long this guy lasts," Corbin says, clapping my shoulder.

"Dude. Seriously. Shut it," I say.

"Oops. Guess he doesn't want the whole team to know he has a thing for the nanny."

Ford grins. "Too late for that. It was one hundred percent apparent the first night he met her."

I am so fucked.

10

MY LIFE AS A LANDLORD

Tyler

Just to prove the guys wrong, I call Sabrina the second I leave the gym. She answers right away in a breathless voice that scrambles my brain. "Hi, Tyler." She sounds upbeat but slightly distracted. "Nope, that one. In the milk crate," she says, not to me.

Jealousy flares. Is a guy helping her move? Is she seeing someone new? And if so, why the hell did I agree to this arrangement? If she's dating another guy while living under my roof, I'll personally smack myself with a wet, smelly sock.

"Just calling to see if you need any help," I say, sliding into my car and turning it on.

She laughs lightly. "I'm all good. I hardly have anything," she says, still sounding like she's half-focused on someone else.

"You sure?"

"Positive. Trevyn is helping me."

I hate Trevyn on principle. "Who's that?" I ask, or maybe I bark it.

"A friend," she says, laughing.

Hmm. What's so funny about friendship? If he is just a friend. And why didn't I offer to help sooner? Oh, right—because I was still reeling from being blindsided by my mom. "I'm nearby if you need help lifting things." I realize I have no clue where she lives. But I can be nearby if she needs someone who can carry heavy things. Heavier things than Trevyn can.

"I think we're good," Sabrina says.

"I'll help you unload when you arrive then."

There. Take that, Trevyn. Two can play at the "help Sabrina" game.

"See you soon."

I'm home in ten minutes, showered a few minutes later. I refuse to be still debating what shirt to wear when Sabrina and her guy inevitably arrive.

I pull on a pair of jeans and a Sea Dogs T-shirt, totally not flexing that I play pro sports.

I head downstairs just as she pulls into the driveway in her little orange Mini Cooper. Yup. Trevyn is with her. At least, someone is, and I presume it's him. He gets out of the car first...wearing silver eyeshadow and some kind of blush on his amber cheeks.

Okay. Cool. To each his own.

He's lean and lanky and gives me a bright wave. "You must be the hot dad," he says.

My first reaction is *hell yes*. I like the way Sabrina has described me to her friend. I like it a lot. My second is relief—since I'm pretty sure Trevyn's not her boyfriend after all.

But before I can say a word—what does one say to

being called a hot dad—Sabrina steps out and rolls her eyes his way. "Those are his words," she says to me, like she needs to apologize for her friend.

I wither a little inside, wishing they *were* her words. Though, really, it's for the best that they're not. Since getting it on with the nanny would be a very bad idea. Something I'll have to remind myself every day since my brain seems to keep forgetting. "Okay," I say coolly, since I'm not sure what I should be responding to—the hot dad comment or the he-said-it-not-me comment.

Trevyn, oblivious, says, "I brought Barbara-dor too! Can she come in?" He points to a blonde Lab mix in the backseat.

"Sure," I say, stepping back as Sabrina opens the door to let the dog out. And maybe Trevyn isn't her guy after all, but I'm still going to carry all her things.

Because she's my kids' nanny.

But mostly because...I can.

I grab her duffel bag, hoist it onto a shoulder, then haul out a couple of boxes along with a milk crate, and lift her roller suitcase out of the car.

Trevyn whistles. "Well, hello there, Mister Muscles."

"Trevyn," Sabrina chides again.

He shoots her an innocent look. "What? That wasn't me. That was Barbara-dor. She likes a hunky guy with a beard."

"Right, of course. It was the dog," Sabrina says, then catches up as I'm heading to the stairs, lined with flower-pots that Agatha planted. Shit. Something else I need to deal with. Taking care of flowers. I'll add that to the never-ending to-do list.

"Wait. Hold on. Did you actually grab everything?"

Sabrina asks, pretty blue eyes roaming over all the cargo in my arms, as if she's counting her things.

I flash her a small smile. "Pretty much."

She shakes her head, like she's surprised, then says, "Wow. And thank you." She takes a beat and says it a second time, softer this time. "Also, thank you again for the job."

We already talked about the job on the phone, but it was mostly perfunctory, going over details and being as businesslike as possible.

Her expression is heartfelt—dangerously so. The look in her eyes is full of gratitude and warmth. And I can't take a chance of letting it melt my heart. My life is too busy. I don't have time for this. And I don't have room to nurture a going-nowhere crush on the nanny.

"This is going to be great," I say, then I lead her up the steps, to the main door, into the foyer, and show her the staircase down to the garden-level apartment attached to my home here on California Street in Pacific Heights. I rented this place a year ago when I joined the team, figuring I'd find a place to buy. But I haven't gotten around to buying yet. Life is too busy. I should though. My agent-slash-financial advisor would tell me to get moving. For now though, I set down Sabrina's things, then gesture to the gleaming white door with the silver keypad. "You can set your own code. It has its own entrance and everything," I say. "Plenty of privacy."

She's practically bouncing. "And I bet it doesn't smell like garlic."

I shoot her a curious look. "Didn't realize that was something you specifically sought out."

"When you've lived above a garlic hot dog place, you

definitely seek it out." She waves in the direction of the place she used to live.

"I hate garlic," I say.

"What do you know? Me too," she says, playfully. "But that wasn't the worst part of the Garlic Palace," she says, and I'm about to ask what was, but she keeps talking, sort of like how she did in the hotel room that night. *Sharing.* "The worst part was I had to stop fostering kittens."

"That sucks," I say, remembering her affection for fostering.

"But I still volunteer at the rescue so I get my kitten fix that way," she says, and I learn something key about Sabrina—she definitely looks on the bright side.

I admire that about her, even though it doesn't quite sit right with me that she had to stop.

As she sets the code, I look away.

She gasps when she walks inside, a hopeful, delighted sound. The apartment is small but inviting, with plush beige carpet and a cozy sofa in the living room. The queen-size bed in the bedroom is topped with a quilt from my mom, adding a homey touch, atop the sheets. Still, there's not much here, and I hope she doesn't hate it. But she says, "It's incredible."

Sounds like she hasn't had a lot of that lately. She sounds, too, like she's excited about this new chapter in her life.

Trevyn and Barbara-dor follow us, and he whistles as he takes it in. "Better than our tiny cruise ship rooms."

Gesturing to her friend, she quickly explains, "He was my skating partner in some of the shows. And we bonded over our hatred of shrimp. They served it all the time. I don't ever eat it, or any fish."

"I stopped eating it. Shrimp is the worst," Trevyn says with a shudder.

They're just friends. Close friends, sure, and I feel a little foolish for letting jealousy get the best of me earlier. There's something nice—warm even—about seeing Sabrina with her friends.

Friends she's clearly chosen. Rather than at her *wedding*, which seemed like it was chosen for her. I relax a little more, letting go not only of my jealousy, but maybe some of my frustration over the complicated situation I've got myself into. It doesn't have to be complicated at all. It can be easy, and it can be businesslike. As long as I don't let my feelings twist me up. And I won't.

"Let me show you around," I say, moving into boss mode.

The dog whimpers and that's Trevyn's cue to excuse himself. As he takes the dog for a walk, I give Sabrina a quick tour. Even though she could obviously figure it out on her own, I want to be a good host. Wait—a good...land-lord, even though I'm not charging her rent. Thinking of myself as Sabrina's landlord is an adjustment given all the things I once wanted to be for her.

"This is obviously the living room," I say. "There's the TV," I add and immediately want to smack myself.

Of course, it's the TV, you dipshit. She knows what a TV looks like.

She gives me a playful smile as her gaze dips to the blue sofa, and she pats the cushion on it. "And this is the sofa?"

"You know, I believe it is," I deadpan then move toward the kitchenette, though, honestly, it's more of a micro-kitchenette. There are two burners on a stove and a tiny fridge. "This is the kitchen area," I say, showing her around. "But it's not much, honestly."

Her blue eyes are thoughtful, curious as she taps the little fridge, the kind you'd find in a hotel room. "And this thing that looks like a fridge is a fridge, right?"

"Pretty sure. But you never know. You should test it," I say as I meet her gaze again.

She's wearing shiny lip gloss and eyelashes—fake I think—that make her pretty eyes even harder to look away from. She has on a sky-blue tank top that covers most of her stomach. *Most* being the operative word. She's paired it with leggings. It's the perfect moving attire, but it's also a perfect distraction, with the way the material hugs her curves and shows off the tight, toned muscles in her arms.

I try to reroute my focus to the tiny stovetop, resting my hand on it. "If this isn't enough for you, you can come upstairs and use the main kitchen. I'm happy to show you that too," I say as I turn around, while tension rattles through me. It's intense being near someone I'm so attracted to in so many ways. It hangs between us—the things that can never be. Or maybe it just hangs in front of me—my own reminder.

"Tyler, I love it all," she says, her tone genuine and no longer teasing.

I look back at her as she gestures to the sea of suitcases, boxes, and milk crates. "I've been living in a micro-studio without a shower. This feels like a mansion to me."

The heartfelt tone in her voice makes my chest squeeze, but her prior situation pisses me off. "Why? What happened?"

Sure, I know what happened on her wedding day and

night. But I mean it more specifically—what went down the morning after.

Trouble is, now I feel terrible that I never really asked how she was doing—*really* doing—all the times I saw her at skating lessons. I didn't truly check in with her. We agreed to pretend that night never happened and somehow, I took that to the letter, never asking about the other things that went wrong. Like with her other job, and her parents.

"I mean, how did you wind up there? In that place?" I ask quickly, trying to course correct.

She brushes some errant blonde strands off her cheek. "Rhonda," she says brightly.

It takes me a few seconds to connect the dots. "The... Lyft driver? With the mismatched slides?"

"Yes! She had a friend who rented me the place. It was all I could afford in the city, since, well...I no longer had a job to supplement my skating business."

"Right. Your parents..." I begin, but it pisses me off to finish the sentence. *Fired you.* So I don't. Because I don't want to let on that I despise her parents for how they treated her.

"Ironic, too, because my mother was the one who was so excited that my run at Glacé was ending at just the right time—her words—for me to devote my energy to wedding planning with her and doing some freelance accounting for my dad." Sabrina waves a hand like she's dismissing all of that. "But it's fine. Really, it's fine. I'd been living with Chad on and off for some time and making extra cash from my parents. I needed to do life on my own. That's what I did this summer."

My throat tightens with unexpected emotions. I'm...a little proud of her. That's hard to do these days.

"And you did it?" I ask, focusing on the details she's sharing.

"Somehow, I pulled it all off. I call it...The Summer of Odd Jobs and Moving On."

Oh, hell. I try not to latch onto those last two words. *Moving on.* But man, are they ever music to my ears. "I couldn't be happier that you've moved on beyond...Fuck Chad."

A smile lights up her pretty face, making her freckles almost shine. "I haven't heard that name in a while."

"Good," I say. "It's best if he's out of your head and out of your life." It comes out sharper, harsher, than it probably should, but hell, that's how I feel. That guy doesn't deserve to be spoken of ever.

"How are things with your parents?" I ask, though I'm honestly dreading the answer for her.

She winces but then seems to do her best to erase the sadness as she swallows, then says evenly, "We don't really talk. I mean, I went to pick up my things and my skating costumes, and my father kind of made it clear...I was a disappointment."

I hiss.

I want to march up to her father and tell him what an ass he is. There's a special place in hell for dads who treat their kids like that. "He's wrong. You're not," I bite out.

When her eyes widen, I try to get a better hold of my reaction, holding up my hands. "Sorry, but I can't stand parents who don't support their kids. Who aren't there for their kids. Who hurt their kids."

She gives a sad smile. "Sounds like you're speaking from experience?"

"My dad walked out on us when I was ten." I don't normally serve up my biggest hurt, but there it is. Something about Sabrina's patent honesty makes me give her some of my own.

"I'm sorry, Tyler. That's terrible."

"It was, and he's gone now. But I learned I never want to be like him."

"Pretty sure you're not," she says.

And hell, I didn't mean to make this conversation about me. And I probably shouldn't be kicking so much dirt on her dad. I hardly know her. "I'm really sorry he said that to you, Sabrina," I say as calmly as I can though my jaw is ticking with irritation. I hate that she went through this, but I'm impressed by how she handled it. But that's not enough, so I add, "You're a legend."

Like I said in the note I left her the morning after her wedding.

The softness in her eyes tells me she remembers. "Well, I try. And hey, my family saying *see you later* all worked out in the end," she says, brightly, and I'm not sure if she's trying to be cheery about it all or if she really did make lemonade out of the whole situation. Knowing her, I bet she made lemonade. "When I wasn't teaching skating, I was a mascot for the Cougars, did some freelance accounting, cleaned the gym sometimes, sold my ring, rented a micro-studio above a restaurant, and spent all summer smelling like garlic. And you probably noticed that during skating lessons."

"Not once," I say, as I file away the fantastic fact that she ditched the ring.

She arches a brow in question. "I don't buy that."

"Scout's honor," I say, holding up three fingers.

Her brow shoots higher. "I call bullshit. You weren't a Boy Scout," she says, giving it right back to me like I did to her that night.

"How do you know?"

"Boy Scouts follow the rules."

I should leave that alone. Truly, I should. And yet I step a few inches closer, lower my voice and say, "And I followed the rules that night."

A small gasp coasts across her lips. Her chest flushes too. She rolls her lips together, and for several long and fantastic seconds, I forget the world beyond that door as I imagine kissing off that lip gloss.

Maybe she does too because she says, a little breathless, "You did, Tyler."

She doesn't say, *What a shame*, but I hear it anyway, humming in the air between us. It drives me a little wild. Maybe the wall she built after her wedding wasn't about me or attraction, but about her. About timing. Because right now? The sparks from that night are back, crackling through my body. And they're not one-sided—I can *feel* that.

It's heady, this awareness. Knowing she wasn't just throwing herself at me because she'd had too much to drink. Every unspoken word, every jolt of electricity between us, is tempting enough to make me want to close the distance, pull her into my arms, and ask for a do-over. A *sober* do-over.

But what's the point? These sparks can't start a fire. They need to be doused.

We can't give in to whatever this is. Not when she's working for me. Not when she's taking care of my kids.

I shove the thoughts aside and return to the conversation. "You're right though. I was never a Boy Scout."

"Too busy with hockey?"

"Abso-fucking-lutely."

"The ice called to you," she says.

"And you," I add. Then, before I get lost in talking about all the things we have in common—we're both athletes and we're also the same type of athlete—I try to recenter myself to the moment.

To my job.

As her boss.

As her landlord.

And really, to my biggest job—being the father to the two best kids in the world. And that means no flirting with their new nanny. I clear my throat. "I'm glad you're not in that micro-studio place anymore, and I'm glad this job worked out." For the first time, I'm really starting to mean it. "Let me show you your bedroom."

"Can't wait," she says. "It's definitely going to be better than the futon on the floor."

"It is," I say, pleased I can provide her with a place to call home for a while.

I guide her to the bedroom, showing her the queen-size bed with a homemade quilt my mom bought at a fundraiser for the local dog rescue. The quilt is covered in dogs and cats.

"There are fresh sheets on the bed," I begin.

"I brought some, but wow. Thank you. It's always good to have extra and I'm sure yours are fabulous," she says, sounding genuinely touched, and her appreciation just makes me want to do more for her, make sure she has everything.

"You're welcome."

"And there has never been a more perfect quilt," Sabrina says, running her hands over it, sighing happily, and sitting down on the bed.

And then she flops onto her back, and I fucking die.

That's it. I just...die at the sight of this beauty on my

bed. At the way her tank top rides up a little bit more, exposing more of her belly—a strip of soft, pale flesh.

It's the sexiest thing I've ever seen. This woman, so strong and so fucking vulnerable, stretched out on this bed in my house. I fight like hell not to think about the fact that while I'll be two floors up in my room later tonight, she'll be down here in this bed after dark. Does she wear sleep shorts? A T-shirt and nothing else? A tank top and white lace panties? Fuck my brain for wandering in those directions.

But if it keeps going, that bet the guys made will be over before it started.

"So, that's the bedroom," I say gruffly, walking away because I can't linger on her in there. The more I see her on the bed, the more I want to peel off those leggings and show her what the opposite of a St. Bernard is.

I scrub a hand down my face as I stalk back to the living room, trying to erase the filthy images, stat. I squeeze my eyes shut, thinking of cold water. Freezing cold water. Bone-chilling showers.

Perfect.

She joins me seconds later, and I move right back into landlord mode, looking around the mostly empty living room.

"Will this place work?" I ask. That's businesslike, right?

"It's great," she enthuses.

"Yeah?" I survey the living room with fresh eyes. The walls are bare. There isn't much furniture either. Agatha at least had a few extra things to make the place home. I should have gotten a reading chair or something. A welcome basket? Or a kitten?

A kitten is not a housewarming gift.

"Did you...want to foster here?"

Sabrina's smile knocks me off-kilter. "That's sweet of you, Tyler. Truly it is. I should probably focus on your kids though."

It's not a correction. But it is a reminder.

Right. The kids. The reason I hired her, and yet here I am tossing out offers to turn this place into an animal sanctuary. I scratch my jaw and mention apologetically, "The place is a little bare."

Sabrina's eyes light up. "Actually, I can picture it perfectly. Everything I'll do here. And *enjoy* here. Like that" —she points to an empty corner—"it's a perfect place for morning yoga. I'll fix it up so cute. Put down a yoga mat, maybe a little table with some candles. I wouldn't burn them though. I just like the smell of candles."

"Do you do yoga every morning?" I ask, hungry for these fresh details about her.

"Once, I did it every day. Now, I try to do it *most days*. If I want to, that is." There's some pride in the addition, like the choice to break the daily habit was good for her —maybe for her soul? "And I usually want to. It's one of the little things in life, you know? And it slows me down. Sometimes I want to do everything, all at once. And yoga helps me take things one moment at a time," she says, then blows out a breath. "And I'm rambling again."

Like she did that night.

I have half a mind to tell her that her ramblings that night fed my dirty mind for days. For weeks. For the whole damn summer.

"I did ask," I say, dryly.

She winces. "I might be nervous. Which is another

thing yoga helps me with. So I will definitely be doing it here in this...Official Yoga Corner."

"Want a plaque with that name on it?"

With a laugh, she says, "Yes please. Because this spot will be perfect for all my downward dogs."

Do not think about her flexibility. Do not think about her arching her back and lifting her ass in the air.

But now that's all I'm thinking about. Her stretching in bed at night, sliding under the covers, and then flinging them off in the morning before she pads into the living room and moves into a downward-facing dog. Stretching, and moaning, and swaying her hips.

I am the dog now because all I can think about is how fantastic it would be to walk in on her just like that.

I clear my throat. "I'm going to..." I pause, unable to find a fucking excuse for leaving before I think any more about the way she moves around this apartment. Finally, I wave a hand and say, "head upstairs."

"Can I help out today?" she asks, stopping me on the way to the door. "Do you want me to pick up the kids from school?"

Surprised, I turn back. I figured she'd move in this afternoon. Get settled and jump into the frying pan tomorrow.

"You don't need to..."

She smiles, but with a touch of desperation. "I want to be useful, Tyler. It won't take me long to move in, and I'd really like to help. You've done so much for me."

Hardly. But if she wants to start sooner rather than later, it makes sense.

"They're out in an hour and a half. I have a team meeting, so it'd help a ton. Why don't you come upstairs in a few, and I can give you all the details? I already put you on the pickup list, and I've told them they're okay to come home with you."

She smiles. "I'm so excited."

"Really?" I'm dazed at my luck and still a little amazed she wants to do this.

"Yes. Hello! I'm a skating coach and teacher. I like kids."

And that's what matters most. "I'll see you in a few minutes then."

When I'm nearly out the door, she calls, "Tyler?"

I turn back, wishing she weren't so fucking pretty.

"The deal is the same, right?"

"What deal? You mean what I'm paying you? Of course. I'd never go back on that," I say, a little shocked she's asking.

"No, I mean the Night of a 1000 Confessions. We're still not talking about it, right? Even though we kind of did today."

Do I detect a note of mischief in her voice, as if she likes breaking the rules?

Well, I sure as hell fucking do.

I scratch my jaw and adopt a quizzical look. "Was it just one thousand, though? Almost seemed like it might've been one thousand and one."

Her smile is too much, teasing and self-deprecating at once. "Please. It was one thousand and two."

"So many confessions, Sabrina," I say, even though I shouldn't keep talking about it. But the look in her blue eyes, the tilt in her lips, the ease in her body—all relaxed. It's hard not to keep going.

"I blame the margaritas," she says, but then straightens her shoulders. "But it won't happen again. I promise."

Once more, I pick up what she's putting down. "I don't even know what you're talking about," I say, in a tone that makes it clear that once again I will play along.

"I don't either," she says.

And I wish she didn't need to forget about it. I wish I didn't, too, though it's for the best for both of us.

But as I head upstairs, I'm flooded by memories. By her words. By the sound of her voice telling me how much she wants me.

I have this whole fantasy that starts with your beard. I keep thinking about how it'd feel. I keep wondering, too, about those arms. How you could pin me down...

Heat roars in me. Desire grips me too tightly. At the top of the steps, I grab the railing and close my eyes, as if I can will away the images.

But they come faster, like the words we said to each other in the hotel room as we inched dangerously closer. Like what I said when she told me about her ex and his mouth. *I bet you'd enjoy it done properly.*

Her reply? *I bet I would too.*

I breathe out roughly, fighting off my fantasies of the nanny.

Get it together, I tell myself before heading into my home, which feels far too close to hers.

11

TELL ME WHAT TO DO

Sabrina

"I deserve a gold star for that feat of strength," I tell Trevyn as we finish dragging boxes into my bedroom. We leave the other items in the living room. I'll sort through them later, though I'm grateful to have had his help today.

"You and me both," he says.

Barbara-dor lifts her snout and pants.

"And her too," I add, stroking her soft head.

"Definitely. Hot Dad was something else, wasn't he, girl?" Trevyn says to his mutt.

I roll my eyes. "Stop making it worse for me."

"Please, you moved in with him."

"I know, and look at this," I whisper, like I'm afraid talking loudly will break the magic spell of this apartment —the magic being the wide-open space, the quiet, the fresh carpet smell. "And it's all mine."

Trevyn gives me a friendly smile. "It's perfect, doll."

"But," I say, plucking at my tank top, "I should change before I get the kids."

"Please, all the moms dress like that," he says.

"And yet I'm going for something a little more... demure."

He gives me an approving wiggle of his fingers. "You're so demure, Sabrina. So demure with your gold star and your resistance."

"I am," I say lightly, but resistance is exactly what I need. From Tyler's thoughtful questions to his genuine concern, the man is definitely boyfriend material.

Not that it matters.

Not that anything will happen.

This place feels like more than just a step up—it's freedom and a fresh start all at once. I won't ruin it, even though I still have the hots for my boss.

As he waits for me, I change into jeans and a simple blue top—something that won't make me stand out at school pickup with the kids. I'd rather blend in.

Then I stand in front of the mirror, take a big breath, and say quietly, "You can do this."

It's what I used to do before my skating competitions when I was younger. When I was older too. My parents would say it to me when I was waiting to take my turn on the ice—one of the few encouraging things they ever did for me.

At the time, I believed both that I could do it and they believed in me. I'm not sure they ever truly did though. They wanted me to train harder, jump higher, eat better, land stronger, wake up earlier. Is that belief in me or hope in a human machine? I'm not sure. But that's okay because I learned how to believe in myself, both on and off the ice. Thanks in large part to Elena, who helped me when I was ready to stop skating competitively. When I had to figure out who the hell I was without the order, the rigor, the rules.

Still, even though I believe in myself, this job as a nanny is brand new. I swallow nervously, picturing making mistakes and fucking up and not having the right answer for the kids. Briefly, the desire to write down every detail of what I did flits through my head, chased by thoughts of training harder, faster. But the thoughts are just that—thoughts. They're also brief.

I'm on the other side of all that perfectionism.

One more centering breath, then I leave the bathroom and the pep talk behind. Grabbing my canvas bag with the fox illustration on it, I head up the stairs with Trevyn in tow. There's only one little problem, and that's why nerves are still chasing me.

"I've never nannied before," I whisper to Trevyn.

"Don't worry, doll," he says, then dips a hand into his bag, handing over a small white kit with a red cross on it. "I got you a first-aid kit."

My throat tightens with gratitude. I love that he thought of this, but the perfectionist in me dies hard. For years, prepping for every competition wasn't just a habit; it was survival. I guess you can take the girl out of competition, but you can't take the prep out of the girl. I dip my hand into my bag and brandish my kit with a smile. This time, though, prepping seemed like a good idea. "Me too. I googled everything a nanny needs."

He whistles in appreciation. "Look at you, slaying already." He squeezes my arm. "You're going to do great," he says, his tone shifting from playful to sincere. "If anyone knows how to thrive under pressure, it's you. And hey, if anyone gives you a hard time, do what we always did on the ice—pick yourself up with a smile and move the fuck on."

"Words to live by," I say.

My friend takes off, popping into the kitchen to say a quick goodbye to Tyler, who's staring at the shelves in the pantry, a little zoned out.

"My Lyft is on its way, so she's all yours now," Trevyn says to my new boss, and I nearly swat my friend.

Tyler quickly snaps out of his stare at the cans of black beans to turn around, brow knit. But his expression clears quickly. "Thanks for helping. It was nice to meet you, Trevyn. If you ever want hockey tick—"

"Yes, sir! Please."

I laugh at my friend, admonishing him. "You are shameless."

Trevyn arches an imperious brow. "Have you seen the warmups, doll?"

I point exaggeratedly to the door. "Don't let it hit you on the way out."

"Oh hush," he says, then turns to Tyler. "One, I'd love to see a game, and not just for the warmups. Two, I'm all about tit for tat, so if you ever want to catch an ice performance, we've got friends who are doing *Ice Spectacle* in New York later this fall."

That's one of the top ice productions in the world, blending an incredible light display with elite performances. "It's supposed to be amazing," I say, seconding Trevyn, but is *Ice Spectacle* even Tyler's scene? "I doubt Tyler wants to see an ice-skating event though."

"I would," Tyler says immediately, owning it.

"Really?" I ask.

"Of course," he says. "I lo—"

Sounds like he's about to say *I love* something... skating?

But then he stops, nodding to Trevyn. "What's your number? I'll get you Sea Dogs tickets, no problem."

My heart gets a little glowy as Tyler trades numbers with my friend simply to give him tickets. When we first arrived, I swear there was a hint of...peacocking in Tyler, a bit of let-me-show-you-how-strong-I-am. I honestly didn't mind watching him carry all my things. It's nice to see the change though.

When they're done, Trevyn waggles his phone. "And the offer stands. If you're ever in New York..."

"Thanks. I will," Tyler says.

"My chariot awaits." Trevyn flashes his winning grin, then coils up the end of Barbara-dor's leash. "Be a good girl and say goodbye to our friends," he says to the dog, who lifts her paw like she's waving.

Then he sails off, calling out, "Don't do anything I wouldn't do," as he heads toward the door.

I'm not sure if the warning is for Tyler or me. But I blush anyway, then point toward Trevyn's exiting frame. "He doesn't believe in filters."

Tyler smirks and says nothing at first—just lets the smile spread. "Something you have in common?"

"Mean," I tease, then wag a finger. "Also, you promised."

"I did. And the clock starts," he says, looking to a brushed silver clock on the wall that looks a little vintage, then back to me and says, "now."

I step into the kitchen, miming zipping my lips. "The filter is on," I say, then nod to the pantry. "Are you trying to figure out what to make for dinner?"

He scratches his jaw. "Yeah. I'll be home in time, but I

just wanted to see if I needed to go to the store. We usually shop at Natural Foods," he says. That market mostly carries organic foods, and it's an inexpensive alternative to some of the bougier grocery stores. I kind of love that he goes there when he doesn't have to worry about the prices. But instead, he chooses to shop where other people do.

"Why don't I go?" I offer, since I want to go above and beyond for this new job. Show him I can be a great nanny. "Do you want to give me a list?"

"Yeah?" He sounds enchanted.

"Isn't that part of the job?" I ask lightly, not because I'm confused but possibly to remind him. His mom did tell me as much when she offered me the post. "Agatha did some of the food shopping, right?"

He blinks, then drags a hand through his hair. "Right. Yeah. She did."

"She worked for you for a while, right?"

"A couple years in Los Angeles, then here."

"She was part of the family?"

He pauses, as if he's considering. "In some ways, I suppose so." He blows out a breath, like he's recentering himself. "Anyway, I'm just getting used to this—this change."

I relax a little bit. This conversation feels awkward but normal-awkward, like it should be this way as we adjust to each other in the house and on the job.

"Me too. But let me tell you something—I know my way around a grocery store." I snap my fingers for emphasis but don't add that my mother trained me to take my time in every aisle, reading every calorie list out loud to see if she'd allow herself to eat it. I understood her urge to track everything—mine manifested differently.

"I can send you a grocery list," he says, sounding more confident now.

"Perfect," I say. But since I don't know his preferences, I figure I should ask. I want to do a good job after all—get the right foods for him. "Now, tell me something—what do you like to eat? Do you want only organic? Do you avoid ultra-processed food? Do you need gluten-free? Dairy-free? Are you all about free-range eggs and so on? Give me the details," I say, eager to learn every single thing.

"The team nutritionist has talked about ultra-processed food lately. It's the new smoking, isn't it?"

I give a little shrug. I don't want to be judgy about food choices. But he sounds like he's on the same page as me. "Personally, I like food made from stuff I can *mostly* pronounce."

"Agree, but one issue—I can pronounce romanesco, but I don't want to eat it," he says dryly.

"I promise I won't pick that up, then," I say, glad we're on the same page about what to buy. Then I pause before adding, "Is broccolini on your no list too?"

"What even is broccolini?" he asks, like how does that vegetable have the audacity to exist?

With a smile, I answer, "It's a mix between broccoli and Chinese broccoli."

"Okay, fine, that makes sense. But riddle me this—why is broccoli so hard to spell? I never get it right on the first try."

"I never get rhythm right on the first try," I say.

"Or accommodate," he adds.

I lift a finger, feeling a little zing of *aha*. "It's the double 'C' for me. It should be abolished from the English language."

"Yes, and broccoflower should be abolished from grocery store aisles," he adds.

"So you want to nix double Cs and designer veggies?"

He adopts a pensive look, then says, "Sounds about right."

"I'll work on the first, though it might take some time, but I can definitely promise not to bring home fancy veggies," I say, adding a dramatic hand-over-the-heart gesture.

His gaze drifts to my hand and lingers there for a few seconds before he snaps his eyes back up. "We're on the same page, then," he says. "And I'll send you a list of acceptable veggies."

List. I get a little excited over that word.

"Acceptable has a double C," I point out, so I don't let on how much I crave order.

His lips quirk. "You know...it does. Maybe we should play Scrabble. Though I think I suck at it," he says, and that thought is entirely too tempting, whether he's bad at it or not. I can already picture us laughing, ribbing each other over playing easy words like "cat" and "dog" instead of tough ones like, say, "broccoli."

"Maybe," I say instead, keeping it open.

Tyler taps his phone and sets it down on the blue countertop again. "And the list is sent."

Yay rules.

"Awesome, thank you. Would you like me to cook too?" I ask.

His brow scrunches as he weighs the question. "I like to cook for my kids," he says, and my heart squeezes a little. It's sweet how he wants to be a super dad and set a good example.

"Got it. Do you want to give me the other instructions? Tell me what to do."

His hazel eyes darken, then almost glimmer. His jaw ticks.

I replay what I just said, and oh shit. It sounds like I'm asking for instructions in bed. Like I did that night at the hotel. "For the kids. To pick them up at school. Since I'm picking them up," I add quickly, perhaps over-clarifying.

Note to self: The ramblings must cease.

"I knew what you meant," he says, then moves closer to the counter, grabbing his phone from it again. "I'll send you the address."

I reach for mine, but as I do, my arm brushes his.

My breath hitches even though the contact is brief and accidental.

Am I really this affected by my new boss?

My arm answers me as tingles race down my skin, from my shoulder all the way to my fingertips.

Yes, you are.

"Please send it to me," I say, but it comes out breathy.

I sneak a glance at Tyler. His shoulders are tense. His fingers curl around his phone, knuckles whitening just slightly. Is he...affected too? The thought sends a pulse of heat through me. My mind slides back in time to the hotel room, the soft sweep of his lips on my forehead, the kind things he said to me—the things I should not be thinking of.

I'm here to do an excellent job as the nanny—not to flirt with the boss. I inch away, pretending to adjust the strap on my bag as he explains the details for pickup.

The whole time, I try not to inhale the woodsmoke scent of my boss that already drives me a little wild. But it lingers in my mind as I leave, hopping into my orange car to pick up his kids for the first time.

And when I reach the private school a mile away, I'm doing my best to ignore these fluttery feelings for the man I work for. I've got a job to do, and I need to nail it.

For a moment, though, I'm back at the edge of the rink, waiting for my name to be called.

Hoping I'll be good enough. No, *great.*

But just like then, I square my shoulders, take a breath, and remind myself: I've got this.

12

WHATEVER, WHATEVER

Sabrina

This shouldn't be so hard. Do I linger in the pickup line or park and wait outside for them?

But I'm a few minutes early, so I keep debating as I circle the block in Japantown. Will they know to look for my orange car? I should park.

Then again, as I make another loop, the Peace Pagoda towering high a few blocks away, I don't see too many available spots. Shoot. I'll need to do the pickup line.

I have Luna's number—Tyler gave it to me at a skating lesson once upon a time. I could just call her and let her know what my car looks like. But as I pull back to the front of the school, I see that the line is already several cars long, starting to snake around the corner. Will they know where to find me if I'm not at the front yet? Are they used to Agatha being at the head of the line?

Best to find a spot. I search for a nearby parking lot on my phone since I can't see any on-street parking, and one pops up just around the block. I weave around the cars forming the line and head to the lot, but my stomach sinks when I see the price: $20 an hour. Highway robbery.

Still, it's my first day on the job, and I can't be late. Can't make a mistake. Pulse racing, I pull into the lot, grab a ticket, and rush to their school, a pretty, three-story structure with an atrium in the middle—or so the website tells me. It looks more like a fancy apartment building on a TV show set in Los Angeles than a San Francisco elementary school as it comes fully into view as I rush down the street. After all that effort to be on time, I'm still hurrying.

I hustle toward the main door, ready to tell the security guard my name, when the final bell rings and kids start streaming out of classrooms, visible through the expanse of windows at the front of the school. *Come on, come on.* I need to time this just right to show them I'm reliable.

So my new employer knows I am as well.

I tell the security guard my name, but he takes too long looking through the list on his tablet. Finally, he says, "Oh, I see you, Ms. Snow. Go right in."

I make it inside the lobby with the mosaic-tiled floor just as Parker walks over, hair flopping across his eyes, backpack slouching down his body. And if I'd thought I was nervous before, it's nothing compared to how I feel now. I've talked to Parker only occasionally at skating lessons—but this is our first real interaction. I give him a wave and a smile.

"Hey! How are you?"

He looks at me like I'm a piece of broccoli that should never have been served in the first place. "You're supposed to pick us up outside. Nobody comes inside."

He walks right past me and out the front door.

Okay, I definitely have my work cut out for me. Tugging on my shirt to adjust it, I follow him out, figuring Luna will meet us there. When I catch up, I say, "Is this a better spot?"

He shrugs and mutters, "Fine."

"How was school?" I ask.

"Fine," he says with a scowl that translates to *get away from me.*

"What did you learn?"

"Stuff."

"What sort of stuff?"

"Just stuff."

Oh man. I don't just have my work cut out for me—I have *all* the work. But little does he know, I'm as persistent as a bee. I shove my hands into my jeans pockets and go toe-to-toe with the kiddo. "Sounds cool. Was it cool?"

"It was whatever."

"Good whatever or bad whatever?" I ask, pressing more.

"Whatever whatever."

A few seconds later, Luna arrives, ponytail bouncing, eyes bright. "Hey, Sabrina! You found it! This place is not easy to find. It doesn't even look like a school—it kind of looks like a weird Art Deco building. Don't you think?"

She knows what Art Deco is? But kids today know all sorts of things.

"Yeah, it kind of does," I say. "Like one of those fancy apartment buildings."

"Exactly! Like on *Nobody Does It Better*," she says, naming a TV show that takes place in, you guessed it, Los Angeles. "Oh, and next time, you can just come to the pickup line."

My stomach twists, and a voice in my head says *you made another mistake already*? But since that sounds a lot like my father's voice, I do my best to silence it, reminding myself I made it here on time and I picked up the kids. "Thank you. I'll do that. Parker already told me not to come in, but for now, my car is parked."

As we walk, Luna chatters about her day. Meanwhile, Parker stops dead in his tracks and asks, "Your car is there? Why did you park there?"

"Because I wanted to meet you at school," I reply.

"But you didn't need to pay twenty dollars. We could've found your car. We're not stupid," he snaps.

Wow. Someone is definitely not a fan of me.

"I wasn't sure if I'd make it on time," I say, my voice firm. Then, because I don't want him thinking he's in charge, I add, "But I don't think you're stupid, and I don't want you speaking to me that way."

He gulps but doesn't say anything.

Maybe it's a small victory, but I'll take it as we climb into the car and head to the grocery store, where I park in the small underground lot, with or without Parker's approval.

* * *

But the détente only lasts as long as the produce aisle. As Luna tells me about a science homework project she's absolutely dreading while I pick out a few avocados, Parker interrupts.

"Can't we get something good?" he asks.

"What would be good to you?" I reply cheerily, perhaps to cover up my faux pas. For all my famous preparation, I didn't even ask Tyler about Luna's and Parker's likes and dislikes. I was too distracted by the brush of their dad's strong arm against mine. I'll do better tomorrow.

"They have gummy bears. Organic," Parker says, and there's a hopeful note in his voice.

But there's also something else—a clever edge. Something that tells me maybe he doesn't usually get gummies. I hesitate as I push the cart toward the bananas. "Are you allowed to?"

"Agatha always got them for us," he says, but this time he's not the sullen, snarky kid of the last half an hour. His voice nearly wobbles when he mentions her name. He must miss her. I bet he feels like I'm stepping on her toes. I should get him the gummy bears—sometimes you just need gummy bears.

I grab the bananas and say, "Let's check them out."

When we get to the aisle with the treats, I pick up a bag and glance at the ingredients under the fluorescent lights. Half of them are unpronounceable. Would Tyler want me to get this for Parker?

"I'm pretty sure this is ultra-processed," I say, a little worried.

Parker furrows his brow. "What is that?"

I quickly explain, trying to keep it light, but his reaction is instant. Parker crosses his arms. "Agatha let us get it," he says, his tone defiant.

My stomach twists into knots. Tyler said he's not into ultra-processed food, but maybe he allows exceptions? But if he does, am I supposed to be exercising those exceptions on day one? I replay our conversation in the kitchen, but mostly we just talked about hard-to-spell words. Crap. I didn't ask about sugar and snacks, and gummy bears definitely have sugar. I don't truly know if he has strict rules for his kids about food, or flexible guidelines. I don't want to be the nanny who trounces willy-nilly on his home life.

I also want to stay firm so the kids know to listen to me.

Feeling a little torn, I make a game-day decision. "Tell you what," I finally say, "I'll buy it for now, but we're going to need to check with your dad before you eat them."

Parker stares at me. "Agatha let me eat them."

Luna rolls her eyes. "Dude, Agatha's not here."

He glares at her. "Yeah. I know."

"Maybe stop obsessing over her."

"I'm not obsessing."

"You kind of are," Luna says, flicking her ponytail, like she's had enough of this conversation.

I have to side with him on this—it's not obsession. "I think he misses her, Luna," I say, cutting in to come to his defense. I'll have to talk to Tyler and ask him how to handle this sensitive area.

But Parker scoffs. "I don't. Mom lets me have them too."

Ouch. There's nothing much I can say on that topic. Their mom is in their life, and I don't want to step on her toes.

"Let's move on," I say firmly, since now's not the time to dive into a tough talk. Instead, I set the bag in the basket and head down the aisle. It hits me then: it's my first day at work. I've barely been on the job an hour, and here I am, breaking up an argument in the middle of the grocery store.

It's almost as if competitive ice-skating is easier.

On the way home, I try to steer things in a more positive direction with Parker at least. Tyler had mentioned I could take the kids out for a fun activity—a park, bowling, something like that. I don't want to be just the "grocery store and pickup" nanny. Besides, if there's one thing I'm good at, it's having fun.

"What do you two like to do after school? Do you like bowling?" I ask, trying to sound upbeat. "Mini golf? Scavenger hunts? Art classes? Bookstore trips?"

"Skating, mini golf, seeing friends. Going to the wildlife sanctuary," Luna says, breezily.

My ears prick, remembering what her dad said on my wedding day when I told him about the doves I didn't get —*She's obsessed with learning about animals.* "Have you been to one? A wildlife sanctuary?"

She shakes her head. "No, but I want to," she says, and I could hug her for being so direct and making my job easy.

"I'll do some research," I say, putting that at the top of my list.

"Also, roller skating," Luna says, then takes a breath, maybe gearing up to rattle off more things she'd like to do.

"Noted. Keep 'em coming," I tell her.

"Hula hooping. I heard that's super fun. I also want to learn to skateboard."

I get the feeling this enthusiastic girl could command a whole conversation, so I make sure to include her brother too. "Parker, what about you?"

"I want stickers for my ceiling," he says. "Moons, and planets, and stars, and constellations."

"That sounds cool," I reply, picturing myself wishing upon shooting stars when I was younger. Maybe we can bond over that. "What about shooting stars? I used to wish on those before my skating competitions. Do you want stickers of those?"

He sighs heavily. "A shooting star is not a star. It's a meteor burning up in the atmosphere," he says, like I'm dumb and he's a rocket scientist.

"Huh. You learn something new every day." I peer into the rearview mirror, catching his blue eyes. "Maybe you can teach me about the stars, then?"

For a second, he's quiet. "Maybe," he says, a little less sharp this time before turning to look out the window.

Maybe, too, I'll hold off on trying to win him over today. Winning him over might take more than gummy bears and hope—but I'm not giving up.

* * *

But if I can't win Parker over right away, at least I can help more around the home. Sure, Tyler said he'd cook, but there's no reason I can't pitch in with prep. I'm here to make his life easier, after all.

As the kids do homework—Luna upstairs and Parker in the open living room—I chop up tomatoes, cilantro, cheese, and lettuce, setting each in small white bowls I find in the cupboard. I grab some rice and beans, putting them on the counter as well, next to an avocado. He'll want to cut that last so it doesn't brown too soon. I remove the chicken breasts from the packaging, even though I don't like touching meat. But it's my job, so it's fine. I can handle it for Tyler and Parker. Luna doesn't eat meat, so I make sure there are enough beans for her. I slice the chicken into chunks for Tyler to cook, put them in a glass dish, close it, and set it in the fridge.

I glance around the bright, sleek kitchen, with its white counters and polished surfaces. All the groceries are put away, the counters are wiped down, and dinner is prepped. Not bad. Not bad at all. Hopefully, Tyler will be happy.

Right on time, the garage door vibrates lightly. Parker perks up, sitting straight on the couch, his ears practically pricked like a dog's. "Dad's home," he says to no one in particular, which somehow makes it sweeter. Then he bolts up.

And my heart—it swells.

A minute later, he launches himself at Tyler, who comes around the corner dressed in workout shorts and a T-shirt. Tyler scoops up Parker easily. "What's up, little buddy?"

"I'm not little," Parker says, but it's full of affection, not any of the attitude he gave me. Good. It's nice to see someone have a good relationship with their father. And I can handle attitude, no problem.

Once Tyler sets his son down, he turns to me in the kitchen and blinks in surprise as I wipe my hands on a towel. He peers at the array of food, then back at me. "You...didn't have to cook."

But he doesn't actually sound mad. He sounds delighted.

"I didn't," I say, feeling a little buzzy from his reaction. "I only prepped things to make it easier for your 'build-a-taco night.'"

Parker snaps his gaze to me. "Build a taco?"

I meet the eight-year-old's eyes, playing my ace. "Yes. I figured you can set everything out and pick your own ingredients for it."

"Isn't that just...taco night?"

"Ah, but is it? You can build the whole thing from scratch—from the rice to the beans to the chicken to the guacamole. Sort of like when you build Lego," I say, feeling a little proud of myself for the comparison.

"Okay, but we already do that," he says, thoroughly unimpressed.

But after years of performing skating routines that rise and crest, I know a thing or two about how to make a point. "Right. *Of course* you assemble your own tacos. But if your dad says yes, maybe if you build something cool out of the taco—like a car, or a house, or a shooting star— you might be able to convince your dad to give you something sweet."

"I want to build my own taco," Parker says to his dad, and yes! Parker's enthusiasm is small, but it feels like one thing going right with him. Score one for the nanny.

"When you finish your homework. And after I cook the beans and meat," Tyler says, then sends Parker to tackle his books.

Parker runs off as Tyler strides into the kitchen, a quirk in his brow. "Build-a-taco night?"

"I figured a name like that might make it seem more fun," I say, but I don't tell him why I want more fun for Parker. I don't want to worry him about his son not liking me.

Tyler's astute, though, because he says, "Let me guess. He was standoffish?"

And he knows his son well. Giving in, I hold up my thumb and forefinger to show a sliver of space. "Yes, but it was the first day. It's all good. However, I have a very important question—can Parker have gummy bears?" My stomach spins with nerves, chased by the raw awareness that I was too caught up in word play with Tyler earlier to nail down the details of what to buy and not buy. Not sure I want to admit that? But then I can hear Elena's voice in my head. *It's okay to admit you need a little help.* "I wasn't sure actually after our conversation earlier if you were good with that or not. Or how you feel about candy and such. I mean, I know you think chocolate chip cookies are scandalous," I tease, reminding him of our wedding night conversation—the one that took place before my 1001 Confessions.

"I'm not a big candy person. Sweets aren't *my* guilty pleasure," he says, and instantly I want to know what his pleasures are—guilty or otherwise. "But I try not to be a hard-ass either. So every now and then can't hurt."

"I agree," I say, relieved that I made the choice to buy them. "And now you have dessert for them tonight."

"They'll love you for sure then," he says, and I hope so. Truly, I do. But I know, too, it'll take time.

I glance around the neat, clean kitchen before looking toward the stairs. Luna seems happily ensconced in her room. It was only one afternoon. Only a few hours. But here we are, and everyone is safe and sound. I should play it cool, but I've never been the cool one. "We made it," I add, letting out an exaggerated, "whew."

Tyler's businesslike demeanor slips away, and a smile takes over. "So I guess you're not quitting?"

My jaw drops. "What? No! Were you worried?"

He shrugs. "No. Yes. Maybe. You never know."

"You're stuck with me," I say, since I will dig my heels into this job like a dog refusing to let go of a one hundred and eighty-seven-day-old bagel it's found on the corner.

"Good," he says, and his shoulders seem to loosen a notch, a sense of ease relaxing his smile as he gathers supplies around the kitchen.

That's my cue to go. I gesture toward the stairs leading to my apartment. "I should leave you to it."

Give him space to be the dad and all.

"Right," he says, but he sounds a little wistful. Almost like he wants me to stay? But no, that can't be it. This is family time, not get-to-know-the-new-nanny time.

Besides, that soft look in his eyes right now? He's probably just tired after the team meeting. Which makes me wonder...

"Are you sure you don't want me to cook?"

"No," he says quickly. "I'll handle it."

And yeah, I should go. "Just let me know about tomorrow's schedule. Text me, maybe. If you can't find me, that is," I tease, since I can't seem to stop running my mouth.

"I will."

"You're leaving soon for an away game, right?" The Sea Dogs season opener is in Las Vegas against one of their main rivals.

"Yes, in three days," he says, and that's when I'll be really busy with the kids—it'll be all me on Thursday and Friday. "Tomorrow you've got some skating lessons in the morning, right?"

"I do. I'll have to rise and shine since it's really early," I say, grateful I can work my skating schedule around the job.

"I'll take them to school so you can get to it."

"You sure?"

"Of course. You'll be busy when I'm out of town. And Elle won't have them till the weekend after this one."

"Right," I say, since Tyler's shared a schedule with me already. The kids are with him most of the time since Elle's swamped with med school, but she's got them a couple weekends a month, and a few nights here and there. I'm glad she's still involved in their life—for them, of course, but also for him. Being a single parent with a full-time job that takes you out of town a lot is *hard*.

I don't want to infringe on the time he has with his children, so I make my way to the staircase that leads to the garden apartment as Luna trots down from the second floor to the main one. But before I round the corner, Tyler calls out, "Do you want to build a taco?"

It's sung, and it sounds exactly like the famous song "Do You Want to Build a Snowman," and it tells me that Tyler watches *Frozen* with his kids.

I can't resist singing back, "It doesn't have to be a taco."

A few seconds later, Luna's joining in, inviting me to build a taco too. It's tempting. Truly it is, especially with the a cappella invite, but I should let them be a family. "Thank you, but I'm all good."

They both serenade me more as I head down the stairs. I nearly turn around and join them.

* * *

A couple hours later, I'm researching wildlife sanctuaries in the area for Luna, how far they are from here and the programs they offer, when there's a knock on my door.

When I open it and see Tyler standing there, he's quick to say, "The kids are getting ready for bed. Do you want to build a taco now? It's pretty fun. Parker made the Big Dipper, which is an asterism, as he likes to remind me, because god forbid I not know every detail about the stars. Luna made a taco cat, with lettuce as the tail, and everyone got gummy bears. And there's more than enough."

My first instinct is to say no. I'm not sure I need any more awkward moments with this sexy man.

But then he goes for the kill with: "And I figured you and Luna eat the same things, so there are plenty of veggies for you."

That does it for me—the way he noticed this little detail. "How did you...?"

"I paid attention," he says, and I replay when he would have figured that out. I haven't mentioned my personal food preferences to him, and we haven't eaten together... except. Holy smokes. He remembered from the nachos on my wedding night? When I said *no meat*. This man's memory is...sexy.

My stomach growls in appreciation for his offer for so many reasons. Maybe especially because Chad was always goading me to eat medium-rare burgers or braised fish or Chicken Pad Thai. Like my not eating meat was some kind of challenge he needed to win. But my *nothing with a face* choice wasn't about control or perfectionism. It is just who I am. It is my choice and mine alone.

"Veggie tacos sound perfect," I say, meaning it. Because he's not trying to change me—he's just listening.

As we head upstairs, I say, "But what did you make with your taco?"

"A puck," he says, his voice low and rumbly, like he knows how that word sounds—a little bit dirty.

And I like it too much.

13

THE FIRST TWENTY-FOUR HOURS
ARE THE HARDEST

Sabrina

It's an age-old question about figure skating—do you ever get used to the early mornings, or do the early mornings get used to you? While I can wake at four-thirty, I wouldn't say I spring free from my bed.

But muscle memory drags me out. To the bureau, where I grab leggings, a sweater, and a sports bra. To the bathroom, where I brush my teeth, loop my hair into a ponytail, and get dressed. Then to the garage, where I hop into my car, spotting a small canvas bag on the floor of the backseat. I must not have grabbed everything in the move yesterday so I make a note to snag that later, pulling out before the sun's even thinking about rising. I drive through the quiet pre-dawn city, cruising along with doctors, nurses, and other early risers, the scent of the car's cinnamon apple air freshener tickling my nose. Soon, I reach Sunnyside Rink where I rent ice for my lessons from the rink's owners. An older couple, Hank and Marla Dawson, were both college hockey players. They met in school, fell in love, and opened this rink together.

With a key I've used countless times, I unlock the heavy double doors, then go inside and punch in a code on the alarm, silencing it before it goes off.

Inside, the familiar blast of chilly air hits my cheeks, and I sigh happily. It's like coming home. It never fails to invigorate me. All at once, I'm wide awake without a drop of caffeine.

My student—Jasmine Morales—won't arrive for another twenty minutes. It's just me, the ice, and the start of the day. I set my bag on the bleachers, slide off my sneakers, and lace up my skates.

After grabbing my travel action camera that Leighton gave me as a "business-warming" gift, I attach it to a stick, adjust some settings, then step onto the ice, holding it.

I don't move right away. I breathe in, inhaling the cool, crisp scent, the bite in the air, the solitude.

When I first laced up at age four, skating was fun. It stayed that way for many years. But at some point, I chased excellence as much as joy. Maybe more. There's nothing wrong with wanting to be tops at something. But it can obsess you. Addict you. Control you.

After I failed to make the Olympics in early college, I had to face some tough truths about myself. I was obsessed with skating, but also with the prep for skating. With the rules and guidelines about how to excel. With the climb up the mountain, and whether I was doing enough—lifting enough weights with enough frequency, skating enough programs with enough electricity.

And smiling through it all. Smiling even when it hurt.

It was a harsh reality, but I learned over time that it's

okay to have fun on the ice. I don't have to obsess over every second, every routine, every workout.

Most of all, I learned I can skate for me.

I'm off, holding the stick with the camera at the end of it, then hitting the ice and flying. It's always felt that way—like flying—even when it's hard. And figure skating is often hard. It's supposed to be hard. And terrifying. And beautiful. It's all of those things. But it's also like meditation as the blades cut into the ice while I skate backward, picking up the pace, arms out, crossing over again and again as I glide around the rink.

Music plays in my earbuds—a fast pop song that makes my pulse speed and my heart soar.

I spin—a scratch spin, with my legs crossed and arms briefly tucked in but still holding the camera, something I've done many times. I move out of it and glide forward, picking up speed again before shifting into a toe loop, landing cleanly, and circling the rink once more, the tiny camera capturing all my moves close up so the viewer feels like they're moving with me.

In some ways, this impromptu routine feels like every morning of my life growing up, when I spent hours at the rink practicing, refining, and aiming for not only excellence, but perfection.

Sometimes reaching it. Always craving it.

Now, though, it feels like freedom. I barely think of the camera, but when I do, it doesn't feel like a judge. It's an outlet for me to express the joy I feel in sport and in movement.

A few more songs, and I'm breathless, exuberant, and ready to teach.

Good thing, because Jasmine and her mom have just arrived. I turn off the camera, then put it away in my bag.

I'll edit the video later and post it, and thanks to modern technology the stick won't appear in the final clip. Yay software.

"Let's do this," I say enthusiastically to the twelve-year-old sporting braids, a beanie and a morning glow.

Then we work—but I try to make it feel like play.

"Yes! You got this," I cheer every time she nails a move.

When she struggles, I help her break it down and find the joy in the sport too. That's what I tried to recapture in college—after taking a year off to see a therapist, work at a coffee shop, and get my mind right again. It worked. I started skating for fun and, eventually, for performance. Turns out I like the performance side better than competition.

But I love teaching most of all. When we finish, Jasmine asks, "Do you think I can go to the Olympics? Or maybe the national championships? It would be so cool to be the first Black girl since Debi Thomas to win a medal."

My chest swells with hope. But tightens, too, since I don't want to say the wrong thing, especially since I love her dreams, and her pride in what they might mean. "I think anything is possible. But the most important thing is to keep showing up—if you love the sport."

"I do love it," she says, resolute and hopeful all at once.

"Then I'll see you at our next lesson," I say, naming the time and date. Tyler is heading out of town in two days, but Jasmine does afternoon lessons too, so I can make those before I pick up the kids.

She smiles, then takes off. Soon, I close the rink, send a thank you message to the owners—Hank and Marla—and head outside as my phone pings with a reply from Marla, a long row of smiley faces and snowflakes. The sun is up now, shining brightly above the horizon as I drive home, energized by the lesson.

Home.

The word drifts through my mind again. I haven't really felt like I've had a home recently, not after bouncing from Isla's couch to Starla's micro-studio over the summer, and before that...well, Fuck Chad's place doesn't count.

What a weird thought—to think of Tyler's house as my home. Well, it's my home for now, and I suppose that's all I can ask for.

I pull into the garage next to his sleek electric car. He's probably inside, getting the kids ready for school.

Since I don't need to "clock in" just yet, I head to my apartment, tug off my skating clothes, and grab a navy blue towel as I turn on the shower. Is this my towel? It's fluffier than I remember, and it smells fresh and new. Must be one of Tyler's guest towels.

The steam begins filling the stall as the water heats up. I'm about to step in when I glance at the shower shelf.

"Seriously?" I groan.

I forgot to bring my shampoo and conditioner inside yesterday. Bet that's what's in the canvas bag on the floor of my car.

After turning off the water, I wrap the towel tightly around myself, grab my car keys, and peer into the hallway. It's quiet, and the garage door is only a few feet away.

I dart across the hall, open the door, and head to my car, pressing the key fob to unlock it.

"Gotcha," I mutter, snatching the bag and shutting the door loudly. But when I spin around, I freeze.

I'm not alone.

The hot dad I work for is standing in the garage,

dressed in a gray college T-shirt and a pair of basketball shorts, staring at me with eyes as wide as Moon Pies.

In no time, I grab at the top of my towel, tugging it higher above my breasts. Decorum and all. "I was getting shampoo. And conditioner," I offer hastily, as if that explains everything.

Even though I *could* have put on clothes. But I took a chance.

Tyler's silent for a beat, his jaw slack. Then he clears his throat and, several seconds later, blurts, "I was… getting some sausage from…" He points vaguely at the white freezer on the far side of the garage.

"The freezer?" I supply, since speech seems to be failing him.

"Um. Yeah. The freezer," he says thickly, his voice rough, sending a rush of heat down my spine.

With my free hand, I smooth the bottom of the towel, making sure it's securely in place. Except…a very naughty devil on my shoulder has half a mind to say, *"So…want to throw me down on the bed and devour me?"*

At least, those *look* like eyes that want to devour a woman. Pupils dilated. Intense eye contact. Heat.

I think?

What do I know?

I only know Fuck Chad.

But I want to know what it's like to be wanted. To be adored. To be devoured. To be…

He exhales sharply, like he's trying to regain control. "I should—"

"Get the sausage?" I suggest, and…oh, does that sound dirty.

"It's veggie sausage," he adds quickly. "For…Luna."

"Sounds good," I say, my voice a little too breathy.

"I can make you some."

That sounds good, too, so I nod. "Yes." I point toward the door, which he's still blocking. "I need to...shower."

He shuffles aside, awkwardly, which is unexpected from a man who moves his body for a living. He winces. "Sorry. I didn't mean to walk in on you."

"You didn't really walk in on me. I'm the one standing here in a towel," I say with a laugh, though my pulse is pounding. "I guess I should probably put clothes on next time."

"It was my fault," he says, though he still hasn't moved completely out of the way.

"I'll make sure I'm dressed next time," I add, but my breath is coming faster now. And his eyes...his eyes look like those of a man who wants to devour.

A devourer.

Is that a thing?

It *should* be a thing.

"I'm just going to...go," I say, backing toward the door.

"Be sure to come upstairs," he calls after me.

I glance at him, up and down, before stepping inside. "Yes. For sausage."

I scurry back inside, clutching the towel tightly. As I reach my apartment, it hits me once more—this is not my towel.

Stopping in my tracks, I spin around and grab the door before it shuts.

"Tyler?" I call out, even though I shouldn't. I shouldn't be this close to him when I'm nearly naked. But my heart is racing, and my skin feels warmer. I feel *alive* in my body when I'm near him, and even though I know I should resist, I can't seem to stop myself.

He turns, his hand still holding the freezer door open,

but he angles the lower half of his body away from me. "Yes?"

"Is this...towel yours?"

The question feels incomplete, and I hesitate. I'm almost afraid to ask what I really want to know: *Did you get this towel for me?*

It's a presumptuous question—too presumptuous to make landfall, so I keep it locked up.

But then he straightens up, letting the freezer door close, and turns fully toward me.

"No," he says, pausing for a moment before adding, "I got a few for you. I wanted it to feel like your home. Is the color okay?"

His words knock the air out of me. I try to fight off the smile tugging at my lips, but it's a losing battle.

It's stupid to be this excited about a towel. A *towel.* But it's big, soft, and exactly what I needed.

"It's perfect," I say, and this time I actually leave, heading to the shower.

Once inside, I set the towel on the rack and turn on the water. Steam fills the space quickly, but as I step in, I can't tell if the water is heating me up—or if it's the other way around.

* * *

I finish the veggie sausage Tyler left for me, rinse the plate, and set it in the dishwasher just as the front door creaks open.

He steps inside, pausing—maybe to kick off his shoes —but then his footsteps fade into the distance. Did he go upstairs or...downstairs?

A few seconds later, the sound of footfalls resumes,

and then he pads down the hall. Finally, he steps into the kitchen.

"The sausage was great," I chirp. First, because it was, and second, because I don't need to quiz my boss about what he just did after dropping off the kids.

"Good," he says, his tone even, his voice deep. His movements are effortless now, unlike in the garage. It's like he's in control again as he pushes a hand through his messy hair and then reaches into the cupboard. He takes out a bag of coffee and waggles it in my direction. "Want some?"

I shake my head. "I'm naturally caffeinated," I reply.

"Good trait in a nanny," he says with a faint smile.

"Yes, I suppose it is."

He sets to work making the coffee, and I know I should excuse myself, especially since I'm on duty this afternoon while he heads to the arena. But before I leave, I say, "The towel was lovely. Really thoughtful. I only had a couple of towels, and they definitely weren't that nice. Mine probably came from the discount bin, and yours are...I don't know—do they even make thousand-thread-count towels? Are towels measured like that, or is that just for sheets?"

The corner of his mouth quirks up as he turns and faces me. "Would you like new sheets too?"

"Oh my god, no. I wasn't saying that. My sheets are fine. You don't have to get me anything else," I ramble, a flush creeping up my neck.

"I want you to be comfortable here," he says, his tone soft but deliberate.

I'd be comfortable with you coming downstairs at night and ripping the sheets off me.

A wave of heat rushes through my chest at the inappropriate thought. I quickly shake it away. "You really don't have to get me sheets," I say, trying to sound casual.

He's quiet for a moment as he measures the coffee, then licks his lips before speaking. "What if I want to?"

He pulls a mug from the cupboard and makes a show of plunking it onto the counter.

My breath catches. It's *that* mug—the one I got him. The one that says: *Sorry About Your St. Bernard Ex, But Here's to Better Dogs Ahead.*

His smile says he knows exactly what he's doing.

But does he know how turned on I am because of a mug?

Except...it's not the mug. It's him. The man who's spoiling me.

"Nice mug," I say, trying for nonchalant.

"What mug? I have no idea what you mean," he replies, his grin mischievous. The grin of a man who remembers the Night of a 1001 Confessions.

And as much as I want to stay, I leave. I rush downstairs to cool off because I'm less than twenty-four hours into my new job, and I already want to proposition my boss again.

I'll splash water on my face, settle down, and work on some skating routines for Jasmine, Luna, and the other kids I coach. I'll do my morning yoga. I'll see my friends.

I stop in my tracks. A pink paper shopping bag with cute little handles sits in front of the door. I snatch it up and peer inside.

There are sheets. Pretty light blue sheets, and the label says they're five hundred-thread count. I know nothing about thread counts, but something tugs at my brain. A question. I google it, and the Internet tells me that while there are thousand-thread-count sheets, five hundred is the best.

Warmth travels through my body, like the sun is shining on me. He got me sheets—the best sheets. Most of all, he did it *before* we joked about it. That's why he was smirking like he had a secret a few minutes ago. He did it on his own. The man is entirely too thoughtful.

Especially since he left another note with the sheets. I read it.

I know you have some already, but...I wanted you to have these.

—T

Already, I like these better. Not for the thread count. But because he got them for me...just because. Stupidly, I hug them. I hold them close for longer than I should, then I go inside, a little giddy.

The door shuts behind me with a loud thud, breaking my thoughts. Breaking the trance too.

He hired me to work in his home. Of course he wants me to have nice sheets. It's just thoughtful. It's not a sign he wants to reconsider my offer from my failed wedding night.

And it's for the best I stop reconsidering it too.

* * *

Later that morning, I pop upstairs to thank him and ask

where the washing machine and dryer are. "So I can wash the sheets before I make the bed."

"Right across from my bedroom," he says, leading me upstairs and down the hall.

I try, I swear I try, not to look in his room.

But I fail, catching sight of the biggest bed I've ever seen. "Is that bigger than king-size? Is it what, emperor size?"

Tyler laughs, eyes twinkling. "Yes. It's for my reign in the bedroom."

And then both our smiles falter. At once.

One day at a time, I tell myself. *One day at a time, and I'll learn how to survive working for this man.*

* * *

On Thursday morning I'm driving the kids to school after a skating lesson when Parker says from the backseat, "My mom knows what a shooting star is."

Damn. This kid pulls no punches. "I bet she's really smart."

"She is. She likes science."

He doesn't say *like me,* but he doesn't have to. It's evident in his tone. "I'm so glad to hear that," I say, hoping he can hear the sincerity in my tone. I peer in the rearview. "And I'm glad you and your mom have things in common."

"Me too," he mutters, then gets out at school with barely a goodbye.

Luna leans forward. "Boys are moody. But I'll see you later." She peers at the dashboard. "Oh, and you need a sign with our last name on it for the window to pick us up. I'll get you one later today."

I smile, a big relieved one. "You're a lifesaver."

She shrugs. "It's easy-peasy."

Then she takes off with a friendly wave that I'm more grateful for than I'd ever imagined I would be.

* * *

The next day, I pull up outside the kids' school like a freaking pro. I've got a blue sign in the dashboard window with the name *Falcon* on it, which honestly kind of makes me feel cool. I'm there at exactly 3:02, which is precisely the best time to arrive for their three-fifteen exit. Early enough so I won't make a mistake. I cut the engine and wait, blasting Amelia Stone and singing along to her girl anthems. A few minutes later, right on time, the kids stream out and Luna and Parker pile into the backseat.

I haven't won over Parker yet. But that's okay. These things take time, and I understand that we all react to change in different ways. But I've got a plan for today. Tyler's in Vegas for the season opener, and I've been managing just fine the last few days. Well, my fancy sheets help.

"How's it going?" I ask as I turn the music down.

Luna dives right into chatter as she yanks on her seatbelt. "I aced my math test."

"You go," I say, lifting my fist in a rocker salute. "Math girls unite."

"And my friend Hannah is having a sleepover this weekend, and I want to go. Can I go?"

"We need to check with your dad," I say as I flick on the blinker.

Parker scoffs at his sister. "I told you she'd have to ask Dad."

"Well, he *is* your father," I point out as I pull into relatively light afternoon traffic.

"Yeah, but Agatha was able to make those decisions," Parker says, but he's less, well, mean than he was when he said it earlier in the week. Less hurt too, I think. Maybe more matter-of-fact.

I sense an opening. "Parker, do you have any plans for tonight?" I ask, evenly, not giving myself away.

"I don't know. Do I?" he asks, curious, like a cat wanting to check out your new food offering but not sure he trusts you.

"You do now," I say. Then I tell him what we're going to do.

And in the rearview mirror, I see his jaw drop.

14

DICK CONTROL

Tyler

The Las Vegas forward is charging down the ice at Mach speed, and Lambert looms in the net, a beast protecting his lair.

But it's my job, too, and I spot an opening. Right when the opponent lifts his stick to slam the puck, I time it perfectly, jamming mine in front of it, swatting it back the other way with a satisfying whiz across the ice. The puck whistles past center ice, landing on my brother's stick. He races toward the Vegas net...

And delivers us a point.

I thrust my glove in the air. A block and an assist all at once. Thank you very much.

The forward curses at me. "Fucking asshole," he mutters.

"Yes, yes, I am," I say to him, flashing the Vegas Saber a *what are you gonna do about it* grin as I skate to the bench and hop over the boards.

After grabbing my water bottle, I chug as the next line jumps over.

Coach smacks me on the shoulder. "Keep that up."

"I will, sir," I say, meaning it. This game is exactly what I need to set the tone for the season: gritty, full throttle, leave it all on the ice.

When the game ends with another W, I head to the locker room, eager to do just that for the next eighty-one games. Right now, I'm ready to head back home and see my kids. They're the reason I play all out.

The better I play, the better I can provide for them, and the last thing I want is to fail as a father. I witnessed that failure for myself growing up, and I won't do it to my kids. Which is why I have something fun planned for Parker this weekend.

As we head down the Vegas arena corridor to board the bus to the airport, Rowan gives me a nod. "How's everything back home?" It's a rare moment when he's not giving me hell.

"Pretty good," I say as we walk.

"Nice. How are the kids doing?"

As if he's summoned them, my phone trills and Parker's photo lights up the screen—a shot of him triumphantly lifting a fork and digging into a plate of pancakes. I took it at a diner they love.

I show it to Rowan. "I should grab this."

"Do it, man," he says, waving me off. He's the same way—always picks up for his daughter.

"What's up, kiddo?"

"Dad! Did you know Betelgeuse is a red supergiant near the end of its life?"

I furrow my brow for a second, then figure it out. "It's a star?"

"Yes! A reddish star in Orion. The planetarium had the coolest exhibit on supergiants, and there was a light show and everything."

Sabrina must have taken him. My chest warms, a mix of gratitude and something I don't have a name for yet. Maybe appreciation for her effort? Her creativity? "Sabrina took you to the planetarium?" I ask, confirming.

"Yeah! It was super cool. They had a whole sky show with music, and we learned about supernovas—like the team you used to play on. Betelgeuse might turn into a supernova someday!"

"That's pretty cool."

"You wanna know what else I learned?"

"I do."

"The Andromeda Galaxy is on a collision course with the Milky Way. But not for, like, four billion years."

I laugh. "All in due time."

"Anyway, we picked up more stickers for my ceiling for this weekend, but we can go shopping when you get home if you want to find more. I just think it'd be awesome to get one of a supergiant."

"A supergiant, huh?" I say.

"Yup! Oh, and I got you a cool T-shirt too. Well, I told Sabrina you'd think it was funny, so she picked it up—but it's really from me."

I'm not sure I'm following the math or money, but I grin anyway.

When we land in San Francisco, I catch up with Miles in the players' lot. We share rides sometimes—better for Earth and all. So I hop into the passenger seat of his car.

"Good thing you're not bringing the Falcon name down so far this season," he says, pulling out of the lot.

"Pretty sure I'm bringing it up," I toss back.

He scoffs. "Not sure it can go higher. Did you see my stats last season?" he says as he drives toward Pacific Heights.

I shoot him a look. "Is there a cup in your house I'm unaware of?"

That shuts him up. But not for long. "Seriously though. We could get one this season. Together. Wouldn't that be something?"

I give him a genuine smile as I offer a fist for knocking. "That would be something indeed."

When he pulls up in front of my home, he gives me a chin nod. "How's everything working out with the house and all? You think you'll buy anytime soon?"

I sigh. "I should, but man, life is busy, you know?"

"I hear you. Don't wait too long though. You'll be here for a while."

I appreciate the endorsement. "That's the plan," I say, then thank him and head up the steps.

When I go inside, the T-shirt Parker told me about is sitting on the kitchen counter. It says: Science is Cool Since It Works Whether You Believe It or Not.

I smile, but not because of the shirt or the good game, or even because of Miles's faith in us. It's because Sabrina figured out my kid. Parker's not an easy puzzle to crack—he's bright, curious, and a little too serious for his age sometimes. But she tried, and it seems she delivered.

It's late, and I'm the only one up. I grab an apple from the counter and crunch into it, taking a moment to breathe in the quiet of the house, the hum of the fridge the only noise. I finish the apple, then toss it into the compost bin and head upstairs, a pang of longing cutting briefly through my chest. I ignore it, since really, what am I even longing for?

I re-center my thoughts as I get ready for bed, chucking my tie and suit back into the closet and tugging on shorts and a T-shirt. As I brush my teeth, I find myself reviewing Sabrina's first week, and I'd say she did a damn fine job. That relaxes me as I slide under the covers a few minutes later.

But once I'm alone in the biggest bed ever, my mind drifts to her. Two flights down. Is she under her sheets? And how do they feel against her body? Are they smooth against her skin? Does she get hot when she sleeps and kick them off?

A groan, unbidden, rumbles up my chest as I imagine the cool blue sheets slipping down her skin, revealing soft flesh and full breasts, and a warm, eager woman.

The longing intensifies, revving my mind and my body.

I could ignore it, but instead I feed it. I reach for my phone on the nightstand. I hop over to her socials, and a fizzy feeling rushes through me when I spot a new video. I've never once commented on her posts, or even "liked" them. But I have watched all her skating videos. Every single one, from the routines and free skates to the tutorials. Yeah, I'm a social stalker. But the woman is stunning and her videos are...addictive. Before I hit play, I grab my earbuds and pop them in. Don't want anyone to wake up and figure out what I'm listening to. I hit play, then settle down under the covers, a hazy sensation filling me as a Jane Black song plays, and Sabrina glides across the ice. She posted this a couple days ago, and it hits me—this routine might very well be from her first morning here. When I ran into her in the garage and she was wearing only her towel.

For some stupid reason, that makes me feel even

more connected to her, knowing what she did *after*. She came here, to my house. With that sense of satisfaction running through my veins, I get a little lost in how she gains speed and power with each crossover, then I'm mesmerized by her spins. I bet they took years to perfect. Of course they did. And she makes it look effortless. When she launches into the air, my breath catches annoyingly, but after two revolutions she lands like it was easy.

I smile. A stupid smile. Because I really shouldn't be watching this.

I hit play again. Then one more time. And I like it so much I'm tempted to hit the heart button.

My finger hovers over it, and I almost, *almost,* do it.

But I catch myself then yank out my earbuds and put the phone on do not disturb. It's me who shouldn't disturb the phone—not the other way around.

I let out a long sigh in the dark, flip over, and pound my pillow a few times. "Get over it, man," I mutter.

But it takes me longer to fall asleep than it should as visions of the woman living under the same roof dance in my head.

* * *

I can balance on the edge of a blade while slamming a puck into the net. But climbing a ladder in my kid's bedroom? While the stunning new nanny hands me sun and moon stickers?

That's an entirely new feat of strength.

It's not because of the ladder. The ladder is fine. The problem is in my pants.

I am that guy now.

That asshole who gets borderline aroused by his kids' nanny's baby tee as it rises up, revealing her stomach.

Am I obsessed with her stomach?

Don't answer that, brain. Just don't answer it.

But my unhelpful brain supplies the answer anyway: *You're obsessed with all of her. Including that belly button ring you just noticed.*

And the problem is, it's making me wonder if she has other piercings. Where they might be. If they're part of what she wanted me to explore.

Thank god I have *some* dick control though. Enough that I'm not sporting wood in my kid's bedroom. For fuck's sake, if that ever happens, I'll have to hang a shame sign around my neck, like a dog who ate his owner's underwear.

Fortunately, Parker and Sabrina are oblivious to my libido's plight. They're busy sorting through the packs of stickers, and handing me moons and stars. Parker's chattering nonstop about astronomy facts while Sabrina hums under her breath, seeming completely at ease. I force myself to focus on their conversation instead of her stomach.

"Do you think this is Betelgeuse?" Sabrina asks Parker as she hands me a sticker with five points even though she's not on the clock today.

"No, I don't think it's the right size," Parker says with the authority of an amateur astronomer. "We need a bigger one."

"Well, you'd better find it," Sabrina says, urging him along. "It's really important to put it on the ceiling. Also, I think you should add the Andromeda Galaxy and the Milky Way Galaxy, so you can be prepared for their collision."

He rolls his blue eyes, but it's playful, not patronizing. "Okay, those are way too big to represent with stickers," Parker says.

"I don't know. That seems like a challenge you'd definitely be up for. Come on, Mister Lego," she teases.

"Oh, those are fighting words," I say.

This is helping matters. This back-and-forth between the two of them is helping. Because I'm focused on that now, instead of the way she looks—entirely too tempting in baggy jeans and a short white shirt.

Parker hands me more stickers and tells me where to place them. I follow his instructions religiously, stretching to reach the ceiling while craning my neck to make sure I get the placement right. This repetitive task is far more helpful to my overactive libido than looking at Sabrina.

But an hour later, with a crick in my neck and a ceiling covered in stars, I climb down and find myself face-to-face with her again.

Wincing as the pain shoots through me, I stretch my neck from side to side. Sabrina flashes me a quizzical look while Parker admires the ceiling. "Are you okay?" she asks, her eyes full of concern.

"I'm fine," I say, rubbing my hand against the back of my neck where a dragon's laid an egg, "but I have a new sympathy for Michelangelo now."

"Aren't you a Renaissance daddy," she says, then pats my shoulder.

Hello, zing. That is not supposed to feel so good.

I am a grown man. A father. And I'm affected by my kids' nanny like a fucking thirteen-year-old boy. But I practice my vaunted dick control, imagining—who would have thought this would be a boner killer—skate blades.

Ha. Take that, hormones. You're not going to get the best of me.

"All right," I say to Parker, rubbing my palms together, focusing on business, the task at hand. "What do you think? Does anything need to be adjusted?"

My son is lying on his bed, staring critically at the ceiling with narrowed eyes. "I think I need to be in the dark to know for sure."

"Well, fortunately, you have blinds." I move around his room to pull down the wooden shutters. It's evening, but it's still not dark enough.

"Why don't I grab some dark sheets?" Sabrina suggests, then hustles out of there, quickly returning with a set of black linen from the closet in the hall. Without using thumbtacks or anything else, she loops them around the top of the wooden blinds as footsteps grow louder—Luna must have emerged from her room to check things out.

"That's impressive," I say with a low whistle as I appraise Sabrina's work.

"I'm a little crafty," Sabrina replies as Luna pops into the room, her ponytail bouncing.

"That's true. Sabrina makes her own costumes," Luna says.

Why does that excite me? I don't even know, but I turn to Sabrina for confirmation. "You made your own skating costumes?"

"Necessity is also the mother of invention. I had to, so I taught myself to sew," she says, twisting the final sheet into place. "What do you think?"

I think I want to know why she *had to*, but I also think she doesn't want to talk about it this second as the room transforms. The ceiling glows with thousands of stars.

Parker gasps. "This is amazing," he says.

"You did good picking these out," Sabrina says to him with a smile visible in the darkness.

"Thank you for helping," Parker says, a little guilt and gratitude in his tone. He's not angling to be her best friend. He doesn't treat her the same way he did Agatha. But he's warming up to her, and I'm glad for that.

"Yeah, I kind of like them too," Luna says, admiring the stars, then tapping her chin. "But I'd want a disco ball instead."

Sabrina's eyes light up. "Disco balls are so cool. I wanted disco balls in my room so badly when I was a kid."

"Did you have them?" Luna asks, hanging on Sabrina's every word.

She shakes her head, her shiny blonde hair swishing. "My parents said I couldn't. They thought it was too immature. But I was a kid—I was supposed to be immature."

"Hello! That's what being a kid is. And now I really want a disco ball," Luna says, clasping her hands together as she turns to me, batting those big brown eyes. "Can I get a disco ball for the ceiling, Dad?"

I pinch the bridge of my nose and shake my head. But it's hardly a no. It's more like *how can I say no to you*? When I let go, I look at Sabrina with a playful accusation. "Look what you've unleashed."

But Sabrina has no remorse. She points to me. "You unleashed it. You put the stars on the ceiling first."

Luna shimmies her hips. "I guess that means I can get a disco ball!"

"Why do I feel like I'm outnumbered already?" I ask.

"Because you kind of are," Luna says, grabbing Sabrina's arm in solidarity.

"She speaks the truth," Sabrina says.

Parker cuts in. "I think there's one set of stars that needs to be adjusted." He points toward Orion's Belt. At least, he's told me it's Orion's Belt. "There are a couple extra stars and they need to be moved." His brow knits. "I can do it."

But he's a little afraid of heights. I go to intervene, but before I can, Sabrina pops up. "I'll do it," she says, and my body heats with warmth that she knows so much about my son already.

In no time, she climbs the ladder, stretches her arms toward the ceiling, and everything starts to rise.

And I do mean everything.

I clear my throat, cough, then make up an excuse about needing a drink. I exit the room so I can cool the fuck off. My chest is a furnace. My skin is sweltering. She is too much.

Down in the kitchen, I fill a glass with tap water and pace. This is the occupational hazard of wanting to bang your nanny: the risk of getting turned on around your kids.

I add ice cubes to my water and consider putting them down my pants.

But the potential deflation is achieved faster than I'd expected. Hell yes. I've still got good dick control.

When I head back upstairs, Sabrina is stretched out on the carpeted floor next to Parker and Luna, all staring at the ceiling, arms parked behind their heads.

"Dad, come look," Luna says. "We can figure out exactly where my disco ball should go by studying how everything looks."

"Your room will never be as cool as mine," Parker says.

"I bet it will," Luna says.

"I bet it won't," he replies.

It's not one-upmanship, it's just basic teasing, and I love that they do that with each other.

"Siblings," I say to Sabrina, like *what can you do.*

"I wish I had a brother or sister," she says, a little wistfully.

"You sure about that?" Luna teases.

"You'd want a brother. One as cool as me," Parker says.

I kneel down to ruffle his hair, but inside my heart tugs for what Sabrina missed out on. For the little comments about how she grew up—with strictness, and rules, and little support. For what her parents are like.

Luna pats the floor, but the only open spot is next to Sabrina. I lie down and my hand brushes hers. I swallow, fighting off the chills that race through me, ignoring the way my skin buzzes, doing my best to stay in this family moment.

This is what matters. She's good with the kids. That is all that matters.

Even though I understand now why I was so excited to learn that she made her own costumes. Because I like learning everything about her. Because I fucking like her. More than I did a week ago, a month ago, at the start of the year.

And that is getting to be a problem.

But my neck's a problem too, so I keep rubbing at the knot. Or trying to.

Sabrina's studying me with those pretty blue eyes of hers. "You know, I have a Theragun if you want to use it."

I have my own, but I say yes so fast. Because accepting her offer means I can follow her downstairs to her place. Where my restraint will be legendary. This will be the perfect test of my dick control and I'll ace it.

I tell the kids it's time for a reading break, and since both are voracious readers, they happily grab books and settle into their favorite reading spots.

I head downstairs with Sabrina. Once I make it to her apartment, my gaze drifts immediately to the corner where she has a purple yoga mat set up.

"Are you doing yoga every day?"

"Yes, Renaissance daddy," she says.

I hold up my hands in surrender. "I didn't mean to make it sound like I was checking up on you."

She gives a playful little shrug. "Maybe you were, maybe you weren't."

Is she being flirty? Or am I far too hopeful?

And the answer is, I'm far too hopeful, because whatever that was ends as she heads to her bedroom. And immediately, I'm wondering what it's like in there. I want to peek around the corner, see her in her element.

I have to fight the urge to follow her.

Seconds later, she comes out waggling the massage gun. It looks exactly like a heavy-duty power tool, and it vibrates like one. While my rational mind knows there's no way she'd use it in bed, my dirty mind wanders there anyway, picturing other vibrating tools and her.

"Sit down on the couch," she tells me.

"Who's bossy now?"

"Me. I can't have my boss going to work with his neck all jacked up," she says, like she enjoys saying that word. "Especially when I can fix it." She looks at the massage gun, then at my neck. "Tell me where it hurts, boss."

She's enjoying saying that far too much. I've got to stay in control, so I lift my hand and rub the back of my neck, indicating where it's killing me.

She presses the button on the gun, and it vibrates with

an intensity that feels like it could send me across the room.

"That thing is supercharged," I say, speaking over the buzzing.

"Oh, it is," she says, sounding way too pleased. But she doesn't press it to my skin. Instead, she studies the vibrating end with some concern before turning it off. "I don't think I'm supposed to use this on your neck. It's too strong."

"Yeah, that makes sense," I say, disappointment creeping into my voice.

Then, in a light tone, she asks, "Do you want me to rub it out?"

If I were drinking something, I'd do a spit take. Because yes. Absolutely yes.

"Sure," I mumble, because I'm too deep into this to say no. Actually, that's a lie. I could say no, but I don't want to. I want her hands on me. Badly.

And I'll take what I can get. She moves behind the couch, pressing her thumbs and her full weight into my shoulders. Her touch is electric. It vibrates through me as she kneads and rubs.

Holy shit, she is strong. Soon she's working over my neck, rubbing out the soreness, getting rid of the knots, and making me feel so damn good that I am groaning.

Yep, I'm sighing and moaning, turning into putty under her hands.

"Mmm. That's fantastic," I murmur.

I can feel her smile. Then hear it in her voice, soft and warm. "That's the point."

"You're definitely making the point," I say.

She digs her thumbs into the knot at the base of my neck, and I'm enjoying this way too much.

Especially since my kids aren't around. It's just her and me. I'm free to think about how much I want to reach for her hands, cover them with mine, pull her over the couch and into my lap, and kiss the breath out of her.

Instead, I reach for the gun on the cushion next to me, so I keep my hands to myself. I busy myself looking at it, pretending it's an oddity I've never seen before. "So...you keep this in your bedroom?" I ask, even though I should keep my mouth shut about how she uses it.

"I do."

I should stop. I really should. "What do you use it for?"

She presses her thumb deeper into the muscles of my neck, harder, massaging out the dragon's egg. "Wouldn't you like to know," she says, teasing.

"I would," I rasp out. "Does it work?"

"It works so well," she purrs.

My famous dick control? Gone. There's no way it's going down while her hands are all over me. So I shut up, close my eyes, and just let myself savor this unexpected massage.

The closeness of her. The way her talented touch works wonders. How she's so willing to help.

I sink into the couch and sigh happily.

Sometime later, I startle awake and look around with a yawn. Shit. The kids! What time is it? Is it night? It's not dark though. I glance at my watch. Oh, it's only forty minutes later.

But I should go check on them. Especially since...I look around Sabrina's place, at her sparse yoga corner, still decorated with only a mat. It's dead quiet in here. I'm all alone. I push up, scratch my jaw, then get the hell out of here.

Once I hit the main floor, I find Sabrina curled up on

the living room couch, reading a book about coaching techniques. She looks up from it and says, "I checked on them as soon as you fell asleep. They're reading, but I figured it'd be best if I stay here in case they needed anything."

Like a responsible adult.

Wincing, I scrub a hand against my neck, relieved but disappointed in myself. "Thanks. I appreciate that."

"No problem," she says.

Sure, this isn't the first time I've crashed midday on them. They're old enough to entertain themselves while we're under the same roof. One time, we were watching an animated movie about a plucky dog leading some kind of resistance movement when I conked out on the couch only to wake up with a bandit mask over my eyes—part of Parker's Halloween costume and pretty damn clever. Another time, I found a cardboard placard on my chest that said *World's Greatest Snorer.*

Still, I should do better. I can't be napping at the nanny's.

Sabrina rises, closing her book with a quick snap. "I'll leave you to it," she says. "I really should prepare for my lessons next week anyway." Once again, she helped out on her own, going the extra mile, like she did with the stars and moon.

"Thanks again," I say as she makes her way out of the living room.

Before she leaves though, she turns around. "I use it on my calves. The Theragun. They get sore."

And you know what? That's still fucking hot. And I still want to be the one to use it on her.

"Let me know if you ever need help," I say, my voice a little gravelly with remnants of sleep.

"I will," she says, her gaze...is it hopeful?

I head to the staircase to check on the kids.

Before I reach it, she says, her voice tinged with nerves but also excitement, "Tomorrow's your home opener. I can bring the kids. We should really all go, don't you think? To cheer you on."

I can't think of a thing I'd rather have right now than all of them in the stands. "Yes."

15

BEDAZZLING

Sabrina

I might have returned the hoodie Tyler gave me on my wedding night, but it seems to have boomeranged back to me. When I wake up on Sunday morning, I find a peach-colored gift bag outside my door with a sweatshirt inside. The same one I returned months ago, I think.

I tug it out, and a note flutters onto the floor.

I don't know if you have any Sea Dogs gear, but I know this —you need it tonight. Don't break my heart by wearing anything but team gear, Snow.

P.S. If you like jerseys better, I left one of those too. The kids will wear theirs. Remember—matchy-matchy is cool. At least I just decided it is.

—T

A smile tugs at my lips as I slip my hand back into the bag, pulling out a jersey in royal blue with his number—forty-four—and his name emblazoned across the back.

My mind immediately whirs with plans for it. I can't help but imagine ways to make it my own. But first, I pick up the note and head back into my apartment. Inside, I cross the small living room, already mentally filing the jersey gift under *perfectly unexpected things Tyler does.*

I set the note carefully into a journal I keep on my nightstand, the one I use to jot down a good thing that's happened to me each day. The journal is pink and white with illustrations of sassy women in flouncy skirts and teetering heels crossing cobblestoned streets.

Isla picked it up for me for my birthday since she's a notebook devotee too—though she's hooked on planners. Well, that's understandable. Planners look fun.

Sometimes I feel a little silly keeping one. Do adults keep journals? But it's a reclaiming of all the tracking I did when I was a teenager. Rather than record the minutes I worked out—and really, in retrospect, would an extra fifteen minutes a day of squats have changed my fate at the Olympics?—I now write down one good thing.

Flipping it open, I tuck the new note beside the one from the sheets and the first one he left—the one from the hotel room that morning after. But I stop and reread it, the kind words hitting me right in the solar plexus all over again, especially this line—*You deserve someone who lets you shine.*

Then I flip forward a few pages and read last night's good thing—*we'll be shopping for disco balls soon!*

Closing the journal, I cross to my dresser and grab a pair of leggings, then throw them on as I mentally prepare for the day. I have some fun plans for activities with the kids. Leighton is an avid geocacher since her guy, Miles, is too, and they do it together. But since Miles and Tyler have game prep, Leighton will take the kids and me on some of her favorite beginner routes.

When I head upstairs, the fading smell of pancakes drifts down the hall. Tyler must have made them before he left for morning skate. I find the kids already in the kitchen. Luna is perched on a stool, swinging her legs, making a playlist—from the looks of it, for her next skating routine—while Parker builds a wing on a Lego spaceship.

"Hey there!" I call, stepping into the kitchen and clocking in for nanny duty.

Luna points to a plate of pancakes. "Hi! Dad said to tell you he left some pancakes for you. They're made with banana, hemp hearts, and whole-wheat flour, and the syrup is all natural."

Tyler knows me well already. "Sounds delish," I say, grabbing a fork, then greeting Parker. Before I dig in, I brandish the jersey. "Hey, Luna. I think this could use some sparkle."

Her eyes widen as she gasps. "Can we add glitter too?"

Parker finally looks up, raising a skeptical eyebrow the jersey's way. "You're going to make *that* sparkly?"

"We are," I say with a confident nod.

Luna's eager eyes light up. "Can you do mine too?"

"Obviously."

Later that day, after we geocache in Dolores Park—tracking down a Matchbox car in a tree, which Luna climbs like a little monkey to retrieve after Parker's spotted it—I order a Lyft, since parking at the arena can be a huge pain, and take the kids to see the Sea Dogs.

Bedazzled.

* * *

But when we arrive, Luna and Parker tell me they want to hang out in the family suite instead of the stands.

Worry digs into me. Is that for wives and girlfriends and their kids? I'd be woefully out of place, wouldn't I?

"Are you sure?" I ask.

"Yes! Mia's always there now. Her dad pays for a sitter for every home game for all the kids, and it's so fun. They have board games and everything. It's kind of more fun than the stands," she says.

"Not kind of. *A lot*," Parker adds.

"Okay, let's go there," I say, but I'm still a little apprehensive about being there myself, and I'm not sure if I'm supposed to just drop the kids off. But I can't call Tyler and ask him. They'll be starting warmups any second. My stomach twists with nerves, but then it hits me—I can call Tyler's mom! She knows everything.

As I'm heading to the family suite, I ring Lauren Falcon and ask her if it's okay that the kids stay there.

"Okay? It's fabulous! Especially since I'm actually hanging out here with Harvey. The food's better here, and we're all about the snacks. Bring those monkeys my way."

"Oh! Great!" I let out a relieved breath. That was serendipitous. I head over to the family suite and say hi to Lauren and her husband Harvey as I survey the spacious room. It's a couple levels above the ice, but it's stacked with food and fun. So I can see why the kids like it. And yes, there are some wives and girlfriends, and kids, but also parents of hockey players from the looks of it. I feel a little better about staying, even though I gaze at the ice longingly.

Lauren nods to it, giving me a knowing smile. "I've got this. You go enjoy the center-ice seats if you want."

She's such a mind reader. "Thanks. I do like being right near the boards."

"Go, go," she says, shooing me out.

I take off, then text my friends, who usually sit right near the center-ice seats Tyler gave me.

Leighton responds first, telling me to get my ass over there. When I make my way down the aisle toward their row, she eyes me up and down. She points to the back of my jersey, which she must have spotted as I maneuvered through the crowds.

"Well, hello, *Rhinestones*," she says, smirking as she christens me with a nickname.

Isla arches a well-groomed brow. Everything about Isla is perfectly put together. "I'm thinking *Squirrel*. Squirrels love shiny things," she says.

"True," adds the redhead next to Isla. That's Skylar— she works at the same podcast studio as Isla. Her show is design-centric, while Isla's is a dating podcast. I've met Skylar a few times—she's bold, outspoken, and resource-ful. Exactly the type of person you'd call to help DIY your way through canning fruit or painting the front door. "But aren't raccoons the ones really into shiny stuff?"

"Are you all saying I look like a raccoon in this?" I gesture to my very shiny, very bedazzled jersey.

"A razzle-dazzle raccoon," Maeve chimes in as she arrives, proudly sporting her *Mrs. Callahan* jersey—a custom one her husband, Asher, made for her a couple seasons ago.

Right next to her is Josie, sliding into her seat. She adjusts her black-and-white glasses as she says warmly, "Actually, she's a bowerbird."

I whip my gaze to Josie, the librarian and resident collector of random facts. Josie has never met a topic she didn't like to research.

"This is going to be good," Maeve says, settling into her seat in the row ahead of us, so we're taking up the first and second rows. The only ones from our girl gang who aren't here are Everly, who's busy working the game as the team publicist, and Fable, who texted that she was on her way.

"Male bowerbirds use shiny or colorful objects to decorate their bowers to attract mates," Josie explains. "They collect things like bottle caps, pieces of glass—"

I raise a hand. "I think I speak for all of us when I ask: what the hell is a bower?"

Josie smooths a hand over her number sixteen jersey —for Wesley, her guy. "It's a structure. Like a house, but fancier. The male builds it to court a mate."

"So, basically," Skylar cuts in with a gleam in her eyes, "a bowerbird would build you a house to get you to fuck him? Sounds like the perfect man. Another reason why I fully intend to take up birdwatching."

After a theatrical pause, Maeve blows on her unpolished fingernails. "Asher built me an art studio."

"Wesley built me a library," Josie adds, in her own not-so-subtle brag.

Isla holds up her hands. "Okay, okay, we get it. Your men are obsessed with you." Just then, Rowan skates by on the ice, glancing up at Isla. Is he bowerbirding for her? I'll have to ask her sometime.

Leighton cuts in, tucking a strand of hair behind her ear and meeting my eyes. "So...how is it working out living with a guy who's been into you since last season?"

I jerk my face toward her. "What?"

"Oh, come on," she says. "When you did your in-game performance, he could not take his eyes off you."

"I was engaged," I say, but inside my heart is beating fast. *Is this true?*

"Remember that picture I took of you after? The man was so eager to stand next to you..." Leighton grabs her phone and flicks through photos at Mach speed, finally landing on a shot of me in a blue—bedazzled—skating costume standing next to Tyler in the tunnel after a game. I reshared the promo shot at the time, but I look with new eyes at the way his arm wraps around my shoulder.

"Really?" I wish I sounded less breathless.

Isla leans closer, tapping my knee. "So how is it, then, living with the guy you wanted to do unholy things to earlier in the summer? Who maybe *still wants* to do those things to you?"

I groan, pressing my hands to my face as I slump in my seat. Of course they know about my Night of a 1001 Confessions. I have no filter around them, and my so-called friends love it. I lower my hands. "The job is great," I say firmly, trying to steer the conversation back to neutral territory.

Skylar snorts. "Yeah, I don't think she was asking about the job."

Heat rushes to my face as memories of last night flood back—offering to massage Tyler, touching his shoulders, running my hands over his back. I was bold. With Chad, I was never bold. Everything with him was so ordinary. But Tyler? Every moment feels supercharged. He brings out something wild in me, and I just want to touch him. Slide my hands along his beard. Tug his shirt off. See if he has tattoos. Does he? I *need* to know.

My face burns hotter, and Isla smiles like she's won the

lottery. "Guess I don't need to offer my matchmaking services to you, then." She pats Skylar on the shoulder. "But maybe Skylar can help you two decorate a bower together."

My friends are too much, and they all break into laughter. "Do I even get to say anything?" I ask as warmups start in earnest on the ice.

But before anyone answers, a few rows up, a group of women start singing "Daddy's Home." That's Tyler's *fan song*, and my gaze snaps to the rink as Number Forty-Four skates past the glass. He does a double take when he spies my sparkly jersey. Even from a couple of rows away, I can see his brows lift my way.

Leighton leans closer, her grin as sharp as ever. "I don't think you need to say anything. It's crystal clear." Then, with a note of seriousness that softens her usual teasing, she adds, "But how are you going to handle working for him and living under the same roof?"

Isla gives me a sympathetic look too. "She's right. That can't be easy. But we know this job is important to you. We want to help you figure it out," she says, always a problem solver.

And suddenly, the mood shifts. Not quite somber, but a reminder of the stakes. If I lose this job to lust, what would I do? Go back to the Garlic Palace? Fine, it's not the worst fate in the world. But this job gives me the freedom to keep growing my coaching business.

I can't lose it by throwing myself at my boss *again*.

"It's fine," I say, trying to convince myself. "I'm ridiculously, insanely, outrageously attracted to him," I say, because why deny it? "But I also used to get up at four-thirty a.m. every day to skate growing up. This girl has discipline."

I turn my focus to the game, cheering as the Sea Dogs attack the puck from the first puck drop. Tyler blocks shot after shot and when he pushes his opponents around, a primal thrill rushes through my chest.

I remind myself: *I am disciplined. I am disciplined. I am disciplined.*

But when Tyler pushes someone into the boards with that delicious scowl? My discipline is definitely on thin ice.

Before the game ends, I say goodbye to my friends and head to the family suite to gather the kids. I thank Lauren again for helping out. "Please," she says. "*Thank you* for giving me a little extra time with the grandkids."

"Did you see that last block by your dad?" I ask Luna and Parker once the Sea Dogs W flashes on the scoreboard and their winning anthem blasts through the arena.

Parker snorts. "No. I'm not that into hockey."

My eyes pop. "Blasphemy!"

His brow furrows. "What does that mean?"

Ooh, a chance for me to teach him. "It means you don't agree with a particular religious belief."

"But...this isn't religion," he says as we make our way out of the suite.

"Hockey is definitely a religion in your home," I say.

He seems to give that some thought. "Yeah, maybe it is."

Luna skips a few steps. "Hey, Sabrina, did you know that a Sea Dog is a nickname for a sea lion, which is more like a seal? Not like a dog at all," she says, then plucks at the logo of a fierce-looking Husky-type dog on her Sea Dogs hoodie.

"Do you think we should let the team know?" I stage whisper.

Luna snickers. "Yes, but I don't know if seals would be a good team logo."

Parker scoffs. "Sounds like blasphemy to me," he says as we reach the elevator that'll take us to the authorized personnel area.

I spin toward him. "Yes, that is indeed blasphemy."

A few minutes later, my stomach is flipping more than I want it to when Tyler emerges from the locker room and heads our way.

In his suit.

It should be illegal to look that good. The suit is forest green, the shirt is charcoal, the tie is absent. The top button is undone, and I can't stop staring at that little patch of skin visible as the man strides toward us in all his towering glory, long legs eating up the concrete floor.

Stop staring. He's your boss.

With more effort than it should take, I snap my gaze up from his throat—dear god, I'm staring at a man's throat —but switching the view to his handsome face doesn't help my cause. Because...that beard...those lips...his eyes.

And most of all, the way he smiles at his kids, warm and welcoming. "Hey, kiddos," he says and holds out his arms.

Luna and Parker run, and as if they weigh nothing, he hoists them both up, one on each side. My throat tightens with unexpected emotion—a poignancy I didn't antici-pate as he says, "Did you have fun?"

"Yeah, even though sometimes hockey's boring," Parker says.

Tyler's jaw drops in mock shock. "What did you say?"

Luna laughs. "It's blasphemy, right?"

I hang back, letting them have their family moment, but Tyler keeps walking, stopping when he reaches me. "Well, as long as you had fun reading books and playing board games, that's what matters," he says to them.

And yup, emotions swim up my chest, higher. His kids are so lucky to have not just his support but his love. It's pure and real. It's not tied to attainment. It's simply there... in the air, in his hugs, in his voice. It's constant—a rudder.

He sets them down, cocks his head, and says, "Does anyone want Mabel's cookies? I hear the Best Ice Cream Shop in the City is selling them now."

"Yes!" Parker says.

Luna waves a hand. "I want them."

"She's a friend! They're the best," I say since I've been following my baker friend's pop-up shops since she started selling her baked goods recently.

"Yeah, I hear she has great chocolate chip cookies," he says. "They're...scandalous."

"Let's go," I say, but then as we're walking to the players' lot, a new worry digs into my chest. Does he just want to go with his kids? Sure, I brought them to the game, but it's Tyler's time with them now. I should let them have it. Even though the thought of not going twists my chest.

After they pile into the backseat of his car, he comes around to open the passenger door for me. "Tyler, you can drop me off at home if you want to have dessert just with the kids."

He scoffs. "Are they one of your guilty pleasures?"

You are. "Yes."

"Then let's be scandalous."

I slide into the passenger seat, and we head off to get dessert after the game.

* * *

The next few days go well enough.

I volunteer at the animal rescue, helping with animal intake, and sending thank-yous to donors. I shop for food again, wandering aisles filled with people buying groceries for the week. It's mundane, but there's a quiet, grounding rhythm to it. I join Trevyn on the occasional dog walk, and he tells me Tyler sent him hockey tickets, and he'll be taking a date to the upcoming game. I'll need to thank Tyler again for that, and for making my friend happy.

I pick the kids up from school—with my cardboard sign on the dash, thank you, Luna—though Elle takes them on the one day she works in the city. It happens to coincide with one of my skating lessons, so it suits me perfectly.

She keeps the kids overnight, but then she has to drop them off unexpectedly early the next morning, an hour before school. Tyler's at the gym, so I answer the door. The kids rocket past me, and I turn to their mother. "Hi, Elle. How are you?"

Elle's an attractive woman with an intelligent air and long dark hair cinched neatly. I'm a hot mess in my pajama bottoms and a T-shirt—no skating lessons this morning. I adjust my untidy ponytail and start to tuck in my shirt. Then stop and let it hang out. Who tucks shirts into pajamas?

Elle's polished and poised, but she's also warm. "I'm well, thanks. And I hear great things about you."

I blink. I wasn't expecting that. But whether it came from Tyler or the kids, it has to be good. "The kids talk about you a lot. All good stuff," I say with a smile. That's the best approach when meeting the mom, right? It has to be.

"Well, that makes my day," she says, then adjusts her bag. "Oh, and if Tyler hasn't remembered Parker's science fair forms yet, give him a nudge for me. He's got his strengths, but paperwork isn't one of them."

Her tone is light, affectionate. There's no tension there, no resentment—just the familiarity of co-parenting with someone she still respects. That's how I read it, at least.

"Got it," I say, smiling back, then waving as she heads down the steps, her sneakers slapping against the pavement.

I close the door and watch her walk away through the window, trying to piece together the story.

She's smart, she's kind, and the kids adore her. Sure, she's busy, but what...capsized for Tyler and Elle? He knows my deal—he was there the day my life went tits up. But why is he a single dad? What didn't work with Elle? They clearly get along, so I doubt there was cheating. It truly seems like a good divorce, but there must have been something? The questions chase me as I move farther into the home, tell the kids to get ready for school, then head downstairs to get myself ready.

As I'm pulling on jeans and a sweater, the thoughts swirl again. What does Tyler want now? Is he looking for love, for marriage, for...that kind of life?

And why do I care?

I shake off the thoughts, trying to tell myself it doesn't matter. It's not my place. I move on and take the kids to school, like a nanny should do.

A nanny should not obsess about her boss.

Somehow, I've managed to avoid any more awkward run-ins with him. No garage moments where I'm wearing only a towel. No heated moments in the kitchen when I sneak furtive glances his way. No massages or naps on my couch. Just the faint reminder of him in small things, like the sheets I curl up in at night or the quiet creak of his footsteps upstairs.

Everything is starting to feel *business as usual*, especially since I turn in the science fair paperwork. On Friday morning, I head to the rink again at dawn where I take another video of my morning routine, then shoot a skating tutorial on how to do a camel spin. After that, my student arrives, and I focus on her.

I'm nearly two weeks in, and the job is steady. Everything I wanted.

I tell my therapist as much when I finally see her again later that morning, catching her up on everything that's gone down since my almost wedding.

"And how are you feeling about all that?" Elena asks, waving a hand as if to encompass the montage of the last few months.

I noodle on her question as I look around. It's...nice to be back in her office. Though, is that the right word for seeing your therapist? Nice? Well, her office has always felt a little like a sanctuary for me. A place where I could escape from the rigors of my parents' expectations. A spot where I could learn to let go of the rules they implemented for me. So yeah, it *is* nice.

Her office is cozy, with a picture of a red, snow-covered cabin on the wall that's always felt homey to me—the opposite of where I grew up, in my parents' pristine, don't-touch-the-vases-on-the-mantel kind of home.

Elena Alvarez feels the opposite of them too. She's grandmotherly, with warm brown skin, silver in her hair, and a crocheted blanket on her couch that her daughter made for her.

"It's…" I say, stopping to fiddle with the yarn, wanting to get the words right. "It's good. It feels…like I'm not the Queen of Chaos for the first time."

"Your summer was a little chaotic," she says, sympathetically.

"Yeah. I wasn't sure what was happening in my life," I say with a shrug.

"And now?"

That's the question. I feel stable for the first time in a while, and I don't want to rock that boat. I probably shouldn't tell her about my feelings for my boss. They can't go anywhere. They won't go anywhere.

"It's good," I say brightly. "I like the job, and I can focus on my business too. I like the kids. It's great."

She nods a few times, her blue eyes thoughtful, as if she's taking my comments at face value. "I'm glad." She takes a beat, her brain clearly working through something.

"Before you almost got married," she begins, and I tense, unsure where she's going. "You never mentioned things with Chad were…less than ideal," she says, since we've got a lot to catch up on. "Were you surprised when you learned he was cheating on you? Was there relief? Were you feeling all along that maybe he wasn't the one?"

Those are good questions—ones I mulled over all summer. Was I simply fooled, or had I fooled myself? "Things seemed good enough," I say, answering truthfully since that's the point of going to therapy.

Elena nods, as if she's absorbing that. "We've talked a

lot about perfection. Your pursuit of it. Letting go of that pursuit too. It's interesting that you expect perfection from yourself but not from others."

Damn. Way to cut to my core. "It's not really fair to expect perfection in other people," I argue.

"True, but 'good enough' shouldn't be the standard either," she says.

And those are some wise words.

Ones I'll have to carry with me if I ever date again.

When I return home later that day, my heart squeezes as I advance toward my apartment. The gift man has struck again.

There's a bag outside my door, but it's bigger this time —overflowing, almost. I feel spoiled and thrilled in equal parts. I paw through it: yoga blocks, yoga bolsters, and a brand-new yoga mat.

I grab the note tucked inside, feeling a little giddy as I rip it open.

Here's a bonus of sorts for an excellent first two weeks on the job. But it doesn't just come with all these fun accoutrements for your yoga corner. I want to build some shelves for the candles and stuff.

—T

The candles have a bright, clean scent—citrusy, like oranges and sunshine. It feels like the kind of smell you'd wear to conquer the day, and I can't help but smile. This is more than good enough.

My mind spins, and my heart feels all sorts of floaty. It's such a thoughtful gift, especially because one of the candles says in rhinestones, *I'm a Fucking Star.*

I roll my lips together like that'll seal in my excitement, but it doesn't work.

I'm far too delighted for any one person to be, so I rush up the stairs. I stop short when I find him in the kitchen, leaning casually against the counter, drinking a cup of coffee and smirking.

He knows what he did. He knows I just discovered the gift.

"Do you want to build some shelves with me?" I sing in tune to the *Frozen* song.

He checks the time. "You know what? I really do."

He sets down his coffee and heads off, presumably to get a toolbox.

And that makes me even hotter.

16

———

OFFICIAL YOGA POSE

Sabrina

He's drilling. I repeat—my hot, single-dad boss is drilling. I might as well strip out of all my clothes right now. Instead, as I hold the bookshelf against the wall, he drills holes into the brackets. He's inches from me, and his woodsmoke scent taunts me, curling past my nose and drifting into my mind.

I swallow roughly as his arm vibrates from the drill.

Pretty sure I vibrate too.

His body is so close. I let myself stare freely—the way the muscles in his corded forearms flex, how his biceps move, how his shirt clings to him.

His focus is intense, his eyes narrowed on the bracket on the second shelf, since he already hung one. A few more seconds pass, then he turns off the drill and shifts his gaze to me.

His hazel eyes radiate hopefulness but also pride, as he asks, "What do you think?"

Like he *wants* me to like it.

But news flash: I love it. And what I really think is that I was today years old when I discovered my new guilty pleasure: hot dad capableness. Yum.

"I think it looks...well hung," I say before I even consider the words leaving my mouth. The second I do, I slam my palm over my lips. I should not be allowed to speak sometimes. Where does this part of me even come from? Little Miss Perfectionist Sabrina never blurted out her dirty thoughts when she was with Fuck Chad.

Tyler blinks. Once. Twice. But when he clears his throat, he's no longer caught off guard—he's in control. "It is, Sabrina. It is," he says, his voice low and amused as he pats the shelf. "Sturdy. Want to give it a tug?"

My heart beats too fast. He's playing with me, and I love it. "Yes," I croak out.

I reach for the shelf, grab it, and yank. Yep. This shelf does not lose its strength at all. When I let go, I scramble for something appropriate to say but completely fail. Instead, I blurt, "Chad was never handy. I like handy."

"Well, that works out for both of us, doesn't it?" Tyler's charm flashes, teasing, a little flirty—but never quite crossing the line.

"It does," I manage, trying to focus on anything other than the inferno my body has become. Almost two weeks in, and I'm a burning fire. There has to be something to gutter these flames.

I roll through conversational topics in my mind and land on the one that's been nagging me all week. Surely, it will douse my desire. "What happened with Elle?"

His brows knit. I probably shouldn't have asked. I wave my hand dismissively. "Actually, it's none of my business. I'm sorry. Forget I even asked."

I gesture to the items on the floor—the yoga blocks, a bolster, a strap, candles that smell like sunshine and orange trees, and all the accoutrements. "I want to set up the shelf now and enjoy the Official Yoga Corner," I say, bending to grab a few things.

He reaches for my arm.

"Nothing bad happened," he says, his voice quieter now. "But nothing great either." His eyes flicker with something like regret.

For the years they spent together? The choices they made?

Or maybe for the end of it.

"Oh." My heart sinks. "That must've been hard at times, being in a marriage where it felt...like that." I hesitate, but the question spills out anyway. "You weren't really in love?" It feels important that I know this.

"Maybe at one point we were, but it didn't feel like sparks. It didn't feel like lightning. It didn't feel the way my pulse beats faster and harder when I get on the ice. You know what I mean? It wasn't like hockey."

Goosebumps rise along my arms. "I know exactly what you mean. I feel that way too on the ice," I murmur.

"Great minds," he says, but it feels like *great hearts*.

Like we have too much in common.

Dangerously so. I turn back to organizing the yoga items, trying desperately to focus.

But I can feel his eyes on me, sense the crackle between us. What is he thinking? Is his mind racing like mine?

"Why did you ask?" he says, his tone surprisingly vulnerable. A little eager too.

Heat races down my spine. I could tell him the truth—

that I'm dying to know all these details about him. But I can't admit that. I really can't.

I turn to him. "I was just curious when I saw her the other day. She's really kind. She seems to know you well."

"We're friends. It's...nice," he says, not quite defeated but resigned. Maybe "nice" wasn't what he wanted from marriage though.

Do you want more than nice? I want to ask, but I know better, so I keep the words to myself.

We finish setting up the yoga corner, then step back to admire it. A purple mat stretches across the floor, a few candles and blocks are neatly arranged on the shelf, and a basket with the strap and the bolster sits in the corner. It's simple but cozy.

"Do you want to do it with me sometime?" I ask impulsively because apparently, I'm an impulsive soul with this man.

He cocks his head, and before the panic sets in, I quickly add, "Yoga. It's good for sports. It's good for hockey players. Have you ever done yoga?"

His smile is magnetic, hooking into my heart and making me forget why we're a bad idea. "Yeah, I'll do yoga with you," he says, glancing at his watch. We've run out of time today. "How about when I get back from the road trip?" he asks, like he doesn't want to miss the chance. Like he's already imagining it.

My breath hitches. It's not a date. It's absolutely not a date with my boss. But try telling that to the flutters in my chest, to the wild thoughts in my head, to the part of me that's checking the clock and counting down the days.

Even as I take Luna to the wildlife sanctuary and Parker to the science museum, as I help them with homework, make dinner for them, and hang out with Trevyn and Barbara-dor one day as we unpack Elphaba.

She just arrived in a box on the doorstep.

"Oh look! Chad didn't even scratch your baby," he says, stroking the sewing machine that I, unfortunately, had to interact with Fuck Chad to retrieve.

"Miracles happen," I say. "But he's also probably too busy getting blown by his new wife to exact revenge via textiles."

"In the immortal words of Glinda, they deserve each other." Then he pats the green machine some more. "And now you're home, Elfie."

But even when I go to the rink while the kids are in school, and even when I go to lessons while Tyler's mom watches the kids, I'm excruciatingly aware of the calendar and the returning of my boss.

It's just yoga, I tell myself.

Nothing will happen.

We're simply two athletes stretching together. That's all.

But I've already picked out which leggings I'll wear. Blue, since he seems to like that color. It's the color of the towels he bought me. Ridiculous, so ridiculous that I've picked an outfit.

A week and a half after he left, the kids aren't the only ones excited to see him return from the road trip late Wednesday night.

And when I drop them off at school the next day and return home, my boss is waiting for me at my door in his navy blue workout shorts and a gray Sea Dogs T-shirt that hugs his pecs and shows off his biceps, a yoga mat under his arm.

"I don't have to be at morning skate for another hour, so I'm ready for the Official Yoga Corner. Are you?"

More than he can ever know.

"Give me one minute," I say, and then my heart nearly explodes in my chest as I race inside. I pull on a yoga tank top that matches my blue leggings, run a brush through my hair, fasten it into a ponytail, then breathe.

Long, deep, and centered.

Like when I hit the ice, reminding myself to enjoy every moment.

I will. Oh yes, I will.

I yank open the door, pasting on a bright smile. "Time for twists," I say, trying to make this seem like we're just two athletes working out. Just two friends.

I almost believe it as we settle onto our mats in the corner. "You set the pace, boss," he says, having fun with that word.

It sends a charge through me. Or maybe he just does.

"Let's start with downward dog," I suggest, stretching my hips back in that pose, lengthening through my arms.

He follows, his movements deliberate and strong. I can't help glancing over, catching how his muscles shift under his shirt as he transitions into the position.

"Tabletop," I call out, my voice a little shaky as I guide us. We both settle onto all fours again, the quiet hum of our breathing filling the room.

"Warrior one," I say as I stand, shifting into warrior one. My arms reach high above my head as I sink into the lunge, and he follows, mirroring my movements.

For a moment, it's quiet—just the soft sounds of our breaths soundtracking my racing mind that catalogues how close we are. A foot apart, as we move together.

This is just stretching, I remind myself. This is just a workout.

"Easy twist," I say finally, stepping into the next pose. I rotate my torso, extending one arm to the ceiling as I pivot on the ball of my back foot.

But when I glance up, my heart stumbles.

He's facing me.

We should be twisting in opposite directions, but instead, his eyes meet mine across the small space between us.

For a moment, neither of us moves. His gaze glimmers with longing, and restraint.

I know both well, and they're racing through me, owning every cell in my body. I feel warm everywhere as I swallow past all this aching want. The moment stretches, and soon, *soon*, it'll break.

He'll move.

He'll shift.

He'll turn the other way.

His chest rises and falls with each breath, but he doesn't turn. His jaw ticks, like he's at war with himself.

After several seconds that feel like I'm on the surface of Mercury, he moves at last—*toward me*. With zero hesitation. "Sabrina," he rasps out, his voice thick with desire.

And I don't know who makes the next move. All I know is we crash onto my mat with a thud and a jolt that radiates deliciously in my bones. He grips my waist. Tugs me against him. Growls. The heat from his body spreads through mine.

All the reasons to resist him burn into ash as his lips crush mine.

And I surrender, shifting under him as he covers me and kisses me like I imagined he would that night.

No, that's not true.

This kiss—chaotic, ravenous, *wild*—is better than my imagination.

17

***

THE WATCH KNOWS

Tyler

My brain is too fried. My skin too hot. My need too high. Every system is overloading, warning me to stop. But I don't. I kiss her anyway.

I kiss Sabrina like it's all I've wanted to do for months. Because it is.

I devour her sweet, pretty lips, sealing my mouth to hers. She tastes minty, with a hint of lip gloss, and it's my new favorite flavor in the world. The orange blossom candle scent drifts past me, like a seductive perfume casting a spell.

Our lips hunt and chase. Our tongues skate together. My teeth clash against hers. It's hungry and ravenous, a kiss powered by the jet fuel of months of lust. Of her living with me. Of me wanting her. Of the memory of the things she said in the hotel room in Cozy Valley.

I keep thinking about your beard.

Your arms.

How you could pin me down.

I wonder about your mouth.

She's obsessed with my mouth. I'm obsessed with her. Especially the sweet, indulgent feel of her lips, and the way I can taste her need, deep and desperate. I know that feeling well—I've been driven wild to touch her, and finally, I am.

Touching her exactly the way she wants.

With the kind of kiss I wanted to give her the night of her wedding. The kind she deserves.

It's hot and deep, a little rough, and all real. I consume her lips, unable to stop, claiming every gasp with my mouth. She rocks up against my hard-on, and every nerve ending crackles. Lust spirals like a tornado, spinning higher, gathering strength and speed. We kiss hard enough to hurt, and I don't want to break this connection. Ever.

But...there is so much more of her to kiss. I wrench away from her captivating mouth and trail kisses along her jaw, nibbling, biting, making her moan and gasp.

"Oh god," she murmurs, and I travel down her neck, inhaling her scent, letting it fry my senses. But I never forget my mission: *give her what she wants.*

My gaze swings down to her strong hands, digging into my arms. A wicked smile forms. Yeah, I know what this woman wants. I grab her wrists roughly, my intent clear.

I meet her eyes. They're wild as she gives a fevered nod.

Her breath hitches as I stretch her hands above her head with a decisive move, pinning her down. My breath comes quickly as I rise up and look down at her. "You said you wanted me to pin you down," I rasp.

She swallows, roughly, quickly. "I do."

So I keep doing it.

Blowing out a harsh breath, I drag my beard against her face, my chest rumbling as I touch her this way.

She gasps, then squirms under me. "Again," she demands—a sweet, sexy beg.

I rub my stubble against her other cheek. She arches against me and we grind. A hungry sway of hips, a press of bodies. A tremor works its way through me, dangerously, as my cock stiffens even more.

She pants, clearly feeling it—feeling *me*. She wraps her legs around my waist, hooking her heels over my ass. "More," she says, as if she's lost to the feeling.

I'm lost to her. With my hands still gripping her wrists, I dip my face, then meld our mouths together, my whole body throbbing. It's too much, too intense, all this white-hot magic. I should jerk away, cool off. But instead, I press harder, need squeezing my chest to almost unbearable levels as we kiss like the world has spun off its axis.

It feels like it—because my world is reduced to her and me, and this yoga mat. To my body moving against hers. To the moans she makes. To the wriggling of her hands. She wants something, so I let go of the grip on her wrists.

Her fingers fly to my hair, and she breathes the sexiest sigh of relief. "I've wanted to do this so badly. Every time I see you, I want to touch you," she says as she rakes her fingers through my hair, and I nearly die of desire.

Her words. Her need. Her beautiful lust.

"You have no idea how much I want this too," I say, and at last—at long fucking last—I confess what I kept swallowed down back in the hotel. "It took all my willpower to walk away from you that night. I never stopped thinking about it."

"Yeah?" she asks, her voice trembling.

"All the time," I say.

She licks her lips, then rocks her hips up against me as if she's seeking out my length. I rock back, my mind spinning dangerously out of control.

Her words echo once more—*I want you to take my real virginity.*

Fuck.

They drive me on, even though I should pump the brakes. Instead, I travel down her neck, pressing a hot kiss to the hollow of her throat. Her breath snags beautifully as she arches into me more, grabbing my hair tighter.

A buzz of electricity shoots straight to my groin.

I want to give her everything, but I'm not sure I can survive the way this feels. The skitters along my spine. The pressure everywhere. The sparks of pleasure.

I remember everything she said that night. Every single thing. I move down her chest, kissing her warm, soft flesh, wanting to give her everything she craves in bed.

I reach the top of her tank top. Guilt lodges in my brain. Am I really doing this? Am I really pushing the boundaries?

But I can't stop. And she doesn't seem to want me to.

She thrusts up against me once more, whispering *please,* and that's it—I'm lost.

I pull the fabric down, exposing her tits, and fuck me.

I had a feeling.

Her nipples are pierced, and they're perfect.

I kiss one, sucking on the tiny barbell. She squirms

and writhes. I kiss the other, flicking the metal with my tongue.

She gasps, then breathes out my name like a dirty prayer. "Tyler."

I nearly lose my mind.

"That—do it again," she says. She sounds high on this moment. Like she wants this. Like she needs this.

And I want to give it to her, even though my head says stop. Don't go any farther. She's your employee. She's the nanny. This is reckless. A mistake.

I should back off. Stop myself.

But one look at her bruised lips, her hungry eyes, and all my restraint shatters.

Her tits are in my face, and there's no place I'd rather be. I kiss and lick and suck as she holds me tight against her chest. We are a frenzy of desire. Unstoppable lust that's been building inside these walls.

Her words flash through my head—*I can't stop thinking about how you might kiss me. Everywhere.*

I want to kiss her everywhere.

My head is a fog. I've lost all sense of reason. And I don't even want to find it.

I just want to find her.

I kiss my way down her body, over the soft, beautiful flesh of her belly. "You taste so sweet," I say.

She murmurs. "Don't stop."

"I can't stop. You're too fucking delicious. Too fucking sweet." I kiss her belly ring, and I'm close—very close—to the waistband of her leggings. To the way it dips in a little V. To the invitation of her spread legs.

She parts them more.

I inch down her body, wanting to taste her everywhere.

My hands toy with the waistband, and she urges me on, pushing my head, shoving me down. Making it clear that all systems are a go. And my cock seems to think so too.

I pull the fabric down an inch and kiss her waist.

She pushes my head harder. "I want you so much."

"I fucking want you too," I growl, grabbing her leggings to peel them off—

Then my watch buzzes. Annoyingly. Persistently. *With an alarm.*

"Fuck," I groan, jerking away. That has to be my morning skate reminder. But it's not. It's a phone call.

My watch tells me Parker's calling. In the middle of a school day.

I bolt upright, hunting for my phone. Where the hell is it? I spot it, knocked off to the side of the yoga mat, and lunge for it.

"Hey, kiddo, what's up?" I say, trying to clear the lust from my voice in record time.

"I forgot my star chart! The science fair is tomorrow, and we need to set up today. Can you bring it to me?"

"Of course," I say, guilt slamming into me, sharp and cold.

Sabrina is already sitting up, adjusting her top, fixing her leggings, her gaze averted.

"Where's your star chart?" I ask, shoving a hand through my hair, like I can finger-comb out the evidence.

"My desk!"

"I'll drop it off on the way to morning skate," I tell him, but one look at the time and—fuck—I'm already pushing it. Morning skate isn't mandatory, but I never miss it. "Maybe I can drop it off after?"

Sabrina lifts a finger, mouthing, *"I'll take it."*

My shoulders relax. *"Thank you,"* I mouth back. Then to Parker: "Sabrina will bring it to you now, buddy."

"Thanks, Dad!" He sounds relieved too.

I hang up, and when I turn back, Sabrina looks at me—a disheveled mess, just like I am.

Flustered, she smooths a hand down her leggings, then twists her hair into a ponytail. "You get the star chart. I'll take it to school," she says, all business.

And I hate myself as I say yes.

I hate myself as I climb the stairs, a fading boner making the whole thing feel even more miserable.

I hate myself as I make it to Parker's room, my pulse still rocketing, my body still buzzing from touching her. My heart slams against my chest *so damn hard.*

I'm sweating, and the lust hasn't even fully left my body as I grab the star chart, feeling like a complete ass.

I should have remembered to tell him to take it this morning.

I shouldn't have let things spiral out of control *so badly* that I nearly missed morning skate.

And I definitely shouldn't have almost tongue-fucked the nanny.

Cooler heads should prevail.

When I make it downstairs, Sabrina is standing in the kitchen, a workout jacket zipped over her chest—not a Sea Dogs one. And somehow, that bugs me. But I get it.

And it's also a reminder.

I hand her the star chart. "Thanks," I say, and it hardly feels like enough.

"No problem." She smiles as she tucks the paper under her arm.

"Sabrina," I add, hating the sound of my own voice—and what I'm about to say. "That shouldn't happen again."

For a second—a split second—disappointment flickers in her eyes. But then it vanishes so fast it's like it was never there at all.

"What shouldn't happen again?" she says breezily, like she did over the summer, when we agreed to never speak of her 1001 confessions.

It's a new truce. A harsh understanding. That we'll both force amnesia to set in.

She sails out of the house, like it was nothing.

Like it didn't happen.

Like I'll have to pretend too.

And I know it's for the best.

18

PUMPKIN ATROCITIES

Tyler

This is not awkward at all.

Not one bit, I swear.

I don't feel like a complete jackass at the kitchen table the next evening, sitting across from the nanny, pretending I didn't almost fuck her.

Nope. I'm not thinking about yesterday at all. I'm definitely not imagining what *could have happened* as I stab a pumpkin with a tiny, ineffective carving knife.

I keep my head down while Sabrina teaches the kids how to make the world's coolest jack-o'-lanterns. A reward, she'd said to Parker, for creativity in the science fair after school today. Not excellence, but creativity, and I appreciate her distinction.

I'd appreciate, too, if I could stop thinking about the yoga corner incident.

She seems to have moved on from that.

Her voice is light, easy—like she's genuinely not thinking about what went down. "So if you slide it like this," she says, leaning over to show Luna how to use the etching tool to make precise cuts, "you can carve some really cute whiskers for the seal face."

Luna squeals a little in excitement. "Yes! And Dad, maybe this should be the new team logo since there really aren't any actual sea dogs."

"I'll take that to management," I say, gripping the serrated carving knife like it's a weapon of war instead of an innocent Halloween tool.

Parker is locked in concentration, his tongue sticking out at the corner of his lips as he carefully slices the visor of his astronaut helmet. Sabrina leans close, guiding him as he works to carve clean lines.

Meanwhile, I...well, I'm creating something that looks —not gonna lie—exactly like the DickNose board my asshole teammates and I keep in the locker room. The one where we draw stick figures with dicks for noses to give each other a hard time. And here I am, apparently bringing that masterpiece into my own home, in front of my kids.

"Um, Dad?" Parker says, squinting at my pumpkin like it personally offends him. "That kind of looks like—"

"A Basset Hound!" Sabrina cuts in, her voice a little too bright.

Parker tilts his head, skeptical. "Really?"

"Sure!" Sabrina nods way too hard. "They have those droopy faces, and, uh—look at the ears!"

I snort under my breath, but I'm grateful she jumped in before Parker could say *dick face* in front of Luna. Or, really, anyone. "Yeah. It's a Basset Hound."

Sabrina has already grabbed her phone from her

pocket and googled Basset Hounds, showing the kids the pics of the droopy dog. "See?"

Parker shrugs like *okay, fair point.* To me, Sabrina says, "You did a good job, Tyler."

It's almost placating, but her eyes linger for a beat too long. Long enough that I wonder—hope—that she's remembering too. But then she looks away, and the moment's gone.

Luna side-eyes me. "Dad, it's okay if you're not good at carving pumpkins. You're good at carving the ice," she says, proud of her comparison. That makes two of us. "And wait till you see my Halloween costume."

She sounds too pleased.

"Is it a cat, still?" I ask, relieved to steer this conversation toward something that isn't my pumpkin atrocity or the world's sexiest kiss yesterday with the nanny.

"I can't tell you," she says, smirking. "But Sabrina is helping me."

Sabrina flashes a pleased smile, wiping her hands on an orange towel with a black cat illustration. "It's going to be amazing, and it was all Luna's idea."

And hell, that *is* great. I should be thrilled that Parker has finally warmed up to her, that Luna is bonding with her more. I should be grateful that everything feels so damn normal.

And yet, some primal, restless part of me is annoyed.

Annoyed that Sabrina has apparently put yesterday behind her so much more easily than I have.

I grip the knife harder as I carve a droopy dick face.

* * *

"Are you ready?" Luna's voice calls out from behind her closed bedroom door at seven in the morning on Halloween.

I still haven't seen her costume yet. It's been one hundred percent classified on a need-to-know basis, she'd told me. Apparently, I didn't need to know.

What I *do* know is that she's been spending a suspicious amount of secret time at Sabrina's place.

"She has a sewing machine, Dad! And it's so cool," Luna had said, practically vibrating with excitement.

Huh. I had no idea. "She does?"

"Her name is *Elphaba,*" Luna had informed me, like I was an idiot for not knowing that.

"The sewing machine has a name?"

"Obviously." Then she'd trotted off to work on "girl" stuff at Sabrina's.

Now, I'm waiting, standing in the hallway outside her door, while my son—fully suited up in his hand-stitched astronaut costume—sits on the stairs, adjusting his helmet.

The door creaks open, and Luna swings it wide.

"Ta-da!" She throws her arms out, sticking the landing like she's mid-routine on the ice.

And—*holy shit.*

She's a figure skater. But not in any costume I've seen before.

Gone are the simple pink and black practice dresses with their little skirts that she's worn for the programs she's performed in showcases and minor competitions. This one is lavender, with sheer long sleeves, fine netting along the neckline, and sparkles everywhere—over the arms and cascading down the front like stardust.

"It's one of Sabrina's costumes! She wore it to nationals, and she took it in for me." Luna beams.

My jaw practically unhinges. This isn't just a costume. It's a gift. A damn meaningful one.

Luna even has white lace-up boots that almost look like ice skates, with silver ribbon tied around the base to sell the illusion. *Impressive.*

"It's perfect," I manage, still reeling.

Luna twirls, then grins. "Are you surprised? I *wanted* to surprise you, Dad. Isn't it the coolest, fanciest skating costume ever?"

"It is," I say, still processing the fact that Sabrina took in one of her old costumes for my daughter.

"And we've seen a lot," Luna adds, since we've spent plenty of time watching skating competitions over the years. Not to mention, my first-ever crush was on a figure skater—*Allison Marchand.* She was eighteen when I was twelve and I could not stop watching her in the Olympics. I could blame my mom and grandmother for their obsession with figure skating, but really I was obsessed too.

"We have," I agree, before pointing toward the stairs. "All right, skater queen, let's get going to school."

"And then we get to trick-or-treat tonight," Luna cheers.

"As if you need any more sugar," I grumble.

"Dad, you can *never* have enough candy," Parker pipes up, slinging his backpack over his shoulder.

We head to the garage, and—because I'm a glutton for punishment—I steal a glance at Sabrina's door. Even though I know she's at the rink for an early lesson.

Maybe she'll post another video.

The thought excites me more than it should.

As I load the kids into the car, I tell myself I won't check. I *won't*.

Hell, I haven't looked at her socials in over a week. I'm trying to break the habit of wanting her.

This is what I planned, right? To move on.

But I picture her skating the whole time I drive my kids to school. I'm chatting with them about their teachers and friends while my mind is taunting me with images of Sabrina gliding across the ice, the spotlight on her alone, one leg extended, arms out wide, and a polished, determined smile on her beautiful face. The pull to check her feed grows stronger all morning as I meet with Corbin and Rowan, catching up with those clowns at the gym.

"Haven't seen you at the bocce ball court," Corbin remarks. It's the first thing he says as I settle in by the free weights.

"Been a little busy with work and shit," I say. "Maybe you've heard of it. It's that thing you do on the ice with blades."

Corbin bristles. "I get plenty of ice time thank you very much," he says, as he parks himself on the weight bench.

"Or maybe you've been afraid to show your face since the bet we made," Rowan says, clearly not willing to let me get off that easily. "I'm guessing you lost," Rowan says.

Oh shit. I pause mid-lift of preacher curls. I fucking forgot that bet—Corbin bet I'd last a week till I was spending too much time with my hand; Rowan bet two days.

Corbin points at me, like my hesitation proves they were right. "Yep! You didn't even last a week till you...gave in," he says, then makes an obscene gesture with his fist.

"Pay up," Rowan says, with a smug smile.

I smirk, shaking my head at these two. "You assume you won."

"Won what?"

It's Ford joining us now, setting down his water bottle with stickers of the mountains and the words *Surprise Them* all over it. His mantra.

"We bet on how long he'd hold out," Corbin supplies, because of course he wants to get my goat.

But the thing is—I've been restrained. So damn restrained in the solo department.

I set down the weights. Wiggle my fingers. "Pay up."

Corbin's jaw drops. "What the hell?"

My smile widens. "I've been such a good boy."

"No way," Ford says, then knocks me with a fist. "Impressive restraint."

"Especially since you're obsessed with her," Rowan adds dryly.

And…ouch.

I bristle at the word obsessed, only because it's true.

But I've resisted jerking off. I've had to since I didn't want to give in to all this desire. Of course, I don't tell them I gave in to *other things* last week.

Nope. That wasn't part of the bet.

Rowan's fishing for his wallet, handing over a fresh green bill. "Man, I didn't think you had it in you."

"You're steel, dude," Corbin adds, forking over the payoff too.

I happily take their money. It feels good, beating my friends, but it also feels like a consolation prize.

We resume working out, but as Ford settles in at a bench, he says, "You might have won, but you're still so screwed."

I keep a stony face even though I know he's right.

* * *

Later that night, as we're grabbing Halloween bags and hustling out the door, Luna is practically bouncing like she can't hold in a secret.

She keeps glancing at the stairs to Sabrina's apartment. Parker's on edge, too, pacing in his NASA-issued astronaut jumpsuit, peeking around the corner.

I narrow my eyes. "All right, what's going on, you little stinkers? Is this another put-a-Zorro-mask-on-Dad moment?"

"No, but *you* need a costume," Luna says.

"What? You don't like my football player attire?" I gesture to my Renegades jersey and eye black. "It's simple. Gets the job done."

"It's fine," Luna says, too quickly. "But wait till you see Sabrina's."

And then—

The door to Sabrina's place snicks open.

Footsteps sound on the stairs, and my pulse beats annoyingly fast in anticipation.

"And now...in the long program, presenting—Sabrina Snow!" Luna announces like a true commentator.

And that's when, for the first time ever, I swear in front of my kids. "Holy shit."

Parker gasps. "Dad."

But I don't even care, because—fuck.

She's wearing a crystal-blue figure-skating costume, the exact shade of her eyes, with a patchwork of rhinestones that catch the light like prisms.

It's one-shouldered—or is it a single-strap thing? Hell if I know the name of that style. All I know is that one shoulder is draped in soft blue fabric, while the other is bare except for a thin strap of delicate rhinestones.

It's entirely appropriate. And incredibly sexy.

It shows off the strength in her arms, the grace in how she carries herself, and the bright, outgoing spirit that made her dress up to match my daughter.

She smiles, seeming completely unfazed by my stunned expression. "What do you think? I wore it in college."

I think it's going to fuel my figure skater crush for a long, long time.

I think I'm probably going to cave later and watch her videos.

"I think it's stunning," I blurt before I can stop myself. Which—fuck.

I shouldn't have said that. Not in front of the kids. Not about her.

Because *stunning* is not a word you use for your nanny.

I never said it about Agatha.

But the kids are too hyped up to notice my slip. They're already rushing for the door, pumpkins made of recycled plastic clutched in their hands, riding that pure Halloween high.

Sabrina, though, is frozen in place. Like she wasn't expecting my reaction. Then, a small smile coasts across her lips, like the compliment meant everything to her. "Thank you," she says, but she clears her expression quickly as we make our way into the late October evening, the streets already filled with zombies and cowboys and Marvel heroes. "I know candy isn't really your guilty pleasure, but if you spot a NutRageous bar, I call dibs."

"That's a rare and special candy bar," I say, lifting a brow.

She sighs, a little wistful. "And it's a Reese's candy bar, so I don't know why it's not more common. But it's incredible. I always wanted one on Halloween as a kid."

I frown. "You didn't have them?"

She laughs. "My dad never let me."

And somehow, some way, I know I'm going to find a NutRageous bar for the figure skater I'm crushing on.

Even if I shouldn't be.

19

SUPER NANNY

Sabrina

It's better than I remembered.

The chocolate, the nuts, the peanut butter, the caramel—it's *chef's kiss* good.

I take another bite of the NutRageous bar that Tyler left on the kitchen counter for me this morning.

I don't think he found it while trick-or-treating with the kids. No idea how he got it this fast. But it's delicious. And it's mine.

Just like the house is today.

The kids are at school, then heading to Elle's tonight. Tyler has morning skate and a game this evening. By the time he comes home in the afternoon to rest before puck drop, I'll be teaching.

It's good—this structure, this routine. It's kept me from thinking too much about last week.

The week where I took a misstep—hard.

If I were making a list of what not to do, right at the

top, I'd write: Don't grind against your boss. Don't tell him how much you want him.

But I've been Super Nanny since then.

I want him to know I can do what he needs—pretend it didn't happen. So I've been excellent at pretending.

Perfect, really.

Isn't that what all my training was really about? Being perfect. Nailing something. Achieving excellence.

I set the half-eaten NutRageous bar on the counter. I'll finish it later.

For now, I grab the laundry basket I brought upstairs earlier and haul it to the next level, where I toss my clothes into the washing machine.

And that's when I hesitate.

Just for a second.

I could check out his room. Just a quick glance. *What would that hurt?*

But what if he has a camera in there? And wouldn't I deserve to get fired for sneaking around his bedroom like a curious cat?

I keep walking away.

Except...when I pass his room, I linger.

Just a little.

His bed is muted green, the pillows a dark gray. The nightstand has a couple of books and a phone holder.

I inhale sharply and force myself to walk away.

Back downstairs.

Back to reality.

I settle in at my laptop, editing some of the videos I shot last week. Then, I post one of my morning routines— a long session where I skated like my soul was on fire.

Pretty sure I was thinking about Tyler.

My phone alarm dings. I hop upstairs, switch my

clothes to the dryer, and start the sheets. Once I move them into the dryer, I have to take off for my afternoon lessons.

By the time I leave, he's still not home.

It's for the best. Truly. It is.

* * *

Late that night, with the stars winking in the sky, the garage opens.

Then the door to the house.

I hear his footsteps, and my chest tightens.

I already checked the score. They didn't win.

Tomorrow, he'll be gone on a road trip. That'll be a good thing. I've made it through the week, pretending nothing happened.

I curl up on the couch with my coaching strategies book, trying to focus, but I'm mostly listening to the house.

I know the moment he goes upstairs. The moment he gets into bed.

I yawn, stretching. It's probably time for me to go to sleep too.

But when I walk into my bedroom, I curse.

I forgot to grab my sheets from the dryer earlier today. They're my favorites, so I'll just quietly grab them. No big deal.

I tiptoe upstairs, careful not to make a sound.

The house is dark and quiet, the carpet soft beneath my toes as I move to the second floor, then tiptoe along the hall toward the dryer.

I pull it open, grab the now cool sheets, then quietly pad back down the hall when I hear a *noise.*

A low grunt from his bedroom.

With the sheets in my hands, I freeze.

Did I really just hear that?

I strain to listen, taking one more careful step.

Everything goes silent. The house is still, and I'm keenly aware of the darkness, the distant sounds of a city quieting for the night, and the hair on my arms standing on end.

Heart pounding, I inch closer, straining to listen.

Then the sound starts again.

A staggered breath.

A grunt.

Through the dim light and the slight crack in the door, I can't really see much. Some movement under the covers, and my brain scrambles to process the scene.

No way. That's not—

Is it?

My breath catches. My pulse skitters wildly, beating so fast it's like a cartoon character scampering down the street at a million miles an hour.

For one wild second, I debate pushing the door open, verifying with my own eyes.

But self-preservation kicks in. And respect for privacy.

I bolt.

Rushing along the hall, then flying down the stairs, I slip away before I'm caught. Before he realizes I was lingering outside his bedroom door for a few dangerous seconds.

Wondering.

Hoping.

Warring with myself over whether I should push that door open or not.

I land in the kitchen and press a hand against my chest. Swallow. Rewind and replay. Again and again.

I'm warm everywhere. My skin buzzes, adrenaline rushing through me.

I better move, though, just in case he gets up, calls out, *"Who's there?"*

I hurdle down the stairs to my apartment, fumble with the keypad, yank the door open, and slam it shut behind me.

A long beat.

I imagine him pushing out of bed, pulling on shorts, padding downstairs, knocking on my door, and asking with a cocky challenge in his gravelly voice: *"Did you want to come in?"*

Or maybe...

"Why did you leave so quickly? Are you afraid it'll turn you on too much?"

A burst of pleasure flickers inside me, then ignites like a firework lighting up the night sky. It radiates from my chest, down my arms, to my fingertips. I tingle everywhere. I'm electric.

And wickedly, completely aroused.

The thought of that sexy man taking matters into his own hands is doing wild things to me.

I can't catch my breath. I'm not even sure I want to. I just want to linger in this hazy, heady sensation where everything is golden and hot.

But I have to get it together.

Make my bed. Go to sleep. Do my job tomorrow at the skating rink since I have lessons.

But even as I yank off the quilt and smooth out the sheets, I can't unsee what I almost saw.

What I wanted to see.

I yank the sheets over the corners, trying desperately to focus on the mundane act to distract my mind. But once I'm in bed under the covers, I picture him again, filling in the paint-by-numbers of a man alone in bed at night. His strong body stretched out. His forearm flexing. Veins protruding. Fist curled around his cock, stroking hard.

I gasp. Then moan.

Oh god.

This is not helpful. I am not going to sleep like this.

I fumble for my phone, needing something—anything —to distract myself.

A book? A podcast? Texting with friends?

All appealing.

But what I should do is focus on work. Yes, that'll do the trick.

I hop onto my social media to check for messages from potential clients. The perfect distraction. When I land there, I see a notification waiting for me.

My brow furrows.

It's a heart on the skating video I posted this morning.

From Falcon Defender.

Oh. My. God.

I click on the profile.

It's Tyler.

He doesn't post much, but this is him. This is definitely him. There are pictures of him with the kids. Laughing. Taking them on a picnic. Visiting an animal rescue. At a hockey game.

And then—nearly a year ago—a photo of him and me the night I performed at a game.

"Big figure-skating fan!"

That's all he says, and it's lovely. But that's not what lights me up. It's the timestamp on the heart on my video.

From five minutes ago.

Five minutes ago.

When I was in the hall outside his room.

Five minutes ago.

When I heard that grunt.

My stomach flips again. He was watching my video in bed.

20

KIND OF

Tyler

I'm nursing my coffee from the un-St.-Bernard-like mug, making small talk with Sabrina about the upcoming schedule as I head out of town for a road trip.

She seems...a little off though. Sure, she's moving around the kitchen like normal—slathering avocado on a bagel, sprinkling sea salt and pumpkin seeds, checking her canvas bag, the one she carries every day with the words *Skate Like No One's Watching, For Fox Sake* on it. But she won't meet my eyes.

When I mention Luna's upcoming field trip for a beach cleanup as part of the school's efforts to raise aware-ness about climate change and rising ocean levels—a topic Sabrina normally loves to chat about—she looks down and says, "That's great that the school is doing that."

She takes a bite of her bagel, studying it like it's some-thing entirely new to her. And sure, I fucking love a good avocado bagel. But the way she's eating it—like she's fixated on it—makes me think something is wrong.

Given what's gone down with us in the last week or so—nothing—I'm not entirely sure if it's my place to ask how she's doing. But I care about her. So I'll do it anyway.

I lower my mug and clear my throat, maybe forcing her to look up. "Are you okay?"

"Am I okay?" She repeats the question like it's in a language she doesn't understand.

"You seem a little off, Sabrina. Is it something with your parents?" I ask gently. Her dad is a world-class prick. Maybe he said something shitty to her yesterday on the phone? Who knows?

"No, not at all," she says, dismissing that quickly, then taking another bite, like she wants to shut herself up.

Hmm. Maybe she had a rough day at the rink. "Was everything okay with your lessons?"

She nods as she chews, her head bobbing up and down like a puppet's, then swallows and says, "Yes! I'm great! Everything is great!"

And that feels like a few too many *greats*.

"Are you sure? You seem a little...not quite yourself," I say. I don't want to say *distracted*—it's kind of rude—but hopefully, she'll get the point.

"Oh, so much going on, so much to do. I have videos to make," she says, and then her eyes slide wide open as she tries to walk it back. "I mean, I don't have more videos to make. I'm not making videos. Well, yes, I am making videos, like the ones you li—"

She cuts herself off, rolling her lips together before she finishes the word *like*. Her face goes pink, the color spreading across her cheeks and down her neck.

And suddenly, I wonder about the videos I like.

"Yeah, I like your videos," I say stupidly, my voice thick, my tongue barely working.

Then...oh, shit.

I've never *liked* one before. Not on social media. But I must have last night. While I was clutching my phone with one hand and jerking my dick with the other.

Pieces of my bedroom indulgence snap back into place, rearranging into a different story.

The moment I thought I heard something late last night. When I hit pause on her skating video, pulled out an earbud, and listened to the silence before shaking it off and continuing—was she really there in the hallway?

The possibility slams into me like a hit into the boards. My chest burns, heat flooding through me. The kitchen shrinks around me, the air too thick, too charged. My pulse hammers out of control. I grip the counter to steady myself.

"I'm so glad to hear that," she says, but her voice is still too high, her eyes darting away from mine.

The pieces assemble the rest of the way in my head. The sound I'd thought I heard last night—it *was* the sound of the dryer opening.

She *was* in the hall. Last night.

And she knows what I did.

I wonder how long she stayed outside my room. Did she stand by my barely opened door for a few seconds? A minute? Was she tempted to come in?

Heat blasts through me.

I wish she had. I wish she'd pushed open the door, leveled me with her sexy gaze, fiddling with the hem of her sleep shirt, and asked—in that Sabrina ramble—for a do-over.

"It should happen again," she'd have murmured, like she'd already decided.

"It really should," I'd have said, voice rough, sheets low on my waist, the lights dim in my room, the heat shimmering between us in the dark. "Right the fuck now."

My throat tightens with lust. My mind pictures her closing the distance between us—climbing into my bed, unstoppable, impossibly sexy. I'd toss the covers off, invite her to join me. Watch me. Climb onto my lap. Sink onto my cock.

A rumble rises in my chest, threatening to break free, but I swallow it down along with all this red-hot, fucking *stupid* desire.

Because then what?

We've been down this road before. Traveled far down it last week. I'm hardly able to resist her as it is, but she's working for me *all season.*

I have to exercise some restraint.

My kids adore her.

Hockey is going well.

I need to keep my focus—on the game, my family, the season.

That's all.

This is not the time to play this kind of dangerous sex roulette.

"Did you like the NutRageous bar?" I ask, changing the subject with zero warning.

As she finishes a bite of her avocado bagel, she rolls with it. "It was amazing. Have you ever tried one? I saved a little bit for you. Even though it's not *your* guilty pleasure," she adds, looking down now again.

She says it like *she's* not my guilty pleasure. Like I've rejected her.

Because you did, you dumbass.

She busies herself with tracking down the candy bar she saved in a Tupperware container, then hands it to me, and I say, "I bet I'll like it."

Like that can erase the rejection from the other day.

"I bet you can't resist it," she says, but it's not said flirtatiously, like she might have said it before. It's said matter-of-factly.

I really need to get back to the way we were. Maybe this candy will help. Hell if I know. I take a bite.

And I can see why she loves it, even if candy's not my thing. The flavors collide in a sweet explosion. "Damn, this is good," I say, focusing on facts.

"Where did you find it?"

"I went online and ordered it for rush delivery yesterday morning. I wanted you to have your favorite candy bar—the one you never had as a kid."

Her smile is soft, a little wistful. "You kind of surprised me."

And I don't think she's had a lot of that. Surprises. Kindness. Gifts.

She had a shitty boyfriend for six years who cheated on her and betrayed her on their wedding day.

And before that, she was raised by a mean fucking man.

"Only kind of?" I ask, playing it light, finding my footing again.

"It was only *kind of* because...I've kind of gotten used to nice things from you."

The breath flees my lungs as the weight of that hits me. The precious, precarious weight of responsibility.

There it is—the reason.

The reason I can't close the distance, grab her face, and kiss her like she's all I think about.

I don't want to mess up anything in Sabrina's life.

I want to be a good man.

The one she hasn't had before.

And good men?

They don't fuck their nannies.

21

DADDY'S HOME

Sabrina

"Fractions are totally cool!" I tell Parker as I explain the math problem that's vexing him.

He shoots me a side-eye. "I don't think I'd call them cool."

"They're the coolest part of math," I argue, taking breaks to help him with homework while I prep an Asian noodle dish. Josie sent me the recipe, since she loves trying new things in the kitchen—and well, so do I.

After I chop the tofu, I move pieces around into a stack, with eight total pieces. "See? Now it's a tofu fraction tower."

Parker squints at it. "How is that a fraction tower?"

I nudge a piece to the side. "Now I've subtracted one-eighth. What's left?"

He leans in, more intrigued than he wants to let on. "Seven-eighths?"

"Exactly! Tofu fractions in action."

"I guess that makes sense. But I still don't know if I like tofu."

"It's all in the seasoning. And seasoning is math too."

From the living room, Luna calls out, "Math would be even cooler if you could do it with chocolate chips." She's working on a history assignment, groaning every few minutes about how boring it is.

"But remember, if we don't learn the lessons of history, we'll repeat them," I say as I toss the kale and tofu into a saucepan and add some spices.

She doesn't even look up. "What's so bad about that?"

I pause. "Uh...there were some pretty bad moments in history."

Tyler's returning from his road trip tonight, but I'm not sure exactly when. Even without him in the home, I'm smiling, having fun, getting excited to spend time with these clever kids with their big hearts and curious minds. It's not skating, but looking after them gives me a different kind of rush and warmth. It's been a fun few days with the kids—school runs, Lego club versus karate debates with Parker, ice skating lessons with Luna, hanging the disco ball she picked out at a thrift shop I took her to in Hayes Valley, and figuring out my own schedule between coaching clients. Tyler's mom helps a lot, sometimes picking them up so I can make my lessons, and I adore her and her pack of Chihuahuas. Elle took the kids one evening, too, so that was helpful as I had back-to-back-to-back lessons with three new skating students. They all found me through my videos—some the tutorials, some the free skates I do. My coaching business is steadily growing. I didn't make it to see Elena these last few days, but it's hard when I have the kids to myself. It's a lot to balance.

Right now Luna and Parker are focused on their homework. Just as I'm finishing up and draining the noodles, the doorbell rings. I tense. I've never liked doorbells—who does? But a glance at the doorbell camera on my phone tells me it's Tyler's mom.

"It's your grandma!" I call. "Does someone want to get the door?"

"I will!" Luna races over and swings it open.

"My little darling! It's been too long!" Lauren sweeps Luna up into a hug, her usual energy filling the house.

"I saw you two days ago!" Luna says.

"My point exactly," Lauren replies, hugging her harder.

When they let go, Luna peers at the bags Lauren carries. "It looks like you brought something."

"What kind of grandmother would I be if I didn't bring gifts?" she says, making her way to the kitchen with a few small packages.

She turns to me, smiling. "Sabrina! I *knew* you'd be perfect for the job." She says it every time she sees me, like she's still patting herself on the back for setting this up. I can't tell if it's because she's pleased with how well things are working out or if she's making sure I never leave. Maybe they're one and the same.

Either way, I'm so grateful for this position—and for her. My coaching business has been growing since I landed this role, and I've been saving money. I'm hopeful I can add clinics next year.

"What did you get me, Grandma?" Parker asks, looking up from his math.

"Oh, just a new Lego set," she says, pulling out a space station kit from her bag.

"Now this is cooler than tofu fractions."

"But you know what?" I tease. "Fractions will help you understand all the pieces."

Luna, waiting for her turn, finally reaches into the bag, and pulls out a book. "Ooh, *Cool Animal Facts!*" Her eyes widen as she flips it open.

"It was inevitable you'd love animals with your last name," Lauren says to Luna.

Which raises an interesting question. "Did you ever want to take Harvey's name?" I ask her.

She laughs, shaking her head. "Changing names is such a pain. And really, why do women have to do all the work in that regard?"

"Fair point," I say.

"Plus, it's memorable and sometimes being a Falcon terrifies people," she says in a stage whisper.

"Nothing like a scary name to get someone's attention," I say as the kids get absorbed in their gifts.

We chat more as I finish plating dinner. Just as I set the dishes down, she taps her chin thoughtfully.

"You know," she muses, "my friend Elsie just introduced her granddaughter to this wonderful engineer. Now they're engaged. It just goes to show how a little push can make all the difference."

It's out of the blue, but not entirely surprising. Moms and grandmothers love dispensing dating advice.

Then it hits me. She's about to dispense dating advice to *me*.

She taps her polished nails on the kitchen counter, giving me a knowing look. "Do you even have time to date? Or is Tyler being a hard-ass?"

Parker snickers. "Don't say *hard-ass*, Grandma."

She turns, bringing a finger to her lips. "Of course I didn't say it."

I laugh awkwardly, caught off guard—then the door swings open again.

Footsteps. A booming voice from the foyer.

"Hey, kiddos!"

Daddy's home.

The kids race to greet him, and moments later, Tyler strides into the kitchen in a beige suit with a burgundy tie and a thicker beard than he left with. My chest aches, and I dismiss it as best I can.

His mom spins around and immediately says, "Tyler, are you being difficult about Sabrina dating?"

Tyler looks like he's about to choke on air. "I'm not—"

"Good. You shouldn't be," she cuts in smoothly, patting his shoulder. "She should get out there and meet someone, don't you think?"

I freeze.

Tyler blinks, looking like he's swallowed something sour, but then—too casually, too easily—he says, "Yeah. She should get out there and meet someone."

I grip the plates hard. His tone is light. Unbothered. Like the idea means nothing to him.

The lack of hesitation settles wrong in my gut.

He wants me to date. Would that make things easier for him?

* * *

A little later, after inviting his mom to stay for dinner, Tyler has shed his suit jacket and changed into jeans and a T-shirt that definitely shows off his arms. His arms, his thick beard, his unruly hair. He makes caveman look so good, even though he's a gentle giant underneath it all. I wish he weren't *exactly* my type.

His mom, still on her matchmaking streak, says, "So I'm going to send her potential matches. I've been listening to that matchmaking podcast and talking to your grandmother about it, and I have some great ideas. I just want to make sure you're being a reasonable employer."

Tyler's expression is blank for a moment, but then he turns stoic. "Of course."

Lauren smiles, like she's just won something.

I'm so thrown off, I don't even know what to make of it. Except...the obvious.

He's doubling down on the whole *it can't happen again.* And the best way to make sure it doesn't? For me to be with someone else.

That shouldn't sting—but it does. Like salt rubbed into a raw wound.

But maybe he's right. Maybe I *should* date. It'd be the fastest way to get over this stupid, going-nowhere crush on my boss.

22

THE SABRINA ZONE

Tyler

It's not my place to tell her what to do. It's definitely not my place.

I repeat that over and over all day long.

Two nights later, I'm back on the ice, and frustration chases me as I slam an opponent into the boards, playing rough, aggressive—because fuck anyone who gets in my way.

Like Chicago's center, barreling down the ice. Not on my watch.

But I get tangled up in a battle along the boards. Before I know it, I'm called out on a penalty.

Miles tugs me away from the Chicago player. "Chill, man," he says. My brother hardly ever loses his cool.

I mutter a curse and skate toward the box, jaw tight as I sit and stew. Chilling feels impossible. I should be getting my head on straight. Instead, the idea of Sabrina dating is lodging deeper in my skull.

By the time I'm back on the ice, we're down by one. And I play like an asshole. A few minutes later, Miles is yanking me away again, telling me to *chill* again. And I'm back in the box. *Again.*

Chicago scores on the power play. Serves me right. But this screws the team. By the third period, we're scrambling.

But the worst part?

We lose, and as I skate off the ice, when I should be thinking about the game and what to do differently next time—I'm still mulling over Sabrina's love life.

I look up toward the family suite, forcing myself to wave at my kids, to blow them a kiss, to make a heart sign. It makes me feel better. They always do.

Luna waves right back at me, making a heart too. Sabrina's with them, though, and I'm right back in the Sabrina zone.

Even though I remind myself—it's not my place to feel anything for her. It's not my place to tell her what to do.

In the locker room, I yank off my shoulder pads with a certain amount of fury.

Images of her going out on her off nights, laughing as some guy picks her up at the door of *my house*, smiling, kissing him as he brings her back after the date to *my home*—are gnawing at me relentlessly.

Why didn't I think of this before?

I toss my gear into the stall, then chuck my uniform into the laundry bin.

Rowan glances at me. "Pissed much?"

"Too much," I admit.

"I guess it's a good thing the kids are coming with me tonight," he says. Since it's a Friday, and our daughters are friends, he's taking everyone home for a sleepover. He also has his sister's son for the evening, so Parker's tagging along too.

Probably for the best.

I shouldn't be around anyone tonight—not with this dragon of jealousy breathing fire down my neck.

But when I leave the locker room, Miles tugs me aside before I can say goodnight to the kids. "Hey," he says, in that calm, take-charge voice he's used since our deadbeat dad took off with barely a word. It reassured me as a kid. Right now, though, I'm in no mood. *For anything.*

"What is it?" I bite out.

He sets a hand on my shoulder and looks me straight in the eyes. "You okay?"

"Fine," I mutter.

"You didn't play like yourself," he says, and that's the thing about my brother. He won't let things slide.

I breathe out hard through my nostrils.

"What's going on?"

"Nothing," I mutter.

Miles stares at me like he can see through my lies. "Is it Sabrina?"

What the fuck? I practically jump away from him. "Are you a psychic?"

"Just your older brother."

I try to let go of my irritation. "I'll figure it out."

"You do that," he says, then nods down the hall toward Leighton, who's waiting for him. "I'm going to take Leighton out. Need a ride?"

The last thing I need is to be near happy people. "I'm good."

He takes off, and I head down the corridor to say goodnight to the kids. I find them hanging out with Rowan already, while Sabrina chats with Isla, Josie, and

Everly several feet down the hall, all turned away from me.

Sabrina's blonde hair is loose, shiny against her pink sweater.

Will she wear that sweater on a date?

I clench my fists.

"Let's get you on the apps," Josie says, tapping Sabrina's arm, and I dig my fingers into my palms. "We can write you an amazing profile."

"And Isla can help you weed through everyone," Everly says, clearly excited by this idea. Then she looks to Isla. "Or did you want to matchmake her?"

Bad idea.

Sabrina laughs. "I don't think I could afford you," she adds lightly, while I breathe in harshly.

"I *am* very exclusive. But you know I'll help you for free. Do you want that?" Isla asks, earnestly.

"Yes, tell us what we can do for you," Everly adds.

Sabrina shrugs lightly, but her voice is upbeat. "I think the apps are probably fine."

Fuck me. She's into this. My muscles are as tight as a steel cable.

"I'm *totally* going to help you," Isla announces. "I'm screening all your matches, and I'm giving you all the tips. I mean, I *am* a dating coach."

Sabrina laughs.

But I don't.

Because if I thought I was pissed off before, it's nothing compared to how I feel now. I am not good at all. I'm going to blow a fuse.

I barely manage a quick goodnight to my kids before I storm out of the arena.

I drive home faster than I should, more aggressively

than I'm supposed to—the way I'd never drive with my kids in the car. The way I shouldn't drive.

I slam on the brakes at a red light, pissed and seething. She's going to date.

She's going to date, and I'll have to see it.

She's going to date, and some other guy gets to romance her.

Worse.

Some other guy gets to give her all the things she asked me to give her on her wedding night.

I hate him with the fury of a thousand fiery hells.

When I reach the foyer, I kick off my shoes, strip off my tie, then pace along the first floor like a caged lion because I can't fucking stand this jealousy clawing at me.

I don't even go up to my room to change out of my suit. I'm too wound up.

I have to do something.

I have to find out what her plan is—so at least I can learn how to handle it.

I need to understand what she's going to do so I can live with it.

The second the garage door rumbles, signaling she's home too, I march to the top of the stairs to head her off before she can duck into her apartment for the night.

Once the door creaks open, I call out, "Do you want to watch a TV show?"

I've never asked her that before. But it's a casual pretext. A way to find out more.

"Sure," she says from the bottom of the stairs, a little tentative. "Let me just put my things down."

"Good idea," I say as nicely as I can, since I don't want to lose this opening.

I beeline for the kitchen, toss my jacket onto a stool and yank off the tie. After I grab a bag of popcorn from the pantry, I dump the sea salt air-popped contents into a bowl.

There. That's nice, right? I can be nice as I hunt for answers.

I bring it to the couch, set it on the table. A minute later, she pads into the living room in that pink sweater, with black leggings now and fuzzy socks.

Fuck, even her socks are cute.

White with pink hearts.

"What do you want to watch?" she asks curiously as she sits down, like she's still trying to figure me out.

Join the club.

I grab the clicker, tune into Webflix, and hunt through shows on the main menu, trying my damnedest to ignore how pretty she smells.

Like orange blossoms and something clean.

Her shampoo, maybe?

Her lotion?

It's flowery, and it's scrambling my brain.

I can't focus on the menu on the screen, so I hit something—I don't even know what. As the credits roll on *The Dating Games*, I figure this will be the perfect show to ask her what's next.

We're silent during the opening scene.

It's awkward since the two assistants who work together are walking on eggshells around each other at the office after hooking up the night before.

Then it's even more tense when the woman meets her friends for coffee, and they ask if she's going to see the guy again, and she hems and haws.

I grab a handful of popcorn and crunch down hard.

Sabrina reaches for some too and stares straight ahead.

We chew.

I stew.

One dating scene rolls into the next, and I can barely take it another second. And once the characters walk down the streets of New York City, gabbing about their worst swipe-right experiences, I snap my gaze to her, frustration boiling over.

"So, are you?" I ask, breaking the silence.

Sabrina looks at me, seeming confused, a cute little furrow digging into her brow, and I just want to touch it and kiss it.

And I'm so pissed that I feel this way as she asks, "Am I what?"

I hesitate, trying not to let annoyance and jealousy own me, as I say as calmly as I can, "Dating. Are you on the apps? Are you already seeing someone?"

But it doesn't come out evenly at all. It comes out full of unchecked irritation. Bursting with green-eyed jealousy.

Her face tightens, but she's not mean. She's never mean, even as she folds her arms over her chest and looks away. "Why do you care?"

"Because I should know."

She jerks her head toward me. "Because you're my boss?"

Sure, let's go with that. "Yeah."

Her jaw tightens. Her eyes narrow. And I said she wasn't mean, but I didn't say she wasn't fierce, since she levels me with a ferocious stare and says, "That's none of your business."

The fuck it isn't.

"It *is* my business," I counter, my tone sharper than I'd intended. "If you're seeing someone, it could affect your job here, and—"

Her lips part angrily. "And what? A guy might stop by? You don't get to tell me who to date, Tyler." She shakes her head, the fumes of rage billowing off her as she pops up with a tight and crystal-clear, "Good night."

She heads downstairs, shutting the door behind her with a loud and irritated click.

Nope. That won't do. That won't do at all.

I'm up and following her in no time.

Banging on the door.

Vision narrowed.

Focus tunneled.

Barely thinking of anything but...

She swings it open, tilts her head, holds her ground with a cool, "Yes?"

She's hurt. I've upset her. I've been a dick when all I want is to be good to her.

That's all I want.

I breathe out, letting go of two days of jealousy. "I don't want you to date anyone. I don't want you to see anyone. Because all those things you asked me for on your wedding night?"

She barely blinks. Just waits, stony-faced.

"I can't stop thinking about them. I haven't once stopped thinking about them. I replay your words to myself every night." Like the fact that she's never had an orgasm with another person. "I wish I could have said yes then. And I can't stand that another guy might be the one to show you everything you said you were missing."

"Tyler," she says, like she's exhausted, like she just

can't handle my going down this road again then backing up.

But that's the thing. I can't stand that possibility either. I forge ahead. "I'm sorry I was a dick tonight. But no one else deserves you. And I want to be the one to show you," I say, my voice raw and honest. I hold her gaze. "Let me. Please just fucking let me."

I'm begging, and I am not above it at all.

She blows out a breath, lifts a skeptical brow. "What about the whole pretend-it-didn't-happen thing?"

I shrug, holding out my hands. "I can't. I can't pretend. I've never been able to pretend."

"You're my boss," she says, but her voice is softening now, less wary.

I don't want to pressure her, but I can't resist her. I take a step closer. "You don't need to go out with someone else. You don't need to 'meet so-and-so.' You already said it, Sabrina. The night of your wedding. That you wanted to lose your real virginity with me. Do all the things with me."

Her breath hitches, and I hold mine.

Hoping for her yes.

The silence between us is thick, charged. It's out there now, impossible to take back.

She steps past the doorway, a couple inches into the hall, her blue eyes fierce.

She grabs my shirt collar. "Then make it worth my while."

23

———

ASK AND RECEIVE

Sabrina

Look, I've only fantasized about this happening ten million times. But in all my fantasies, I somehow pictured variations on the same scenario—how I thought Tyler would pin me down, like he did the other week.

A rough, hard kiss.

A scrape of stubble.

A squeeze of my ass.

But instead, he scoops me up into his arms and carries me back into my own apartment. I never pictured this, but it makes me feel giddy, makes me glow.

The symbolism of carrying me across the threshold is not lost on me.

I don't want to read anything into it, even though it feels like a do-over of my failed wedding night—both the failed wedding and my failed proposition to him.

But when he kicks the door closed without even

looking at it? With just a decisive thump of his foot? That feels fresh and new. And fucking hot.

Tyler doesn't take me to the bedroom. He strides all the way across the living room, then sinks down on the couch, settling me on his lap, adjusting my legs so I'm straddling his ambitious erection as I face him.

I'm shimmering, vibrating with the need to touch him, the need to be touched. But I'm also waiting for him to go next. To spread me out on the couch.

To devour my mouth.

To kiss me everywhere and take me apart.

To do anything. To do everything.

Once again though, he surprises me when he lifts his hand—slowly, like a tease—and cups my cheek, stroking softly. "Tell me what you want, Sabrina. And I'll give it to you."

Like it's that simple—ask and receive.

It's a wild thought, and a wildly arousing one too. I melt a little more as I sink deeper onto the hard ridge of his erection, growing more turned on as I feel his length against me.

But I can't fully consider what I want, not when he dips his face to my jawline, kissing me there—an unhurried tease of his lips across my skin—as he whispers, "Whatever you want. Whatever you need."

My head swims with too many ideas. "I don't know where to start."

He chuckles as his mouth meets mine once more, then leaves a trail of kisses across my jawline before he stops, holds my face in his big hands, and says, "Remember—you are the deal. And it's a big deal." It's a callback to the Night of 1001 Confessions, when he told me my pleasure was *the* deal. The point of it all—of sex. This feels like a promise renewed that he'd make it happen. I nod urgently and he keeps going. "But I don't want to assume you want the same things you asked for in June. I need you…to tell me how you picture me making you come when you're alone at night."

I gasp from the boldness of the statement. The sheer accurateness of it too. "How do you know I do that?"

"Educated guess," he muses, then meets my gaze again. "Plus, you did tell me that night. Your exact words were—*My solo time? I've enjoyed that. And I've spent a lot of it picturing all the things I want. So many things.*"

Holy shit. He's quoting me back to me. I shiver.

He drops a scorching kiss to my mouth, claiming my lips with a possessiveness that sends pleasure rocketing through my whole body, straight to my core.

But he wrenches back, asking again, "So, what'll it be?"

That's the million-dollar question.

What do I want from this man now that *this* is happening?

Images flash through my mind. Desires. Wishes. Positions. Role-play. Games. I'm not sure where to start, but since we're being honest, I start with that.

"I don't know. I just want it all," I admit, feeling too ravenous to know where to start at the Tyler sex buffet.

He dips his face to mine once more, tugging on my lower lip with his teeth, then letting go. "Want me to find out what you want?"

"Yes," I say, trembling, gasping.

After sliding a thumb down my jawline to the corner of my mouth, he presses, parting my lips for him. And I gasp.

My breath stutters. But he doesn't rush. He just

watches my lips fall open around his thumb. Like he's testing me. Like he wants to see if I'll beg.

I don't.

Not yet.

I might not have much experience, but I'm good at listening to my body. Knowing what it needs and wants. Right now, my body says it wants to be wound higher. I want him to push me, to make everything feel excruciatingly good.

"Tell me more," he urges, coaxing my mouth open, pushing his thumb inside. "Like, does this feel good?"

I had no idea this would be such a turn-on. I wriggle against him, then nod. "Yes," I say around his thumb. He slides it farther inside my mouth, slow and seductive, a simulation of how he wants to fuck me.

A promise of later.

Controlling. Purposeful. A man who knows how to use all his equipment.

He lets his thumb fall from my mouth and runs it down my throat, over my chest, before sliding that hand up and inside my shirt, against my skin, toward my tits. Then he squeezes—hard. "This? Does this feel good?"

I shudder, my mind flashing bright neon. "Yes," I say, arching my back.

Tyler rumbles out a raspy, "Good."

Threading his fingers into my hair, he tugs my head back, exposing my neck. More kisses, more touches, then more words as he says, "Tell me something."

"Anything." A flush races up my throat, impossibly warm.

"Do you picture coming on my face?"

The sound I make is animalistic. Like a cat in heat.

His smirk is satisfied. Too confident. As if he already

knows what I do alone in the dark. And maybe that should embarrass me, but it doesn't. It makes me reckless.

"You think I picture it?" I challenge, curling my fingers into his shoulders. I haven't technically said yes. I've just groaned. "Or you just want me to say it?"

He leans his face closer to mine. "You don't have to say it."

I swallow past the heat surging everywhere in me. "Why?"

"Because I know it. I know you do because of the way you look at me," he says, with a confidence that electrifies my body, my soul. "The way you've looked at me since that day here on your yoga mat when I was this close to burying my face between your pretty thighs. This close to tasting your sweetness. This close to learning if you're as wet and hot and fucking delicious as I imagine you are right now."

I'm wetter. Hotter. Greedier.

Electricity crackles in me as I grind right back against his cock. He's right. I don't have to say I picture that. Because he clearly knows it. But still, I ask, "Can you feel me right now? How much I want it?"

I'm only wearing leggings. He's wearing his suit pants still. And I'm soaked. Can he tell? I need to know.

His answer is a nod and a growl. "You bet I fucking can." His hazel eyes are midnight as his gaze rolls over me like a heat wave. "And you need to know something, Sabrina."

"Yes?" I ask, desperate for whatever he has to tell me, whatever he plans to do.

He levels me with a dark, feral stare, as if he's making sure I'm focusing on him. "I picture you coming on my face," he grits out. "All the fucking time."

My belly coils, low and tight. A pulse beats between my legs.

"Yeah?" The question is breathy. But it's hardly a question. It's more like the most delicious realization I've ever experienced in my entire life.

With a bitten off moan, he grips my hips, moving me against his hard-on, setting the pace as he makes me dry hump him. Though *makes me* barely covers it—I am ready and here for the dry fucking. The full fucking. Any fucking from Tyler.

"I get off to it every night," he says, like it's been driving him mad to be this worked up, this aroused. I love the way he's been so frustrated by his desire. Same here. "I fucked my fist last week, picturing how you'd taste coming all over my face."

I'm officially boneless from the admission. "That was the night I—"

"The night you stopped outside my door," he says with a smug, satisfied smirk.

"You knew I was there?"

A cocky grin curves his lips, like his pressure's been loosened, the frustration abated from all these bare admissions. "I heard something in the hallway. I'm guessing it was you. And I bet you were tempted to come in," he says, then gives a lazy thrust of his hips.

"I was," I say, rocking back against him, seeking out as much of his arousal as I can get.

He strokes my face, and I'm painfully aware he still hasn't stripped off my clothes, still hasn't told me what he'll do to me.

"But you wanted to watch me," he continues. "You wanted to see how fucking wound up I was."

A shudder rolls through me as he thrusts again, thick

and hard. But I don't give in yet to the questions or the pleasure. "Did I want that?" I ask, shameless, because I'm a fast learner. I can play this game.

He curls his hand around the back of my skull. "You would've stayed," he rasps out. "You would've watched. You would've pushed that door open a little more, just to see my cock in my hand. Maybe even stepped into my room, leaned against the door, and thrust your hand inside your panties while you watched me come so fucking hard. *To you.*"

I barely even know what's happening to my body. Pleasure is everywhere. It's racing through every single nerve ending. I'm on the verge of coming. I've been so worked up since the second he touched me, since before he even carried me inside, that every little movement winds me tighter. Every word makes me hotter.

I can't form words. I just moan.

With a low, pleased noise, he thrusts up again.

Again.

Then again.

A long, slow stroke.

I cry out, bracing for the onslaught of pleasure he's delivering to my body.

"And you knew what got me off," he says, a challenge. Like he's daring me to admit everything from that night. How all the clues added up.

"I had a feeling," I murmur.

His grip tightens on my hips, rough and demanding. "Tell me, Sabrina. Tell me what did it for me. Tell me what made me come harder than I ever have before."

"You watched my video," I blurt out and I'm so close. So fucking close. All I want is for him to touch me.

And I swear this man can read my mind because he

moves so quickly I can barely process what's happening. But he's lifted me off his lap, set me back on the couch, and is peeling off my leggings and fuzzy socks. Just like that.

He kneels on the floor, yanks down my panties, and lets out the lowest, dirtiest rumble. "Fucking beautiful. So fucking pretty."

No one has ever praised me like this. No one. And it makes me even wetter.

"Yes, that's it, baby," he says, as he spreads my thighs wide, then meets my gaze and says, "this is what got me off."

Then his mouth is on me with a hot, open-mouthed kiss that sends a jolt right through my body. I grab his hair, gripping tight, curling my fingers through it as he kisses my pussy—a man unhinged, a man showing me exactly what turns him on.

Me.

He sucks and licks, worshipping me with his mouth. It's incredible, the way he touches me, with flicks of his tongue and drags of his lush lips, and a blow of air here and there, then a suck on my clit that has me crying out. But most of all, it's his noises that send me to the cliff. Hungry, eager noises as he feasts.

Showing me what turns him on the most.

Making me feel like I'm drowning in his desire.

And I don't want to come up for air.

With his tongue cartwheeling over me, I lose my mind, gasping as I detonate.

The powerful release steals my senses. It blasts through my body and mind.

I moan for days, gripping his hair as the orgasm seizes

me. Sparks burst behind my eyes. Bliss radiates in my cells.

I'm still gasping from the orgasm, my body loose and noodle-y when I finally flutter open my eyes.

Tyler's wiping a hand across his wet mouth.

Sexiest. Thing. Ever.

Before I can even say a word, or a thanks, or a wow, he shifts back on his heels, grips my waist, and lifts me, tossing me over his shoulder in no time.

I'm half-naked, and he's already carrying me across the room.

"What are you doing?" I shout, then smack his back playfully.

His palm lands on my ass, a quick, sharp swat that zings through me. I shudder. No one has ever spanked me before. I kind of want to ask for another, but before I can get the words out, he says, "I'm giving you your second orgasm—that's what I'm doing."

Oh well, I can table the spanking for now then.

He rounds the corner and tosses me onto the bed. Then, he drops his palms to the mattress, bracing himself on those strong arms, muscles bulging, and stares down at me. "If memory serves, you wanted this too."

He grabs my wrists, pushes them above my head, and straddles me. "Am I right?"

I look up at him—his overpowering frame, his intense eyes, his coiled strength.

"Yes," I say, my breath staggered and needy, matching how I feel inside.

Because this—this is everything I've wanted. For him to hold me down, fuck me hard, wreck me.

"Fuck me like this now. Please don't make me wait," I beg, and I don't even care.

His eyes flicker with dirty delight. He lets go of my wrists and sits up, grabs my hand, and says, "Take off my shirt. I know you fucking want to."

"Presumptuous," I say, but I'm reaching for the top button, hastily undoing all of them and spreading it open.

He does have tattoos. Like I wondered. Like I hoped.

I yank that shirt off so fast, then fling it to the floor. I press a hand to his right pec, tracing the dates inked there, recognizing them instantly. "You tattooed your kids' birthdays on your chest?"

He presses his hand over mine, holding it tight. Gripping it like we're both holding something sacred. "Yeah."

He doesn't have to say they're what matters most to him. It's clear. It's clear in the way he holds my hand so my fingers can stroke the ink on his chest. So I can touch what matters most to him.

I'm mesmerized—not just by the ink, but by the feel of him.

The strength of his chest. The sturdiness of his body. The dark trail of hair traveling from his pecs down the ladder of his abs to the waistband of his pants, making my mouth water.

"I want these off," I say, tugging at them now, boldness overtaking me.

I've never been bold in bed before—not because I'm shy, but because I've never really enjoyed sex.

Now though? I think I'm going to love it. "Get naked," I demand.

If I blurted things out that night we were together in the hotel, that's nothing compared to how I am now. I'm unleashed, and I have so many things I want to say.

He drags a hand down his face. "Holy fuck. I can barely keep up with you."

I blink. "Is that bad?"

He dips his face, brushing his lips tenderly against mine. "It's all good." When he breaks the kiss, he tugs at my sweater. "And I could say the same to you. Get naked. Now."

"Yes, sir." I strip off my shirt and sports bra, suddenly naked before him.

His eyes don't settle. They travel. Up. Down. Over every inch of me.

"I am going to have a field day with this beautiful body," he says, flicking a finger against my right nipple and the slim silver barbell that runs through it. "And we're going to come back to this. I want to spend a good long time with these beauties."

"Have me. Do whatever you want," I say, trembling from the pleasure and the promise of more. Especially since someone is finally appreciating the piercings I had done a few years ago. I did them for me—I like them. But wow—to be with a man who enjoys them so shamelessly is entirely new. It might even be my new guilty pleasure.

He slides his hands to my waist, then stops. "Shit. I don't have condoms." He scrubs a hand over his jaw. "I haven't had sex in...a long time," he admits. "More than a year."

And I didn't think it was possible, but I'm even more turned on by his restraint.

"I'm very good at preparing." I reach into the night-stand and grab a condom, adding quickly, "For us. Just in case."

His lips twitch. "In case I ever stormed in here and told you I wanted a redo on the Night of 1001 Confessions?"

"Yes," I say, smiling, even though that's not entirely

how I came to be in possession of this, but that's a story for later.

Tyler stands, sheds his pants and briefs, and stands naked before me.

And oh my god.

He's glorious.

His cock is as beautiful as the rest of him. Everything is wonderfully proportional. He grips himself and strokes from base to tip, squeezing out a drop of liquid arousal. I part my lips. I barely know what's come over me, but I stick out my tongue—asking for it.

He drags his thumb across my lips and slides it inside my mouth. My eyes flutter, and I moan around his thumb, tasting him. When I open my eyes again, I can't wait any longer. "Please fuck me."

Withdrawing his thumb, he drags it against the corner of my lips. "Such a beautifully filthy mouth. But so impatient. You'll get my cock, but only when I'm ready to give it to you."

I whimper.

He smiles again, a closed mouth grin. "Beg me, baby. You beg so sweetly."

"Please, Tyler. I want you. *Badly*."

"You sure?"

"Yes!" I practically bang my fists.

"Spread those pretty legs so I can make sure."

I'm on edge with desire as I part my thighs, feeling vulnerable and wildly turned on. He stares at me approvingly.

"So fucking ready." He climbs back onto the bed, settles between my thighs, and, with intense focus, rolls on the condom.

Then—he spreads my legs wide.

Nudges the head of his cock against my wetness.

Draws a sharp breath.

"Fuck, baby," he grunts out. "You feel so good."

"You're not even in me," I protest.

"I know. And you already feel incredible."

I wrap my hands around his shoulders, urging him closer.

But he pauses—stilling himself, like he needs to catch his breath.

And in that moment, in that hesitation, my heart pounds so loudly, so...wonderfully.

Because I swear his does too. When he opens his eyes, his voice is low and strained. "Tell me if it hurts."

He remembers everything—including the fact that I don't have much experience.

"I know it's going to feel good," I say, then urge him on.

He pushes in—gritting his teeth, as if he's fighting off a groan.

I gasp from the pleasure, from the way it spreads, deep and slow, as he sinks all the way into me.

"Ohhh," I moan, chased by a little cry.

He breathes out hard too. "This is..."

For the first time, he seems speechless.

He freezes. "I need a moment."

I stop breathing. I didn't expect that. I didn't expect him to have to pull himself together. "You do?" I ask, a little giddy.

"I've wanted this so badly. Need to make it good for you."

"It is good," I say, and what a thrill to reassure him.

So I do it with actions too. Reaching around, I grab his ass. He's so firm, so strong, and I can't wait to hold on as he fucks me.

But he doesn't start pounding into me like I'm used to.

Instead, he reaches for my right hand, peels it off his ass. Then my left. I'm not sure what to make of the move until he says, "Hands over your head, Sabrina."

Yes please! I comply.

He stretches over me and pins my wrists down.

Then—he pulls back, slow and lingering.

Taking his time.

Then he slides his cock back in, filling me deeply.

And I moan as my legs shake from the pleasure.

He pulls back, almost all the way out, leaving me empty, wanting.

Then he thrusts deep again, sending hot sparks pulsing through my entire body.

As he holds me down and fills me he stares into my eyes in a way that should be unnerving.

But it's not.

It's hot. It's thrilling—the way he wants me, the way he can't hide it.

A shudder wracks his strong body as he eases out, then drives back in. "I should've done this a long time ago," he murmurs.

My toes curl. "You should have," I toss back, breathless.

He fucks me slow and deep, holding me down the whole time. "I've wanted this for so long."

And maybe it's the endorphins talking, maybe it's the aftershocks of the most intense orgasm of my life, but I say, "Then stop telling me to pretend it didn't happen."

His eyes flood with heat and longing. "I won't, baby. I can't."

And I can barely process the weight of those words before he shoves into me again—rearranging my view of the world, of sex, of possibilities with every mind-bending thrust.

With every pump of his hips.

With every press of his body against mine.

My mind goes hazy, my body aches everywhere, and the world blurs as he takes me in deep and slow—everything I never knew I wanted.

Then, he picks up the pace—harder, faster—sending me spinning as I fall apart beneath him. And seconds later, he follows me there, grunting, tensing, and giving me everything.

This is what I've been missing. And all I can think is— I want so much more of him.

24

THE GAME PLAN

Tyler

After I return from the bathroom, I fiddle with the condom wrapper left on the nightstand. I didn't notice it before, but the packaging says, *Put some protection on that erection.*

As I sit down on Sabrina's bed, I arch a brow, waggling it her way. "This is...interesting."

A splash of pink colors her cheeks. She's still stretched out on the bed, all loose and languid, skin glowing, hair a perfect mess. "Trevyn gave it to me. Turn it to the other side."

I flip it over and snort. The words *Large* are written on the back, then in small print: *Just tell him it's X-Large, sweetheart. He'll love a good ego stroke, among other strokes.*

I laugh. "Way to knock me down a peg," I say.

She gives a faux pout. "Aww, did I hurt your feelings with the novelty condom?"

Novelty. That word sends a zip of worry down my spine. "They work like regular condoms though?"

She sits up. "Yes! They're just in fun packaging. And I'm on protection too."

I breathe a sigh of relief. "Good."

"Trust me, I don't want to get pregnant," she says.

And damn, we are racing right into the serious conversations faster than I'd expected. I drag a hand through my hair, hoping to reset. "Sorry. I didn't mean to make a thing of it."

She sits up and sets a hand on my arm. "I'll be right back."

She rushes out of the bedroom, and I can't help it—I watch her go, admiring her heart-shaped ass for the first time ever. I let out a low moan of appreciation at her fading form, then take a deep breath, looking around her room.

There's a notebook and a pen on the nightstand. A couple books. Some necklaces on her bureau. And a few framed photos of her and her friends.

That ought to make me smile—all this normalcy.

But my chest tightens, and I rub my sternum to try to loosen the tension. What the hell happens next? Where do we go from here? No idea. Since I've disposed of the used condom already, I grab my boxer briefs and pull them on, then my pants. Seems presumptuous to just lounge around in the buff, and honestly, I haven't thought beyond this point.

Well, I didn't think beyond immediate gratification when I banged on her door. And now that the lights are on and the deed is done, I'd better think fast.

Sabrina turns the corner back into her room, eyes me up and down quickly, then hustles to grab a long T-shirt from the bureau and fish out a pair of panties. In no time, she's covered up too.

I'm standing here stupidly, thanks to a novelty condom wrapper, unsure what to say. But I can read her body language loud and clear. She thinks I'm going, so I sit down and pat the bed. "Come here."

She walks toward me, but apprehensively, like a small dog who doesn't trust me yet.

When she sits, I reach for her hand. She takes mine, and we thread our fingers together. My heart settles a bit. Just a bit though. I study our clasped hands for a beat. "Hey," I begin.

She closes her eyes, her shoulders sinking. "Just say it."

"Say what?"

When she opens her eyes, she looks tough, resolute as she says, "Pretend it didn't happen."

But I can hear the pain in her voice. I squeeze her hand tighter. "I'm not going to say that," I try to reassure her. "I'm just not...good at this. This is all...like learning to ride a bike again."

A small smile shifts her lips. "News flash: you're a quick re-learner."

I don't mean the sex though. I mean the post-sex. Sorting my thoughts, I rub my thumb along her fingers. It's such a privilege to touch her like this. "What I'm trying to say is—" I stop, make sure I'm meeting her eyes. "I meant it when I said it earlier. I mean it now. I won't pretend this didn't happen."

And then, maybe because I'm better with physical things, I tug her onto my lap, then flop down on the bed with her, sliding under the covers together, pulling the quilt to my waist—and hers too.

"Tell me more about this condom gift," I say, finding my way back to intimacy like that. "When did he give it to you?"

Her lips quirk up, then she admits, "A few weeks ago."

I feel like I'm in on a secret, but then I wonder—was it because her friends were encouraging her to date again? Does she even still want to date? I didn't come in here asking her out to dinner. I stormed in here wanting to take her to bed, so how the hell do I reconcile the two? "Any reason in particular?" I ask, fishing for intel.

"If you must know, he said it was because he knew I would never be that presumptuous, but he wanted to be presumptuous for both of us," she says, gesturing from her to me. "And then he said he wanted to be helpful for both of us. And then he basically said he was trying to manifest it for us."

Her grin makes me grin. "So he was the wingman I didn't even know I had?"

She laughs. "Evidently. He manifested tonight, it seems."

"Fucking love that guy," I say. "Can he manifest a Cup for me too?"

"I can ask," she says, settling into the pillows now, perhaps believing that I'm not going to take off and shut this down. "He was wing-manning you from day one."

I turn toward her, still holding her hand. "Good. This thing with us feels a little inevitable, doesn't it?"

"Well, considering I threw myself at you on my wedding night, I'd say you read the room pretty well."

A laugh bursts from me. "I suppose I did. And I was a perfect gentleman back then."

"Don't remind me," she grumbles.

"But I don't have to be one now," I say, dropping my voice as I slide a hand down her stomach.

"Thank god," she says.

Which brings us to the point of this moment. "I want this," I say, even though we haven't defined what *this* is. "But it also could get messy."

She sighs. "It could."

I flash back to last summer when I swallowed down my wishes. Not the night of her wedding, but at the ice-skating lesson, when she brought me the sweatshirt and the mug as a thank you.

I held back then. I didn't ask her out on the date I wanted to. And I'm not sure I really *can* ask her out on a date now. I can at least tell her the truth of that day though.

I push up a little higher in bed. She follows suit. I clear my throat. "You remember that day, a week after your wedding? When you came to the ice-skating rink and asked to talk to me after a lesson?"

She nods immediately. "Yes, of course."

"I was going to ask you out on a date." I lay it all out there.

"You were?" she asks, fighting off a smile.

"I was so damn ready," I admit. "I was going to ask you to go to a baseball game and debate the umpires. I was going to see if you wanted to play mini golf—and then ask if I could make you scream in pleasure. I had a whole plan. Anything to spend a little more time with you."

"Why didn't you?" she asks.

"The sweatshirt," I say like that makes everything crystal clear.

"The sweatshirt I returned?"

"Yup. It felt like a sign. You were returning it. You were

apologizing. You were blaming the spicy margaritas. Didn't take a genius to know it wasn't the right time."

And wow—my shoulders feel lighter. Was this a burden I was carrying? Not exactly. But it was definitely a secret. It's one I've held onto for a while.

"News flash, Tyler." She gives me a teasing look. "I would have said yes."

I mutter a thousand curses under my breath. Fuck. I should have asked her then. "Let me put that on a list of things I regret."

"But," she adds wistfully, "I also wasn't in a good place."

And that raises the question: What exactly kind of place are we in tonight? "What about now?" I ask.

Slowly, she pulls her gaze back, giving me a very quizzical look. "Are you asking me if we can date?" It's like she wants to be absolutely certain of the score.

I'm going to sound like a giant ass if I say we can't. But I don't have to because she beats me to it.

"I think that would be...really complicated, wouldn't it? The kids and all."

Relief floods me. I'm so glad she's the one who said those words. "Yeah. I think it would be...but," I say, my mind leaping ahead, trying to find a loophole, an answer, when I flash back on tonight's hockey game.

It was messy because I didn't follow the game plan Coach laid out. I took stupid chances. I acted on my emotions, letting them get the better of me. If I'd stuck to the plan, maybe we'd have won.

"When things get messy in a game, I always find it's best to go back to the plan," I say, tentatively, but strategically too.

Her eyes sparkle with curiosity. "Same for me. When

I've made mistakes on the ice, I need to return to the program. The choreography. Go on."

"What if *we* had a game plan," I say, gesturing from her to me.

"A way to keep things from spiraling into something we're not prepared for?"

"Yes, like a quid pro quo."

She laughs. "I mean, I like your quid. I think you like my quo."

I grin, running my fingers along the soft skin of her stomach under her shirt. "I definitely like your quid and your quo." Then I frown. "Actually, I have no idea what either one of those means."

But I know this much—I fucking loved fucking her. And I think she's fantastic. If she still wants all those things she asked for this summer, I really, really want to be the man to give them to her.

My gut churns. I'm going to sound like an ass, but this whole dating thing has to be addressed. "But I also know you were looking into dating. And I just don't want to be the guy to stand in your way...even though I came in here tonight and said I don't want you to date."

She tilts her head. "You're kind of sending mixed messages. Do you want me to date or not?"

"No," I say instantly, emphatically. "I really don't."

And then—fuck it. I wrap my arm around her waist and jerk her against me, facing her as I hold her. I run my hand from her shoulder down to her wrist, watching as goosebumps rise on her skin. "I want you all to myself."

Her smile is soft, a little teasing. "I wasn't actually going to date. Everyone was pressuring me because it's fun for people who are coupled up to try to connect their single friends. But honestly..." She exhales wistfully.

"Honestly what?" I press.

She gives me a sly look. "Honestly, for a long time I was hoping that you'd bang on the door, bend me over the bed, and fuck me to pieces."

That image is scorching hot. And it's seared into my brain. "You want me to bend you over the bed? Because that can definitely be arranged."

"I want it all, Tyler. That was the first time I've ever had an orgasm with another person. And…I've got some other things on my list."

I clear my throat dramatically. "Two, baby. I gave you two," I point out. "Do not shortchange me."

"I would never. In fact, they're both going on my list of good things that happened to me today." She pushes up in bed, like an idea's struck her. "That's it. We need a list."

"A sex list? Count me in."

"Yes, a game plan for sex. A list so we can work through all the un-St. Bernard-like things I want you to do to me."

I am so there. "Let's do it. Maybe you put a list of three things you want?"

"Only three?" she teases.

"I didn't want to be presumptuous. You tell me how many you want."

She's a match ready to strike. "All I can eat," she says. "But we could start with five."

That's two better than I'd hoped, so already this feels like winning. "I like five. And what if we check one off… once a week?"

Her eyes pop. "Well, you have better restraint than I do."

"Maybe I'm just trying to stretch this out."

She hums, as if she's considering, then a glint shines in

her eyes. "If that's the case, how about every other week? Just to make sure we don't get in over our heads."

How did we go from once a week to once every other week? But what I really hear is that she wants to stretch it out too. "That sounds fair for the first rule," I say, keeping my cool so I don't let on how much I like this plan.

It feels like a wide-open window. A long, winding road with beautiful views and barely an end in sight. It feels like the promise of pleasure, stretched out before us, with no complications.

"It's like a workout plan," she says.

"A sex workout?" I smirk.

"Yes. But we're going to need more rules," she adds, staying on task.

"You're right. We really can't do anything in front of the kids."

"Yes. Definitely no kissing, no hand-holding," she adds.

"No little sneaky displays of affection."

"And no sleepovers."

That last one doesn't sit well with me though. Hanging out here in her bed late at night? This is the best I've felt in a long time. "You mean when the kids are home?" I ask, hoping she likes that technicality too.

"Sure, but also because we don't want to get used to this."

"It's every other week. You can't get that used to it," I say, trying to convince her.

"True," she says, and I want to pump a fist, because do I ever want to wrap her in my arms tonight.

"And no one says 'pretend it didn't happen,'" I add because I know how important that is to her.

"Yes. Good," she says, then hesitates like something is weighing on her.

My gut twists with worry, but it's best to be upfront. "What is it, baby?"

"When it's over, it's over. We move on. I enjoy my job, and I want to keep doing it," she says, sounding so damn vulnerable, and it hits me exactly how much she has to lose. "Is that okay?"

I don't want to hurt her like others did. Like Chad did. Like her dad did.

I don't want to take all the things away from her that she needs and depends on.

I want to be a man she can rely on.

"You're not going to lose your job," I try to reassure her. "You're a fantastic nanny. You're great with the kids. I need you desperately."

She smiles, warm and pleased. "Good. Because I'm kind of falling in love with the gig."

That is music to my ears. But it also means we need to be smart and logical. "We'll be adults. It's a promise. It's a game plan, and we'll follow it. When the game is over, it's over," I say even though the words taste sour on my tongue.

She sticks out a hand. "Deal."

I take it and shake. This is exactly what we need. And exactly what I hate. But it's necessary.

After jerking her closer, I drop a kiss to those sweet lips. "Sealed with a kiss," I say, focusing on touch again.

She rolls her eyes. "You're such a cheeseball."

I scoff. "Am not."

"A little."

"Would a cheeseball want to fuck you to pieces?"

She seems to mull that over. "Maybe."

"We should find out then for sure. What's on your list?" I ask. "I'm dying to know."

"That's a surprise."

"Really?"

"Yeah. Wouldn't that make it more fun, if everything was a surprise?"

Actually, she's right. "You keep me on my toes, Sabrina Snow. You know that, right?"

"I think I do."

I tug her closer, sweep her hair off her cheek. "I'm going to be counting down the days to your next surprise."

"Or the minutes," she says, letting the words roll off her lips seductively.

My eyes pop with curiosity and dirty hope. "First one?"

She taps her chin, like she's deep in thought. "Never have I ever been fucked hard twice in one night."

And I'll be thanking Trevyn for giving her more than one condom, because I rip that wrapper open so fast and put her on her hands and knees.

25

———

A SEX SCHEDULE

Sabrina

I'm counting down the days until the next time. Counting and researching. Watching videos, reading *very* naughty books, and jotting down ideas for our Five Sessions of Sex School.

And who better to brainstorm with than my girl-friends?

With Tyler at the arena for a workout and the kids at school, I head to Moon Over Milkshakes, the retro-themed diner my friends love. The beachy music plays at a reasonable volume now, which is a nice change—it used to be *way* too loud.

I spot my crew right away, wave, and slide into the booth with a bump of my hip against Isla's. I'm just in that kind of mood.

It's been a week since Tyler turned my legs to jelly, and I am *ready* and waiting for the next round.

"You might be wondering why I called this meeting,

ladies," I say, addressing the assembled crew—Isla, Leighton, Skylar, and Maeve. Everly and Josie couldn't slip away from work.

Maeve arches a brow. "Well, considering your text told us to bring our *dirtiest* ideas, I had a clue."

"Fine, fine. I wanted to be dramatic," I say, grabbing the menus and doling them out. "Now, hurry. Order. We need food, and then I need ideas for naughty, dirty, *filthy*, toe-curling sex."

"Yes, ma'am," Leighton says, smirking.

Once we order, I nod toward her. "And thanks again for asking them to turn the music down. It's so much nicer here now."

"I agree," Isla says.

Leighton just smiles, then taps the table. "Have you considered hand necklaces?"

I blink. "Do I *want* that?"

"I *highly* recommend it."

"Noted." I type it into my phone, then turn to Isla for her input but she snatches my phone.

"What was that for?"

"For doubting me," she says, holding my phone hostage behind her back as she dips her other hand into her purse.

"What are you talking about?"

She whips out her hand theatrically, clutching a red hardcover journal with foiled gold letters on the front— My Tiny Sex Diary.

A laugh bursts from me. "Shut up."

"No, you shut up. How dare you take notes on your phone when you're with me?" she says, giving me the hardest of hard times.

I dip my face obsequiously. "Forgive me, notebook queen."

"Seriously, what were you thinking?" Leighton teases.

"Evidently I wasn't," I say.

Isla hands me the notebook ceremoniously. "As soon as you mentioned your sex lessons the other night, I ordered this just for you."

"Please tell me it doesn't have one of those embossed *From the library of Sabrina Snow* stamps on the first page," I say.

"No, but I can add that," Isla says helpfully and the thing is—she would. She'd special order the stamp from an Etsy shop in seconds.

"That won't be necessary."

"But here you go," she says, gently opening the book. The beginning offers pages for lists, and then after that it includes a section for the date, the "Summary of the Experience," and ratings on a five-star scale. "I always find it's best to take notes by hand. They stick longer."

"And we want that man to make things really, *really* stick," Maeve puts in, unable to resist that one.

I laugh, then set the tiny book on the table, accepting the pen, too, that Isla hands me. I ask her, "Okay, what do *you* think I should add to my list of five pleasures?"

She exhales dramatically. "I wish I knew. It's been *forever* for me. Honestly, at this point, if the right man just blows on my *ear*, I might come."

I lift a brow. "Ear play?"

Skylar chuckles. "My dog licks my ears. And my face. Every single night."

I tilt my head. "Ears *and* face? He sounds very thorough."

"He *is*." She sighs, like she's resigned herself to this

fate. "I mean, I can't be mad about it. I *do* cuddle him every night. And he's a Doxie mix, so how could I not?"

"And is there a sex tip somewhere in that?" Isla asks dryly.

Skylar holds up her hands. "Oh god, no. But since dogs know all our secrets, if you *asked* him, he'd probably recommend," she leans in and lowers her voice, whispering the name of a porn site.

I perk up. "Ooh, *role-play section*. Noted." I write that down on a page.

Maeve leans forward. "I'd also suggest some toys. I'm a *big* fan of bringing another party to the bedroom."

I shift in my seat, already warming to the idea. "What kind of party are we talking? A *guest star* or more of a *supporting role*?"

Maeve winks. "Depends on how adventurous you're feeling."

I nod, adding that to my growing list. The possibilities are stacking up fast, and I'm *very* into it. The server swings by with our drinks, and we thank her. Once she's gone, Isla says, "I feel like I should be taking notes too. You know, for...science."

Skylar grins. "Right? This is basically a public service."

Maeve lifts her milkshake. "I'd also suggest you might want to ask him to—"

She mouths the words, giving me a wild idea.

"Oh, that does sound like fun," I say, raising my glass to meet hers.

And if Tyler had me screaming his name last time, he has no idea what's coming next.

* * *

But first, there's a bag outside my apartment when I return after lunch before picking up the kids. A little shimmy runs through me as I cross the distance from the garage and pick it up. This man and his surprise gifts.

This bag is the smallest one yet. It's orange and blue—the team colors for the city's football team. I dip my hand in, fishing past light blue tissue paper to find...two tickets to a football game.

For this weekend. When Elle has the kids till shortly after the game.

I clutch the tickets to my chest a little too long. I smile a little too wide. And I probably assume a little too much. But his words from a week ago ring in my head.

I was going to ask you to go to a baseball game and debate the umpires. I was going to see if you wanted to play mini golf —and then ask if I could make you scream in pleasure.

When I reach inside the bag once more, I find a card.

Wanna go with me?
   —T

My stomach flips. Forget last week's words on what might have been. I'll take these brand-new ones now on what *will be*, thank you very much.

I hold the card tightly and go inside, tucking it into the notebook by my bed, right with all the other ones he's given me. The one from the morning after my not-wedding, the one from the gift of sheets, the one from the Sea Dogs hoodie. And the bag with yoga gifts.

At this rate, he'll have a whole notebook to himself to go along with the sex diary. Fitting.

After I text him my yes, his words echo in my head for the rest of the day—*Wanna go with me?* They're written, but I can hear them as clearly as if he'd spoken them. I can hear the vulnerability in this subtle way of asking me out.

Now, there's something else I can't wait for, and it's not just because I love football. But as I swing open the car door so I can pick up the kids, my phone buzzes. It's an email from Elena, confirming our next appointment.

Hot shame washes through me. She encouraged me to turn my list-keeping habit around. To use it for good with my list of good things that have happened. Does that really include keeping track of sweet notes the man who signs my paychecks leaves for me?

I sink down in the front seat, pausing before I start the car so I can mull over what the hell I'm doing.

On the one hand, this whole sex list is ridiculously risky. But then, so is doing a triple loop with blades on my feet, and I still do those. I've done them for decades.

I confirm the next appointment, then head to the school.

* * *

"Are you kidding me? That was holding!" I shout from our sweet seats on the fifty-yard line. "Are you paid by the other team?"

The ref doesn't answer me, of course. He just stalks down the sidelines, completely ignoring the way the Dallas team's offensive lineman tackled the pass rusher—

and seeming oblivious, too, to the sea of boos swelling around him.

Like the stocky Renegades fan in front of us, who sloshes his beer as he throws his hands up in frustration.

I snap my gaze to Tyler, but he's already on his feet, a fierce energy radiating from him. "C'mon! That's the second time you missed a holding call," Tyler shouts to the field, chastising the officials.

The stocky guy in the Slater jersey (repping the Renegades quarterback Holden Slater) in front of us spins around. "Right? These refs suck," he says.

"They're worse than the refs who suck up to the entire Kansas City team," I put in, pointing angrily past the sea of blue and orange jerseys to the guys in black and white who are ruining this game.

Tyler scoffs, then snorts.

Oh. Did I just say that out loud?

The guy in front of us lifts his nearly empty beer cup in approval. "You called it. The refs are obsessed with KC."

Tyler looks at me, eyebrows arching.

"Sorry, was that rude?" I deadpan.

Tyler just laughs. "To whom? The refs? Nope." His eyes glint as he leans in closer, his shoulder bumping mine.

When we're seated he slips his hand across my lap and into the pocket of my sweatshirt—it's a Sea Dogs hoodie, the one he gave me before the team's first home game of the season.

His fingers find mine inside the pocket, and he threads them together, sending sparks all over my skin.

Then, he shifts closer, his beard whisking across my cheek, his mouth near my ear. "Want to debate the refs some more?"

A shiver runs through me. Not from the words, but from his tone—low and raspy. "Is that code for something?" I ask.

"Maybe it is," he murmurs, then sneaks in a nibble on my earlobe before pulling back, turning his attention to the field.

"C'mon, D! Let's do this!" he shouts as the Renegades defense holds off the Dallas offense, forcing a punt.

He cheers, and a few minutes later, the offense is back on the field, the team's quarterback leading the charge.

"C'mon, Slater! You better throw a football better than you hit a golf ball," he says.

I arch a brow, then whistle in appreciation. "Hello, trash talker. What was that about?"

"He's one of the guys I played golf with over the summer. We were teammates in that tournament in Cozy Valley."

"Does that mean you stink at golf too?" I feign innocence, as if I don't know that I'm pushing his buttons, but I'm secretly eating up these details about Tyler's life outside of hockey.

"Hey, watch it," he says with a smile that tells me he likes my teasing.

"Do you guys need to start a club for pro athletes who flounder on the links?"

"Damn, woman, you pull no punches."

"And you wouldn't want it any other way," I say, feeling bold. Because he likes my style of bold.

Briefly, though, I wonder—am I doing such a good job at being a super nanny? Does a super nanny flirt with her boss like this?

But then I shove those thoughts away. I'm not nannying right now, and we're just having fun.

Just in case, I shift gears when there's a break in the action. "Do you go there a lot to see your friends?" I ask.

"I do, yeah. Holden lives there with his kids. Some of my other dad friends do too," he adds. "We get together whenever we can for bocce ball and other lawn games."

"A single dads club?"

He seems to give that some thought. "You know... maybe it is."

I lean closer. "Cheeseball."

"Watch it, Snow," he warns, but he's still squeezing my hand. He shoots me a look—the kind that lingers just a second too long. The kind that feels like it should've happened months ago.

And this? This feels perfect in a new way.

Like a perfect date.

Especially when the Renegades pull out a win, and as we make our way out of the packed stadium—along with the spilled popcorn, the beers, and the happy fans—Tyler asks if I want to meet Holden.

"Sure, but what if I think he's cuter than you?" I ask, all innocent.

His eyes darken, and he tugs me toward him. "I'll have to spank you for that."

"Promise?"

His expression turns feral.

And we're not heading toward the authorized personnel area any longer.

It takes forever to get out of the stadium lot, and once we do, there's a whole city to traverse. But as we go, Tyler keeps one hand on the wheel, the other on my thigh.

Sliding it up and down, up and down.

And I had no idea I'd be ready to climb him just from his hand on my leg. But I am. I'm a hot, wet mess.

"Are you trying to break our schedule?" I ask.

"Been thinking about that sex schedule," he says as we near the house, and right now, I wouldn't mind if he threw it out. I really wouldn't.

"What about it?"

We reach his home, and he lets go of my leg to open the garage. "We never said we couldn't do..." As soon as he parks the car and cuts the engine, he grabs my face and says, "this," before he pulls me in for a hot, searing kiss.

My brain pops. My senses fry. And I melt in the car. Then I heat up when he tugs on my lower lip with a growl.

He kisses me harder, recklessly, the kind of quick make-out in the front seat that feels like it could lead to more.

But even as he kisses me like I'm his new guilty pleasure, I can feel his restraint too. It's in his arms, his muscles coiled. It's in his stance—close but not too close. And it's in the clock, ticking in my mind.

The kids will be home soon.

Elle will be dropping them off.

I don't want to be a disheveled mess in front of her.

But I also really want this man to kiss me some more. So I grab his face, running my fingers through his beard, and I turn the table, kissing him hungrily. Then I can barely take the distance between us, so I take my chances, swiftly moving into his lap.

Then I smile at him. "We're not having sex."

"So we're not breaking our schedule," he replies as he curls his big hands over my ass and grinds me up and down.

I glance back at the clock.

They'll be home soon.

Any minute, really.

I should stop.

But I keep rubbing myself on him, and he keeps working me up and down on his dick, his breathing growing more staggered with every passing thrust.

"Fuck, baby," he grits out. "This is hard to stick to."

"I know," I breathe out.

And I'm nearly ready to throw in the towel this early. I dip my face closer, seeking out a hot, messy kiss that'll blow my mind, but instead...he grips me tighter—then gently moves me off him, setting me back in my seat with a clear intention.

"I'm sorry, but I need to get a grip because all I want right now is to fuck all that sass right out of you," he says. "And I also do not want to answer the door with a raging boner, so I'd better go inside and think about...I don't know, kittens or *Frozen* tunes."

A laugh bursts from me at the image of this man trying to hide the flagpole in his pants, but inside I'm dying. The ache between my legs won't abate, and my whole body is screaming at me to climb back onto him.

"I can answer it," I offer, grateful to be helpful again. To play Super Nanny. "I can hide my lady boner."

And now it's Tyler's turn to crack up. "Would you do that for me? I don't think I can deflate that quickly."

Is it weird that I love that he's asked me to help on this count? If it's weird, I don't want to be normal.

Less than four minutes later, I've smoothed out my hair, dusted powder against my flushed cheeks, and I'm swinging open the door, pushing our sex schedule out of my head as fast as I can.

"Sabrina!" Luna shouts. "Mom took us to the wildlife sanctuary in Darling Springs. They had foxes. Foxes! Like on your bag! There was a fox who was injured, and he can't live in the wild anymore, so the sanctuary helps him. And we learned that foxes eat rabbits and birds and stuff, but they eat berries and fruit too—like us," she says, without taking a breath.

And wow. "That's a whole lot of fox facts," I say.

"Don't forget they can see in the dark. They have a layer in their eyes...what's it called, Mom?" Parker asks, turning back to Elle in the doorway.

"The *tapetum lucidum*," she says. "It reflects light back through the eye."

"You should be a vet, Mom. That'd be cooler than a doctor," Luna says, skipping inside and dropping her bag.

"No problem. I'll just see if I can switch from treating humans to animals," Elle deadpans as the kids rush past me toward—I presume—the kitchen.

Elle looks at me with a pleasant smile. "How's everything with you? How was the football game?"

Great. I rode your ex-husband's huge cock in the front seat of his car. I'm still on edge with the way I want him. And I'm totally not thinking about the fact that you're his ex-wife at all right now.

"So fun," I squeak out.

"And the Renegades won, I heard. But I was not forced to hear about it," she says, sounding relieved. "Did he go on and on about all the bad calls?"

I bristle for a second. Just enough for it to feel irrational. Why does it bother me that she knows he does that?

Because I like when he does it with me? Because I want to be the only one who knows the way he rants about refs, the way his voice gets all low and grumbly, the way he throws his hands in the air when he's really fired up?

Or because I'll never be the only one who knows him?

Tyler once said he didn't feel the sparks with her, but he must have felt something. She's smart and capable and a good mom, and even if she's not into sports...she's got her act together.

I bet she doesn't bang her boss.

I swallow down the unexpected shame. "There were so many bad calls, we couldn't stop," I say as footsteps echo in the hall, and a few seconds later, Tyler rounds the corner.

I can't help it. My eyes roam straight to his jeans, hunting for a bulge.

It's all gone, and maybe—maybe I take a little bit of pride that it took five minutes to deflate. Even though I should not be feeling any kind of boastfulness about banging my boss. On a schedule no less.

In fact, as I say goodbye to let them have their co-parenting talk about what the kids are up to this week, I'm not actually sure where I should be.

I'm off for the rest of the night.

But I didn't make any plans.

The longer he talks to her in the doorway, the tighter my chest feels. I shouldn't care. But that doesn't stop me from feeling like an outsider. So, I do what any rational adult woman does when she's getting way too in her head —I lean on a friend.

I message Trevyn, and invite myself on a dog walk.

Before I go, I swing past Luna in the kitchen and tell her I'll be out if her dad asks. Then I make myself scarce, meeting Trevyn at a nearby park with his Lab mutt.

"What's gotten into you, sweetie?" my friend asks suspiciously as I fall into step next to him and his dog.

"Just missed you."

He arches a dubious and well-groomed brow. "I can see the lie radiating off you...just like I can tell you almost fucked your boss today."

I swat his arm. "Shut up."

"And you didn't deny it."

"I mean, I wanted to see Barbara-dor, not you," I say as we wander into the park, lit by streetlamps.

"Understandable," he says, but then shoots me another side-eye glance. "So...did you almost fuck him?"

I groan. "How is it obvious?"

And Trevyn cracks up, doubling over. "Sweetie, I guess I know you well."

With a sigh of admission, I say, "You do."

But when I return after we've done a few laps of the park, ducking into my apartment, there's a knock on my door a minute later—and concern on Tyler's face when I answer. "You okay?"

"Of course."

"Why did you go?" It's asked with only concern, not accusation.

Dishes clink in the kitchen. The kids must have had dinner already. "I went for a walk," I say, answering *where* not *why*.

Tyler shoots me a look that says bullshit. "You took off right away."

"I told Luna I was going," I point out, but now I feel stupid in a new way.

Was I rude to him? Should I have told him too?

We might have a game plan for sex—we might be

mostly sticking to it—but what's the game plan for...well, life?

"Was it seeing Elle?" he asks gently.

My chest tightens. Am I this obvious to everyone? I hesitate.

"I had to talk to her about Thanksgiving and Christmas," he says, and the first of those is coming up soon. "Just a lot to figure out."

"Oh. Sure, of course."

"Did it bother you?" he asks quietly, and I am see-through.

"Not really."

"But a little?"

"There's no reason for me to even be bothered," I say, raising my chin, staying strong.

"Don't be bothered," he says, then cups my cheek and sighs longingly. "I can't stop thinking about you," he says in a low, hot whisper.

And I'm not bothered anymore.

Wait, that's a lie.

I'm hot and bothered.

"I saved some dinner for you. Come upstairs," he says, and it's hardly a demand. It's a thoughtful invitation.

So I say yes.

And then I enjoy the hell out of the mushroom and lentil dish he made.

* * *

We're two floors apart. Me in my bed. Him in his.

Is he even asleep?

But that question is answered a minute later when my phone buzzes.

. . .

> Tyler: Watching your videos again. Swore I wouldn't. But I can't stop. And I'm so fucking turned on. And it's All. Your. Fault.

I gasp as heat rolls through me.

> Sabrina: Which one?

> Tyler: The last one you posted. I can't stop watching it. Your lips. Your hair. Everything. Just everything.

His text comes out frantic. Bitten off. Like maybe he's dictating it while fucking his fist. Then another one comes.

> Tyler: Tell me you're fucking yourself too.

> Tyler: Tell me your fingers are in your panties.

> Tyler: Tell me now.

I type out a desperate *yes*, then slide my hand into my panties and finish what we started in his car.

* * *

When I see Elena the next day, I don't mention the sex diary, or the football game, or the night with Tyler. Instead I focus on a new skating student who's eager to compete at the highest levels. I ask questions about how I can coach her differently than I was coached.

And really, that's a good use of this hour. Maybe even a better one than if I'd spent the time confessing my sins. Since I'm not exactly sure how I'd tell her that *I'm sleeping with my boss, but don't worry, we have a game plan on how not to fall.*

It's one thing to tell my friends. It's entirely another to tell someone who's been helping me navigate complicated emotions for the last six years.

But maybe if I can keep this thing with Tyler entirely *un-complicated* I'll be just fine.

26

SHREK DADDY

Tyler

Admittedly, I've been spoiled by Sabrina and Agatha. I've hardly set foot in a grocery store in years. But with Thanksgiving coming up, I don't feel right handing Sabrina a list of the things I'll need to cook.

And it's not just because I'm hosting this year—pray for me—but because I want to make sure I do right by the vegetarians in my life.

Luna and Sabrina.

Since my brother is the real cook in the family, he's handling most of the meal, but I still want to contribute. So I enlist my sister one afternoon when she's in the city for a meeting with business partners for her punk rock bar. She's been a vegetarian her whole life, and I figure she's my best shot at getting this right.

We head to Natural Foods while Sabrina is at the rink for her skating lessons. As I push the cart down the nut aisle—since Charlie assures me that the best stuffing is made with nuts—I brace myself for her sisterly inquisition about my true motives. After all, she gave me the third degree about my unrequited crush when I hired Sabrina. But she's too busy singing the praises of pecans and pistachios.

"I could marry mixed nuts," she says, grabbing a bag and tossing it in my cart.

As we leave the aisle, my phone buzzes with a text, and I pull it out.

> Sabrina: While you're at the store, could you please get me some Popsicles?

Popsicles? It's an unusual request. But one I like.

"Who's that?" Charlie nods to my phone and I quickly stuff it back in my pocket.

"Sabrina," I reply, then hightail it out of that conversation and head to the frozen meat section, figuring that's where the fake meat is too, like the veggie sausages Luna likes. I stop in front of a display case of Tofurky, scrubbing a hand over the back of my neck, trying to decide which one of these fake turkeys to get.

"So, how do you choose?"

Charlie laughs and flicks her pink-tipped hair off her shoulder. "You don't, unless you want to train the vegetarians in your life to secretly hate you. Let's go."

I furrow my brow. "What do you mean? It's Tofurky."

"It's an abomination of food," she says.

"Ouch. I'll make sure the Tofurky people don't hear you say that." I glance at some other options—ham substitutes, Cornish game hen made of rice and mushrooms, a loaf of something with wheat protein and lentils—then a... "How about a Field Roast?" I ask, looking at the vaguely ham-like thing.

She pretends to gag.

I hold up my hands. "I'm so lost. I have no idea what I'm supposed to get. Don't I just buy a fake turkey?"

She pats my shoulder, her expression shifting from playful to understanding. "First of all, I love the sentiment. But here's the thing—most people think vegetarians are climbing the walls for meat substitutes. We're not. Most of us actually really and truly like vegetables and rice and lentils."

I blink. "But isn't that all the stuff in these things?"

She smirks. "Sort of. But let me tell you a little secret. What's the best part of a Thanksgiving meal?"

I narrow my eyes, like this is a trick question, but then say, "The rosemary mashed potatoes? The stuffing? The cranberry sauce with orange slices that Mom makes?"

Her whole expression lights up like I've just won a game show. "Yes! Exactly. It's the sides. The sides are better than the main course."

"So...I need to stock up on sides?" I ask since that kind of makes sense.

"Yes! Think about it—creamy mashed potatoes, roasted vegetables with rosemary, sautéed Brussels sprouts, fresh-baked rolls straight from the oven, a savory butternut squash soup, a delicious salad...That's the good stuff."

I nod slowly. "That does sound good."

"If you really want to make something substantial, do a mac and cheese with a breadcrumb topping, a butternut squash risotto, or a rice pilaf with cranberries. But you don't have to replace the meat," she explains. "And you definitely don't need to make it look like meat. Most of us aren't craving things that look like meat. Personally, I can't stand those fake beet burgers that 'bleed.' It's just wrong."

"That does sound disgusting," I say.

"And look, the fact that you're thinking about this and making sure your guests have a variety of things to eat? That says a lot."

Good. I'm glad. I want Luna and Sabrina both to know I'm thinking about them. That I care about their choices, and that it's a privilege to be able to accommodate them, not a pain in the ass. But I also would never have known this.

"Thanks, Charlie. I would never have thought of that," I admit.

Charlie squeezes my shoulder. "That's why you brought me." Then she points at me, shooting me a searing stare. "Also, don't you dare forget pumpkin pie. No soul alive can resist it."

"True."

"Do you think you can make one?"

I scoff. "I can buy the fuck out of one."

"That works too." Then she grins mischievously. "But there's one more thing most herbivores love above everything else."

This is going to be good. "Tell me. I need to know all your secrets."

"Are you ready for it?" she asks, lowering her voice.

"I sure am."

She leads me toward the beauty aisle.

I stare at her, baffled, as she picks out several face masks, cruelty-free shampoo, and some ethically sourced face serum. I glance down at my cart, then back at her. "For them?"

She bursts out laughing. "Oh, no. These are for me.

Service fee for today." She winks, then tosses a few extra face masks into the cart. "But I bet they'd like them too."

I laugh. She was always the sneaky one.

As we wander down some more aisles, I let out a sigh of relief. Charlie hasn't cross-examined me and I've gotten what I came for.

But I've definitely spoken too soon. When I'm grabbing some edamame, she says, "So I'm guessing if you're making food for her, that crush might not be so unrequited?"

It's like an icy dose of cold water. My grip tightens on the handle of the cart, and I focus way too hard on the bag of edamame in my hand. "What are you talking about?"

She laughs at me. "It's funny how you play clueless."

"No idea what you mean."

"Fair enough. You are often naturally clueless. But I think in this case, we both know exactly what I mean." She levels me with a shrewd stare. "You're shopping specifically for her. Is this because of your unrequited crush, or has it turned into something more?"

I couldn't be more transparent, but I've got to find a way around this. "It's for Luna. And Sabrina is a great nanny, so I really want to make her feel at home. She hasn't had a lot of that," I say, and that's the truth and the whole damn truth. "Her parents didn't even invite her for Thanksgiving. Her dad is a grade-A asshole. The least I can do is cook for her."

Charlie's teasing expression vanishes, and she sets a hand on her chest. "You kind of made me tear up a little bit with that. That's really sweet."

"She deserves some good in her life. You and I know what it's like to have a dad who's let us down, but at least we have a great mom and an amazing stepdad. We have Miles and we have Birdie. And we have each other too."

She rests her head on my shoulder, sighing in a contented, relaxed way. "We do. We really do," she says.

"One hundred percent," I say quietly as I pat her hair, grateful she knows she can count on me. That she's always known that, since it's the same for me with her. And with my brother. I'm lucky like that—so damn lucky.

She lifts her face and says, "On that note I need to grab some bread. I'll be right back."

"I assume that bread is on me too?"

"You know it," she says with a gotcha grin.

Once she's out of sight, I glance around the corner to make sure she's gone, then double back to the frozen section and grab some Popsicles.

Well, Sabrina did say she wanted them, and what she wants, she gets.

* * *

On the team jet the next night, after barely eking out a win at home, I sink down in my cushy seat in the dim light of the aircraft, figuring I'll get some quiet time to watch a few more of these cooking videos.

My brother's in the row in front of me, already absorbed in a book—knowing him, I'm guessing it's an allegory about the state of the world. Anything to make his big brain bigger.

It's fuck-all late, but I'm not tired yet. With the team settling into quiet nighttime vibes and most of the guys trying to catch some early shut-eye, this'll be a good chance for me to make sure I know what the hell I'm doing when we get back in a few days. I pop in my earbuds and toggle over to some videos I've downloaded on my tablet.

As I watch a YouTuber assemble mushroom risotto, Rowan drops down in the seat next to mine, and Ford hovers behind me in the next row.

Well, so much for my plans. I hit stop.

"You in a recipe club?" Rowan asks, checking out the video I just paused, his gaze flicking to the ingredients listed on the screen.

"Ooh, do you exchange faves? I've got a couple Crock-Pot meals that you'll flip for," Ford taunts from behind me.

"Dude. Stop holding out. Give them all to me," Rowan says, tossing his black suit jacket onto the empty seat between us.

I can never catch a break with these guys. "Can't a man plan a meal on a plane?"

"Oh, is it a private meal?" Ford teases, pushing his hair back from his eyes.

"Hey, if that's your thing, that's cool. I mean, we get that you're *really* into solo stuff. Just didn't know it included cooking too," Rowan adds dryly, with a wink and a jerk of his fist.

"Do you cook in the nude?" Ford bombards me with questions. "Wait, scratch that. I don't want to know."

Rowan snaps his gaze to the troublemaker behind me. "Thanks, asshole. Now I'll have to bleach my brain."

I snap the device closed and scrub a hand against the back of my neck. "Do you clowns have anything better to do than give me a hard time? How about watching some cooking videos yourselves?"

Rowan turns to Ford, his green eyes glinting mischievously. "Nope. I definitely don't have anything better to do. Devon, do you have anything better to do?"

"Fuck no," Ford says emphatically. Then he leans over the seat, clapping my shoulder. "Don't turn it off, buddy. Come on, we want to learn too."

Unknotting his tie, Rowan smirks and lowers his voice. "It's for the nanny, isn't it?"

I try to maintain a straight face, but they make it nearly impossible. "It's for Thanksgiving," I correct.

"We get it," Ford says with faux sympathy. "You've got it bad for her. You want to impress her with all your skills."

Miles pops up from his seat, turning around with a shit-eating grin. "You're gonna need my help for that then. I'm the cook of the family."

Guess he's been listening in after all. "We'll see about that," I say.

As much as they drive me bananas—Rowan and Ford mostly—there's a part of me that wishes I could say yes out loud. That I could say: *Yes, I do. I have it so bad for her. And I can't wait to do something nice for her.* That I could add: *I'm counting down the days—for so many reasons.*

Especially when a photo lands on my phone the next morning—Sabrina, Luna, and Parker heading to a Thanksgiving food drive with other students from their school.

There she is. Teaching my kids to give back. And looking like she belongs.

It's a real good look.

* * *

I've driven home after logging two wins on the road, and I'm pulling into the garage, eager to see the kids.

When I trudge up the stairs and kick off my shoes, I stop in my tracks as I'm rounding the corner.

The three of them—Sabrina, Luna, and Parker—are camped out on the couch under blankets, watching an animated movie, eating popcorn...with face masks slathered all over them.

They can't see me yet. At least, I don't think they can. My chest feels fizzy as I drink in the sight—Sabrina's mask is gold, shiny like her, making her a little glowy. Luna's is a soft lavender, her favorite color. Parker's is painted on like a raccoon's bandit mask. I bet that was Sabrina's creativity.

Parker pats his charcoal-black cheeks, a serious look in his eyes. "Is it ready to wash off, Sabrina?"

Luna leans over, inspecting his face. "I think you need about five more minutes, right, Sabrina?"

Sabrina studies Parker and nods. "Yep. Almost. And your skin is going to be so smooth, you're going to love it, you little bandit."

He shoots her a skeptical look. "I don't know..."

She pats his knee. "At least you're trying it. That's the thing—sometimes you just have to try things in life. You don't know until you try."

From around the corner, I listen like a little spy. They don't even realize I'm here.

But I'm okay with my secret mission. Because my heart is thudding powerfully against my chest at the sight of them on the couch.

Having a good time. Settled in. Comfy. Cozy. And as I take in the scene, all I can think is...*I could get used to this.*

But I don't just want to watch it. I want to be a part of it. *Now.*

I turn the corner and say, "Got an extra one for me?"

Luna pops up, grinning. "Yes! Put it on."

A few minutes later, I'm in a hoodie and basketball shorts, green goop smeared over my face, parked on the couch with the nanny and my two favorite people in the world.

And they've all left their face masks on too.

"We should take a picture of you," Luna says, nudging my arm.

I can only imagine the hell Rowan and Ford would give me if that shot went anywhere. "Maybe not," I say.

But Parker's waggling his phone, siding with his sister for once. "It'll be funny."

"It'll be ammunition for my teammates," I grumble.

Sabrina gives me an *I dare you* look. "Like Rowan wouldn't do it for Mia," she says.

Damn. She's right. He's the guy who braids his daughter's hair every day. Of course, he'd wear a face mask.

"Put it on your socials, Daddy," Luna says, wearing me down.

Sabrina's eyes twinkle. "Do it."

"Do it," Parker echoes.

"I hardly ever use socials," I point out, but I'm already remembering one of the last things I posted—a picture of me meeting Sabrina about a year ago.

And yep, here's my daughter cuing up my feed to show me. "Let me make the post for you," she says.

"You haven't even taken a picture yet," I say, but I'm losing this battle hard and fast.

Luna urges us all together, and before I know it, my daughter is snapping a selfie of the four of us on the couch in our face masks.

As she posts it on my feed, I glance at Sabrina, trying to ignore the way my heart catches being this close to her. And absolutely ignoring the thoughts of tomorrow night, when I'll have her all alone before Thanksgiving.

"Figured yours would be fancy," I say softly to her.

She sits up taller, all mock serious. "I really should have worn my tiara."

"Next time," I say, and I'm already picturing the next time.

Yeah, I could definitely get used to this.

But that's also the problem.

* * *

Sometime later, as the moonlight streams in through the window, and the hum of the refrigerator is my only companion, I wake to a cardboard sign on my chest that says "*Shrek* Daddy!"

I'm all alone in the living room, but I hardly feel that way as I wash off the face mask.

* * *

Not gonna lie, I'm raring to say goodbye to my kids. If that makes me a bad dad, slap the label on me.

I drop them off at Elle's place in Darling Springs on Tuesday night, where she's going to medical school, say my goodbyes, and then peel the fuck out of town. I'm already showered and ready to go.

As I pass the sign for Cozy Valley on the drive back to San Francisco, I swear my friend must feel the disturbance in the force because my phone rings. It's Corbin. I hit answer on the console.

"Dude, I just drove past your town," I say.

"Thanks for stopping by."

"I'm sure you love pop-ins."

"True. Thanks for not popping by," he says, then gives me a date and time for the next dads' group get-together.

"I'll be there."

"Good. I need someone who really sucks at bocce ball so my team can win."

I groan. "Go fuck off." But I can't strip the excitement out of my voice. Nothing can bring me down tonight.

"Love you too." Then he pauses, like something's on his mind. "What are you doing tonight?" His tone shifts, and he seems intrigued as I pass the sign telling me San Francisco is only thirty miles away. "You sound way more pumped than you usually do."

Well, that's one way to put it.

"Just having the place all to myself," I say, smirking. That's the secret I'm keeping. The one that's just between the nanny and me.

"Ah, a date with your hand. Good luck."

There's no point in arguing. So I shift gears, and we shoot the breeze about sports the rest of the drive back. Then I'm home. Ready to turn off the world.

Lesson two is about to begin.

27

———

A POPSICLE LESSON

Tyler

When I walk into the kitchen, Sabrina is standing in front of the fridge, music playing—Amelia Stone's newest album. There's an excited look in her eyes. I texted her that I'd be home soon.

"You're wearing my favorite color," I say, eyeing the sky-blue top she has on. She's also playing one of my favorite singers, but I keep that little detail to myself for some reason. Maybe to focus on her.

"Oh, is it?" she asks.

"It sure is. It's the color of your eyes," I say, advancing toward her.

"You like it on me?" she teases.

"So much," I murmur.

She waggles a little red book at me.

I furrow my brow. "What's that?"

"A sex diary," she says.

She just gets better and better.

"Does it say, 'Dear Diary, Tyler Falcon fucked my brains out tonight?'"

"Yes," she says. "And you got five stars."

My heart does a little jig. That's so her. And I fucking love it.

I love it so much, I close the distance between us, grab her face, and haul her in for a hot, scorching kiss that fries my brain. I kiss her deeply, savoring the sweet lip gloss taste of her mouth, the sexy sigh she makes, and the way she melts into me, her body pressed to mine.

I devour her, needing all of her as the kiss rockets through my cells. My head is a haze of orange blossoms and the woman I want.

When I let go, she steadies herself against the counter, blinking as a shudder wracks her body, like an aftershock.

"Wow," she breathes. "That was a five-star kiss."

"They all are with you." I shake my head, amazed I lasted over two weeks without having her in my bed. "I deserve a fucking medal for my restraint. I missed you."

Her smile is bright and beautiful. "But I've been right here the whole time."

I close the distance between us again, threading my fingers through her soft, shiny hair. "I know. And I still missed you."

Then I show her just how much. Kissing her again, grabbing her ass, hooking her legs around my waist.

I want to haul her up onto the counter, get down on my knees and eat her, then finger her, then fuck her.

But she said she wanted to surprise me, and she's calling the shots.

So I let go and ask, "What'll it be tonight?"

She spins around, yanks open the freezer, and takes out the Popsicles she asked me to buy last week. I'd be lying if I said the shape of the dessert hadn't crossed my mind, and what that might mean. But I didn't want to assume.

She takes one out, meets my gaze, and says, "I want you to coach me."

My brain pops. My cock thickens to steel in my jeans.

It didn't take a genius to figure blow jobs were on the list tonight when she grabbed the box. But I didn't expect those words. The earnestness in her voice. The hope in her tone. The want in her eyes.

"I will. Under one condition."

"Name it."

I slide my hand around her waist.

"I'll coach you. But you need to know this—I'm going to love every fucking second of it."

She rolls her lips together like she's holding in all her excitement. "Me too. Can I unwrap it now?"

"You'd better," I say, my voice rough.

She unwraps the Popsicle—a long, cherry one, then sets the box back in the freezer. "What do I do now?"

Her eyes are wide. Guileless. Innocent, but also filthy at the same time. Flickering with desire. With her wish to learn.

"Part your lips just slightly," I tell her.

She complies.

"Yeah. That's perfect. Do you know why?"

She shakes her head. "No idea."

I lift a hand, tucking a strand of hair behind her ear. "Because it looks like you really want it. That's the best part of a blow job. When she wants to give it to you."

She shudders slightly. "I want it. I want you."

Best words ever. "Same here, baby. Same fucking here," I say.

Her lips remain parted as she lifts the Popsicle, waiting for my instruction. And I am an inferno, burning everywhere.

Somehow, I manage to speak. "Just the tip. Just past those gorgeous lips."

She brings the icy treat to her mouth and I nearly lose my mind.

I grip the edge of the counter, holding tight so I don't ruin this lesson by ending it too soon. "Now, flick your tongue around the head."

And I watch as she swirls her tongue around it. It's the sexiest thing I've ever seen.

Then it's even sexier when she draws half an inch of red ice into her mouth. A jolt of pleasure slams into me, barreling down my spine.

I can barely stand how good she looks right now.

"Wrap your lips around it," I grit out, mesmerized, unable to look anywhere else.

She gasps as she sucks the tip of the Popsicle.

A sharp breath hisses out between my teeth. *Fuck.*

My face is on fire. My cock throbs in my jeans. I am turned on in every single cell of my body.

"Does it taste good?" I manage to ask.

She nods against the Popsicle, murmuring, "Delish."

"Now draw a little more between those sweet lips," I tell her.

She pulls it out of her mouth for a second. "Like this?"

Then she draws it back in.

Sucking it deeper. Moaning around it.

Holy fuck.

I don't know how I'm gonna last through this lesson.

The icy treat slides past those pretty pink lips. I'm mesmerized as I watch her suck, her cheeks hollowing out, her eyes fluttering closed. She moans around it, then stops. Taking a breath, she lets it fall from her mouth, holding it just in front of her chin. A drop of cherry juice slides down the length of the frozen treat. I watch it go. Even the Popsicle is so turned on, it's close.

I clench my fists. My chest is tight with anticipation.

"Does that work?" Sabrina asks.

"What?" I can barely think. I'm not sure I can speak in anything but grunts.

"Did I do it right?"

She's such a good student, and so eager to please. And if I'm only getting one night with her every couple of weeks, I want to make the most of it. With more restraint than I'd ever thought I had, I step closer, curl a hand around her throat, and say, "Do it one more time."

With my thumb pressing lightly against the sides of her neck—not too tight, just enough to make her breath hitch—she brings the Popsicle back to her mouth, gliding it in. She asks me with her eyes if this is okay.

"Farther," I instruct.

She takes it deeper, and I gently rub her throat. "Remember, baby. Just relax. Just like that."

Her muscles loosen under my palm, and I groan as the awareness hits me—she takes instructions so damn well. So well, she's now dragging the treat all the way past her lips, so only the wooden handle is exposed.

My nostrils flare.

My eyes widen.

And I snap.

"That's enough," I say, letting go of her delicate throat. "Practice on me now."

She pushes the Popsicle out of her mouth and sets it hastily on a plate on the counter. "It's a good thing I practiced beforehand on all these Popsicles. To drive you wild."

On that mic drop of all mic drops, she falls to her knees, yanking at my jeans in a flurry. She's all messy and aggressive, and that heats me up so I help her along, shoving my jeans down and freeing my cock. She's on me in a second, and my mind short-circuits with cracks and pops of pleasure. Lust floods my body. I stumble backward against the counter, gripping it for balance.

"Holy fuck," I say. Her mouth is icy, and sensations zing through me. I've never felt anything like this. "Your mouth is so cold."

"Want me to stop?" she teases, dropping me from her lips.

I grab the back of her head, gripping tight. "Don't you fucking dare."

With a wicked smile, she drops her mouth back onto me, sucking me past her lips again.

She's icy cold. And it's so fucking hot. She sucks with fervor and zero finesse, and I don't care. Because her enthusiasm is the sexiest thing ever.

She's not artful. I'm not even sure she's doing anything I just told her to do in that briefest of brief tutorials. And I'm entirely sure I don't care—because I'm gripping the counter, clenching my teeth, and holding on for dear life.

Sabrina Snow is on her knees, sucking the chrome off my cock, the loudest, filthiest slurping noises I've ever heard echoing in my kitchen. It's wet and messy, and I am being eaten alive by the flames inside my body.

Her hands are everywhere, like she can't stop touching me. Her fingernails scratch up my abs, then down my legs, then inside my thighs. She sucks my dick, plays with my balls, and slides that deliciously cold mouth up and down my shaft again and again.

I feel like a pinball machine. She's playing me, pulling levers, launching the silver ball inside me this way and that, where everything is lighting up, and I have no idea where anything is going—except it feels like she's about to hit the high score on this machine.

And then, she draws me in deep, lips stretched wide, hand gripping the base, the head of my cock hitting the back of her throat—until she coughs.

I pull out, stroking her cheek as I meet her eyes. "You okay, baby?"

She grabs my dick and yanks it right back between her lips. "I'm all good," she says and she takes me in, then resumes her enthusiastic, extraordinary pace, sucking with ferocity.

With the same rabid desire I feel for her.

Spit dribbles down the side of her mouth. And she doesn't stop. She keeps going.

That's all it takes.

I'm shaking, shuddering, gripping the back of her head, fucking her throat—until I'm spilling in her mouth. My world goes offline. Pleasure steals all my senses. This filthy bliss rattles my world as I groan and grunt for days.

When I ease out and blink open my eyes, there's a wicked look in her baby blues. I don't even know why—until she parts her lips.

She's been holding my come in her mouth.

She pokes out the corner of her tongue, coated in my release, and flicks it against her red-stained lips—slow, deliberate—a red-and-white finale, a work of dirty art before she presses her lips together and makes a show of swallowing it all.

I swear, I nearly come again. "I'm giving you an A for artistry and filth," I say, my voice as drained as I feel.

She gives a little shimmy of her shoulders as I reach down and tug her up. I loop my arms around her, my legs still shaking. When I rest my forehead against hers, my synapses fire in little bursts of pleasure, my brain a neon canvas.

But as I begin to reconnect to reality, my mind returns to a few minutes earlier. "Did you say you practiced?"

"I'm an athlete. That's what we do."

"You fucking practiced?" I ask again.

I shouldn't be astonished. This is super on-brand for her. And yet, something about it is kind of ridiculously touching. It's hitting my heart in ways I never would have expected.

"I wanted to get it right. I wanted to be good at it. You practice hockey," she says, like she's proving a point too. That practice makes perfect? Or maybe that athletes just love to play, whether practice or games. We crave movement. We crave competition. We chase excellence.

Is that what she wanted? I drag a hand down the side of my face, blown away by this woman who wanted to be so goddamn good *for me* that she practiced.

"Fair," I say, still gobsmacked, but damn curious too. "How did you practice? With...Popsicles?"

Her smile is full of pride—pride in a job well done. "Check the box. It's more than halfway empty. So maybe I've had a bit of a sugar rush the last few days. I read some online articles on technique. And I wanted to...surprise you."

She asked me to show her what good sex is, but this woman is showing me what great attention is. And I'm learning, too, that this kind of attention doesn't just make my dick happy—it makes my heart happy as well. "You came to class prepared," I say, but I'm not sure that covers the half of what I feel. I hope my tone of voice does some of the work for what I'm not sure how to say though.

"I did," she says, but her smile softens as she asks, "was it good for you?"

Like it's all she wants to know.

I stroke her cheek softly, looping my other arm around her to tug her closer. "Out of this world, Sabrina. You blew my dick and my mind. I still can't believe you practiced."

Her smile widens. "I used to get up every morning at four-thirty to practice ice skating. Sucking on a cherry Popsicle so that I could give you an excellent blow job was no hardship."

I wrap my arms around her and pull her into a deeper hug. Is this a normal reaction post-blow job of my dreams? To just hold her? I don't even know. But I don't want to let go. "I didn't need to teach you," I say softly.

"But I wanted you to," she says, her hand gripping my shirt as she looks up at me. "I wanted it to be so good for you, Tyler."

I hear the vulnerability in her voice. And the desire too.

I pull back, tucking a finger under her chin. "You nailed it, sweetheart. And that means it's my turn now."

I zip up my jeans, adjust myself, and grab a tumbler from the cupboard. Taking my time, I reach for a bottle of scotch my brother gave me when I joined the team, pour two fingers, then grab an ice cube from the freezer and drop it into the liquor. Sabrina watches me with avid eyes as I pluck the ice cube from the glass and pop it in my mouth. I suck off the whisky and swirl it around on my tongue, making sure I get my mouth nice and cold. Her eyes widen, and I let the ice cube fall from my mouth back into the tumbler with a plink.

"And now, here's the next lesson…"

I peel down her leggings, grab her hips, then set her on the counter. I slip off her panties, press my palms on either side of her strong legs and bend so I can lick a slow, cold line along her sweet, wet pussy.

She shudders, then shivers. "Oh my god," she breathes as she wiggles.

I stand, meeting her eyes. "I'm going to eat your pussy. And you're gonna tell me exactly how you like it. Or I'll have to stop."

Her eyes sparkle, lighting up like she's just won the lottery. "Really?"

"Yes."

"Do it. Please," she says, and the excitement is impossible to miss. My god, I'm so damn glad I was the guy at the bar in Cozy Valley the night she almost got married. I'm so glad I was the one she shared her 1001 confessions with.

And I don't want anyone else to have her. But those thoughts are too much for right now, so I jostle them out of the way to focus on the here and now.

I lick her again, savoring her, her taste mingling with the memory of the scotch on my tongue.

"Your mouth is so cold," she says, but it comes out trembly, breathless. She doesn't pull away.

I reach for the Popsicle on the plate and take a slow lick, making sure I coat the tip of my tongue with its coldness. Then I return to the wet paradise between her thighs. I press my tongue right up against her swollen clit. She practically jumps on the counter, moaning at the same time.

"Oh my god, it's so cold and so good at the same time," she gasps, her fingers curling in my hair, keeping me in place.

Yesssss.

That.

Right there. I want more of that. "Tell me what you want me to do," I whisper against her pussy, holding back, making her work for it.

"Do it again," she pleads, her voice barely above a breath.

I take the Popsicle back into my mouth, suck on it, let it melt over my tongue, then press a hot, open-mouthed kiss to her clit.

She wiggles against me, but she doesn't push me away. She pulls me closer, her thighs squeezing around my head, her breath catching.

"More," she demands.

And I give it to her.

I bury my face between her thighs, licking, lapping, letting her ride my tongue as she trembles beneath me.

"Yeah, just like that. More of your tongue," she urges, gripping my hair.

When her moans turn into long, helpless cries, I stop, wrenching away. "Say it," I tell her—a firm demand.

She groans, twisting against the counter. "Lick me."

"Good girl," I say, then I give her a teasing flick of my tongue.

"Kiss me."

I press my mouth to her pussy, soft and slow.

"Fuck me with your tongue."

It's my turn to groan salaciously, then I comply. But I do it with a pause here, a stop there—I make her say every filthy word describing what she wants me to do before I give her exactly what she's begging for. Until she's gripping my hair, writhing, gasping, throwing her head back and coming on my tongue.

By the time she's done, I'm rock hard again.

I push to my feet, my chest heaving, my gaze locked on her. She looks wrecked and beautiful, her skin flushed, her lips swollen.

"What else is in that sex diary of yours?" I ask, reaching for the little red book on the counter but not opening it. I wait. "Can I look?"

She hesitates for half a second, then meets my gaze, her eyes dark and trusting. "Page fourteen."

Pleasure ignites in me all over again, chased by something warmer, something steadier, something I don't quite know what to do with. Why do I love that she practiced on Popsicles for days? Why am I caught up in her knowing the page number? Is it just because all this tonight turns me on?

No. There's more to it. My chest feels fizzy, and something's stirring deep inside me that has nothing to do with sex. Something that feels a lot like more. But when I flip to page fourteen and read her words, everything else drains away. There's no room left inside me for anything but lust.

"Ask him to bend me over the counter," I read aloud. I haul in a breath, letting it fuel me, then meet her gaze. "Ask for it, baby."

She bites the corner of her lip, teasing, tempting—then whispers, "Bend me over the counter, Tyler. Now."

"There's nothing as good as a fast and furious fuck," I tell her.

She blinks up at me, all innocence and wicked delight. "I wouldn't know," she says, coquettish as hell. "But maybe you could show me."

"With so much pleasure," I promise.

Then I grab her off the counter, spin her around, and press a hand to the small of her back. I push her down, lining up her body into a seductive L shape for me. She's wearing only her top and this half-naked look is hot as fuck.

I reach into my pocket, rip open a condom, shove my jeans down my thighs, and slide inside her in one smooth stroke.

And fuuuck.

She's tight. I'm steel hard. And I don't want this to end. I stop for a beat, just savoring the way we fit. "When everyone's here for Thanksgiving…" I begin on a harsh pant.

"Yes?" she prompts as I start to move, slow and deep.

"I want you to think about the way I fucked you in the kitchen."

"I will," she breathes.

"Want you to look over here, and think about me fucking you so hard on this counter," I growl, slamming into her, reaching a hand around to stroke her clit.

"It'll be our dirty secret," she says.

"I'm going to be thinking of you the whole goddamn time," I say, and that's the truth, the whole truth, and nothing but.

I swivel my hips and drive back into her, playing with her, making her feel everything as I tell her exactly what I want her to be imagining when everyone is in this house in a couple days. How I've fucked her. How good it felt when we fit together, my cock plowing into her over and over again. How I've tugged on her hair, how she's groaned my name, and how I'll be thinking about this too every time our eyes meet.

And soon, she's gripping the counter, screaming my name.

And I'm following her there.

I was right. There's nothing like a fast and furious kitchen fuck with the woman I can't stop thinking about.

The woman who practices to make me happy.

Who knows what she wants.

Who plays the music I like. "I like these songs," I say, and it's just about music. But it feels like a bare admission.

"I had a feeling," she says.

"That I like female pop singers?" I hold her tighter.

"I noticed what you play in your car. What you listen to in the house. What you sing along to with your kids," she says.

And suddenly, I don't just want to make her happy in the bedroom tonight.

I want to do something special for her.

And I don't stop thinking about it as I carry her upstairs to my room.

* * *

The water pounds down, hot and fast, but I take my time washing her in the dim light of my rainfall shower, wiping away the last traces of the Popsicle from our hands, our bodies.

She murmurs under the hot stream, eyes half-closed, and I'm thinking. Hard. Wracking my brain.

I want to do something for her beyond tickets to a game or yoga supplies or even soft sheets.

I want to tell her she can use my shower anytime. I want to tell her she can sleep in my *emperor-size* bed whenever she wants. I want to tell her I want her here tomorrow night too.

I know all of those things are too dangerous. We're trying to stick to a game plan.

But there's one thing I keep returning to.

One thing I know she wants.

Something she hasn't had in a while.

When we're standing under the spray and I'm rubbing my hands over her skin, I stop and say, "Let's get you a foster kitten."

She freezes. Then blinks up at me. "What did you just say?"

"You want to foster kittens again. We talked about it briefly the day you moved in. And I always felt like you missed it. Like you wanted to. Let's do it," I blurt out.

Her mouth parts, surprise flickering across her face as she turns around, studying me. "Why are you saying this now?"

"Because you loved it. I know you miss it. It was really important to you," I say, my voice quiet but certain.

"It was. It is."

I cup her face, my thumb brushing across her cheek. "I'd like you to have the things you want."

Her smile lights up my soul. "Okay then."

It's said simply and softly, but full of a gratitude that melts my heart. And I can't wait to bring this kitten home either.

28

THEN AND NOW

Sabrina

A year ago on Thanksgiving, I walked up the steps to my parents' home next to Chad, a huge knot in my chest. I looked up at the brass knocker on the familiar doorway of my parents' stately white mansion, but it hardly felt like I belonged there.

I turned to Chad, nerves twisting inside me, and smoothed a hand over my silk blouse as I asked, "Do I look okay?"

If I didn't look the part, the criticism would come. I'd worn a long, flowy skirt, a demure navy shirt, and pearls.

Pearls.

"You look fantastic," he said, then gripped my hand, squeezing my monster-sized ring.

But the knot in my chest tightened even more uncomfortably then. I held a tray of oven roasted turkey in my hands. My mother had asked me to swing by the caterers to pick it up because, as it turned out, she didn't have enough for her special guests from the club.

She'd even asked me to taste it, to make sure it was good. I had asked Chad to try it instead. The whole time I spent there that day, I was sure I would be critiqued—for the turkey, for the clothes, for my life.

But I was with Chad, the son of my father's business partner, so everything was fine for a while. A respite, when I was free from the critiques, thanks to a choice they approved of.

Now, I'm walking up the steps to Tyler's home, bouncing along in my sneakers and jeans, with Luna and Parker by my side. I took them to the park with Trevyn and Barbara-dor to burn off some holiday morning energy. And because Tyler said he had a surprise for us.

When I walk into the foyer with the crew, the voices carry all the way from the kitchen. But they're different than the voices at my parents' home, where everyone was tense, clipped. Now, the voices are teasing, playful.

"Dude. You do not make risotto until the end, okay?" That's Miles.

"That makes no sense," Tyler replies.

"It makes all the sense," Miles says. "You can't reheat it. It tastes bad reheated. You need to serve it fresh."

"Seriously?" Tyler sounds doubtful, but worried too— like he wants this risotto dish to be just right.

"Just trust me on this," Miles says, warm and reassuring. "We'll tackle something else instead."

There's rustling in the kitchen as we kick off our shoes. Trevyn raises his eyebrows, curious. "What's the surprise?"

I turn to Luna. "Do you have any idea?"

"Nope," she says, unbothered, but that's life for a ten-year-old.

"Don't ask me," Parker says with a shrug. "Cooking is hard. Science is easy."

"Little man, cooking *is* science," Trevyn says to Parker, ruffling his hair.

We all head into the kitchen, where Tyler and Miles are wearing aprons.

Miles's apron is covered in illustrations of dogs and the words *Dogs—For Whom Everything Is Exciting*. And Tyler's black and red apron says, *Don't Ask Me. I'm Just Here for the Food.*

Miles swats Tyler's hand as he tries to sneak a taste of mashed potatoes. "Watch it, Little Falcon."

"I made them," Tyler says, indignant.

"And I know your style. You'll eat them all before we sit down. Let's focus on the cranberries," Miles instructs, and both the brotherly diss and the brotherly love make me smile.

They must realize we're here since they look up at the same time. Tyler turns his gaze to the clock. "I didn't realize you were back yet from the park," he says, sounding a little concerned.

"I hope we didn't ruin your surprise," I say, feeling bad that maybe we walked in too soon. On the risotto perhaps?

Miles punches Tyler's arm. "Nope. Because Little Falcon got it wrong, but I'm here to save the day. Like I told you I would on the plane."

Tyler scoffs. "Pretty sure I did that already with my epic mashed potatoes."

"I love mashed potatoes," I say. "And really, all sides."

I scan the evidence of Thanksgiving prep across the

counter: the sliced-up Brussels sprouts, the mashed potatoes, the fresh cranberries. The smells of the holiday mingle—rosemary and butter, tart cranberries, and fresh rolls.

And then I catch a hint of Tyler. That woodsmoke scent that catches me off guard in the best of ways.

He looks caught off guard too, though almost bashful as he glances from Luna to me. "Anyway, the surprise is still happening. But it's not a surprise anymore. I thought I'd make you a mushroom risotto for a main dish. One we serve with the turkey. For the vegetarians in my life. But I have to do it last, it turns out."

Luna gasps, then runs over to him and gives him a side hug. "You're the best, Dad."

Tyler hugs her back, and joy warms his hazel eyes. But relief does too. Like he's glad he did right by her. I want to do the same as Luna—rush over and hug him in thanks. But I can't, and a twinge of sadness digs into me for a few seconds. I clasp my hands behind my back, twisting my fingers together like I need to hold myself back.

Trevyn tosses me a look that says, *Girl, you've got it bad.*

My heart squeezes even more as Tyler gives Luna a kiss on the forehead.

"I wanted you two to have something special," he says, then looks to Parker. "And I have plenty of turkey for you."

"Thanks, Dad. You're a turkey."

"You're a turkey," he retorts, then gobbles, and Parker cracks up.

As he laughs, Tyler swings his gaze my way, his eyes hopeful. And the twinge in me vanishes. "Thank you," I say.

It's the nicest surprise, his risotto plans. What's nicer is that those twisting, corkscrew feelings from last year never surface.

* * *

Later in the day, as Trevyn and I build a Lego tuxedo cat with Parker, a warm nutmeg scent drifts through the living room. Trevyn nudges me and says, "Is *someone* baking a pumpkin pie?"

Parker's eyes light up. "Does it have gummy bears in it?"

Trevyn shudders Parker's way. "That sounds nasty."

"Have you ever tried pumpkin pie with gummy bears in it?" Parker counters, never one to back down from the scientific method.

Trevyn pauses, as if he's giving that some thought. "Actually, no. Have you?"

"Nope. But I'm willing to take my chances."

Trevyn shakes his head but laughs. "Then I will too."

Soon, other family members arrive. Tyler's mom and Harvey, then Leighton with her camera, then Tyler and Miles's grandmother Birdie, with a tray of toffee caramel bars.

Charlie's here too, checking on everything in the kitchen and I instantly develop a friend crush on their little sister. Tyler's moving around in a focused flurry, getting advice from Miles every step of the way. The man of the house looks both overwhelmed and focused, like he's got this even as information comes at him from all angles and he opens ovens, stirs pots, and chops vegetables.

The kitchen is buzzing, but I can't simply sit on the couch. My job is to be a helper. To help with kids and the house, and the kids are occupied with Lauren right now, working on a puzzle of the solar system since the Lego cat is done. So I slip into the kitchen. It's more natural for me to offer a hand anyway, so I tell Tyler to let me work on the Brussels sprouts.

"Thanks," he says with a big sigh. "I'd appreciate it."

I had a feeling he needed that. And I like being there for him. Especially when he sets a hand on my back as he moves past me, sliding his fingers across the fabric of my shirt.

It's out of sight from anyone else. But still, I keep thinking of our rule: *No little sneaky displays of affection.*

It feels like he broke it.

And I like it.

But Tyler refuses to let me touch the pumpkin pie. As it's baking (without gummy bears), I peer across the open kitchen to the dining room. "I'll finish setting the table," I say.

He grabs my arm. It's not overly romantic, but I do scan around to see if anyone's looking. No one is. "You don't have to do...that stuff," he says, with a hint of...worry perhaps in his voice?

"I don't mind," I say, and really, this is so much more fun than last year when hired help scurried around my parents' home, setting everything up. I sat awkwardly in the pristinely appointed living room, entertaining my mother's rich friends from the country club, asking about their grandchildren and bridge clubs and book clubs where no one read anything by an author who didn't look like them.

Tyler pulls me deeper into the kitchen, closer to the hallway, out of earshot of everyone. "I don't want you to feel like you have to do this. To set the table. And stuff."

I think I know what he means by *and stuff*. He doesn't want me to feel any expectations—that sex means we're a couple.

But my desire to help isn't coming from there. It's coming from me wanting to do a great job. "I'm the nanny. It's okay. My job is to make everything easier for you."

"Sabrina." He whispers my name with a plea. "You've made my life easier. It's okay. I want you to sit down and enjoy yourself."

"I will. I promise. I want to help." Maybe there's a bit of a plea in my voice. But it's hard for me to abandon this intense desire to do a good job.

"You can hang with Trevyn. You are doing a great job. You don't have to be...perfect," he whispers, seeing straight through me and serving up a shot of truth right to my heart. A truth I didn't expect, but maybe one I need.

I think of Elena. The things we've worked on over the years. The letting go of my perfectionist tendencies. True, I haven't told her about Tyler, but at least I can honor *this* —the things she's helped me with.

"Thank you," I say.

But before I go, he asks with anticipation and nerves, "Have you heard anything?"

It's adorable. The way he's as eager to hear from Little Friends as I am. I re-signed up for the foster kitten list and have been waiting. It's been two days—slightly less than forty-eight hours—and nothing.

"Not yet. I keep checking," I say.

"Let me know the second you hear."

"I will," I say, promising once again.

And I'm about to head into the living room, but he doesn't let go of my arm. Instead, he rubs his thumb against my wrist in a subtle pattern that melts me and turns me on at the same time. My heart speeds up, and I wish fervently he'd yank me against him and kiss me—a quick, chaste kiss that would be a promise of more.

But he doesn't of course. We have rules that we're mostly not breaking. "Remember what I said the other night? When we sit down at the table?" he says, his voice low and raspy, his eyes fiery with the reminders of the way we fucked the other night.

A rush of pleasure zings through me. "Oh, I remember."

"Me too. It's all I can think about—how you looked when I bent you over the counter. I'm going to be thinking about the way you sound when you come as you're eating my risotto. Well, when I'm not thinking about that kitten."

I laugh. "Do you even like kittens?"

"What do you think I am? A monster?"

"I don't know. You've never talked about kittens before."

"Well, watch out. I'm gonna be talking about them now. Why don't you check your email? Maybe you got something in the last few minutes."

I roll my eyes, but I'm totally loving his pre-smittenness. I take out my phone and check. It's empty.

His shoulders sag. "Soon," he says, and I'm hopeful too.

Before I can retreat to the living room to join my friend, Tyler's mother wanders into the kitchen. "So, how's all that dating going, Sabrina?"

The question makes me go rigid. What the hell do I say to her? Tyler gives me a look that could wither mountains, but I don't know what it means. We've never talked about what we're saying to his mother. And I wait for him to say something.

But he doesn't. The green-eyed jealousy I saw before in him flares again. So I step in and improvise. "I haven't really met anyone I've wanted to go out with."

Lauren sighs, like she's bummed for me. "Really? No one?"

And impulsively, since that's my middle name, I go for it. "Well...there's one guy. But it's complicated."

"Why is it complicated?"

How do I even begin? I start to answer, but she cuts in with, "Is Tyler being difficult about you dating?"

That gets Tyler's attention immediately. He nods to her, gesturing toward the hallway, then pulls her aside.

I'm dying to know what he's saying.

Dying.

I take my time heading to the living room, furtively stealing glances at the two of them. I can't make out their words—they're talking too quietly. But there's real emotion in his warm eyes—a plea maybe for his mother to understand his situation? His mother exhales, like she's making peace with something, then opens her arms and gives him a hug.

My throat catches as I watch them embrace. His love for his children is all his, of course. But he learned it too. From her, from his brother, from his sister. From all this love around him. And I love that about him.

* * *

Later, when we're all at the table, passing ceramic dishes of mashed potatoes and scooping seconds of a fantastic mushroom risotto, and food moaning over these delicious Brussels sprouts, Birdie clears her throat and says to me, "Did you know Tyler used to have a thing for *Allison Marchand*?"

I blink, then turn my gaze toward the man who pays my checks. "The figure skater? Who won a silver medal in the Olympics?"

"The one and only," Birdie answers.

Tyler lowers his face, groaning as his family cackles.

"He was so enamored with her," Charlie pipes in. "He had a poster on his wall and everything. He couldn't stop watching her compete, Sabrina."

"Weird," Parker says. Because he's not one to say *ew*, though it's clear that's what he means.

But to me this news is delightful. "Tell me more."

Trevyn raises a finger. "And leave out no detail," he adds.

"My dad and I watch figure skating together all the time," Luna puts in as she grabs a buttery roll.

I sort of knew this—his figure skating interest—but I also didn't really know how far back it went, or how deep. "And you've always been into this?" I ask Tyler, but inside I'm thinking—*his nighttime habits with my video make even more sense now*.

Tyler doesn't need to answer since his mom is here to handle it. "He watched every televised competition she was in when he was younger," his mother supplies, far too pleased to share this.

Lauren Falcon is such a troublemaker, and I adore her for it.

I have a million more questions for him.

But then my phone buzzes in my back pocket, loud and obnoxious. Shoot. I forgot to silence it.

From across the table, Tyler points at me. "You'd better check, in case that's it."

"I don't want to open it in the middle of dinner," I whisper back, but there's no point. Everyone can hear us.

"What if it's the kitten?" he says, in a tone that brooks no argument.

"Is a kitten texting you now?" Leighton asks.

"Sabrina, check it," Parker puts in with more urgency than I'd expected.

"Is it them? Is it them? Is it them?" Luna begs.

Clearly, there's no way to ignore this. I take out my phone and beam when I spot a message from Nia, the foster coordinator at the animal rescue.

I read it out loud, trying to rein in my excitement. "We know it's Thanksgiving, but we got these new little cuties on our steps. Can you foster one of them? We need a foster for the next couple weeks."

Tyler looks at me with so much intensity I'd swear he just scored a goal. "Say yes. Say it now."

And Luna and Parker just about lose their minds as I do.

* * *

Later, as everyone zones out to a Christmas movie on TV, I help Tyler in the kitchen with the last of the cleanup, then turn to him, something still nagging at me, but not in a bad way. More like I can't stop thinking about it. "What was that all about with your mother? When you pulled her aside?"

He sighs, peers around, then says quietly, "I told her she has to stop asking you about your dating."

"Why?" I press since I can't resist.

His eyes are fiery. His tone, firm. "Because I can't stand hearing it."

My heart stutters. "Did you tell her...about us?"

"Some of the truth," he admits. "Not the private details. But that I've had it bad for you for a very long time," he admits.

A flutter moves through me, even though I already knew how he felt. He'd told me our first night together he'd wanted to ask me out. To take me to mini golf or a baseball game. But hearing him say it again? It's a lovely reminder.

Trouble is, the more he says sweet, swoony things, the more I start to want them—those dates, those nights, those times with him.

What if I let myself want them? Just for a second?

But I have to ignore that want. There are too many other things at stake. The job. His kids. His life is one thing; mine is another.

"What did she say?" I ask, trying to focus on the conversation.

"She said she's not surprised." He exhales, a wry twist to his lips. "My brother and sister teased me about my crush before you even started. But my mom also said I shouldn't stand in the way of you being happy."

My heart sinks a little.

I get it. Truly, I do.

And he's not standing in the way of my happiness. He's making me happy. But he's also making it clear—that this thing between us is just *this*. And it's not ever going to be something else.

And that's fine by me.

Isn't it?

I have plans for myself. A life I'm rebuilding. A business I'm growing. And I'm doing it all alone—with no family to support me. Just friends, like Trevyn and Leighton, Isla and Skylar. Friends who are like family.

But I can't mistake Tyler's family for my own.

They belong to him.

I don't belong to anyone.

* * *

The next morning, he goes with me and the kids to pick up a kitten at Little Friends. All at once, four people fall in love at the same time with a two-pound black-and-white creature with a pink nose, white paws, and the loudest meow in the world.

Inside the shelter, Tyler reaches into the kennel through the grates and scratches the little critter's ears. "Hey, Drama," he says to the tiny thing. "We're going to take care of you till you find a family."

We're.

This kitten was never just mine, and that's more than okay with me.

Even though as we drive home, a dark thought flits through my mind—am I getting too comfortable with my life here with them?

29

———

WHISKERS AND KISSES

Tyler

Show me a hockey player who doesn't know his rating, and I'll show you a liar. We know that shit cold.

I know this season is much better than my last one. Two months in, my ice time is higher, my shot blocks have improved, and my penalty minutes have gone down.

This is what I wanted. To have a great season in my eleventh year in the pros. To line up a solid final contract. To be able to provide for my kids for the rest of their lives, no matter what hockey throws my way.

And I'm managing it. While also managing a—how shall we say—*unconventional* relationship with a woman who lives with me.

A woman who, somehow, has got me hooked on a tiny little two-pound creature a little more than a week into fostering.

Before I left the house for an afternoon game, I said goodbye to Drama, like I do every time I leave these days.

But now, as I hop off the exercise bike at the arena and make my way to the locker room, I fire off a text to Sabrina to check in on the kitten.

> Tyler: How is the cutie?

> Sabrina: Well, I'm at the rink so I wouldn't know.

> Tyler: Should I have the neighbor check on her? My mom? Harvey?

> Sabrina: She's a cat. She's fine.

> Tyler: She's a kitten.

> Sabrina: Tyler, she's fine. I promise. She's probably sleeping on the couch in my apartment.

I round the corner toward the locker room, tapping out a reply.

> Tyler: Are you sure though? We can set up a cam. Miles has one for when he dog-sits our mom's dogs.

> Sabrina: That's where she was when I left for my lessons.

> Tyler: But you're going to be there for a while. You have so many lessons—which is awesome—but the kids are with Elle tonight, so they won't be able to check on her either. Maybe I shouldn't go to Cozy Valley after the game.

Sabrina: I'll be home around eight. She'll be fine.

Tyler: But I'll be done by seven. I should just swing by and check on things. And get a camera.

Sabrina: Cat Daddy, stop. Go see your friends tonight. Friendship time is important.

Tyler: So is pussy…cat time. :)

Sabrina: You're so thoughtful.

Tyler: But seriously, you think she's fine?

Sabrina: Seriously—she's fine. Go! Socialization is key to happiness. Studies prove it.

I scoff and type out a reply.

Tyler: I bet orgasms are on that list.

Sabrina: Fine. Orgasms and friendship.

Tyler: Like I said, I'm always thinking of … cats.

Sabrina: That's clear.

Tyler: And I might still get a cat-cam.

I step into the locker room, the clang of gear and the chatter of teammates thick in the air. But I'm still weighing whether we need a cat-cam or not. Rowan tugs on his uniform shorts in his stall, then tips his chin toward me.

"You good, man?" he asks, then smirks. "Or are you just stressing because you know I'm gonna destroy you in cornhole tonight?"

I snort. "You figured me out. But it's lucky I've got my cheat codes for cornhole, buddy."

He nods toward me, a serious look in his eyes. "Actually, you really are wound up. What's going on? I don't need you getting on the ice all stressed."

Despite our penchant for trash talk, I appreciate that Rowan's reading me right. I drag a hand through my hair, sighing heavily. "It's okay if the kitten is in the house alone for six hours, right? She's three months old."

Across the room, Max is strapping on his goalie leg pads, his chest protector already in place. He glances up, eyes narrowing. "You got a kitten? Is she getting enough stimulation? Does she have enough toys? Did you make her little tinfoil balls? Cats love those more than anything in the world."

I tense. I haven't done any of that. "I think we have tinfoil at home. But I can check," I mumble.

Max nods like this is life-or-death. "Yeah, you'd better. Kittens need all sorts of things. Ball up some tinfoil and she'll go wild for it. Also, you know what their favorite toy in the world is? The little cardboard roll inside the toilet paper. Oh, and boxes of tissues. That shit is so fun for kittens. But you also need a ground scratching post. Do you have one?"

"What is that? We have a regular scratching post."

"Oh, you have to get a ground scratching post. And some of those toys with a ball inside it that they bat around. They go nuts for that stuff."

I blink, overwhelmed by all this feline information. I had no idea there were so many toys for cats.

"The OG cat daddy has spoken," Asher chimes in from his locker, pointing to Max.

Max plunks down on the bench and tugs on his skates. "Dude, the cat economy is crazy. There's so much stuff for them. They need laser pointers, toys, feathers, little plastic balls..."

My brother strides across the room to my locker and grabs my phone from my stall. "Better get all this down. OG Cat Daddy doesn't dole out advice very often."

I open the Notes app. I'm going to need all of these things. "What else, guys?"

Wesley chimes in from his locker. "What about a cat tower?"

Rowan points at him approvingly, then back at me. "Dude, Bryant's right. You definitely need a cat tower."

I scrub a hand over my tight jaw. "Shit. We don't have one."

Rowan claps me on the shoulder. "There's a cute pet store in Cozy Valley—Whiskers and Kisses."

"Whiskers and Kisses?" Ford chimes in with a chuckle as he tosses his tie into his stall. "That's fucking cute."

"No kidding," Rowan says, turning his focus back to me. "We're going there tonight and stocking up on all the cat things you need. I got your back, Falcon."

I breathe a sigh of relief. "Thanks, man. We're going to have to do that for sure."

Max tugs on his jersey, adding, "I'll send you a list. Better yet, I'm going to write it on the DickNose board."

With full gear on, he heads over to the board, where my brother has already started writing Cat Shit. Max joins in, jotting down the list of all the things I need. I snap a photo, then get ready for the game.

And I try not to worry about the two-pound tuxie while battling for the puck in the corners during the second period.

I put her out of my mind as I shove an opponent out of the way, snagging the puck and whipping it across the neutral zone to Bryant, who takes it right into the net.

Yes!

He sends it screaming past the goalie's leg pads. A goal for him, an assist for me. And my stats keep getting better.

We smack gloves, and when I hop over the boards for the line change, I feel like I can balance it all—the game, the kids, the woman, even all this cat shopping. And a night out in Cozy Valley with the guys. Well, Sabrina said it's a good idea for my happiness.

When the game ends, I hustle the hell out of the arena with Rowan. We hop into his car, then head out of the city to the small town not too far from here. Along the way, I toss my suit jacket and tug on a hoodie instead.

Before we head to the bar to meet up with Holden and Corbin, we swing past Whiskers and Kisses off Main Street—a shop that has literally everything.

I don't know why I didn't do this sooner. But a short while later, I'm loading up Rowan's car with a cat tower, all sorts of scratching posts, a red laser pointer, and even a rotating toy with feathers—like a baby mobile but for cats.

As I survey the gear, I breathe out a sigh of relief. "This is good. This is exactly what a foster kitten needs."

Rowan smirks. "And exactly what a man who's completely smitten with his foster kitten needs."

I don't argue. Because he's right. He shuts the door to the trunk, then we walk down Main Street, which is decked out for Christmas already with garlands strung around the lampposts. Rowan side-eyes them, grumbling about too many decorations.

"Do you hate Christmas?" I ask.

"And Christmas hates me," he says as we pass a bookstore where a big, orange cat sleeps soundly on top of a stack of Christmas books in the window display.

"Then I won't invite you over when we decorate our tree," I say.

"Oh, you can invite Mia. She's great with decorations since she's got a good eye. I'll keep myself busy walking the dog."

"That's the spirit," I say as we turn the corner to The Gameyard to meet our friends. Holiday music plays overhead and Rowan grouses about that too for a bit. After we order some beer—with a club soda for the Grinch—and start a round of cornhole, my mind swings back to San Francisco. Not just to the cat.

I'm picturing Sabrina.

Is she home now? Coming in from her lessons? Unlocking the door to her apartment? Saying hello to a cute little critter who stretches up from the couch and greets her? Is she picking up Drama and holding her? Giving her a kiss? A pang of missing lodges in my heart.

"Earth to Falcon."

I spin around. Holden is staring at me as I toss a beanbag absently in my free hand.

"We'll have to kick you out of the club if you keep drifting off like that," the football star says, admonishing me.

Corbin grins as he lifts his beer glass. "Maybe it's time

for another bet. When you *finally* break, since you're still clearly all tangled up in wanting the nanny."

"She has a name," I say sharply. "It's Sabrina."

Corbin holds up a hand in surrender, even though he didn't really say anything wrong. "You're into Sabrina. Really into her."

Shit. I did overreact. "Sorry. My bad," I say, not answering him. Instead, I toss the beanbag toward the top of the board, but I miss the hole.

"What are you going to do about it?" Holden asks, and the fact that he's not harassing me about missing speaks volumes.

Plus, it's a reasonable question. "Honestly? I don't know. I really don't know."

There's quiet for several seconds, just the chorus of a rock song coming from inside the bar. A heaviness descends on me—the weight of decisions, of conflict.

"What do you *want* to do about it?" Corbin asks thoughtfully. It's a rare moment when these guys are serious, which means it's all the more important to pay attention.

I exhale, rubbing a hand over my jaw. "I mean, the whole situation is complicated. It's early days, and I really shouldn't be thinking about this. I've got the season to focus on. The kids. Everything."

Rowan nods thoughtfully. "Yeah. Stuff can get complicated real fast."

Holden shakes his head. "Relationships are nothing but a hot mess."

"That can bite you in the ass," Corbin adds.

We all lift our glasses and drink.

I put relationship thoughts out of my head and focus

on beating my friends in lawn games. Since that equals happiness.

And, evidently, so do a few more beers.

* * *

When the night is over and we're driving back home with Rowan at the wheel, I'm honestly, maybe a little buzzed. A little eager too.

To see Sabrina.

And Drama, of course. But mostly, I want to see her. "I wonder if I should text her and tell her what I picked up at the store or just surprise her," I muse as we cross the Golden Gate Bridge, my foot tapping on the floor of his car.

Rowan cracks up laughing. "Dude. You're a little obsessed."

No point denying it. "I'll surprise her," I say, nodding to myself as the city lights grow brighter, beckoning me home. "She'll like that."

Rowan smirks as he slows at a light. "Do you need help carrying it all in? Or are you afraid that when she sees I'm stronger than you, she'll think she picked the wrong guy?"

I flip him off. "I'll carry everything."

I'm already thinking about walking through that door, about the way Sabrina's face will light up when she sees what I brought home for Drama.

And maybe—just maybe—about the fact that no one else is in the house tonight.

30

HURTS SO GOOD

Sabrina

"Are you tipsy?" I ask the man who can't stop touching me.

"Are you saying I'm not usually affectionate?" Tyler counters, nuzzling my neck as we stretch out on the couch.

"You're just kind of...extra happy."

He brushes his lips along my shoulder now. "You said time with friends led to happiness," he says, tossing my words right back at me.

I shove him lightly. "And you said pussy...cats."

His gaze drifts to the little gymnast in the room, who's climbing the Everest of the cat tower now. "And I was right." He drops a kiss to the shell of my ear. "But do you want me to stop?"

I shiver. "Nope," I say. But I also didn't expect this from him tonight—all the cat gifts, all the playfulness, all the Tyler-ness.

"And to answer your question, I had a couple drinks in

Cozy Valley, but that was a few hours ago. So honestly, this is just me." His voice dips slightly, a little vulnerable with that admission.

My resolve melts even more. Still, I tease him with, "Just you, Falcon?"

"I'm naturally affectionate. Accept it, Snow."

And I do. *Mostly*. Sure, he's affectionate on our sex dates. But tonight isn't even on the calendar. Which I suppose brings me to my real question. "Tyler," I whisper before he melts me with another kiss.

He looks up again, his gaze soft and earnest, like he knows what's on my mind. "Yes, baby?"

The way he says that, with such tenderness and fierceness, makes my bones feel like they're dissolving. It's been a little over a week and a half since the Popsicle lesson. Still, my mind is tracking dates with him, like I used to track workouts and competition prep. It's tracking spicy lessons and late-night plans. It's trying to make sense of this...unconventional arrangement with my boss. "We made a game plan," I say gently. "This isn't in the calendar. Tonight isn't on the schedule."

"I know," he says, his voice full of heat and desperation. "But I'm going out of town soon for a road trip. And I won't be able to see you again for a while."

"True," I say.

"And it's too hard to resist you," he adds, then lavishes my neck with open-mouthed caresses, tender brushes of his lips that heat me up from the inside.

Maybe this was inevitable. This shoehorning in of extra days. But it also worries me. I don't want to get too used to him. Or any of this. History tells me it'll all fall apart and probably at the worst possible time. I can't get accustomed to any of it, from the foster kitten practicing her climbing skills on the cat tower Tyler bought me to this man hanging out with me on a rare night when it's only us in the home.

"But what happens if we start bending the rules now?" The protest dies on my tongue when he slides a hand down the side of my body and cups my breast through my shirt.

"Is this on your list?" He squeezes my nipple piercing. Pleasure shoots through me, making my toes curl, and I've forgotten everything else but *this*.

"Yes," I gasp.

Nipple play is definitely on the list, but it's mixed with a little something else too. Something I kind of want to do. Something I've never really gotten the hang of.

There's only one issue. "It feels a little selfish though," I admit.

"If it's selfish, we're doing it," he says, his tone practically demanding we start right now.

I laugh. "Why?"

"Because if you think it's selfish, I want it. Because it means I get to focus on you the whole fucking time." Then he brings his face close to mine, drops a hot kiss to my lips before whispering, "Because I like you getting what you want."

In that case...

"Turn to page twenty," I tell him.

He rushes to my bedroom and returns seconds later with my tiny sex diary. His lips curve in a sexy grin, a little lopsided, a little hopeful. The look in his eyes is pure candy. This is his guilty pleasure—*my pleasures*.

Discovering them. Delivering them. And reading them out loud, which he does next.

His voice is a low rasp, his eyes flickering with heat,

the bulge in his slacks getting harder with every spoken word like he can't believe his luck.

* * *

Fifteen minutes later, I'm tied up in my bed, my arms stretched above me and tied to the slats on the headboard, my own silk scarves holding me in place.

My breath stutters in anticipation. I rub my thighs together, trying to ease the ache. But the ache is me now.

Especially since Tyler's half-naked. His sweatshirt is long gone, and his shirt has been cast off, but he still wears the slacks from his post-game suit. It's a hot look—especially considering how those beige slacks stretch against his thick thighs. And how his strong muscles flex in his arms as he checks the knots one more time.

I'm dressed in only panties and a bra. Somewhere in my apartment a little cat roams, but she's fine.

And I'm more than fine as he kisses his way down my body, his lips trailing over the lace of my bra. With his teeth helping, he pushes the cups down, revealing my tits and hard nipples that might as well boast a neon sign flashing the words—*Touch Me, Play With Me, Have Some Fun.*

He sucks in a breath as he gazes lasciviously at them.

"Tell me," he demands, flicking a finger against the right barbell. "Tell me why nipple play is on your list."

A rush of pleasure spreads through me, heat and sparks filling my cells. Do I tell him? Do I say it?

Fuck it. "I like to play with them when I get myself off," I admit.

His eyes darken. He sucks in a staggered breath. "You

playing with your tits when you're alone is the hottest thing ever."

Then he straddles me and unhooks my bra from the clasp in the middle, letting the cups fall to the side. His big hands palm my tits.

I grow wetter by the second, arching into his touch.

He squeezes both a little bit harder.

I squirm.

He kneads them roughly.

I gasp.

He flicks his finger against the barbell on the left one, and my voice pitches up.

"Oh god. So good," I cry out.

He teases the right one. I nearly scream.

The look on his face is pure satisfaction as he moves off me slightly and issues a command: "Spread these thighs, baby."

I comply, and when his gaze lands on the wet patch of my panties, his hazel eyes go feral. "Fuck, baby. You do like nipple play," he says.

And the answer is *fuck yes*. He returns his hands to my breasts, rubbing, squeezing, making me writhe against his touch.

A flush crawls down my chest, and my skin warms everywhere. A pulse beats between my thighs.

Tyler dips his face, buries it between the valley of my tits, then draws one nipple between his lips and flicks his tongue across the barbell.

Then he does the same to the other.

Soon, I'm panting, arching, and—I'm dripping. I'm so wet, so turned on I can't stand it. My arms strain against the scarves.

As I try to break free, his laugh cuts through, but then

it vanishes as he palms my right breast another time and draws my hard nipple back to his mouth, his tongue swirling across the piercing again and again in a dizzying, intoxicating motion.

I nearly come. "Keep doing that," I urge.

And he does one better. He kisses and sucks, while dipping his other hand into my panties.

And the second his fingers meet my slick heat I lose my mind. Less than a minute later, I'm gasping and falling apart. I jerk against the scarves, losing myself to him, and moaning for a good, long time until the dramatic cry of a kitten pierces the air.

"Ha. Told you she needed something," Tyler says, triumphant, pointing to Drama sitting in the doorway, meowing for attention.

"Fine. You're right, Cat Daddy."

"I knew it," he says, then hops out of bed to fetch the furball.

I peer over at the big, strapping hockey stud cradling a tiny kitten against his chest. I sigh happily. "I think she wants you to throw her one of those tinfoil balls," I say.

"Perfect. I get to play with both of you," Tyler says.

And a few minutes later, he's multitasking—tossing tinfoil balls to the kitten while stroking my pussy again, bringing me to another orgasm.

We've broken our number one rule. It feels like we're breaking an unwritten one when a few minutes later, he says, "Tell me about your lessons."

I snort. "Is that a condition of untying?"

His eyes shoot to my wrists, still shackled by the silk scarves. "Oh shit," he says, then hustles to untie me.

He stretches across me, and wow, I have quite a nice view of his chest. It's so strong and sturdy, and there's a bruise right there. As he frees my right hand, I reach for the bruise, gently touching the inky lake on his right pec, just under his kids' birthdays. "Does this hurt?" I ask as he shifts to my left wrist.

He glances down at me, pausing his knot work. His lips shift. "If I say yes, will you kiss it?"

The flirt is strong in him.

"I guess you'll have to find out." I suppose it's strong in me too.

He frowns, playing it up. "It hurts so much."

I stretch closer, pressing a kiss to the slab of muscle. His breath hitches as I touch him, and a thrill rushes through me.

He unknots the scarf on my left wrist, freeing me and catching my left hand in his. He strokes the faint red marks the material's left on my arm. "Does this hurt?"

Well, two can play at this game. "Yes."

He kisses it, then my other wrist. I shiver from his soft touches, these after kisses to my once-bound wrists. From under him like this, I scan his upper body, spotting a scratch on his forearm. With him still leaning over me, I drag a finger across the cut—it's maybe a week old, nearly healed. "This?"

He pauses, then perhaps gives in completely, letting me take the lead in this game as he says, "So much."

I kiss him there, a slow, sweet kiss that makes his breath catch once again. I didn't know these soft kisses could affect a man like this. Could affect *this* man like this. I study his face, hunting for any marks and bruises from the rough sport he plays for a living, then run my finger down his cheek, traveling to a small cut along his jaw. "And this?"

Tyler pouts. "Hurts a lot."

Happily, I kiss there too, brushing my lips slowly across his skin. Savoring every hum, every murmur. I relish it—this power I'm only now realizing I have over this burly defenseman, who looms over opponents on the ice and smashes men into the boards, but then melts into my kisses. It's a power I want to use for good. So I drop another slow, hazy kiss to his jawline.

He sighs, and I want to capture that sound. The sound of him relaxing into me after a long day. Another soft murmur comes from him as I continue to kiss him. He settles down next to me on the bed, looping his arm around my waist. He's so warm right now.

I touch the corner of his mouth with my forefinger. "And this?"

"So much pain," he whispers.

I press my mouth to his and kiss him, a little more deeply. He parts his lips, swallowing more of the kiss, drinking it up like it's brandy. I kiss him back luxuriously, taking my time as his hands wrap around my waist and he holds me close. It's a tight grip like he doesn't want to let me go.

It lasts an intoxicating minute or maybe many more until our kiss is interrupted by another meow—loud and demanding.

Drama is stalking the foot of the bed like a tiny black and white lion, looking entirely put out.

"Kitty girl wants to join us," Tyler says, then sits up and reaches for her, cradling her in a palm. He places her on a pillow, but being a cat, she doesn't sit still. She parades around beside the headboard, testing each section while Tyler returns to me, kissing me tenderly. Then more urgently. And I can't resist.

My lips travel down his chest to his abs, then to the

zipper of his pants. I tug at it, arching a brow. "Does this hurt?"

"Unbelievably so," he says.

I free his cock, take him in my mouth, and drive him wild as Drama curls up at last under his arm.

After he comes hard and loud, and I wipe a hand across my mouth, I say with a pleased shrug of my shoulder, "Told you I like practice."

He reaches for me, tugs me to his other side, and traces my mouth with his finger. "Practice anytime."

It sounds like he means it—the *anytime.* It sounds like an open invitation for us to come together.

Which is what tonight is dangerously starting to feel like—like a night without an end. And that scares me a little. I don't want to get hurt. I've been there, done that, and rearranged my life last summer because of it. I went full garlic to make it on my own, and I don't want to backtrack, especially as I'm finding my footing.

But when Tyler pats the pillow and urges me to sink closer to him, I stop thinking about what might hurt, and I give in, like the cat. I could learn a thing or two from her about embracing the moment.

"So, tell me about your lessons," Tyler says, returning at last to the question he asked earlier.

Funny. I'd expected him to forget his question. To be distracted by sex and orgasms. To notice the ticking of the clock and rush out of my place, hell-bent on returning to his own room two floors and a lock away. But with Drama resting her little furry face in the crook of his arm and purring loudly enough to shake the bed, Tyler seems to be staying put too. "You said you had a new student today?" he adds.

He really does pay attention. But then again, he always

has. This is the man who bought me yoga gear and sheets and towels and a NutRageous bar.

"Yes," I say. "A girl with curly hair, a bright smile, and ADHD. It was the first thing she said when she showed up to the lesson. She stuck out her hand and said, *I'm Tiffany and I have ADHD*. And honestly, it was cute how much she wanted me to know."

Tyler nods. "That's pretty good of her, owning it."

"I thought that too. Well, her mom had actually told me in advance over email, which was helpful because I googled it and did some research. I read some articles on how exercise can help a lot with mood and focus in people who have ADHD."

His eyes spark. "Really? How so?"

I tell him more about the research I did and what I learned about how physical activity often improves concentration in people with ADHD.

"That's impressive, that you put all that work into it," he says.

"Former perfectionist here," I say, owning it. "I really need to do something with all that energy, so it works well in that regard—research, that is."

"I'm glad you have that knowledge about yourself," he says. "Is coaching fulfilling you?"

That's a good question. I mull it over for a beat before I answer with the truth. "It is. It feels natural. I love figure skating, but I did get pretty obsessed with it when I was younger. And when I tried out for the Olympics, I was at the peak of my obsession. I didn't make it," I add, but he probably knows.

His eyes hold mine with not quite sympathy, but empathy. The empathy of someone who understands what it's like to chase a goal and not always reach it. "Was that hard for you?"

I sigh, remembering with excruciating clarity the shattering disappointment when I didn't make it past the Olympic trials. "It was devastating. But in some ways it was also a relief. I don't think I realized at the time that it was. It was only after going to therapy for a while that I learned all that perfectionism and pursuit of excellence had been taking a toll on me. It was affecting my mind and my emotions. I obsessed over every second I spent prepping, exercising, practicing. It was all I could think about. I had to learn to let go of it—all that order. All that list-making and tracking. And then finally, when I did, I was able to skate again—for fun."

A soft smile crosses his lips. "In your videos, I can see the joy that you feel. It's in your eyes."

That warms my heart in a brand-new way. "I'm glad you can see it."

"That's one of the reasons I love watching them," he admits, then gives me a sheepish look. "Not just because I have this thing for figure skating—well, now for one skater in particular." He stops to drop a kiss to my forehead, and it feels like it spreads through my body, down to my toes. When he pulls back, he says, "But also because it's so clear you're having a good time."

"I am. I truly am."

He runs a hand along my hair, touching me absently through our pillow talk. "Is that how you teach? I mean, I see you with Luna, and she's always having fun and so are you. But is that your goal—to help students feel that joy too?"

It's just a little thing, but he seems to understand me so well already, and I don't think it's simply because he's been privy to my lessons as a parental spectator. "I think so. I hope so. I want to help them with their goals and meet them where they are—if they're ambitious, if they're competitive. But also to help them just have fun, too, if that's what they want."

He exhales softly, then tries to fight off a yawn. He's unsuccessful. The yawn shakes his whole body. I laugh. He must be so tired. I rub his shoulder, perhaps a subtle way of letting him know he's free to go if he wants to. I'm not going to hold him back. "You played a hockey game today, went on a feline shopping spree, hung out with your friends, drove back down here, fucked me with your fingers—you must be exhausted. You should go to bed."

Tyler sinks deeper into the pillows, his eyes floating closed. "Yeah, I should...get to sleep early." He doesn't make a move to leave. "We should skate together sometime."

I blink, a little taken aback. "Skate together?" I want to make sure I actually heard him right.

"At a rink. For fun. You know, for the joy of it," he says, his voice getting a little slurry at the end.

It sounds like a date—a date that's not at all in the tiny sex diary. That's not part of the game plan. The plan we're veering far, far away from already.

Briefly, he opens his eyes again to kick off his pants. Then he pulls up the quilt and slides his legs under it. His eyes flutter closed without even a mention of going upstairs.

It feels like another rule is broken as he falls asleep with the kitten in his arms and his head on my shoulder.

31

THE HIRED HELP

Sabrina

But morning always comes, the sun rising on our choices and their consequences. As the sun streaks through the window, my phone trills, rousing me from a dream with a jolt. Grabbing it from the nightstand, I spot Elle's name on the screen.

What the...?

Snapping my gaze to Tyler, who's soundly sleeping—and soundly snoring—I bolt out of bed, then answer it the second I hustle past the doorway.

"Hey, what's going on?" I ask without bothering to mask my concern. She was supposed to drop the kids off at school...I glance at the time on the TV. Fifteen minutes ago. Panic rushes through my veins.

"Hey!" Her tone is bright, and that's somewhat reassuring. "I called Tyler, but he didn't answer, and I'm walking up the steps right now, about to knock on the door."

She's here?

I spin around, hunting for clothes in my living room. "Oh, okay."

"I can just leave their bags on the porch but I figured if he was home it'd just be easier," she says, apologetic.

I rub my eyes. "Their bags?"

"They didn't want to take their overnight bags to school. I guess I kind of understand; it's a pain to lug them around."

That's a fair point. A lot of times she'll drop the bags off in the morning or in the afternoon when she's had the kids for a sleepover. I spot a sweatshirt on the carpet by the couch. I make a run for it as she says, "Sorry. I shouldn't have bothered you, Sabrina. I don't really know what hours you keep or what the rules are about calling you for this," she says. She sounds flustered for the first time, like she's crossed some sort of line with the hired help.

I wince as those words flash through my brain.

Hired help.

Yep, that's what I am. I'm the hired help, and my tits are flying free because I banged my boss last night. Fine, he didn't technically bang me, but...semantics. As shame courses through me, I jam on the sweatshirt, stuffing my arms through it then readjusting the phone. "I'll be right up," I say, then hunt for jeans. But I don't have any pants out here. My stomach tips as I hang up and tiptoe furtively back to my room, opening the door as quietly as I can.

I don't want to wake him and explain this shitshow.

Tyler rustles in bed, but the man isn't a lover of sleep for nothing. He doesn't wake—just snores a little louder as I slide open a drawer quietly and grab a pair of leggings. I dart into the bathroom, yank them on, then douse my dragon breath with some mouthwash. A ten-second gargle later and I'm grabbing a hair tie and yanking my hair into a messy bun. I stuff my phone into the pocket of my leggings then race up the stairs to the front door, swinging it open when I realize—I grabbed Tyler's hoodie from the floor. It's the same color as mine, and I'm swimming in it. It hits me mid-thigh.

But there's no time to change.

I flash back to all the times I've performed on the ice.

When I wobbled during a competition. When I missed a jump. When I fell flat on my ass and had to get right back up. You pick yourself up and you smile, then skate on. I paste on the brightest *never let them see you sweat* grin ever and skate on. "Good morning."

Elle blinks, looking down at my clothes. "Oh, I didn't mean to…" She thrusts the kids' bags at me. "Here."

I take them and set them down in the foyer. "Thanks."

She waves a hand like it's nothing, then she tears her gaze off of my torso and focuses squarely on my eyes. "If you could just let Tyler know that I dropped them off. And that he doesn't need to return any of my text messages or phone calls about them. We're all set now." She spins around, ready to fly down the steps. But then her shoulders pinch and she turns back toward me, holding up a finger. "Though he does need to return my messages about Christmas because I should definitely be able to put the kids on a flight to New York on the twenty-third or the twenty-fourth. I'll get unaccompanied minor tickets," she explains quickly.

I freeze.

I didn't know she had the kids right before Christmas Eve. Sure, he mentioned they were discussing holiday plans, but I didn't know what those plans were.

He didn't share them with me. All I know is the last hockey game before Christmas is in New York on the twenty-third.

Christmas is around two weeks away. I don't know if he expects me to work. We didn't talk about this. It never even came up, and now I feel so unbearably stupid.

What kind of employee doesn't ask their boss what the plans are for Christmas? Do I have the day off? The week off? What kind of boss doesn't tell the employee if they have the day off?

My chest feels like concrete.

Is this what happens when you start sleeping with your boss? You just take all sorts of things for granted? My head throbs and I barely listen as Elle tells me the details.

When she's gone I shut the door, feeling sick all over. I have no idea what to do next. And I definitely don't know what I'm going to do in a couple weeks when I'm all alone out here in his house, and he's in New York for the holidays.

I trudge into the kitchen, trying to get my bearings. I stare briefly at the living room. There's no tree yet, but will he even do that? I don't know. Maybe I'll just be alone in a tree-less house. I guess that's fine too.

I hunt for a piece of fruit to munch on. A minute later, heavy footsteps echo on the stairs, and he rounds the corner, then appears. He's wearing his slacks and nothing else, bleary-eyed as he scrubs a hand across his beard. He looks impossibly sexy, all messy morning hair and soft eyes. "I think I overslept," he says, his voice rusty with sleep.

I can't let it affect me though. I straighten my shoulders. "Yeah, I think you did."

His gaze drifts to the duffel bags in the foyer. "Are the

kids here?" He goes ramrod straight, pointing to the staircase toward his room. "I should—"

I hold up a hand, waving that off. "They're at school. Elle just dropped off the bags." I swallow down my pride and add, "She said she called you, and she also said to tell you that she's going to book a flight for the kids to join you in New York for Christmas."

"Oh," he says, then looks at me with perhaps a touch of guilt flashing in his eyes. "That's helpful. I have them for Christmas."

I take a beat, ignoring the hurt, since I have no right to feel hurt. *Skate on.* "I guess that means I have the holiday off," I say chipper and bright. Like a little fucking Christmas elf.

He freezes, his eyes flickering with embarrassment. "Oh. Yeah. I guess so. I'm sorry. I hadn't thought of that before," he says, sounding genuinely remorseful. But for what? For not telling me? "I should have said something sooner. I mean, Agatha used to take the holiday off every year."

Right. Because I'm just like Agatha. His last nanny.

Of course you're like Agatha. You have the same job.

In fact, I should act like the nanny, not like his girlfriend, who's annoyingly hurt that she wasn't invited for Christmas. Clearly, that ice-skating invitation last night was nothing more than a sleepy, offhand remark—not a real request. We're not dating.

"It sounds great," I say, laying on the holiday charm so thick. "I'm going to be hanging out with Trevyn for Christmas," I say, improvising. "We made some plans. It's like a Friendsgiving. Actually, like a Friendsmas. With Isla, and Skylar," I say and I am babbling. It is like the Night of 1001 Confessions all over again, but it's the Morning of a

Million Holiday Lies. But maybe Trevyn is free. Maybe we'll do karaoke. Or watch a movie. "I really appreciate the time off, so thank you."

His brow knits, but he manages an awkward, "You're welcome." His gaze drifts over me, slow and deliberate, lingering just a second too long. "Is that my sweatshirt?"

And I didn't think it was possible, but now I feel even worse. "Yes, it is. I grabbed it by mistake. Would you like it back?"

His lips part like he's torn on what to say, but he eventually says, "No."

And I have no idea if he feels guilty or if he's trying to figure me out. "Don't worry. Elle didn't say anything," I say crisply, trying to get out of this awkward conversation. I head toward the stairs, abandoning the fruit pursuit too. "And I won't wear it this afternoon when I take the kids to the science museum."

He grabs my arm before I can go, his grip firm but hesitant. "That's not what I meant, Sabrina."

"What did you mean then?" I snap.

He lets go of my arm, looking...chastened. "It just threw me off. I didn't mean to—"

"Fall asleep in my room?"

He tilts his head. "No, that's not what I was going to say."

"So you *did* mean to fall asleep in my room." Holy shit. What am I doing? Am I giving my boss the third degree? I shake my head, embarrassed now too. "It's all good. Let's just move on," I say, trying to erase this entire uncomfortable moment. "I should work on my skating lesson plans. And I have to do some prep for the science museum visit. You have community service with the team this afternoon —distributing compost bins in the neighborhood." I'm reminding him of the schedule so he knows I've got my act together. And so he knows I'm well aware of my place. I'm not the girlfriend. I'm the nanny, and even if he didn't tell me the holiday schedule, I still know the daily schedule and it's my job to make sure everyone else does too. "Anyway, you should probably charge your phone. Elle only called me because you didn't answer, and I was rushing to answer the door without waking you up. I guess your phone died."

He grabs it from the pocket of his pants and looks at the technological carcass. "Fuck. The kids could have called. I need to be more responsible," he says, and now he's beating himself up.

This morning could not have gone any worse.

I pluck at the sweatshirt. "Me too. I should have been more careful about the sweatshirt."

He reaches for my hand again. "There's nothing wrong with you wearing that," he says, his voice firm and full of meaning.

But the sweatshirt is causing problems. "I guess we should be more careful."

He parts his lips but doesn't say anything for several seconds. His loss for words speaks volumes, then he says, "Yeah, I mean, we talked about it. For the kids and everything."

My throat tightens, shame rushing through me, but also real concern for the two young people in his life—Luna and Parker. I know their parents have a so-called *good divorce*. I know they get along. But the kids are still young. They're being shuttled back and forth between two homes. They don't need to be more confused. They don't need to think of me as their dad's *sidepiece*. They need to see me as the nanny who plans amazing visits to science museums, teaches them math in cool ways, and tracks down disco balls at thrift shops.

"I should probably give you your sweatshirt back then," I say, starting to take it off, catching a whiff of his woodsmoke scent, and it nearly stops my heart. But then his hand comes down on mine once more.

"Wear it. Don't take it off," he says, his voice firm and commanding as he tugs the neckline back down on me. His eyes hold mine, his gaze full of longing, and something else—something I can't place. "I want you to wear it. I like the way it looks on you. I don't care if she knew it belonged to me."

A muscle ticks in his jaw. His fingers twitch, like he wants to touch me, but he won't.

My wild heart settles the slightest bit, but only the slightest.

He looks at the time and swears under his breath. "I have practice."

And just like that, he's gone.

32

A NEW VICTORY

Sabrina

"Okay, if you two can work together as a team, you can play with Drama when we get home. How does that sound?"

On the steps outside the children's science museum, Luna and Parker nod so fast it's a wonder their heads don't fly off.

Ah, kittens—the universal motivator for nearly all kids.

"Perfect. Because I also created a scavenger hunt for you today," I say, holding open the door.

Parker's eyes widen. "You did?"

"What kind of nanny do you take me for? The kind who scrolls on her phone the whole time, or the kind who actually gets involved?"

"The kind who's involved," Luna says, tugging on my jacket and pulling me toward the ticket counter.

Yep, I'm the nanny who does her job well. And that job

does not include sleeping with the dad. I'm not even thinking about him this afternoon at all. I'm focused on teaching and playing with the kids. Because that's what I was hired to do till the hockey season ends and that's a ways off.

After I buy the tickets, we head to the Forces and Motion Exhibit, which I researched online earlier today. I turn to them. "Okay, pop quiz. What happens when you rub a balloon on your hair?"

"It creates static electricity!" Luna announces, thrusting her hand in the air.

"And that's an example of a force in motion," Parker adds, pointing to a nearby sign that reads Electrostatic Force. "Electrons move from your hair to the balloon, and that makes your hair stand up."

"Exactly! It's an invisible force," Luna adds, beaming as she reads the sign.

"Great teamwork," I say as we move into the next exhibit—a recycling maze that makes a game of learning which items go in compost, recycling or the landfill.

Parker holds up a pizza box, with his brow furrowed. "Cardboard recycling, right?"

"Not if it's greasy," Luna says with the confidence of a kid who just read the exhibit info.

"Oh! That makes sense. The oil might prevent the cardboard from breaking down."

Now it's Luna's turn to be confused. "So how do you recycle pizza boxes?"

Parker studies the exhibit info. "You ask for a layer of paper between the pizza and the box!"

And since this box isn't greasy, they toss it in the recycling bin together, where a cartoonish voice coming from the bin says, "Recycling one glass bottle saves enough energy to power a lightbulb for four hours."

As we go, I toss them more questions, and they work together to find the answers in the exhibits. Then I lead them into a dimly lit room with midnight blue walls and displays all about ice and motion. Even if they don't love hockey, I think they'll get a kick out of this one.

"Next question. How fast do you think a hockey puck glides on ice?"

Parker scrunches his forehead. "Uh...fifty miles an hour?"

"A little more than that. And it all has to do with friction," I say. "Do you think there's a lot of friction on ice or not much?"

"Not much," Luna guesses.

"Exactly. Because there's so little friction, pucks can glide at speeds over a hundred miles per hour."

"That's really fast," Parker says.

Luna's jaw drops as she spins toward her brother. "We have to tell Dad later—that's one of the coolest things I've ever heard!"

"Sabrina, can we look up more hockey facts?" Parker asks thoughtfully. "Because when Dad talks about it, it's sooo boring. But when you do, it's actually interesting."

That makes me happier than it should. And for all the wrong reasons. I shouldn't be pleased that they enjoy my approach more. But I'm still a little pissed at their dad—and mad at myself too—so I'll take the win.

We move through the rest of the Ice and Cold Exhibit, and I point to a display about ice before asking, "So, why is ice slippery?"

Parker and Luna exchange a glance before Parker guesses: "Uh...because it's wet?"

"Kind of! It's because pressure from your foot or skate creates a thin layer of water, which reduces friction."

Luna gasps. "Wait. Suddenly, my dad's job is so much more interesting."

I laugh. "Well, I'd hope you're interested in ice—you're a figure skater."

She squares her shoulders, clearly taking that as a compliment. "I know," she says, then shoots me a conspiratorial grin. "But what we do is way cooler than a bunch of guys whacking pucks."

Parker nods. "She's not wrong."

I shouldn't be pleased. I really shouldn't. But I kind of am.

And I'm especially pleased because, once again, I am Super Nanny. Exactly who I was hired to be.

* * *

At home, Luna and Parker fly down the stairs toward my apartment.

"I want to hold her first!" Luna declares.

"I do!" Parker insists.

"She likes me better," Luna retorts, reaching the door ahead of her brother.

"Not true," Parker argues.

"You know what she loves most?" I counter, tapping the code into the keypad.

Both of them pause. "What?"

"Food," I say with a grin. "How about we feed little Miss Drama?"

Right on cue, I lean toward the door, cupping my ear. Drama's high-pitched wail filters through—a sound somewhere between a whistle and a demand for immediate attention.

They both chuckle. "She really wants to see us," Parker says.

"Of course she does," I say.

I push open the door, and they instantly scoop her up. Together. It's the sweetest brother-sister moment I've seen, with Luna cradling the kitten's head and torso and Parker holding her bottom half.

Drama makes a show of resisting before melting into the attention, stretching luxuriously in their arms.

Luna gasps as she notices the brand-new cat tower, tunnels, and toys scattered across the living room. She hands the kitten to her brother and races to check out all the gear. "Oh my god! You got so much stuff for her!"

My heart goes a little squishy as last night flashes through my mind—Tyler hauling everything in from Rowan's car, setting it up without a word.

"I got some gifts for the kitten," he said. "I know she's only a foster, but you can use them for the next one...and the next one...and the next one."

And just like that, I feel like a jerk for being mad at him at all.

Fine, I didn't let on that I was mad at him, but still, I feel bad for my pissy thoughts. So, he forgot about the Christmas holiday. That's not the worst thing in the world.

We feed Drama, and when she's done eating, I scoop her up and announce, "Okay—who's ready for a kitten play session?"

We take out every toy—feathers, balls, and the laser pointer—and Drama zooms around like a tiny rocket. Luna dangles a wand toy, Parker sets up a triangular cardboard scratcher, and I lounge back, watching them fall further in love with this little cat.

Then, the garage door rattles. A minute later, footsteps echo as Tyler must head upstairs. Then, the footsteps grow louder as he comes back downstairs. We all snicker, co-conspirators in hiding out in KittenLandia.

A knock sounds at my door.

I tense but remind myself just to be a good nanny. And I am—clearly.

Luna hops up and swings it open. "Daddy, we're playing with the kitten, so you'll have to come back later."

Tyler blinks. "Okay...I just wanted to check if you needed—"

"We don't need anything," Luna interrupts, waving a hand. "You can go out, or do your weights, or...do your things. We're playing with Drama."

Tyler hesitates, looking half amused, half uncertain. "Oh. Well...do you want to play a board game later? Lego?"

Parker barely looks up from where Drama is batting a feather toy across the floor. "No, but thanks."

Tyler glances at me, like maybe he expected a different answer. Then he nods. "Okay. Have fun."

For a second, I almost call after him to invite him to join us in the kitten love fest. But I don't want to get too cozy as a family. Best if I focus on my role here—taking care of his kids. I sit back, watching the kids play with Drama.

As he walks away, it feels like a different kind of win.

Not the small, selfish victory I felt earlier—but a real one.

Especially when I think back to when I started this job —when Parker barely acknowledged me.

Now, he does more than that. And I'm really grateful for it.

* * *

Later, as the family's eating dinner upstairs, I head out since I'm off duty. I make my way to the bustling Fillmore Street, its shops lit up with Christmas displays and bright festive lights. I dip into An Open Book, thumbing through some coaching books, then picking up some gifts for Trevyn, Isla, Leighton, and Skylar for Christmas. At the checkout, I grab a blank card, adding that to my haul too.

Once I'm home, I keep it simple.

Tyler,

Thank you so much for all the kitten supplies. I'm truly grateful that you opened your home to fostering again—it means a lot to me, but even more to the animals. It's really kind of you to help give these animals a second chance.

—Sabrina

Then, without overthinking it, but making sure all the lights are off, I slide it under his door.

I don't linger. I don't listen for him. I simply return to my home and go to bed. Before I turn out the light, I put the tiny sex diary away. We haven't talked about another lesson. I'm not even sure we'll have one.

And really, that's okay.

* * *

The next morning when the kids are at school, I head to a skating lesson with Tiffany. She has a long break in the middle of the day so is able to do lessons then. At the rink, I say hello to Marla at the front counter, then meet my student on the ice where I show her how to skate backward.

And pretty soon, she's nailing it. "Look, Mom!" she shouts to her mother in the bleachers. "You should do it too."

Her mom smiles and doesn't say no immediately.

When the lesson ends, Tiffany skates to the boards. "Seriously. It's so fun. You should do it."

I turn to her mother, give a hopeful shrug, and say, "Figure skating is always a good idea."

"Maybe I'll try someday," her mom says, and I like that attitude.

A lot.

* * *

When I head into my next session with Elena that afternoon, the guilt I felt last time over withholding intel from her is gone. What am I even keeping from her now? I'm not sure I'm still having a *thing* with my boss anymore. Tyler's out of town for an away game, and we didn't set a date for a fourth lesson.

If we even will have one.

There's really nothing to discuss about him.

But Elena wants to know how I'm feeling about the upcoming holidays. "It's your first Christmas since the wedding," she states. "And since the things your father said to you last summer. Will you see your parents at all?"

My throat tightens all at once—uncomfortably. The memories rush back. The things my father said to me that day. The things my mother never said.

The gaslighting.

And then, images of Chad and Madison flicker through my mind too—them enjoying the blenders and napkin rings, the ones that were meant for us.

Let them. Just let them enjoy them.

Feeling strong and certain, I answer her: "And I won't be seeing them—my parents."

"How do you feel about that?"

I see my parents' home, cold and immaculately decorated. "Fine, actually. I don't think I'll miss them," I say, but then I picture Tyler's living room, imagining him decorating it with his kids when he returns from his road trip. I think about their excitement for Santa, and suddenly, everything feels complicated in a whole new way.

"I need to get in touch with my friends and see what they're doing," I add. "It'll be weird being in the house by myself."

At least that is the truth.

And it feels...a little freeing to say it.

No, *a lot.*

I look at Elena again, at her warm eyes, her shrewd gaze, her laugh lines, and the kindness in her expression.

I walked through her door for the first time many years ago so I could make changes. Those changes started with honesty. I don't know what changes I need to make now. But whatever they are, they ought to at least start with honesty.

"And the other thing is," I say, and it's not as hard as I'd thought it would be to finish the thought: "I have feelings for my boss."

Elena nods, then listens without judgement as I tell her more.

33

FUCK-UPS AND FIASCOS

Tyler

The second we step out of the hotel near the Space Needle, I'm drenched.

"Are you kidding me?" I say to the sky. It's pelting raindrops down.

We're in Seattle, having flown up this morning so we can play tomorrow afternoon. I'm heading to the arena for a workout with Rowan and Miles.

"It's almost like you barely grew up in this town," Miles says, adjusting his collar but heading into the downpour regardless. The arena's not far from here.

"Want an umbrella?" Rowan mocks.

"No," I grumble, since there's no way I'd ever admit to needing one. The guys would give me hell.

"Maybe you can get a cup of hot chamomile tea at the arena and a warm footbath," Rowan teases.

"Do you like getting soaked?" I counter as we walk quickly toward the grounds.

"Fucking love it," Rowan says, lifting his face to the dark sky, inviting the rain. "Makes me stronger. Something you should consider sometime."

"Thanks, appreciate it," I say, but then I go quiet as they shoot the breeze about the local music scene.

I'm quiet too, as we head into the arena and make our way down to the visitors' locker room. I can't stop thinking about Sabrina. I can't stop thinking about when Elle showed up, and I barely knew how to handle the moment after. And I definitely can't stop thinking about my own fuck-up with Sabrina—the whole Christmas fiasco. Although *fuck-ups* is more appropriate—I'm pretty sure there were several.

I stew a little longer as we hit the weight room, then I move through bench presses, flies, and triceps with barely a word while Miles and Rowan debate punk rock versus classic rock.

When I set down the barbell on the weight bench and push up, Miles turns away from the rack of weights on the wall and meets my gaze in the mirror. "You're grumpier than usual. What's up?"

"Nothing."

Rowan snorts but doesn't stop his crunches. "Bullshit. What'd you do?"

I narrow my eyes. "Why do you assume I did something?"

"Because that's how you act when you're mad at yourself. You get all grumbly and quiet. You complain about the weather..."

What the hell? Are they holding up a mirror to my dark soul?

I don't deny it, but I don't answer them either. I don't even know how to begin to open up about everything that's wrong. Where would I start? This is all new to me in its own way. I was married for eight years in a very friendly, very lackluster marriage. We grew apart.

There is *nothing* lackluster about Sabrina. She's fiery and feisty and passionate and completely off-limits, and I am so out of my element.

Rowan points at me. "You're thinking way too much."

I heave a sigh. Maybe I should tell them. I haven't been able to swim my way out of this murky gray quicksand I've been in since yesterday morning. "The thing is...I've gotten involved with Sabrina."

Rowan thrusts an arm in the air. "I just need to say—I was the first one to call it. Back at the gym before the season started."

Miles smacks his shoulder. "Dude, my girlfriend called it a year ago when Tyler met Sabrina the night she performed at a hockey game. She told me then that she thought he had it bad for her."

"So you're claiming first-sies because of your girl-friend? Real classy, Captain," Rowan retorts.

I drag my hands through my hair and cut through the madness. "Guys, I really fucking like her. And I messed up."

They snap to it, their expressions suddenly serious.

"What happened?" Miles asks with big-brother concern.

I look around, making sure the door is still shut, and then I say, "I didn't make any plans with her for Christmas —not for work, not for anything. The kids are joining me in New York after our last game, and I never even asked her what she was doing. Never said if I needed her to work or not. And I didn't invite her—but the second it came up, I realized I probably should have. Plus, she found out about the plans through Elle, and it was just... fucking awkward and uncomfortable and...What am I even doing?"

Miles blows out a long breath, adjusting his glasses. "That's a lot, but what part is bugging you the most?"

That's a damn good question, and I've had enough time to formulate an answer. Still, it's hard to say. "I don't want to screw this up. Not with her. Not with my kids. Not the way Dad did."

Miles nods, getting it immediately, of course. "Heard."

"And she works for me. She takes care of Luna and Parker. So the entire situation is so damn complicated."

Rowan holds up his hands. "Shit, man. Romance sucks, so I don't know what to say. But I feel for you since that's a lot."

"It is a lot, but let's break it down," Miles says, pinning me with a stare. "Do you want to invite her?"

"Yes," I say, desperation coloring my tone. "But I don't know if it's too late or if it'll look like I'm inviting her as the babysitter or something. Or if it'll look like I want her to be my—"

"Your what?" Rowan cuts in pointedly.

I'm silent for a beat because this vulnerability is new for me too. "My girlfriend," I say, but then my chest tightens. "But that's not what she wants right now. She just got out of a shitty relationship where she almost married the guy, and I don't know how to figure that out in front of the kids—dating and all," I say, and I hate the sound of my voice. I feel like I'm whining, but I'm in uncharted territory. "And she works for me, like I've said."

Miles laughs, but it's clear he's laughing at himself. "Relationships are hard. I fell for the coach's daughter—

I'd know. But you have to communicate what you want. Do you want to spend Christmas with her?"

"I do, but I've made it too complicated now by not asking her. And now if I ask her, what if she's not ready for...a trip with her boss and his kids? For fuck's sake. Saying it out loud makes it sound ridiculous."

Miles smirks. "Dude, you're spiraling. You're not asking her to be your girlfriend. You're inviting her on a trip."

Rowan shrugs. "If she says yes, she wants to go. That's it."

Miles moves next to me, claps my shoulder. "One step at a time. This isn't a proposal. It's a trip. Just tell her you fucked up and invite her."

I grab my water bottle and down some. He's right. This isn't a grand romantic move—it's what I should have done in the first place. Invite her to join us for the holidays. "That's it?"

"Yep, that's it."

Miles turns to Rowan. "I bet even the Grinch would say it's that easy."

Rowan scoffs. "I'm the last person who should be giving you any romantic advice, but in this case? Just tell her the truth."

That seems easy enough. This isn't about putting a label on us. It's about making sure she knows she's wanted.

And as I'm leaving, I flash back to something Trevyn mentioned the day I met him. Something Sabrina would *love* to do in New York. And just like that, I know—this isn't just something I *should* do. It's something I *want* to do. Something I want to do with her and the kids. Something she'd want too.

I leave the weight room, and I text her to see what she's up to, trying to figure out if now might be a good time to call.

A few minutes later, she texts back.

> Sabrina: I'm OK! I wanted to let you know that Parker isn't feeling well. I picked him up from school early, and he's got a fever, but he's going to be fine! He's taking Tylenol, and we're cuddled up together watching cartoons.

I call her *stat.*

34

NURSE KITTEN

Tyler

"Hey little buddy. How's it going?"

"I'm okay, Dad," Parker answers, his voice a little froggy and a little sad. I pace down the hall of the corridor at the Seattle Arena, my phone pressed tight to my ear.

"I heard you're not feeling so hot," I say, rounding the corner. I just called Sabrina for the update—it's a flu-like bug that's going around, she told me. Some of the other kids at school have it.

"Actually, I *am* a little bit hot," Parker says, then forces out a laugh at his own joke. I manage a small smile, relieved he's retained his sense of humor. "I'm one hundred two."

"That's no fun. I wish I were there," I say, and my heart hurts since it's eight hundred miles away from here in San Francisco, with my little boy.

"Me too," he says, then coughs, before saying in a softer voice, "Sorry, Sabrina."

"It's okay. Coughing is fine," she replies, her voice easy to hear. She must be right next to him on the couch. And my heart squeezes a little more, knowing she's there with him.

"But we get to watch *Space Dogs*," Parker tells me, managing to sound a little upbeat. "Sabrina found it from YouTube, and it's funny, and the science mostly makes sense, so it's not that bad. Also, I want to talk to you about the science of Santa sometime soon," he says, but his voice fades and he coughs again. "But not right now. Love you, Dad."

"Love you too," I say, my chest hurting, full of longing and the wish to be there and take care of him.

A few seconds later, there's a rustling on the phone, then Sabrina's voice. "Hey, it looks like he's going to snuggle up under a blanket for a nap," she says, then pauses. "Wait. Spoke too soon. Be right back."

I stare at the phone and the line that went dead. My pulse spikes and panic grips me, hard and cold. I pace down the hall, then tap out a quick text to Sabrina— *What's going on?*—but before I can send it, my phone rings. This time it's Luna. I swipe it so fast. "What's going on?"

"Dad, it's me. I'm upstairs. Like, literally at the top of the stairs and I'm watching them downstairs. But don't worry, I have a mask on because I really don't want to get sick, because I don't want to miss Secret Santa, and Sabrina already helped take me shopping for Secret Santa," she says, and I want to say *speed it up*, but I don't want to be rude. "But anyway, she just called up to me and said Parker is barfing but don't worry. He's almost done barfing."

"Shoot," I mutter, feeling utterly helpless.

"I've got a view of the bathroom door from here, Dad," she says, then like a play-by-play announcer, she narrates what's happening downstairs. "Oh my god, Sabrina is so strong. She's carrying him across the hallway and back to the living room."

My throat tightens with emotions as I picture her taking care of my little guy. "Tell Sabrina to call when she can," I say gently. "I love you, Luna."

"Love you too, Dad."

A little later, as I'm walking back to the hotel in the rain, every cell in my body on high alert, my phone rings once more. It's Sabrina, and I answer it immediately. "Hey, how's it going?"

"He's okay. I think he feels better now that he's thrown up a little bit. He's actually curled up under a blanket on the couch right next to me, sound asleep. Oh, and Drama is right here with him too. She's purring on his neck. It's okay that she's here? In the house?"

"Of course," I say instantly.

"She has to go back next week to Little Friends. For her final vaccine and then her spay. But for now, she's being a little nurse kitten," Sabrina says, cheery and chipper, like she's trying to make me feel better about Parker being sick.

"Does he need to go see a doctor? Does he need anything? Do you need anything? Some meds? Cough syrup? Dinner? I can send you all that right away. An appointment at the doctor?" I hope she says yes to something, anything.

"Actually, we went to urgent care when I picked him up from school. They had an appointment right away, and that's when they said it's probably a twenty-four-hour bug. I texted you as soon as we left urgent care."

"Oh," I say, stopping under the awning at the hotel. Parker's the kind of kid who rarely gets sick, and on the odd occasions he has, I've always been around. I never felt more useless in my life. Or more grateful. "Thank you for doing that."

"They said there's really nothing to give him. It's just a virus, but it tends to run its course pretty quickly," she says.

"Can I get you something? Something for dinner? I don't want you to think about cooking or even zapping anything in the microwave right now."

"I'm sure there's some food in the house," she says. In the background, a voice calls out, "Dad, I love those sand-wiches from Happy Cow."

I laugh.

Sabrina does too. "Luna won't venture downstairs, but she sure doesn't miss a thing," she says with a laugh.

And it feels like we're sharing a smile over the way we know my daughter so well.

I go ahead and I place an order for some sandwiches and some Gatorade, and then some crackers for when Parker is feeling better. I send a note along too—just for Sabrina.

I can't tell you how much it means to me to know you're there.

—T

Then I try not to gnaw my leg off with worry.

* * *

I do my best to put my worries out of mind as we battle Seattle in a rough, physical game the next day, jostling for control of the puck every second it seems. I'm slammed into the boards nearly as many times as I shove the team around. But we trudge off the ice with a hard-fought win, and as soon as I'm in the visitors' locker room, I text Sabrina.

Tyler: How is he? How's Luna? How are you?

Sabrina: Parker stayed home today, of course, but he's doing so much better! No more barfing, and he's been fever-free without meds for nearly twenty-four hours, so that's good!

My shoulders relax.

Tyler: Thank god. And Luna?

Sabrina: That girl has some serious germ avoidance skills! She's practically sealed herself in a bubble since yesterday. She's all good.

I breathe a huge sigh of relief as I sink down on the bench in front of my stall.

Tyler: Thank you so much for taking good care of him.

Sabrina: It's the job. Glad I could do it!

I wince at those two words—*the job*. It's the truth. Of course it's the job. But it's a reminder, too, that I have my work cut out for me. I made her feel like she's only my employee. I'll need to show her when I return home that she's so much more, even if it's not the time to articulate exactly how much. For now though, I shower, put on my suit, and head to the jet, grateful this was a short trip and I'm on my way home.

We land in San Francisco in the evening and I jump into my car and drive home. But when I pull into the garage, I spot my mother's car parked on the curb. I check the time. It's nearly nine. That's odd. I didn't think she'd be here at this hour. It's a little late for a pop-in.

I go inside, head up the steps to the first level, and run right into them at the front door. "You've got everything," my mother says to Luna and Parker as they hoist their bags onto their shoulders. "So we should be all set. And you can play with all the dogs tonight at my house."

She looks up at me with a smile. "Oh, hi, sweetheart. How are you?"

"I'm fine, but what's going on?"

Parker looks great, his eyes bright, his cheeks rosy. He flings himself at me. "Dad! I'm all better."

"I heard," I say, giving him a big hug. Then I do the same for Luna, but that still doesn't answer the question of why they're taking off right now.

"Sabrina texted me," my mother begins. "She's not feeling so great. So I came over to collect my babies, and I'll get them to school tomorrow. I didn't want Sabrina to worry about making sure they got to bed on time and having to make them breakfast, and she needs to rest herself," my mom says, going into full mom mode and grandma mode too.

My muscles tighten and I'm antsy to check on Sabrina as soon as I can, but I give my kids a kiss and a hug, and we chat a moment before they leave.

The second the door is locked I march downstairs and knock on Sabrina's door. "Are you okay? Can I come in?"

"Go for it," she says weakly. The door's not locked, so I open it, and my heart stops. She's curled up under the blanket on the couch, her face pale, her blonde hair a wild mess and falling out of a half-made bun. She looks both beautiful and tragic, cocooned with a kitten in her arms.

"Hey, baby," I say, and I close the distance, sitting right next to her.

She pushes a hand out from under the blanket, trying to stop me. "Don't get too close," she says, her voice cracking like Parker's was yesterday. She tugs the blanket up higher over her mouth and coughs into it. When she stops a second or two later, she says, "Go. Save yourself while you still can."

I smile. "I'm not scared," I say. Then I touch her forehead. She's burning up. "Sweetheart, did you take any Tylenol?"

She shakes her head. "Not one hundred two."

"I bet it is." I hunt around for the thermometer, but I

don't spot it on the coffee table or anywhere in her living room.

She points weakly toward the stairs. "It's upstairs. Kitchen."

And that's that. I scoop her up, blanket, kitten and all, locking her door on the way out, and carry her toward the main living room, Drama meowing dramatically of course as I go.

"Tyler," Sabrina says, but her protest is half-hearted. "You can't carry me upstairs."

"I can and I am," I say.

"I'll be fine," she says, as I round the corner to the living room, heading straight for the couch.

"You'll be fine because I'm going to take care of you," I say, in a firm, clear voice.

Her shoulders curl inward. "But I'm gross."

"You're not gross."

She coughs into her elbow as I set her down. "I'm gross."

I laugh. "Hush, baby."

I set her gently on the couch and Drama readjusts herself, giving me a slightly haughty look like she can't believe I've dragged her two-and-a-half-pound cuteness upstairs. Sabrina clutches the tuxedo kitten a little more tightly. I head to the kitchen, find the thermometer on the counter there, then return and quickly scan her forehead.

I shake my head, tsking her. "You're one hundred two. You're getting some medicine."

She pouts but nods. I give her Tylenol, pour some Gatorade, and hold the cup for her as she sits up and drinks from it. She doesn't drink that much, so I say, "A little more."

She takes another sip of the cherry-flavored drink, then hands it back to me.

But I give it back to her. "You need to get liquids inside you, baby," I say.

She sighs then drinks some more.

"Now you need to rest," I tell her. She settles into the couch, but I shake my head and once more I scoop her up along with the kitten, and I carry her up the stairs again.

"Tyler, why are you taking me up here?"

"Because you're sick, and you need the emperor bed."

She rests her head against my chest and that feels like exactly where she should be.

* * *

She falls asleep in my bed, tucked under her blanket and my cover, with Drama curling up on top of the pillow. I change out of my suit into basketball shorts and a hoodie and check on Sabrina constantly, making sure she's comfortable and not burning up. She coughs faintly a few times but doesn't wake. The lights are low and I'm sitting in a chair, reading on my tablet.

Her eyes flutter open around ten-thirty and she stares at me, a little confused. Then says, "Where am I?"

"My room, baby."

"Where are the kids?"

"With my mom. They're spending the night there."

She nods, a sign she's remembered everything. She pushes up and swings her legs out of bed. "I have to pee."

I'm up and out of the chair in no time, offering her a hand.

"I can stand," she says weakly.

"I know, but let me help you," I say with my hand still

held out. She takes it and I walk with her to the bathroom door, then leave her be.

She shuts the door, and a few minutes later, trudges back to bed. I help her into it. She shivers a little, and I check her temperature again. "You're one hundred one. That's good," I tell her. "Can you drink some more Gatorade?"

"Maybe," she says.

I grab a water bottle that I already filled with the cherry drink. "Your favorite flavor."

"A Popsicle might be good," she says, with the tiniest tease in her voice, and that makes me smile over the memory of the Popsicle and the fact that she can make a joke right now.

"If you want a Popsicle, I'll get you one," I say.

"Maybe later," she says, then takes the water bottle and drinks more. She hands it to me and I set it down on the nightstand.

Drama stretches her way across the bed, padding closer to Sabrina.

"Do you want to go back to sleep?" I ask.

She shrugs, but then says, "I don't think I'm sleepy right yet. Maybe I'll watch something."

"What do you want to watch?" I say, then I don't give her a chance to turn me down. I hop into bed right next to her.

She stares at me like I'm losing it, shirking away. "You shouldn't get that close. You might die."

I laugh. "I'm not going to die."

"I really don't want to get you sick."

"I'm pretty tough."

"There's a difference between this virus and someone trying to beat you up with a hockey stick."

"You're right. I'm not going to lose my teeth here," I say.

"Tyler," she says. She's so tough but the thing is, I'm immovable in this regard.

"I'm going to be fine. You can't stop me. Best to just give in."

She sighs, acquiescing, then says, "You want to watch some skating?"

I smile. "A woman after my own heart."

Then I hunt through the Chromecast and I find some old skating videos. We watch together, pointing out triple loops and axles, camel spins and twizzles, and oohing and aahing over the jumps.

When she yawns, I say, "Do you want to try to go to sleep again?"

She nods, so I turn off the TV and dim the lights a little more, checking her temperature once again. She's one hundred one, but that's good. She's not getting worse.

I help her settle into the covers, gently take the hair tie from her half-bun, and stroke her hair. "Do you need anything else?"

She shakes her head.

"Sabrina," I say, since I haven't said I'm sorry yet and really, I need to.

"Yes," she says softly.

"I'm sorry," I say, blurting it out.

She's quiet for a beat, then she says, "S'okay."

I keep stroking her hair as I speak. "I'm sorry about the other day. I handled it badly. This is all new to me. The way I feel for you and balancing it all, and I should have done a better job. I just want you to know that, and I want you to come with me. With us. If you want to. I want you to come...just because I want you there," I say, my heart jumping around as I think about taking her to New York.

But when I look down at her again, she's fast asleep and probably has been for the last few minutes. I tuck the blanket tightly around her and drop a kiss to her warm forehead.

Tonight is for healing, not exoneration.

35

—————

PRETEND I NEVER SAID AVOCADO

Sabrina

It's a new day, and the sun streams through the windows, bright and, mostly, welcome.

With a deep sigh I push myself up in bed, blinking, orienting myself. I look down at the sage green cover, the dark gray pillows. At the spacious bed. At the huge en suite bathroom. This room is so...not mine.

Oh. Right. I sit up. Rub my eyes. Scan my surroundings. On the navy blue chair—the same chair where Tyler sat last night and read on his tablet—is a neatly folded sweatshirt.

I swing my legs out of bed, taking my time to gauge how I'm feeling. The verdict? Surprisingly good.

I stand. Wow. Is this what it feels like to be normal again?

My head doesn't hurt. I don't feel hot all over. I'm not really achy anymore. I'm still a little tired though, and my breath is foul.

I need to go downstairs and brush my teeth, but when I look more closely at the chair, my heart squeezes. Underneath the hoodie is a pair of leggings—my leggings—and in front of them, a white card. Something warm and hazy runs through my bloodstream.

Tyler and his notes.

There's also some white panties and a sports bra too. A stupid smile spreads as I unfold the note.

Hi.

Hope you feel better. You slept all night. Okay. Not the WHOLE night. You woke up once in the middle of the night and we had a very brief conversation, but I promise you only divulged your social security number and all your bank account information. In any case, if I'm not here, it's because I went downstairs to change the cat litter and feed the kitten— like Drama would let me do anything else. She's demanding. Also, I did grab some clothes for you in the middle of the night in case you want to shower. I left out a toothbrush on the bathroom counter too. Since I know you're obsessed with minty breath. And I shut the door in case you just want to spend the day in bed doing none of those things.

But if you're up for food, I'm ordering some bagels right now since I know you love those.

With avocado.

Unless the thought of avocado makes you want to hurl. In which case, pretend I never said avocado.

—T

My heart swells even more. I do love bagels so much. I also want to feel human again so I head straight for Tyler's spacious rainfall shower and indulge.

When I'm out of the shower, I pull on the fresh clothes, towel-dry my hair, then twist it into a makeshift bun since he left my hair tie on the counter for me.

Of course he did.

I pad downstairs still feeling a little tired and slow but mostly better. When I reach the first level, the faint sounds of a familiar song drift from the kitchen. It's Camden, the pop singer, and her bold, brassy voice is like a calling card that tells me Tyler's in there.

I feel weirdly...shy.

Having him see me like that last night was uncomfortable.

I walk into the kitchen, where he's putting something in the fridge. I stop at the island. When he turns around, the fridge door shutting, his hazel eyes light up. He gives me the warmest smile. "Hey."

"Hi."

"Are you feeling any better?"

"Yes," I say, then quickly amend it to "mostly." I shift gears since I don't like talking about how I feel. "How's Parker?"

A smile shifts his lips. "All better. I talked to my mom. He's back at school, and Luna too, of course. She never caught it."

"Good. That's a relief. Thank you for everything." Then I'm quiet for several seconds, weighing how far to go. But he carried me upstairs and gave me meds and Gatorade, and watched skating videos and left out clothes for me. I swallow down my pride. "I hate being sick."

His eyes soften, and he gives a gentle nod. "I had a feeling. But it's okay, Sabrina. It happens to everyone."

"But I don't like it when it happens to me," I say, with maybe a pout.

"Well, no one does."

"I know. I just really don't like it," I say, and he seems to sense I'm not whining. I'm actually admitting something hard.

He takes a step closer to me. "Because you're afraid of not being perfect."

It's said gently, like a soft gust of wind through a window that flutters open the pages of a book, revealing a twist in the story you didn't see coming. The twist is that he's figured me out. The thing I usually try to hide behind doing too much, being everything, trying hard.

"Maybe," I say softly, crossing my arms over my chest, like I'm hugging myself. "Probably."

Tyler looks like he wants to reach for me, to wrap me in his arms, and I wouldn't object. But instead he says, "It's okay. You don't have to be the super nanny. You don't have to be super Sabrina. It's okay to be you. And I really wanted to be there for you. To take care of you."

My throat tightens so hard, so uncomfortably, I can feel tears building in the back of my eyes. I fight them off. "Well, thank you," I say. Then I say one more hard thing. "I guess I'm not used to it."

"I'm going to go out on a limb and say Chad never took care of you?" Tyler doesn't sound bitter or angry at him—just matter of fact, like he knows that's what Chad would've been like.

"He's not really a caretaker."

"And I'm guessing your parents weren't either?"

A mirthless laugh falls from my lips. "You'd be right."

"I'm glad it was me last night then," he says, "because I'm not like that."

I wince, but it's not because what he said was painful. It's because the past still aches. The way I grew up still hurts. Because the armor I had to wear doesn't always shield you when you're sick, when you're vulnerable, when you can't do everything. But it's hard to linger in this conversation. "What about you? Are you worried about getting sick? Or are you an ox?"

He flexes a big arm. "Ox, baby, ox."

It's like he knew I needed a little teasing to break up the serious moment, but my mind latches onto that word again—*baby*. The way he says it so easily, the way he's saying it...again. I hang on to the sweetness of his tone too.

I still don't know what's happening between us. But maybe that's okay. "Well, Mister Ox. Where's the little Drama queen?"

"Shockingly, she's sound asleep. In your apartment," he says, then he adds, "I hope you didn't mind me going downstairs to your place and getting some things."

That raises a good point. "How did you get in there? I don't mind but I'm curious."

"You gave me the code. In the middle of the night. I asked if I could get some things for you."

I laugh. "I don't remember that at all."

"You were pretty sleepy. You're cute when you're sleepy. And you're cute when you're sick."

I growl, wiggling a finger his way. "Now that's taking it too far, you ox."

He holds up his hands in surrender, then gestures toward the counter where he's taken out a cutting board, and left some bagels and avocado. "Can I make you a bagel?"

I set a hand on my belly, and it's rumbling. "You know, I think I am hungry. But let's pretend you never said avocado."

"I never said avocado."

He slices the bagel and toasts it. And I take this care-taking for what it is.

Care.

Care given freely. Without expectation of perfor-mance. Without the requirement of excellence. It's just care, and maybe I don't have to figure out what this thing between us is all the time. Maybe I can simply accept it as something new and lovely in my life.

And I like new and lovely a lot.

When I'm halfway done with the bagel, he clears his throat. "Sabrina," he says, and he sounds serious.

I tense. A Pavlovian reaction. Something tough is coming.

But then his lips curve up like he has a secret. "I called Trevyn the other day. I hope it wasn't too presumptuous, but I really needed his help with something."

He hands me another note card.

Sabrina,

I should have done this a while ago. I should have asked if you had plans for the holiday. I didn't and I'm sorry. And I should have said something, too, the last morning we spent together. I'm sorry for not figuring it out sooner.

A lot of this—well, all of this—is new to me. So I'm not sure I'm so good at figuring any of this out. And I don't even know if you've already made Christmas plans with your friends. If you have, I understand. But Trevyn said he thought you were still free. And I just can't imagine taking the kids to see Ice Spectacle *in New York without you since I know you wanted to go too.*

I'm not asking you to babysit. I'm not asking you to work. I'm just asking you to go...with us.

—T

* * *

Luna makes an announcement after school a few days later. "Since we're not going to be here for Christmas, we should gather all the toys we don't use and clothes, too, and donate them, instead of getting a tree."

"We talked about how to help others in my classes too," Parker puts in. "Maybe we can get gift cards for unhoused families and donate them too. A lot of shelters have holiday giving programs."

And I fall even harder for these kids. "Just check with your dad," I say, fighting off a lump in my throat.

Tyler doesn't need to be asked twice. He says yes and helps the kids gather items that afternoon. After we drop off some donations at a local shelter, we pop into its secondhand shop and pick up some gently used garlands and a wreath too, and decorate the house that way, as Parker discusses the science of Santa with his father, and Drama plays with a few stray ribbons.

It feels like a new tradition, but I don't want to get too attached to it. It's like fostering. You give the animals so much love for a short time, knowing you're only a stop along the way.

And that's okay.

We return Drama to Little Friends the next day. That was always the plan—to take care of her until she was big enough to be spayed and fully vaccinated.

Still, Luna pouts, and Parker's lower lip quivers as we walk into the animal rescue in the heart of the city. A little pink crate swings in Luna's hand. Inside, a tuxedo kitten is curled up peacefully on a blanket.

I spot Nia quickly. With a shirt that reads *I Work For My Cat* and flower tattoos winding down her bronze skin, she's hard to miss. She's microchipping a little silver tabby at an exam table in the cat wing, but she looks up and sees us, finishes popping the chip in, hands the animal to a volunteer, and turns in our direction.

Once she peers in the crate, she says approvingly, "She looks a little chunkier."

"She sure is," I say, handing the kitty over.

"Aww, we're going to have people lining up for you," Nia coos, scratching Drama's chin as she opens the crate.

The kitten happily accepts the adulation, purring louder as Nia cradles her.

But when I glance at the Falcon kids, my heart squeezes. Their frowns dig deeper into their cheeks. My chest aches for them. I've fostered before—many times. You grow attached, but you learn to let go so you can keep helping.

These kids though? It's their first time. I kneel so I'm closer to eye level. "I know you'll miss her," I say gently, one hand on Parker's arm, the other on Luna's shoulder. "But she's going to find an amazing family, and when she does, do you know what that means?"

Parker sniffs, valiantly fighting off tears. "What does it mean?"

"It means we can keep fostering. The more we foster, the more stray animals we can help find homes. Every time we open our home to another foster, we're giving an animal a second chance."

"It helps so much," Nia adds with a sage nod. "We always need fosters. So, so badly."

Luna octopuses her arms around me. "I want to keep saving lives."

"Me too," Parker says, his voice wobbly but determined.

I glance at Tyler, who's standing as stoically as possible by the cat cages. His jaw is tight but his eyes are a little wet. He strides over to Drama, scoops her up, and presses a soft kiss to her tiny head.

It's not really goodbye.

It's the start of a new hello—with a new family, whoever they might be.

36

MEOWY FRIENDSMAS

Sabrina

Tiffany barely says hello when she arrives at the rink for her lesson on a Sunday afternoon. "I want to learn the bunny hop," she declares as she hangs over the boards, waving her phone at me, cued up to YouTube. "Look!"

I know both how to do a bunny hop and teach it, but still, I skate over to her to watch the video she's tracked down. A minute later, her mother catches up. She's a few paces behind Tiffany since it's hard to keep up with the busy girl.

"That's an intermediate move but we can work toward that," I tell my student. "How does that sound?"

Tiffany sighs, like she's so put out, but then she nods excitedly. "Yes, please!" She peers at the video again. "Wait. Mom, that's *your* account on my phone. Were you watching YouTube on my phone? Last time you watched all those Ukrainian TV shows." Tiffany doesn't sound accusatory so much as curious.

Her mom gives a small, proud shrug. "They remind me of home."

And I think I know what's going on here. "Ms. Kovalenko. Do you want to take a lesson someday?"

"Mom! Do it, do it, do it," Tiffany encourages.

"Perhaps," her mom says, and it feels like she's one step closer than the last time she said *maybe*.

I seize the chance: "I'd love to put together some intro moves just for you. Think about it."

"I am," she says.

And I hold on to that bit of progress as I teach her daughter some backward wiggles, then spend the rest of the afternoon with other students.

* * *

That evening I'm exhausted from coaching all day, but it's a good kind of exhausted. Mostly, I'm energized at the thought of seeing my friends tonight since it's time for Friendsmas. Isla, Miss Christmas herself, is hosting at her house.

After I tug on a thrifted Christmas sweater—it has a gold sequined cat wearing a red scarf with actual jingle bells and the words *Meowy Christmas* under the animal—I head to her home.

The kids are with Elle, but I'll pick them up bright and early tomorrow for the flight across the country.

No need for them to fly as unaccompanied minors since I'll be with them now—Tyler worked with Elle to rebook all the tickets, and since he played in Montreal the other night, we'll meet him in the city tomorrow. But I put the trip out of my mind as I knock on Isla's door. She swings it open, and a sonic blast of Sia's "Candy Cane Lane" hits me.

"And a *Meowy Christmas* to you too," she sings, then hustles me inside. "Also, excellent work on the ugly sweater."

"I take issue with the word *ugly*. I think this is quite fabulous," I say, flicking a bell a few times, adding a little tinkling harmony to the soundtrack.

"Wear it in June, then," Trevyn shouts from the living room as he scratches Barbara-dor behind her reindeer ears.

"Um, June is hot."

"Not in San Francisco," Leighton calls out as she sets a tray of mixed nuts on the table.

Maeve swoops in from the kitchen. "Did someone say mixed nuts?"

She grabs a couple and pops them in her mouth, and I set the gifts on the table, then hug everyone.

Skylar's here too, and so are Everly and Josie—they wave from the kitchen as they mix drinks. Spiked hot cocoa, I think.

Or really, I hope.

Soon, we're all huddled in Isla's living room, the lights of the tree twinkling, laughing and toasting to the holidays.

When Isla snaps her gaze to me with a pointed look, I know I'm about to get a friendly grilling. "So, word on the street is you're ditching us for the hot boss you have a sex diary with."

I blush. I mean, they all know what's going on, but still, I'm not sure anything's going to happen with Tyler in New York. Nothing *has* happened for a while anyway, with his travel and me getting sick and our...argument?

Yes, it was an argument. A temporary estrangement, really. One that—Shoot, I need to answer my friends.

"It *is* true, but I am not ditching you," I say, then gesture to myself. "Hello. I'm here right now."

"True, but I'm pretty sure you were pretending you were busy with us when you needed to get out of things with him," Trevyn points out.

"I hate you," I tell him.

"Sorry. Not sorry. But it was impressive finagling," Trevyn adds since he knows how I used my friends as a cover-up.

"Did you use us as a shield?" Josie asks salaciously, leaning forward in the chair. "I love that. We were like your secret excuse."

"And why does that thrill you?" Everly asks her.

"Because it kind of makes me feel like we're enabling this clandestine love affair. Like you had with Max," Josie says to the team publicist. Then, to Leighton, "And you with Miles."

"And you *kind of* with Wesley," Maeve counters, then adds saucily as she plucks a cashew from the bowl, "but *I* was not clandestine. Mine was simple and splashed all over socials."

"Oh please, you were complicated in the most Maeve-ian way," Josie says.

Maeve just flicks her hair off her shoulder, owning it. "Of course I was."

Skylar clears her throat. "And now, Sabrina? Now it's not forbidden with Tyler?"

I wince. I don't know what it *is* other than...*good luck with, well, everything.*

"I honestly don't know." I sigh, but then brighten. "But I'm trying to be okay with that. You know what I mean?"

The mood turns serious for a moment, not surprising since the tune does too, with *Please Come Home for Christmas* now playing.

"That makes sense," Isla says thoughtfully. "Sometimes relationships have to live in the in-between before you can figure out what's next."

"The in-between," Leighton says thoughtfully. "I spent a lot of time there with Miles."

Everly raises a hand. "Same here. You don't always get to the other side until you've made it through the in-between."

"And on that festive note, let's open some presents," Trevyn says.

"Yes, let's do that," I say, eager to move on to something certain, something knowable—friendship.

And when the night ends, Isla says, "Have fun in New York with your..."

She stops, clearly not knowing what to call Tyler.

I don't either.

* * *

The flight takes off in the morning, with the kids settled into their comfy seats in the first row. I relax into my big seat right across from them. As the plane climbs higher, I scroll through pictures of Drama with her new family. A couple adopted her—two young moms who have two young kids. They've been posting pictures of the kitten on their social media, dubbing themselves *Cat Ladies With Kids Too.*

I heart the pics, then turn off my phone and stare out the window as the plane hurtles across the country for the holidays.

It's a little surreal—six months ago, I was wearing a wedding dress and running away from a gaslighting ex and a mean father, straight into the arms of a hockey star.

Now I'm flying toward him. To spend Christmas with him and his kids.

Life moves fast when you least expect it.

Even though I still don't know what to call Tyler in this in-between state.

I wish myself luck and hope I'll figure it out soon.

That evening, we drop our bags off in Tyler's suite at The Luxe Hotel on Fifth Avenue with a decadent view of Central Park. He booked it for all of us, and I have an adjoining room because...appearances. We don't want to confuse the kids, after all.

After they brush their teeth, I hustle them to the street to catch the town car Tyler ordered for us to take us to his game against the tough New York team.

The city is a blur of holiday lights and bustling sidewalks full of last-minute shoppers, but all I can think about is how this doesn't feel like just a work trip.

It feels like a...

I stop myself from thinking the words *family vacation* too much. This is just...all of us hanging out.

No need for labels.

And when I think of how close I was to saying *I do* just a little while ago, but for an accidental voice message, this uncertainty is a good thing.

It has to be.

We reach the arena, where the energy for the last game before Christmas is electric. The crowd is rowdy since New York fans always bring their A-game when it comes to support.

But so do I. I'm bedazzled, after all, in my number forty-four jersey.

And when the sexiest, most caring man I know flies onto the ice, he turns to our side of the rink and makes a heart gesture for the kids.

Then his eyes travel to me.

And stay there.

My breath catches. My chest flutters.

I still don't know what to do with all of these feelings. Especially since I keep wondering what it's going to be like later tonight when we're in the same hotel suite, him and the kids and me.

* * *

The answer?

It's hard. Really hard.

Especially since I'm here all alone in my hotel bed, reading, and wishing—in this moment—that things were more clear.

At least in my head. I wish I knew what I wanted. What I'm ready for. What I can handle. I just don't know yet. So much has changed in my life in the last several months.

Am I even ready for...anything more?

I turn off the lights, willing myself to sleep.

Then comes the knock on the adjoining door.

37

SOMETHING ELSE TOO

Tyler

It's been too long.

The need to touch her is like a heavy weight on my chest. Like claws in my heart.

I've already put the kids to bed in the suite I'm sharing with them—that wasn't hard. They were zonked after a late hockey game, yawning on the car ride back. Once in their jammies, they both collapsed into the big bed in their room, crashing fast and hard with me only reading a few sentences from *The Peppermint Patrol*—Luna's pick, and Parker didn't even protest.

With the lights out, I paced around the suite like a caged animal, shoveling a hand through my hair until I couldn't wait any longer to see Sabrina. Now, just five minutes later, I'm here, slipping away from them because I have to act.

I've got to touch her.

I need her.

This is dangerous. I can't be the guy who leaves his young kids alone to sneak around for a quickie with the nanny next door.

And yet, I can't tear my gaze away from her in the faint light of her hotel room. A soft night-light glows by the bed. Her tablet sits on the covers. She was probably reading before she answered my knock. City lights glimmer in the window. The sounds of a New York night—faint honking, a siren somewhere in the distance—remind me that this is a city that never sleeps. Sabrina stands right in front of me, loose blonde hair curling over the straps of a light blue cami. She wears pajama pants and fuzzy socks with foxes on them, and this detail—her love of foxes—does unfair things to my heart.

"Hi," I say softly, my fingers itching to touch her, my palms eager to slide up and down those bare arms, to feel her skin. To see her shiver as I touch her. Hell, I feel like I'm shivering just from looking at her.

"Hey, you," she says.

The sound of her voice makes my pulse soar. I'm so far gone.

"I had to see you." That feels like the truest thing I've ever said.

"Yeah?" A smile teases me at the corner of her lips.

"On the car ride back from the arena? I was dying to reach across the seats and hold your hand," I say.

Her smile widens. "I wanted that too."

More confessions pour out. "On the elevator ride up here? The four of us?"

She nods for me to keep going.

"Same thing. I just wanted to wrap my arm around you. Bring you to my side. Hold you."

Her blue eyes dance. "I could feel it—you wanting that."

I am so transparent, and I don't mind at all. "And then when you went into your room, and I went into ours, I just felt anticipation climbing through me," I say, and at last, at long last, the weight is lifting. I needed to say all this. I can't keep it to myself anymore.

She takes a step closer, and her scent swirls around me —that orange blossom perfume. I thought it was her candles, but it has to be her lotion too. Another detail about her I file away.

"So what are you going to do about that?" she asks.

That's the question, isn't it? The million-dollar one I keep asking myself. It's a question I've been asking myself since I left her that note card back in San Francisco. Since I booked the tickets for her and rebooked the ones for my kids. Now that she's here, I keep thinking—this woman flew with my children across the country to spend Christmas with us.

Us.

What was I thinking when I didn't want to define this? I need to define this fast. I can't leave this open-ended. I can't just go with the flow. That's not fair to her. And it's definitely not fair to this too-tight, too-big feeling in my chest.

Briefly, I think of the text Corbin sent me earlier, and a plan begins to form.

But before I fuck-up again by saying the wrong thing or saying nothing, I shut my mouth—by sealing it to hers. And all is right in the world as we connect again.

I slant my lips to her soft, sweet mouth, groaning at the taste of her minty breath. My Sabrina loves her toothpaste. The more spearmint-y the better, and I love knowing this detail about her. I love knowing all the things about her. Her affection for foxes and for rescue animals. Her love of bagels. Her soft spot for shiny objects. Her need to keep lists and the way she tempers it by keeping good lists. Her love of skating and her bigger love of the joy in the sport. Her strength in standing up to her family and her boundless spirit in making every day fun for my kids. How she teaches them about Earth, and giving back. The way she cares for them. And for me.

As all of this knowledge swirls in my head, I kiss her more fervently, her body molding to mine, her heart beating against my chest, and I know something else too.

These sparks I feel?

This intensity that has me hostage?

This clawing feeling that consumes my chest, my cells, my bones? This unfamiliar emotion that's swallowing me whole?

I'm falling in love with the nanny.

I groan into her mouth, tugging her impossibly closer, wanting to gather her in my arms, to haul her up, have her wrap her legs around my waist. But the weight of responsibility in the next room bears down on me. I can't fuck her in the adjoining room, even with the kids out for the count. Besides, they just fell asleep. They might wake up.

But I can do something else.

I break the kiss, panting hard. Her breath is coming in staggered gusts too. She's clutching my shirt like she doesn't want to let go.

And the plan is fully formed. "Corbin is in New York," I begin.

Her brow knits. "Yeah?"

"He's from here. His family is here. He texted earlier to

invite the kids to Christmas cookie decorating tomorrow afternoon with his family."

Her lips twitch, but she waits for me to say more.

"We can have some time alone," I say, the words spilling out now. Tumbling on top of each other. But the last thing I want is for her to think I'm asking her for another sex date. I cup her face, hold her gaze. "Let me take you on that ice-skating date in the afternoon."

She twists her fingers tighter around the collar of my shirt. "I can't wait to skate circles around you, Falcon."

I tip my head back and laugh.

Forget falling. I'm already there.

I drop a kiss to her lips. "It is on."

* * *

The massive Christmas tree looms over the ice rink, festooned with ornaments and the sparkling lights that flicked on before dawn. It's noon right now, so they're soft but still visible. The sun is shining brightly above us at the packed rink at Rockefeller Center.

No surprise—it's Christmas Eve, but I snagged some last-minute tickets for a slot on the ice.

Now, with hordes of tourists and New Yorkers—some wobbling, some whizzing by—Sabrina skates backward, showing off gorgeous crossovers as I skate toward her, unable to take my eyes off the figure-skating beauty.

"Come on! You challenged me to a skills competition that night in Cozy Valley." She wiggles her mittened fingers toward me. "Let's see what you've got."

"The taunting," I say. "The taunting."

But I can handle my own on blades, thank you very

much. I spin around and skate backward right past her, then come to a fast hockey stop, spraying ice.

"Show-off," she teases, and I push off, skating around with her, but then I stop in my tracks. A young couple wobbles nearby. I grab Sabrina even though she probably has noticed them too. But I yank her against me regardless.

"That's the thing about a big public rink—it's not the best place for a skills competition," I say.

She rolls her eyes and swats my chest with her mittened hand. "Oh, please, you just don't want to admit I'm faster," she teases.

I drop a kiss on her nose, overwhelmed briefly by how much I want this. These dates, these moments, this time with her. And I'm about to toss out a witty comeback, like *let's do it again when we get back home*, when the wobbly guy gets down on one knee.

"Oh," I say, blinking.

Sabrina gasps. "Oh my god."

The man takes out a small velvet box from his jacket pocket, and the woman's nodding, smiling, giving her *yes*. Sabrina claps and cheers, and I join in too.

"Congrats," I say to both of them.

They smile back.

When the woman tugs him up and they kiss on the ice, we resume our pace, passing them as Sabrina calls out, "Congratulations."

As we loop around the rink, she says to me, "Let's hope it all works out."

I'm quiet for a beat.

It's a stark reminder that romance usually starts with the best of intentions. A date at a skating rink. A football game. Nights cuddled up together. But it can end like it did for Sabrina—in infidelity, humiliation, and estrangement from her family. And for me, it can fizzle out into two people who are better off as friends.

But maybe it doesn't always have to go wrong. Maybe sometimes, two people can figure it out.

Maybe I can too, and that starts with focusing on the here and now. On this holiday. On this date. On this time with her. Now is not the time to think too hard about the future.

I take her hand, pull her close, and as I skate with her, I say, "Would you do something for me?"

She arches a curious brow. "Maybe?"

"Do a camel spin."

She laughs, shaking her head. "You really do have a thing for figure skaters."

"No. I have a thing for you. And I fucking love watching you skate for me."

She bobs her shoulder, lets go of my hand, and glides effortlessly to an open spot in the middle of the rink, where she leans forward, lifting her right leg behind her. Then she spins around and around, her arms out wide, her face bright, her smile shining.

When she's done, I'm not the only one clapping for her. But I'm the only one she skates over to.

I take her hand once more.

So what if we don't know what the future holds? I know what this moment holds. *Her and me, finally going out together.*

I tug off her mitten, stuff it in my jacket pocket, and curl my fingers through hers as we skate round and round together. Even if the future is murky, the present is perfect.

When our session is done, our skates turned in, I'm pretty sure I'm ready to ask her a big question. To finally put a name to what we are. But she grabs my wrist, checks the time, and then wiggles her eyebrows.

"Do we have time for our fourth lesson?" she asks, reminding me that it's been a while. "Because there's an item on my list. Page twenty-two. I've always wanted to have hot, up-against-the-door hotel sex."

I hail a cab so fast.

* * *

I set a timer on my watch. I make sure my phone is on. I'm not fucking up again.

Any of this. For anyone.

We have ninety minutes till we need to get to Park Slope to pick up the kids. And the second the door to her room is opened, I push Sabrina against the wall and grab her face.

"You should get everything you want," I rasp out as I kick the door closed.

She hums, flicking the tip of her tongue against the corner of her lips before her gaze drifts down my torso to my jeans. "Like your cock inside me?"

I groan, then run a finger across her bottom lip. "What a filthy mouth on such a sweet woman."

She lifts her chin. "You like it that way."

I love it that way, I correct in my head. Out loud, I say, "I absolutely fucking do."

She gives a sassy little bob of her shoulder. "Get moving, Falcon."

I kiss her hard—a punishing one for this sassy, feisty woman who deserves it. I pour all my lust, all this pent-up longing, into a searing kiss that vibrates to my very core.

Our tongues skate together as we tug off jackets, toe off boots, fumble at belts and waistbands.

But it's winter in New York, and a quickie against the door isn't easy. As we get a little tangled in layers, we laugh and break apart. I focus on sliding her leggings down her legs, trying to tug them off.

But then once I'm down here...

Well, fuck it.

I yank down her panties too, and once they're at her knees, I bury my face between her thighs.

She gasps, clearly surprised. "I thought you were going to—"

"Fuck you against the door?" I stop to ask.

"Yes."

With a cocky smirk, I look up at her. "I will, but you should know by now that I really like to eat first."

Her breath catches. A second later, she drops both hands to my shoulders and pushes me down, dragging me right against her again.

Exactly where I want to be.

My entire body heats as I lick and suck, making the most obscene sounds as I devour her sweetness on my tongue, savoring every drop of her pleasure. At the same time, I manage to help peel off her leggings the rest of the way—then her panties.

Multitasking for the win.

When she's free of both, I tap her ankle. She spreads her legs a little wider, giving me even more room. A carnal groan escapes my lips.

Yes. Fucking yes.

I eat her up, sliding my tongue through her pussy, lapping up every taste of her as my bones buzz with pleasure. She rocks against my face, seeking friction, messing up my beard in all kinds of ways, and I fucking love it.

The taste of her is all over my face.

She's moaning and groaning, and I am too. I'm grunting as I consume my woman.

And it's beautiful—so fucking beautiful—how she shudders out of nowhere, then says, "Oh, god, oh my god."

Like the orgasm surprised her.

Well, it surprised me too, as she trembles, her whole body shaking as she comes on my lips faster than she'd probably expected.

My cock throbs in my jeans, aching to visit her, but I want one more taste of her sweetness. I flick my tongue against her sensitive clit, then rise, swiping my hand across my mouth.

With her eyes a little glossy, she murmurs, "That's so sexy."

"That?" I ask, meaning my hand across my mouth.

"Yes. But the look in your eyes too."

I hold her gaze as I grip her jaw. "Know this—I fucking love eating you. For every single meal."

Her hand darts out, stroking the outline of my hard-on. "I can tell," she says in a purr.

Then a flash of nerves crosses her eyes, chased by vulnerability. "Tyler, when you said earlier I have a filthy mouth?"

"Yes?" I'm unsure where this is going.

"I want you to know—the way I talk to you...the way I touch you..."

Nerves thread in her voice, and I nod for her to keep going.

"It's you, Tyler. It's just you. You are the second guy I've been with, as you know. But when I'm with you, I feel confident. I feel free." She pauses, like she's thinking, really mulling over what to say. "And most of all, I feel safe."

My heart glows. It's like a light spreading all through my body, in every single cell. I hold her face tighter. "That's the sexiest thing you've ever said to me."

She grabs my hips and yanks me closer to her. "Get inside me."

"Okay, that's sexier."

"Also, you know I'm on protection right?"

She told me that before, but I'm picking up what she's putting down, and the sound I make is unholy. "Okay, that's the sexiest."

She pushes down my jeans and frees my aching cock, then runs her nimble hand down my shaft, sending sparks of pleasure forking through my entire body. Flames shoot through me as she strokes from base to tip and back, rubbing her thumb across the crown.

"I'm negative. What about you?"

"Me too."

Then she guides my cock toward her. But I stop. Point to the door. Move her from the wall to the door, hike up her leg, and hitch it around my hip.

Then I notch the head of my cock against her slick wetness and slide home.

Filling her all the way.

For a moment, neither one of us moves. I just stay there, trembling. Fucking trembling—my nerves frying, my circuits overloading.

Then I whisper the words that keep echoing over and over again in my head. "It's different like this," I say.

She nods savagely. "Yes, it is."

But it's not because we're bare.

It's because I know—I just *know*.

I fuck her the way she wants. Hard and fast and full of passion. But something else entirely.

This growing, soul-deep connection between the two of us is so much more than sex dates. So much more than lessons. So much more than something undefined.

It's becoming something incredibly clear to me.

I run a hand through her hair, look her in the eye as I drive deep, and I say, "Because I feel closer to you."

"Me too," she says, like her voice is breaking.

I check the clock, and we've still got time, so I tap the brakes. I fuck her in a slow, deep rhythm that I hope starts to tell her everything I'm feeling in my heart.

That I want to get closer.

That I want her to be mine.

That she makes my heart feel bigger, brighter, happier.

That I don't just want a career and happy kids.

That I want more.

That I want *her*.

And like that, with those thoughts relentlessly pressing into my mind, she comes undone once again, and I follow her.

* * *

A little later, after we've cleaned up and hopped into the town car, I can't wait any longer. I reach for her hand, clasp it in mine, and I say, "We can't keep doing this."

38

THIS LABEL

Sabrina

I freeze.

In the back of the town car, zigzagging toward Park Slope, passing last-minute shoppers rushing down the sidewalks, swinging red and white shopping bags, my body goes cold.

Is he really ending this while holding my hand as we pick up his kids? After he screwed me against the door? Is this the next about-face? I tug my hand away from him so I can raise all my drawbridges.

What was I thinking? Believing in...whatever this even is. That was so stupid. "What can't we do?" I ask, my armor on.

I'm suiting up, grabbing a shield and a sword when he reaches for my hand once more, urgently.

"I can't pretend," he says, squeezing my fingers, his voice intense. "I can't pretend this is just sex and trysts and lessons for me. It's not. I didn't want to put a label on this thing when I asked you to come here. I kept it all open-ended because of my past and your past. And I didn't want you to feel any pressure," he says, the words tumbling out in a heap, just like I laid all my confessions bare the night of my almost-wedding.

I turn my gaze toward him, mesmerized by the words falling from those gorgeous lips. "But I can't keep doing that. I just can't, Sabrina," he says.

Hope dares to poke up, like a flower bud in March. "Why is that?" I ask, trying to mask the trembling in my voice.

"Sabrina, I said it before—this is all new to me. I've never felt anything like this. It's like sparks inside me all the time," he says, and I'm shot back in time to the day he built the yoga shelves, when I asked him about Elle and he said *it didn't feel like sparks. It didn't feel like lightning.* I hold my breath because maybe this thing between us *does* feel like lightning to him. Pretty sure the crackles in my chest are a sign it's that way for me. "I'm crazy for you," he says.

And I was wrong.

He's not backing off.

He's coming closer.

It's like all the Christmas lights flickering on in the city are inside me now, like I'm powering them. Like this hope and this joy can illuminate the entire metropolitan area. And if I could tell Elena how I felt, I can do it with Tyler.

"It's the same for me," I say, grabbing his shirt collar, since I need to hold him now. I have to. And it's such a relief to tell him. It's such a relief to leave the in-between. I feel like I've shed a coat as the clouds parted and the sun broke free. "I'm crazy for you too," I add.

Tyler's smile is full of disbelief and happiness, maybe in equal parts. "Yeah?"

"Obviously," I say, my fingers twisting tighter in his shirt. But even though I love everything he's saying, and I adore the jolts I feel in my chest, there are two big questions.

Luna and Parker. "But what about the kids?" I ask, with some concern.

No, *a lot* of concern.

I let go of the hold on him so we can face this big issue.

He scrubs a hand across the back of his neck, as if he's thinking. "Do you want to tell them?"

My stomach twists. That's a huge step. We've only just walked out of the in-between. Am I ready for something that big? I've barely hit the six-months-post-failed-wedding mark. And this is the first time Tyler and I have truly talked about our feelings.

Is now the time to tell the kids?

But if I'm asking the question, the answer is no. "Probably not yet," I say gently.

He nods immediately, making it clear he's on the same page I am. "I'm not sure what I'd say yet either, to be honest. And I know this is probably a lot for you and it's all coming on quickly," he says, and once again, he sounds just like me the night of my 1001 confessions, and I love his confessions as much as I think he loved mine. "But I couldn't go another second without you knowing how I feel for you. Maybe we can figure out the details sometime in the new year, whenever you're ready. What to say, what it means, how it works, your job and the kids and... everything."

Yes, everything. Because there is so much to figure out.

"But I couldn't wait another second. And I just wanted

you to know," he says, stopping to take a breath, a necessary one. He grabs my hands again, and this time I let him. "Does this mean you're my...girlfriend?" But he laughs as soon as he says that. "I want you to be my girlfriend, but that's such a ridiculous word. Such a young word. Lover is worse. But I just couldn't pretend that I'm not thinking about you all the time, wanting all the best things for you, and needing you to be mine."

I squeeze his hands tighter, his confessions wrapping around me like the warmest embrace of my life. "Is that what you want for Christmas?"

He smiles. "You. All I want is you."

I don't know the answers to all the bigger questions either, like how we navigate this, or how we act in front of the two little people we both love, but I like this label—*his.*

"You can have me."

* * *

That night, the four of us go to the Christmas Eve show of the *Ice Spectacle*. I dress in black pants and a pink sweater with sparkly little silver threads in it, and a snowflake necklace that Tyler gives me when he slips into my room for a minute before we're about to leave.

"This is for you," he says, and he puts it on me as I hold up my hair. He kisses the back of my neck and whispers, "A snowflake for my Sabrina Snow."

We leave with Luna and Parker. We don't have to make a plan to know how to act. Intrinsically, we're on the same page. I don't want to confuse them either. My life's been so topsy-turvy and I need time to adjust to whatever this means. So Tyler and I don't hold hands in front of the kids. We don't kiss in front of them, and we don't make little inside jokes.

But after we enter the arena and take our seats right by the ice for the skating extravaganza, he stretches an arm across the back of the seats, squeezes my shoulder, and whispers, "Merry Christmas, Sabrina."

I turn to my boss, who doesn't seem like my boss right now. He seems like the man who put his heart on the line. For me. "Merry Christmas, Tyler."

And as the four of us settle in and watch the show, I feel like a new label fits.

Family.

39

WATCH ME

Tyler

It's a little like playing hooky in my house.

I pull Sabrina close to me on the couch one afternoon in early January when we're both free in the middle of the day. She's heading to pick up the kids from school in twenty minutes, right around when I'll leave for a game. For a little while, though, it's just us.

This feels like a new kind of lesson—in living together, maybe. In quiet, lazy moments. In togetherness when we can get it.

"Tell me something, Snow," I say, fiddling absently with the silver snowflake that snuggles against the soft skin of her chest. I love to touch it. To steal kisses on it when I can. To run my finger across it when no one's looking.

"Something," she says saucily.

I slide my hand down her belly. I am undeterred by her sass. "What else is on your sex list?"

She rolls her eyes and looks up at me. "Don't you have to go to work any minute?"

"I do. But I'm still asking."

"And you still get sex off-list with me," she says, then gestures to the kitchen counter, which I bent her over minutes ago—at her request—for an afternoon quickie. Well, we had a free hour. Of course, we made use of it. "You just did."

"But I love off-list sex and on-list sex. Can you blame me?"

She taps her chin, then flashes me a naughty smile. "I guess I can't."

"And I still want to work my way through your list."

We made it through those four lessons before the holidays, but finding alone time for extended romps through her checklist has been challenging since then. Shortly after we returned from New York, I had to hit the ground running and take off for a long road trip, including over to Toronto to play the Terror and to Tampa Bay to play the Ospreys. A week and a half later, I returned. But we didn't even crack open the tiny sex diary when I slipped into her room the night I landed back in town and showed her exactly how much I'd missed her.

But still, I'm dying to know what else is in that little book. "Just tell me," I whisper in her ear, then lick the shell since that always gets her. She shivers against me.

"You're trying to weaken my resolve," she says.

I flick my tongue against her again. "You like it when I weaken your resolve," I say.

"I do. But I thought you liked surprises."

"I like giving you what you want more."

She sighs heavily, but not like she's annoyed. More like she's...breaking, and I love it when Sabrina breaks. She turns around and fixes me with a serious stare. "Remember the night outside your room? When I was getting my laundry from the dryer?"

Heat flares in me. I remember it perfectly. "When you almost came in?"

She licks her lips. "Yes. You were watching the video of me," she says a little breathily. Like that turns her on. Well, it fucking turns me on too.

"And I was getting off," I add, owning it completely. My bones buzz from the memory.

"I wanted to walk in on you," she says softly.

I groan, thread a hand through her hair, and tug her face toward me. "Baby, you should have come in."

"I was so tempted, Tyler."

"Then do it sometime. It's fucking hot, the idea of you watching me. Is that really what you want?"

She nods several times, her eyes glittering with desire. Her gaze drifts down to my lap. "Wow, you really do like the idea of me walking in on you."

I grab her hand and slide it over my growing erection. I breathe out hard. "So much. Like I told you, I'll give you everything you want."

But before either of us can say another word or do another thing, her phone buzzes on the coffee table. "It might be Everly," she says, with hope in her tone. "She said they want me to do another intermission performance at an upcoming game. That could be good for business."

"I hope it's her then. Or Little Friends," I say, tempted to grab it myself. The rescue told her we'd have another foster kitten any day, and I can't wait.

"You are too cute, Cat Daddy," she says.

"Meow," I hum, and I adjust myself as she slides a

thumb across the screen.

Then she breathes out hard and mutters, "My father."

It's like a bucket of ice water. Instant deflation. "Has he even contacted you since the day you went to get your skating costumes?" I bite out, trying to hold in my venom, but it's no use.

"No. Not at all," she says heavily. Then she takes another breath but doesn't move to open the message.

I rub a hand across her shoulder. "You don't have to open it if you don't want to," I tell her.

Her eyes are hard. Determined. "It's okay. I want to know what he has to say to me."

I drop a kiss to her cheek, letting her know I'm right here with her. Then she slides it open, her jaw ticking. "He wants to know where the final accounting report is that I worked on last summer. The one I emailed to him then."

What a prick. I pinch the bridge of my nose. "I swear, Sabrina, if I ever see him..."

She turns to me, lips quirked up, like this delights her. "What would you do?"

"I'd let him know that he missed out on the most incredible person ever," I say, in no uncertain terms.

She smiles. "I almost wish you could give him a piece of your mind over text message. I think I'd like that."

"I'd go to battle for you, baby."

"I'd love to see it."

"Yeah?"

She lowers her voice, like she's sharing a secret. "It kind of excites me when you play rough—hockey, that is. So yes, I would."

Nothing would thrill me more. "You have no idea how much I love giving you what you want."

With soft eyes and softer lips, she gives me another

kiss. But then she checks the time again and says, "I need to get the kids, and you need to go to the arena."

I stand, but before we leave, something nags at me. "Are you going to answer him?"

"No. Let him search his email for that report instead."

I drop a kiss to her forehead. "You're a legend."

* * *

I'm not the only one who likes her videos though.

The next night at dinner—we all sit down together around the kitchen island to build tacos and warble the *Frozen* soundtrack off-tune—Luna clears her throat while making a snowman out of beans. "I have an idea for this weekend," she says.

"Do tell," Sabrina says, and I love how easily she fits in.

It's no surprise, of course. She takes care of the kids, but she's been spending more time with us post-New York when she's off-duty too. And each time we hang out—no touching of course—I think we're closer to telling them we're...together.

The thought worries me though. They've already had to adjust to so much—new routines, new places, new people coming and going. I don't want to create another change they have to brace for. I want them to feel stable. Certain.

"I've been watching some skating videos, and I want us to shoot one together—of Sabrina. Outside. It's so pretty when the sun is rising, and we can shoot a clip of her at an outdoor rink doing a beautiful free skate. I love those so much. The sun will reflect off the ice, and, Dad, wouldn't that be cool?"

"Did you know that ice is slippery because your skate creates a thin layer of water, which reduces friction?" Parker interjects as he builds a spaceship from shredded cheese.

"I didn't know that," I answer, then look to Sabrina, picturing her skating at dawn—the sun shining brightly as she glides across the ice, the mountains and hills framing her, the trees witnessing her glory. She's weightless, effortless, like she belongs there spinning on blades, flying through air, landing on one foot.

Yes, I love watching her videos alone at night.

But I love watching them, period.

I've always crushed on figure skating. Maybe it was because I was always waiting for *her*. "I'll be your videographer," I offer.

Sabrina's never been shy. She's never backed down. She's always gone for it, so I'm not shocked when she says, "Let's do it."

And it feels like we're not just planning for the weekend. We're building something bigger.

40

CATCH ME IF YOU CAN

Tyler

But getting the kids up before sunrise on Saturday is an ordeal. Even though one of them had the idea. Hell, *me* getting up before sunrise is a challenge. But I do it, and ten years of early mornings as a dad is good training. Still, Luna yawns and Parker grumbles as we load into my car, the sky still inky dark.

The only one with real energy is Sabrina—she's the earliest riser of us all.

"You can take the girl out of four-thirty a.m. wake-up calls, but you can't take the early bird out of the girl," she says as she slides into the front seat, caffeine-free.

Meanwhile, I need a serious jolt. I can't believe I forgot to brew coffee, but before I can even suggest swinging by a drive-thru espresso hut in the Marina, Sabrina hands me a travel mug, a tendril of steam curling from it.

Fuck, I think I love her.

"Thank you," I say, leaning in. I'm this close to dropping a chaste kiss on her lips across the console when her eyes widen—right as I come to my senses.

The kids are in the backseat. I can't kiss her in front of them.

I yank back at lightning speed, by stealing a glimpse in the rearview mirror with a guilty gulp. I hope they didn't notice my *almost* mistake, but I can't tell. Luna is still yawning, and Parker is staring at something on his phone.

"By my calculations, we have forty minutes to get there, Dad. If you go seven miles over the speed limit on the highway—"

I pull out of the garage and step on it.

Sabrina turns around and offers sliced apples to the kids, along with Rowan's homemade peanut butter to dip it in—probably a Christmas gift from Mia to Luna. That perks them up, along with the promise to snag pancakes when we're done.

Before the sun pokes its head above the horizon, we arrive at the rink in Cozy Valley. It's an outdoor rink, and I reserved it the other night. We hustle out of the car, check in, and head outside.

The thing about Cozy Valley is that it's nestled in the rolling foothills at the edge of Wine Country. Even though it's California and we don't get much snow around here, the tiny peaks are gorgeous in their nudity—no white caps, but all powerful rocks rising amidst trees still green.

It's chilly, in the high thirties, though it'll warm up soon.

Sabrina wears black leggings, and she's pulling on pink leg warmers and a white jacket—light enough for her to move freely in. We hit the rink as the kids huddle on benches.

"I'll be your backup, Dad," Luna says.

"I'll be the director," Parker adds.

"Perfect," Sabrina tells them as she laces her white skates while I tug on my black ones.

The thing is, she can shoot videos herself, using the stick and the stabilizer thingy.

But I *want* to do this for her.

I want to be the one capturing her.

We step onto the ice in this rink that looks like a frozen lake in winter. It's still and bracingly beautiful in the chilly dawn air. I've got her phone in my hand, the video settings already adjusted for movement and tracking.

"Let's do it, Snow," I tell her.

"Catch me if you can, Falcon," she says.

I want to RSVP with a *hell yes.*

An *always yes.*

She pushes off on one foot, then glides on both blades, quickly gathering speed, her blonde hair flying like a mane behind her. I keep pace with her the whole time, filming her as she moves—graceful, athletic—while the sun peeks over the horizon, peach and pink painting the morning sky.

She races backward, a blur of black and white and pink motion, shiny and strong, and I do my best to capture every crossover, every spin, every jump.

And as she builds strength and momentum, her arms widen, like she's inviting all of us into her world—of ice, of beauty, of strength, of grace, of confidence.

I can't help but think of the hand she was dealt by her family, by her ex.

But here she is.

As resilient as the morning. As strong as the ice beneath her blades.

As brave as the birds soaring past her while the sun climbs above the horizon, bringing on a new day.

When she spins—head back, arms wide—it's like she's melting into nature itself.

And I can only hope I've done this justice.

Then she finishes, and her breath comes fast as she skates over to me, cheeks rosy, face glowing. There's a look that says she's about to come in for a celebratory kiss too.

And it's my turn to hit the brakes.

I give a quick nod toward the two little kids rushing toward us on their blades.

It hurts to keep holding back.

Especially when they ask to skate with us, and the four of us take laps around the rink together.

The four of us.

This is what I want.

More than I want to have a great season. More than I want to win every game. I want to catch her and keep her. *With us.*

But how the hell I'm going to do that is still up for debate.

* * *

We meet Corbin at The Cozy Griddle, where we demolish more stacks of pancakes than I can count—most with hemp hearts and bananas, of course. When we're done, it's past nine, so the town has fully woken up.

From the other side of the booth, Corbin's daughter, Charlotte, clears her throat, straightens her spine, and says, "The way I see it, we can either go to the bookstore now, then to Hey Nice Nails for a mani-pedi, or check out the pop-up board game exhibit on Lily Lane."

"Is there really a Lily Lane here?" Sabrina asks, intrigued.

"Yes! I can show you. But first, you have to tell me which one you want to do," she says to Sabrina in a no-nonsense tone.

I turn to Corbin, laughing. I've met Charlotte before, but every time I see her, I swear she's ten times smarter.

"She's organized. What can I say? She keeps me on top of things," my friend says with a *what can you do* shrug as he pushes messy hair off his forehead.

"No doubt," I reply.

"Looks like that's a good thing," Sabrina says to him with a playful rib, fitting right in with the crew.

That makes me smile stupidly, but I wipe the grin off my face so fast.

Corbin lifts his empty coffee cup in a toast. "Sure is."

Charlotte, efficient and focused, swings her gaze to Sabrina. "You seem to be in charge. My vote is for the board game exhibit. Do you second it?"

Yup. Total take-charge kid. "As long as they have *Operation*," Sabrina says.

"Let's find out," Luna chimes in, and just like that, the kids are wiggling out of the booth, off to hunt for the next thing to do.

"Excuse me. We're not done," I point out, gesturing to the cups of coffee.

Luna waves me off. "Oh, but you seem like you're about to do the dad talk thing—blah, blah, blah, hockey. Blah, blah, blah, my back hurts. Blah, blah, blah, I can fall asleep anywhere. Last week, it was the barber."

I whistle. "Damn."

"I feel triggered," Corbin mutters.

"Looks like someone knows you both well," Sabrina

observes. Then she slides out of the booth. "I'll take them."

And just like that, she's off.

Funny how a few months ago, she would've asked if it was okay, and I would've wanted her to check in. Now? I don't need her to ask. I trust her completely with the kids. And it feels like...it feels like she's a partner.

I sit back in the dark green booth, walloped by that realization, the weight of it, the scope of it.

Corbin must notice, too, because once he confirms they're gone, he leans back, draping his arms across the booth, and gives me a knowing look. "Looks a whole lot more than you just *having it bad* for her."

I exhale, dragging a hand over my jaw. He's not wrong. "It's definitely more than that. I told her in New York I was...well, pretty much in love with her."

He jerks back, blinking. "You said the L-word?"

"Well, not yet. I said I was crazy for her. But close enough."

"Not really," he says as no-nonsense as his daughter right now. "But it's a start."

That's a fair point, I suppose. "True. But that's what I was going for. To let her know my feelings were real."

"Like I said, it's a start. A good one," he adds before he gives me a long, assessing look. "So what's next, man?"

I shrug, my chest twisting as I try to navigate the road in the dark. "I guess we tell the kids that...we're *together* together."

Corbin arches a brow. "*Together* together? That's how you're saying it?"

I scrub a hand across my beard. "You know what I mean."

"Yeah, but do *you*?" He leans forward, resting his forearms on the table. "Because telling the kids is one thing. But if this is real *real*...have you thought about what that looks like for you?"

I know what he's asking. Have I thought about where this could go? If it's long-term? Marriage again? Another ring, another house, a whole new future I wasn't planning on?

That twisting feeling intensifies, but it's not bad. I'm not afraid. I just want to do it...right. I don't want to make mistakes. Don't want to set the kids back. Don't want to promise too much too soon to anyone.

I drag a hand over my jaw, my mind zigzagging with all the next steps I'm not sure how to take. But they're ones I *want* to figure out. "I'm working on it," I say, meaning it.

"Good to hear. I'll be here for you," he says, and that's another thing I like about the move from LA—I'm close to family but close to all these new friends too.

"Appreciate it," I say, but then Corbin gets distracted as a brunette with blonde streaks in her hair, wearing jeans and a sweater with a line drawing of a slice of cake on it, walks by. No, *rushes* by. Like she's late.

"Hey, Mabel," he calls. "Did you forget to say hello?"

Mabel stops, then backtracks. For a split second, something flickers in her expression when she sees Corbin, like she didn't expect to run into him. "Sorry. There's a space I need to go check out."

"Oh sweet," he says, "let me know how it goes."

"I will, and speaking of," she says, lips curving up in a smile, "did you forget to answer my email?"

Corbin smirks. "Of course not. I'm still mulling it over."

"It's a good idea, and you know it," she teases.

I glance between them, noting the way she holds her

own but teases him too. Then I turn her name over in my head. She must be Mabel as in Mabel's Cookies. The one who did a partnership with a San Francisco ice cream shop a few months ago.

As if reading my mind, Corbin nods to me.

"Mabel, this is Tyler. He plays hockey for the second-best team in the city. Tyler, this is Mabel. My best friend's sister," Corbin says, his tone lighter now, "also known as the best baker in the world."

"Nice to meet you, Mabel," I say.

"You too," she says.

"Her cookies are the best," he adds.

Mabel lifts a shoulder and holds his gaze. "You know that sounds vaguely dirty, right?"

Corbin wiggles his eyebrows. "I do."

Mabel rolls her eyes. "I'll catch up with you later. We can talk about that idea."

"Absolutely."

"And nice to meet you, Tyler. Also, I'm sure your team is actually the best."

"We are," I say and once she takes off, I glance at him. "What idea?"

Corbin tells me the plans, and color me intrigued. "Will you do it?"

"I think so."

"Sounds like a recipe for trouble," I say, thinking of the way he looked at her when she nearly passed him by.

Corbin grins. "But I like trouble." Then he clears his throat. "But back to you. What's the plan with Sabrina?"

That's the question. And I need to figure it out fast.

* * *

On the drive home that afternoon, my mind spins with how to make it real. What to say to Sabrina. How to figure out if she's even ready. How to tell the kids we're...well, into each other.

And fuck, it's hard.

They've only ever known me with their mom. Since the divorce, I've been decidedly single. They've been introduced to exactly no one.

Do we just skip ahead and say, *Hey, we live together now?* And then I move her upstairs?

I really need to talk to Sabrina. Tomorrow, I've got morning skate, and then a game in the afternoon. Maybe we'll have the talk tonight, after the kids go to bed.

Yeah. That's a good plan. Because all these *almosts* are getting hard to manage. Pretty soon, I'll loop an arm around her in front of them without thinking—and that's not the way for them to find out.

But Corbin's words keep pressing on my brain. *"Have you thought about what that looks like for you?"*

I need to figure out what this looks like for all of us.

I put those thoughts aside when we swing by Little Friends and pick up our newest foster—a calico named Olive. Sabrina holds the carrier in her lap the rest of the way home, peeking inside as the kitten lets out a soft meow.

"She's perfect," Luna whispers from the backseat.

Parker nods solemnly. "I think she likes us already."

Sabrina laughs. "I bet she does."

By the time we pull into the driveway, the kids are plotting how to introduce Olive to her new temporary home and debating when she'll use Drama's cat tower. They race ahead as I grab the bag of kitten supplies from the backseat.

Once inside, Sabrina heads for her apartment and unlocks the door. "Oh my god. Maybe I didn't leave the heater on," Sabrina gasps, her teeth chattering. "It's freezing in here." Sabrina hugs herself.

"The cat can't stay there then," Luna announces.

"Sabrina can't either," Parker points out.

"Obviously," Luna says dryly.

"It's not *dangerously* freezing. Just, like, fifty degrees," Sabrina says.

Which is still *way* too cold for a home.

I check the thermostat. Adjust it. Check it again. Fiddle with the Nest.

Twenty minutes later, her place is still an icebox. I call the repair place, and they say they'll come in the morning.

"Sabrina, you'll have to sleep upstairs with Olive," Luna announces, then wiggles her brows. "Slumber party in the living room!"

"Can we?" Parker asks, clearly already planning the movie and popcorn situation like he did the last time we had one. We've got a massive couch with ottomans that slide into the middle, turning it into an even bigger bed.

"Does that work for you and Olive?" I ask Sabrina.

She grins. "All I have to say is...we'd better get in jammies now!"

So, no *big talk* tonight.

Instead, we're all bundled under blankets in the living room, with a new foster cat exploring the home, watching *Frozen* for what has to be the fiftieth time.

And as Anna arrives at the ice palace, I decide I'll talk to my mom, my sister and my brother as soon as possible. Yeah. That's it. They can help me figure this out.

I send them a text, and somewhere between Kristoff grumbling about ice sales and Olaf singing about summer, I drift off under the covers, with my kids sandwiched between me and Sabrina.

In the morning, I wake up to—what the hell?

Is that a carrot hanging around my neck?

And a sign that says: *Be Right Back. Auditioning for Olaf.*

Sabrina's sound asleep, but my two kids are smiling at me, like they're up to something.

What, I have no idea.

41

HYPE MAN

Sabrina

On Sunday morning, Tyler's busy with the heating repair woman—I wanted to shout, *Go, lady boss* when a tall lady with coiled hair and blue coveralls arrived from the company she owns. My car is charging, so I grab Tyler's from the garage and run the kids to see their friends—Luna is going to spend the day with Mia and Mia's grandma (and Mia's dog, Luna points out), and Parker is going to his friend Jamal's house since he got a "sweet new volcano kit" for Christmas.

When I return, I park right outside since Tyler needs to leave any minute for the arena.

Once I'm inside, the repair woman is shoving her work boots back on at the front door. "It's toasty downstairs now," she says, pointing to my apartment as she grabs her toolbox. "Don't hesitate to call if it goes bananas again though."

"We won't," Tyler says as I come to stand beside him. "Appreciate you coming out on a Sunday."

"That's the job," she says, then tilts her head, brow furrowed like she's studying us. "You look familiar."

I'm sure she's about to say something to Tyler about blocking some shots today against Phoenix. But she doesn't look at him twice. She's studying me.

"Hey! You do those skating videos. Sabrina on Ice!"

Oh. I've never been recognized before. I feel a little *glowy*. "That's me," I say, beaming from the inside out.

"A few months ago, I got hooked on all these adventure sports videos. I watch them in between calls, and then you showed up on my feed and I watched all your performances."

"Wait till you see the new one she's going to post. It's stunning," Tyler says, with so much passion and pride. "We shot it yesterday outdoors, and it's incredible."

"I'll be watching," she says.

Before she can open the door, Tyler adds, "And she's going to be performing at a Sea Dogs game next weekend."

I swat his arm. "Tyler," I say, admonishing him—but secretly loving that he's telling her about me. Everly did reach out after all and confirmed a time for me to perform again, and I can't wait.

"I'll be there," the woman says.

"I'd be happy to get you good seats," Tyler offers, and wow, he is my hype man.

"You're a doll," she says.

He waggles his phone and says he'll be in touch with the tickets.

When she leaves, I give him a look. "You're like my personal publicist," I say.

"Damn straight," he says, then grabs his wallet from the table by the door. "And I need to get to morning skate. Then the game. Dinner tonight? Here?" His voice pitches up, full of hope, like he's asking me on a date.

"Of course," I say, and I'm loving these *dates*. They make me feel like the next steps are possible, like it's not too soon for me to fall again. Like maybe I got it right the second time around.

He loops an arm around my waist and tugs me close. "No kids here now," he says, then drops a quick, hot kiss to my lips that leaves my bones buzzing.

He trots down the steps. "See you later, Sabrina."

As I watch him stride to the car, I feel...settled, calm and happy. Peaceful too. I sigh contentedly.

But then my attention snags on a man walking toward the house. He's polished and put together in tailored slacks and a blue oxford-cloth shirt on a Sunday.

My father.

42

A LITTLE BIT RIGHT

Sabrina

Two questions prick at me as I stand in the front entrance.

Why is he here and how does he know where I live? Not...how are you? Not...how is Mom?

But as soon as that last thought lands, worry crawls up my throat, turning into dread. That has to be it. "Is Mom okay?" I ask, some ancient, primal concern jostling to the front of the line.

I don't want her to be sick. I don't want her to be gone. Why else would he be here? Or could it be...for me?

He strides up the steps, pressing his hands down, as if to say don't make a scene. "She's fine, Sabrina. Of course she's fine," he says, dismissing me. "Don't raise your voice."

I jerk my head back, then hold my arms out wide. "I didn't! That was a normal tone."

"She's fine," he says again, crisply. "How are you?"

Wait. My head spins. Did he actually ask that? Does

he...care how I am? For a second, I relax my shoulders. Maybe this is a détente. Maybe he came to say he's sorry. A kernel of hope lodges in my heart. "I'm fine."

"Good. I'm glad," he says, then stops a few steps down and looks around, as if he's assessing the steps and the front porch with its flowerpots, filled with native plants. "This is a nice place," he observes.

"Thanks," I say, but if this is an olive branch, call me wary. There's something in his tone, like he's laying a trap.

I cross my arms. "How did you know where my home is?"

His lip curls. "You want to know how I figured out where you live? It's not *your house*."

Why is my father so mean? "How is that relevant?"

But what I really want to say is—*why are you so awful*? Was his father like this to him? Is that where he learned this behavior? Well, if that's the case, it stops with me. I will never be like him. I will never treat people the way he does.

"Because it's not accurate," he says. "And I would think as an accounting major, you'd care about accuracy. But you've proven accuracy isn't important to you."

I grit my teeth, anger lashing at me, hurt storming my chest. "Dad," I begin, but fuck him. He doesn't deserve to be called a father. "David, how did you figure out where I live?" I ask again.

"Chad gave me the address," he says matter-of-factly.

"Chad?" That doesn't compute.

"Yes, Chad, the man you were supposed to marry but instead threw a childish fit about in front of two hundred and fifty people."

Oh. So we're still mad about that. Got it. "You're going there again?"

"Sabrina, I'll be going there for a while," he bites out, as I try to figure out how Chad has the address but then it hits me—Elphaba. I wanted my sewing machine so I could make a costume for Luna, and he needed to ship it to me. And naturally, when my dad needed to find me, he asked his minion.

Trying to hold my own once again, I speak as evenly as I can to this man. "Well, you found me. What do you want?"

"I've been texting you and asking you. Is it really that hard to send me the report? We need it for our year-end accounting. I'd have thought you'd know that."

That treacherous ball of hurt rolls faster down my veins, presses harder against my insides. Of course he came here for business. Of course that's all he cares about. "I sent it to you," I say, and I can't believe I ever thought he'd show up just...*for me.* "Like I told you when you first asked for it."

"Well, the file is corrupt. Is it so much trouble to send it again? Especially since I came all the way down here."

Like that was hard. He has meetings in the city all the time. "You could have told me that over text," I say, then whip my phone from my back pocket.

"You don't answer my texts."

"I wonder why." I stab my finger against the email search bar, find it in fifteen seconds, and resend. "There. Check your email."

He glares at me. Then, like it pains him to the soul, opens his email and clicks on the file. With an aggrieved sigh, he says, "There, that wasn't so hard, was it?"

My jaw ticks. "Nope. And now you have it," I say, my eyes swinging pointedly to the curb. *Time to go.*

But he doesn't leave. Instead, he stares at Tyler's house

curiously. Studying it. It's a nice home of course, by any standards. It's a modern Scandinavian style, slate and beige, with big windows and a sleek design, and it's located in one of the fanciest sections of the city. "So, looks like you leveled up."

What did he just say? I tilt my head. "Excuse me?"

"Traded up," he says, like I didn't understand his meaning when it was crystal clear. He waves a hand toward the home. "I saw you kiss that man just now. You live with him. Is this why you fabricated that whole nonsensical story about a cat and a voicemail? Because you were really sleeping with someone else?"

Something in me snaps. Like a branch breaking off a tree in a windstorm. One loud crack and it's crashed on the ground. I point to his car on the street. "Go away. Now. Just get off my property."

He laughs. "Oh, Sabrina. You're still making things up. It's not yours. It belongs to the rich hockey player you're" —he stops to sketch air quotes—"*working for*." He shakes his head, like he's tsking me. "I should have reached out to you to get VIP tickets for the game I'm taking clients to next weekend instead of buying them for face value. You really tried to play us all for fools. But when Chad gave me the address, I did some searching, saw who rented this home, and then learned Tyler Falcon also just so happened to be in Cozy Valley for a *charity* golf tournament the same weekend as your wedding. Only ten minutes away from the venue. Cozy Valley, where you like to use the rink. Tyler, who you met more than a year ago when you skated for the Sea Dogs. You two looked awfully cozy in that photo you posted that night while you were engaged. It's all incredibly convenient, isn't it?"

I'm reeling, a boxer slammed in all my soft spots,

stumbling, slumping against the ropes as he hits me every place it hurts.

"That's not what happened," I choke out.

"Sure. Of course it's not. You got close with him quickly, didn't you? Moving in with him. Doing face masks with his kids," my father continues, leveling his lowest blow yet, and I didn't think he could hit lower.

But when the person who was supposed to love you unconditionally slams you into the wall, your knees give out. I grab the post next to the railing, my breath coming fast and hard, my heart exploding.

My father never loved me.

I've never been good enough for him. "Go away," I seethe, but it fast becomes a sob, wrenched up from the depths of my trying-too-hard-for-him soul.

I spin around, grab the door handle, and yank it open in a tear-streaked haze, then slam it shut as big, gasping breaths wrack me.

I feel like I can't get any air.

Like I've been crushed as I cry and crumple to the ground.

He's an awful, cruel man.

But as I drop my face into my hands, one thought keeps shoving its way to the front of my mind—what if he's also a little bit...right?

I am sleeping with my boss, and that's what hurts too. That shard of truth, jagged and sharp, cuts me.

43

PRESENTATION TIME

Tyler

On the ice that afternoon, I get up in Phoenix's business, cutting off passes, stealing the puck.

I race behind the net, fighting it out in the corners with a kind of loose and easy pace that sends adrenaline rushing through me.

It's a natural high.

This is why I play hockey—for games like this. When everything comes together, and you feel on top of the world. Every pass, every blocked shot feels a little like magic.

The magic that comes from years of practice, performance, experience.

And...joy. In the third period, the Phoenix center charges ahead on a breakaway, chasing down the net, but I cut him off, smacking the puck far, far from him and right toward my brother's stick.

Where Miles spins around and takes it the other way.

He sends it skipping past their goalie's leg pads, and it lodges in the twine.

The lamp lights. Yes!

We hug, because why the fuck not? We're three goals ahead and everything on the ice is going my way. And maybe soon, everything else will too.

We hop over the boards, and I tug off my gloves to grab my water bottle and down some. "Falcon to Falcon," Coach McBride says, clapping me on the shoulder, then Miles.

"That's the way we like it, sir," Miles says.

"Keep it up," Coach says, and when he heads back down the bench, Miles turns to me. "Got your text. Let's have lunch with Mom and Charlie tomorrow, 'kay? We'll figure it out."

"Thanks, man," I say, feeling like everything is possible.

"I'm stoked for you," he says with a genuine smile.

"Me too," I say, then we hit the ice again, and soon, we wrap up the afternoon with a W.

Yeah, everything feels possible.

* * *

When I return home, I pull into the garage, then knock first on Sabrina's door downstairs. Maybe she's with the kitten. But there's no answer, then the sounds of pots and pans drift downstairs.

Ah, they're upstairs.

When I reach the first floor, I toe off my shoes in the foyer and head to the kitchen, but I stop short. Holy shit. Sabrina's alone and cooking...like five things. In a whirl, like she's an executive chef in a Michelin-star joint, she grabs a saucepan from the heat while stirring a different pot. On the counter sits a huge metal bowl with a salad.

This is...Thanksgiving-level stuff.

"Hello," she says evenly as she lowers the ladle for the boiling pot, while dumping the sauteed veggies into a serving dish.

"Hey, Sabrina," I say, impressed she's moving so quickly and efficiently, but concerned, too, since there's something almost robotic to her right now. "Are you okay?"

She lifts her face and flashes a closed-mouth smile as she spreads the veggies in the serving dish. "I'm great. Just making dinner for you and the kids. And the kids are upstairs putting on their jammies. After they came home this afternoon from their friends' homes, I made sure they did their homework. I double-checked everything. Their math is so good now. Yay. And they both showered and cleaned up their rooms. So after dinner, you can put them to bed. They even fed the kitten and measured out her food, so that helped with fractions too," she says, and holy shit.

Something is really wrong with Sabrina. She's slid into Super Nanny mode for some reason.

"Are you okay, baby?" I ask softly.

She shoots me an admonishing stare, then presses her finger to her lips. "We don't want them to hear."

But maybe we do. "What's going on?" I ask, stepping toward her, really looking at her.

Her eyes are...rimmed with red.

She doesn't answer my question though because the clatter of little feet grows louder. And like a summer rainstorm that comes out of nowhere, two freshly showered, wet-behind-the-ears children skid into the kitchen.

"Hi, Dad," Luna says, then hugs me.

"Guess what, Dad?" Parker says, but Luna shushes him.

They look like they're up to something, and I feel entirely unmoored. "What's up, kids?" I ask, trying to get a handle on the situation.

Luna sighs, but bounces. "Fine. We were going to surprise you at dinner. We have a presentation for you."

Oh. This should be interesting. They haven't done a presentation since a year ago when Luna campaigned for a dog. She went full PowerPoint and everything. "Okay," I say, going along with it. I'll have to talk to Sabrina later. Maybe she's only focused on the to-do list of the day.

This is a good reminder. I need to focus on these kids first too. "Give me a minute," I say, then I head to my room to change out of my suit and into jeans and a T-shirt.

When I return downstairs, the table is immaculately set and Luna and Parker sit like angels, waiting for me. Sabrina stands though.

My brow furrows. "Are you joining us?"

She shakes her head. "I need to..." She stops, like she's collecting her thoughts briefly, then says, "tend to some things downstairs."

Okay. "But you usually do...join us," I point out, and really, I hope she will every night. I hope these dinners become our norm—us doing all this together.

"Right, but I don't want to intrude," she says, brightly, as if she's doing us a favor. "You should have your family time."

Her words are a gut punch. But...have I been assuming too much?

Is this too much for her? Too presumptuous of me? I look around at my kids. They're the loves of my life, but that doesn't mean she wants to have dinner with them every night. Or take them to school every morning. Or help them with homework. Or have their schedule be her schedule.

It's one thing to do it as the paid nanny. It's entirely another for me to ask her to take on...being the girlfriend of a busy single dad with a complicated schedule.

Just because we're into each other doesn't necessarily mean she'll want to have every meal together.

Hang out with us in the kitchen, the living room, the car.

Do things together whenever I'm home and not playing hockey.

My pulse spikes annoyingly. I got far out on my skis, didn't I?

Just because she's great with my kids as the nanny doesn't mean she'll want to become an instant family.

Shit. My chest tightens.

They're my kids, not hers, and it's not fair to think she'd want to jump from taking care of them for a season while she's paid to being saddled with...*us.* As what—the twenty-six-year-old girlfriend to a single dad who travels half the year?

Fuck. I need to think this through. See my brother, sister, and my mom. Figure out my life.

But manners are manners, so I roll my shoulders and shove those thoughts away. I gesture to the dishes. "You made plenty of food though. But you can take a plate downstairs if you'd prefer," I say.

Sabrina's expression falters. Hurt flashes briefly in her blue eyes. And...that was probably the wrong thing to say.

I shake my head. "I didn't—"

"Don't leave yet, Sabrina," Luna jumps in. "We want to do the presentation first."

"Yeah, we worked on it together," Parker says. "Can you stay for it?"

Parker sounds so desperate, and it must work on Sabrina, since she says, "Of course I can."

She takes off her apron, wipes her hands, but still doesn't sit. "Let's hear it," she says, and I guess it's time for a PowerPoint now.

Sabrina stands on the other side of the island, across from the kids and me.

Parker swipes the tablet, opening a PowerPoint that says Our Big Plan. He clicks to a picture of...us doing face masks. "Let's start with Exhibit A."

"Yes, Parker, excellent idea," Luna says, adopting an adulting tone. "We call this...the beginning. See how much fun we had?"

They wait for a response, so I nod and say, "Yes."

Sabrina doesn't say a word.

"And here is Exhibit B," Parker says, clicking to the next slide.

A photo of the four of us from last night. I'd fallen asleep and Luna looks to be taking a selfie of her, Parker, and Sabrina with me and my carrot nose. I couldn't be dadding any harder.

"And this was the best," Luna says, "wasn't it? But then there was...this." She clicks to the next one.

"Exhibit C," Parker says in an announcer voice as he gestures to the photo of the four of us from Halloween. He's wearing his astronaut costume, I'm a football player, and Luna and Sabrina are skaters. My heart swells.

"We all had so much fun here too," Parker says.

"We did," I say, unsure where this is going.

The next photo is a picture of us at the *Ice Spectacle*. "And here is Exhibit D. We all went to New York together," he adds.

Then Luna is practically bouncing and...

Oh, fuck.

Everything snaps into place. How did I not see this sooner? They're onto us. But I steal a look at Sabrina, and she's tight, tense.

This is bad. I should stop this. "Kids—" I begin.

But they're running the show. Luna straightens her spine and cuts in. "And we know you two like each other, so this is why we think it's time for you to get married."

44

———

ABORT MISSION

Tyler

A sharp laugh sputters from me. "Are you serious?"

Luna blinks.

Parker furrows his brow.

Sabrina rolls her lips, but her blue eyes flash with something closer to alarm than mirth. No—not just alarm. This is abort-mission levels of panic.

"Yes, we're serious," Luna says, more emotional than I'd expected.

Ah, hell. She really means this. The crease in Parker's forehead tells me he does too.

"We thought—" Parker starts.

Sabrina jumps in, her voice bright—too bright. "Kids, maybe this isn't the best time."

But what I hear is—there will never be a good time for this.

My thoughts spin out. Did I misread her? Misjudge everything? My kids, at least—that's the only thing I might be able to fix. So I try, turning to the two little people who depend on me, their faces confused. "That's not how it happens," I explain. "People don't just get married because—"

Because what, idiot?

"But don't you two like each other?" Luna asks, so guileless. So damn innocent. And it's moments like this that remind me—she's still just a kid.

A kid with big dreams. *Kid* dreams. Not teenage dreams. Not adult ones.

"Of course we do," I say, because I'm not going to lie about that.

But a quiet voice inside me whispers—*While I was busy protecting the kids and Sabrina, did I ever stop to consider she might not see a future with me?*

That being crazy for someone isn't the same as...whatever this family thing is that I want?

My pulse spikes. She's already been pulling away from me—has been ever since I returned home tonight.

"Then what's the issue?" Luna presses.

That's a damn good question.

I'd thought I had a handle on this in Cozy Valley. I was gearing up to tackle things properly. But now? Now I feel like I'm not just back at the starting line—I'm not even on the damn track.

I steal a glance at the woman I adore. She's standing tall, shoulders back, chin up.

Like she would after finishing a routine. Is this the Sabrina who landed every routine under pressure, who never let a stumble show? Not the Sabrina who melted in my arms every time I touched her?

And have I misread her too? Was she ever wanting the

same thing I was? My mind is reeling and I can't even grasp at answers.

But I try. "That's just not how it works," I say to the kids, my voice sharper than I'd intended. I need to cut this conversation off before it spirals further.

Sabrina takes another step back, her posture shifting, and my gaze snaps to her. Her face is unreadable, but there's something off in her eyes. Like she's holding back more than just words. She looks to the kids, "This really seems like something you should discuss with your father. I'm going to let you all have some family time."

Then she's gone, her footsteps fast fading down the stairs.

She leaves—because she can.

But I stay because that's my job—*them*. And it's a job I love, but now I'm left alone standing here—staring at the huge dinner she's cooked with two confused kids and one colossal mess of a problem.

I drag a hand over my beard. "We should eat," I mutter.

"But, Dad," Luna presses, just shy of whining. "Why can't you two?"

Ah, hell. I can't brush them off. They've put together a whole damn PowerPoint.

I exhale heavily, trying—really trying—to explain. "It's not that easy, kids. You don't go from liking someone to getting married."

"Fine," Parker says, with a thoughtful sigh. Then—"So what are you two? Boyfriend-girlfriend?"

Are we even that?

In my rush to tell her how I felt in New York, I never actually put a label on us. I insisted we keep things quiet. Said we'd figure out how to tell the kids on our terms.

And yet—here they are, telling me their terms. They want us to get married.

By keeping quiet, I let it get to this point where my kids have completely misunderstood things. But maybe... so did I.

My chest hollows out as my gaze instinctively drifts toward the hallway. Toward the space where she walked away. The hall's empty now, without her. And, so am I.

But for the first time, a thought crashes into my mind, heavy and suffocating. Maybe she was never mine to have.

I let out a slow breath. "Honestly, I don't know," I admit. "I'm sorry I confused you two."

Luna frowns. "You kinda did, Dad," she murmurs, her lower lip quivering.

I've made everything worse by not coming clean.

I reach for my little girl, pulling her close. "I'm sorry, honey. I care deeply for Sabrina. I just..."

But the words don't come. Because for the first time, I don't know what comes next.

Nowhere in the dating handbook did it occur to me that my kids would see marriage as the next logical step.

Suddenly, I can't shake the fear that maybe—maybe I was never the next step for her at all.

And if she doesn't see a future here...what the hell am I even doing?

45

——————

FULL SKATER MODE

Tyler

When I have a bad game, I'm itching to hit the ice again. To prove myself. Do it all over. Show the team and myself that I can play and play well.

Later that evening, I'm crawling out of my skin. I'm antsy and aching as I clean up, as I read to the kids, as I make sure they brush their teeth, then tuck them in.

Because as I do all this—these daily chores, these wonderful daily chores—they're my reminder.

This is my life.

These two people.

The second they're asleep, I pad downstairs and knock on Sabrina's door. But all I hear is a faint meow. No shuffling of feet. No *I'll be right there.* Just a plaintive little cry from a kitten.

Guilt and frustration climb my throat as I open the door to the garage, already dreading what I'll find.

My heart sinks when I spot her side empty, her little orange car gone.

She left.

Because she's not on duty tonight.

Because I stupidly, foolishly assumed she'd want to hang out with the kids and me.

This is her job though. And I need to treat her with some fucking respect. I can't take advantage of whatever *this* was.

I can't take advantage of her. I trudge upstairs and open a text.

Tyler: Hey. Let me know when you're home so we can talk.

A few minutes later, a reply arrives.

Sabrina: Of course.

No exclamation points. No warmth. Well, it's not like I deserve them.

I settle onto the couch and put on a rerun of *Tacoma FD*, one of the funniest shows I've ever seen.

It's funny all right.

But I don't laugh.

When the garage finally opens again, I sit up straight, like a dog waiting for its owner.

Do I go downstairs right away? Or do I give her time?

Ah, fuck it. It's late.

I count to sixty, then head down. Best to deal with things stat.

I knock. She opens the door a smidge, and I still can't get a read on her.

"Can I come in?"

"Of course," she says, opening the door all the way. And that's when I spot Olive, curled up in her arms. A tiny, purring calico shield.

Or maybe not. Maybe this isn't a shield at all. Maybe this is just business as usual for her as she plays with a kitten.

Which only bolsters my resolve.

"How was your...night?" I ask.

That isn't awkward at all.

"Fine. I went to see Trevyn," she says. "We grabbed some dinner."

I wince. Right. Because she didn't want to eat with us.

Because she didn't feel welcome, you dumbass.

But they're one and the same, aren't they? Two sides of the same coin.

"Cool," I say, scratching my jaw, needing to do this. For both of us. But especially for her. "Listen, Sabrina—"

"My father stopped by today."

It's like I just walked into a wall. "What the—? He did? How did he—?"

"He wanted that report. The one he texted about. I resent it," she says, quiet. Like she's testing something. But I don't know what. I can't read her.

"That's all?" I ask, and I can't hide the anger in my voice.

She sighs, her lips trembling the slightest bit. "He said...some things."

I growl. That man. "Like what?"

"Just..." She closes her eyes for a second, then opens them. "That he should have asked me to get him VIP tickets to the game, since...he saw us. Kissing goodbye. He...made assumptions. That it had been going on for a while. That it had happened before the wedding even."

I see red. "That asshole. That flaming fucking asshole," I say, ready to rip him to pieces.

Her eyes shine, and it hits me like a punch to the ribs. He's why she cried earlier.

And I'm adding to her stress. With the kids, with the presentation, with the pressure. She's barely free of that asshole ex, and now her gaslighting father has shown up again, and the last thing—the *very last thing*—she needs is pressure from a guy like me.

I breathe out hard, letting go of my anger. Anger I have no right to feel.

"I'm sorry, Sabrina," I say, lifting a hand, reaching out to hold her, pull her close, and comfort her. "I'm sorry he said that."

But she just strokes the cat's head, nodding. Like she's saying she's okay.

I lower my hand. Stay in my lane.

"It's fine," she says, her voice quiet. Stoic.

Is it though?

I don't know. But that's the problem. I don't know a damn thing. Don't know if she wants comfort or space. A shoulder to lean on or just a good time for a little while. A secret or something all too complicated.

"What did you want to talk about?" she asks, her voice stripped bare of emotion.

She deserves better than me.

I'm not a safe, easy place for her to land after a terrible ex and a shitty father. I'm the worst next thing for her.

She needs a laid-back guy, with an easy life and zero baggage.

"I don't want to add to the stress in your life, Sabrina," I say. "You deserve to be happy, and if I'm making things harder for you, we should stop now."

Her brow pinches. Her lips part, like she's about to say something.

For a second, I see *everything* flicker across her face—pain, hurt, disappointment.

But just as quickly, it vanishes. And she's poised again.

The skater.

I want to grab her. Hold her. Tell her that we can figure it out.

But her dad thinks she's screwing up. My kids put her on the spot. And she does not need another person adding to the shit she has to sort through.

She needs a job, steady and dependable. She needs to build her business. She needs to move on from the assholes in her life.

And I've given her zero fucking space to do that.

"Okay," she says, even, toneless.

And the dead sound of her voice breaks my heart.

I press on, like I need to convince her. "You just got out of something serious. You shouldn't want something serious right now." I tap my chest—no, I stab it. "I'm nothing but serious. I'm a dad with two kids who travels half the time. You deserve to have fun, not be tied to a life like mine that you didn't sign up for."

She nods, crisp and businesslike. "Got it. I'm one

hundred percent clear." She pauses. "Do you want me to quit?"

What? "No! You're an amazing nanny. I want you to keep your job."

"That's fair," she says, her voice unreadable. Then, firmer, steadier, she adds, "It makes sense. We can pretend nothing happened."

My chest caves in. But I'm the one who drove the bulldozer straight through us. "Yeah," I say. "It's the right thing to do."

I don't believe it. Not one bit. But that's what I tell myself the rest of the night, because I have to do this—for her.

46

BUNNY HOPS

Sabrina

If I got through my un-marriage, I can handle this.

Wait—let me revise that.

I did survive not only being jilted, but running away, embarrassing myself in front of a hot hockey stud, getting fired, and being disowned. And after that, I lived in a garlic palace.

This heartbreak? It's nothing.

This ache in my chest is easy.

This hollow feeling is cake.

I tell myself that the next day over and over when the kids are back at school and Tyler's off doing...hockey things. Pumping iron. Grunting with the guys. Stalking around with the weight of the world on his shoulders.

Whatever.

I go to Sunnyside Rink, say hi to Hank and Marla at the front, then meet Jasmine for a lesson. And holy hell, this girl is fire. Her loops and axels are next level.

"I can feel it, Jasmine. The way you want this," I tell her. I never promise medals or glory. But I *do* want to encourage passion.

"Thank you, Sabrina. I've got a plan. I know what I want," she says, skating off the ice.

Her mom looks on knowingly. "She sure does."

"A plan is good," I say.

And I have one too—to build and grow this business. That is what I'm going to do. And I don't need the distraction of a man getting in the way.

And he, clearly, doesn't need or want the distraction of me.

So I don't give that to him.

I take care of the kids. I pick them up. I chauffeur them to their activities. I coach Luna on her single axel at the rink. I visit High Kick Coffee with them, say hi to their great-grandmother while they do homework and try out her newest treats.

If I were keeping a list of all my nanny accomplishments, I'd be acing it. Because I am excellent at this.

And really, that has to be good enough.

* * *

Tiffany is working on her bunny hop, making progress faster than I'd expected.

"Go you! You're acing it already," I say as she shows me her moves at our next lesson.

"I *told* you I could do it," she says.

"You were right."

When the lesson ends, her mom beckons me over to her spot on the bench.

"So...I've been thinking."

My heart skips faster. I have a feeling. "Yes?"

"I've been thinking about lessons," she says.

I want to squeal, but I keep my composure. "And?"

"And I kind of want to do a girls' night out on the rink. Just me and my besties. What do you think?"

Goosebumps rise on my arms. I think that sounds amazing. "I would *love* to host it," I say, already thinking of ideas, things to teach them, basic moves, the fun we can have.

"Perfect. Let's do it."

* * *

Later that day, before I pick up the kids, I slide into a booth at Moon Over Milkshakes with Isla, Trevyn, and Leighton. Beach music plays faintly overhead and servers bustle by with plates of burgers and fries, sandwiches and salads.

"How's everything going?" Leighton asks me, her tone lined with concern. Like she senses I might be going through some shit.

But I am not dwelling. I am not wallowing.

"Great!" I say, then urge them to order and once we do, I dive into updates about my students' progress. "And it occurred to me—I should do girls' nights out. I should offer that. Isn't that a great idea? Especially since I'm skating this weekend at the Sea Dogs arena again. It would be a great opportunity to capitalize on that. By having girls' night out options on my site," I say, then snap my fingers. "Oh, that reminds me—I need to post the skating video that Ty—"

But I swallow the word *Tyler.*

I don't want to go there. Don't want to rehash the hurt.

The more I throw myself into work, the less I'll feel it. The faster I'll move on.

"Tyler," Isla supplies, tilting her head from across the mint green booth. "What's going on, friend?"

My heart squeezes. My throat tightens.

"Sweetie," Trevyn says, reaching for my hand. "You can tell us."

He knows some of it. He saw me Sunday night and helped me through that evening. But that was before Tyler knocked on my door and yanked the rug completely out from under us.

But truly, it was no surprise. It's better if we pretend nothing happened. It's always been better that way. We were foolish to think we could magically jump from working together in his home with his kids to being... together.

Besides, he has too much on his plate.

I swallow past the tightness, trying to will it away.

"It's just..." I wave a hand, trying to dismiss all these mounting feelings.

"What happened?" Leighton asks, her voice calm and steady.

I draw a breath. "We broke up. Well...really, *he* did."

"Oh no," Leighton says gently.

"Really?" Isla asks, her eyes sad.

"Yeah. Really," I say, then I tell them everything.

Everything I didn't tell Tyler.

Everything about my father's visit.

Exactly how awful it made me feel.

Isla nods, absorbing it all, then says, "So when you were already at rock-bottom, his kids suggested marriage, he didn't jump on it, you shut down, and he walked it all the way backward because he couldn't figure out what the hell was going on with you."

I blink. "How did you get all of that from what I just said?"

She shrugs, like it was easy, or easy-ish. "I'm a dating coach. My job is literally to study romance and help people find happily-ever-afters."

"And so you figured out he couldn't figure out what was going on with me?" I ask, still incredulous at how she read us like that.

She doesn't back down. "Sabrina, you're really good at being great."

I feel like I've just walked into a pole. "What does that mean? Are you saying I fake it?"

Isla reaches for my hand. "No, no. But I am saying you've had to learn self-protection. You've had no choice —because of your parents, but also because you have uncommon talent. You're really damn good at throwing yourself into skating, into success. And I'm not saying you shouldn't throw yourself into your business. I'm just wondering...is it possible Tyler had no clue where your emotions were at? And maybe he made some stupid assumptions?"

Trevyn nods sagely. "Because men *can* make some really stupid-ass assumptions."

I swat his arm. "You're not supposed to side with him."

He squeezes my shoulder but doesn't let my comment slide. "I'm not siding with him. I'm siding with...*seeing all sides.*"

Leighton gives me a thoughtful look. "And you know, the thing is—he's *really* caught up in being a great dad, because his dad wasn't. Miles felt similar pressure—he felt like he had to be super responsible at all times. Move forward. He was so focused on being responsible, on doing the right thing, but sometimes it tripped him up. A lot of that pressure came from their dad and the way he walked out. And Tyler? He is a dad, so I bet he's dealing with that in his own way. He probably feels the pressure to do the opposite of his dad too."

I frown. I'd never really thought about that. I hadn't considered how much he carried. "What do I do with that? I can't go back and have him un-break up with me because we both have daddy issues."

Leighton takes a beat, then nods slowly. "I'm not sure. But maybe...the two of you aren't done talking."

I mull on that as the server brings our lunch.

"It's something to think about," Isla says, nudging me toward this new...realization, perhaps.

Maybe I should think about it.

But first, I eat lunch with my friends, and afterward, I finally post the skating video from Cozy Valley with the caption: ***It's like lightning.***

I wonder if Tyler still watches them.

I don't know.

But Chad clearly does, since he leaves a comment that evening.

Good job, Sabrina.

Maybe if he'd done this a while ago, I'd have cursed, spat, or sent a million *Can you believe this?* screenshots to my friends.

Instead, I just delete his words.

And I make another appointment to see Elena. But how to handle Tyler isn't so easy. I don't know what I'll say to him or if I'm ready to open my heart to hurt again.

And I don't know when I will be.

47

LET ME GET THIS STRAIGHT

Tyler

"A dog walk?" I ask my mother on the phone when she calls after morning skate on Saturday.

"Yes, that thing where you put leashes on pooches and they bark at every other dog that dares to pass by."

I heave a sigh as I trudge down the corridor toward the players' lot, a few paces behind my brother. "I know what a dog walk is."

"Are you sure? You seemed confused."

"Because you don't usually call me to join you on a dog walk."

"Do you have something against dogs?"

"Mom. No. Obviously," I say, exasperated, even though it's only been a short call.

"And you're free today since Elle has the kids," she adds.

My mother knows everything. Is she a superhero? Well, probably. "She has them all weekend," I admit.

"Perfect. Then your brother knows where to meet me."

"Miles knows?"

As if on cue, Miles spins around and flashes me a smile and a thumbs-up.

I groan as I near the door. "Why do I have the feeling I'm walking into an ambush?"

My mother laughs. "Sweetheart, you're the one who reached out to us on Saturday."

"And we never met for lunch," I point out with a grumble, because I'm feeling grumbly.

"Because you cancelled," she says, matter-of-factly.

Right. Because what was the point? I'd originally planned to meet with them to talk about next steps with Sabrina, and, well, those became clear as day. "So you changed it to a dog walk?"

I'm pushing back because I know my mom. The woman is always ten steps ahead of me.

"Yes. Charlie has to work, but like I said, your brother knows where to meet me. Bye!"

She hangs up right as Miles reaches the door, swinging it open. "Good thing I drove us today."

I narrow my eyes at him. "You trapped me, dude."

"Did I?" he asks with a smirk.

"You fucking did."

He claps my shoulder as we stride across the lot to his car. "Maybe you need to be trapped."

The long-haired Boppity leads the pack of Chihuahua rescue mutts. She's tiny—maybe seven pounds, but she's the biggest dog in the world in her mind, so she barks her presence to any mammal that enters her fifty-foot pack radius. My mom holds her leash and Boo's as well. I've got Cindy while Miles has Bippity as we walk the fearsome foursome along Marina Green, the Golden Gate Bridge rising majestically in a clear blue January sky.

"So, why did you cancel with us the other day? Does it have something to do with the..." Mom pauses, adjusting her sunglasses so she can look at me over the tops of the big cheetah shades, "breakup?"

This superpower of hers is hard to keep up with. "How did you find out about that?" I shoot my gaze toward Miles. He must have told her.

My brother holds up his hands in surrender. "Not me."

"Had to have been you," I say.

My mom cackles. "I figured it out. You've been a grumpy turd, and when I picked the kids up from school yesterday they said you and Sabrina were acting, and I quote, *weird.* Then they told me about a certain presentation last weekend," she says. "And I put it all together."

There you go. Secrets and my family don't co-exist. "Okay, and?"

"And, young man, why are you being so surly with your mother?"

"And your brother?" Miles pipes in.

"Are you here to echo her?" I snap to Miles.

He slows his pace and stares straight at me. "And are you going to be a big dick?"

Ouch. "I'm not being a dick."

"Bullshit. You've been a surly, sullen bastard since Sunday night. You were like an ogre on our Los Angeles trip," he says, mentioning our quick midweek road trip down the state.

"It's my old hometown," I say, like that justifies my mood.

"Boys!" My mother cuts in with a sharp and clear order. She doesn't yell, since she doesn't have to. But we all stop. Including the four dogs. They turn their snouts to Mom, waiting for an order from on high. Miles and I look at her, chastened.

Well, I do. I'm mostly the chastened one, because I'm the asshole.

"Stop this snipping. Now, let's talk," Mom says, with authority and love. "I understand you prefer to grunt like a caveman. But I'm not going to let you swing your arms and scratch your chest. Why did you break up with a woman you clearly care so deeply about?"

I consider the question for about two seconds, then jump in with the cold, unvarnished truth. "The kids asked us to get married. Married! She practically choked when they said that. Her eyes popped and she bolted from the room. So yeah, I did the right thing. Because she doesn't need more stress in her life. She doesn't need a guy with two kids. She doesn't need a boss who's also a boyfriend. She doesn't need to have her job in question. Don't you two get it?" I ask, exasperated all over again.

Miles nods, nice and long, then strokes his chin. "So you assumed you knew what was best for her. How'd that go for you?"

My chest tightens, like someone's tied a belt around it. "She shut down. She didn't even fight me on it. Hell, she was probably glad."

My mother stares at me, like she can't believe I'm selling this line. Boppity does the same. She's so over me. "Tyler, do you really believe that?" my mom asks. "That she was probably *glad*?"

"Yes!" I shout, doubling down.

"Why?" she asks. Boppity barks. Cindy barks louder.

"Because of how she was acting," I say, annoyed I have to rehash this hurt all over again, but rehash it I do, letting them know what went down the night my heart splintered into pieces.

When I finish with how Sabrina was just petting the kitten at the end, Miles stares at me with ferocity in his expression. "Did it ever occur to you, even once, even at all, that maybe she wasn't shutting you out because she didn't care? Maybe she shut down because she was already dealing with enough from her father?"

Mom gives me a sympathetic look. "Sweetheart, that has to be so hard for her," she says, and her words are a jolt.

They're jumper cables restarting my engine. "Wait," I sputter. "You're saying she just went along with it?"

Boppity lifts her chin and barks again at me. It sounds like *you idiot* in canine.

"Listen to your fur sister," Mom says.

Miles chuckles under his breath, then mutters, "Yeah, Little Falcon."

"Tyler, her father showed up that morning," my mom says. "Do you think maybe that threw her off? Maybe it sent her spinning? Maybe it made her feel like her world had tipped upside down. From what you've said, he's never supported her."

"It's so much worse than that," I hiss out, the venom back in my voice. "He puts her down. He blames her. He twists everything. He accused her of having an affair with me *before* she almost married that tool."

"That's my point, sweetheart," Mom says, reaching up to ruffle my hair. "She must have been hurting so much."

Miles clears his throat. "And then, let me see if I've got this straight. Right after she has a run-in with the man who makes her feel worthless, she pulls back from you just a little. Maybe out of self-protection. And you assume that means she doesn't want you," Miles adds, pulling no punches.

How did I miss it? "Shit," I mutter, dragging a hand through my hair, feeling like the world's biggest idiot. She was robotic, yes. But she was also overperforming. She was making a million dishes at dinner. She was telling me every little thing she did for the kids. She was—a stark realization slams into me—making a spoken list *for me* of every damn thing she'd done. Like she used to do to track her skating performance. And she was in full skater mode Sunday night.

I didn't connect the dots. She was protecting herself because of him. She was trying to be perfect *for me* because he'd been horrible to her. And then I proceeded to presume it was all about me—but it was all about her and him.

My heart aches horribly with all the hurt she must carry over that man.

And I didn't even connect the dots. "I'm the world's biggest idiot," I mutter.

Miles holds his arms out wide. "At last, he learns!" Cindy twirls around Miles in a little doggie victory dance.

"Seriously. I am," I add as my stomach drops and I replay how quiet she was when she told me about his visit. Like she could only get out a few words, here and there. She wasn't holding back from me. She was holding in a dam of hurt, while clutching a kitten like a shield.

I should have been her shield. Not a little baby cat.

"What do I do now?" I ask, feeling utterly helpless, like I did when Parker was sick and I was hundreds of miles away.

My mother comes closer, squeezes my arm. "If you want to be a good dad, teach your kids what it means to stay. Don't show them how to run."

With that final blow, I'm knocked dead.

But it's time to pick myself up from the ground and start over. I check my watch. It's noon. It's a game day. And a VIP night. We have warmups, and also a couple quick photo opps as some VIPs tour the arena before the game against the Vegas Sabers.

The game where Sabrina's performing tonight. She'll arrive early, knowing her. Probably five-ish, to be safe. To stretch. Get in her costume. Take some pics.

I need to talk to her before she heads to the arena. I grab my phone like I'm an Old West gunslinger. Call her right away. But it goes to voicemail.

She's probably practicing her routine a few more times before tonight. She'd want to be one hundred ten percent ready.

I make a promise to myself to find her as soon as I can. And somehow I'll need to prove to her I can be the man she deserves. A man she can depend on, no matter what.

An idea lands in my head. "I need to talk to Leighton," I say to Miles.

But that's just the start of my busy afternoon. Especially since it ends with another idea, bright and shiny, shortly before I head into work.

48

SHOOT YOUR SHOT

Tyler

When you know what you want for, well, the rest of the foreseeable future, you want the foreseeable future to start right now.

But responsibilities get in the way.

Like games and such.

Still, when I arrive in the locker room, I set the gift for Sabrina carefully in my stall, making sure it's safe and sound. I'm the first one here, and since I'm early, I spin around and track down Everly in her office.

Her eyes widen with surprise when she sees me, but then the polished publicist with the sleek blonde ponytail quickly says, "What can I do for you, Tyler?"

"Some of the players are doing photo opps with the VIPs, right?"

"Yes. And a quick tour. Just of the entrance to the tunnel, the locker room, the corridor. It'll be about five minutes. And we have them staggered right before warmups. I had you on the list to do one," she says, then clicks on her tablet, calling it up. "Since you got tickets for…" She scans it, then meets my eyes like she's impressed. "You got a lot of tickets. Isla Marlowe, Trevyn Storm, Skylar Haven. Jasmine Morales and her parents. Tiffany Kovalenko and Anaka Kovalenko. As well as Nia Brown. Tonya Jackson. And, let's see, a…Rhonda McConky."

I grin, not too wide, not too proud. I invited Tonya earlier this week—she's the repair woman who adores Sabrina. And right after lunch I made some last-minute calls to Sabrina's students, tracking down their names through Leighton, who's photographed some of Sabrina's practices with them. I called Sabrina's good friends. I wanted them all here tonight for her big performance and to be treated like the stars they are to her. And I tracked down both the woman who runs the animal rescue, and the Lyft driver who helped Sabrina escape from her wedding day. I want Sabrina to see everyone who loves her.

Including…me.

I asked Elle to come too, snagging her center-ice seats with the kids. She's always loved hockey so she said it's no hardship. I also told her something else…about how I've caught feelings for the nanny. Elle laughed and told me she already knew.

Now, I need to let Everly in on a few more details. "But I kind of want it to be a surprise for Sabrina," I say, a little sheepish as I sort of reveal my hand to Everly. But she's a pro, so she just listens as I add, "Maybe you could wait to post the photo of that group with their tour guide till after Sabrina goes on."

She laughs softly but smiles. "Sure, Tyler. I'll make sure Leighton knows. She's here tonight."

I give a virtual high-five. "Perfect."

"And you'll be ready in your uniform since your tour starts at five-thirty?"

"Absolutely," I say then, and this is the hard part. This is the part I can't entirely control. But as I make small talk with Everly about the game, I give it my best shot. I've got laser vision. Twenty-twenty, thank you very much. And her tablet is resting on her lap at just the right angle for some upside-down reading. There are four VIP groups coming tonight, and I do my best to scan the names for one in particular. Or really, two.

Finding them, I finish the chat, then thank her, and head down the management corridor and back to the authorized personnel area, where Rowan's dropping his dog at the doggie daycare the arena opened recently. When he's done, I catch up to him, clapping him on the shoulder.

"Favor, man," I say.

"Name it."

"I need you to switch VIP groups with me for the tour. Can you do yours at five-thirty? And I'll take your five-forty group."

He gives a *why not* shrug. It's that easy. "Done."

Friends. They've got your back. Then I beeline for my brother in the locker room and pull him aside. "Need something from you."

"Another ass-kicking?"

I roll my eyes. "Along those lines." Lowering my voice, I add, "Think you can make sure Leighton keeps Sabrina out of the corridor before the five-thirty tour, then brings her *to* the corridor by the tunnel around, say, five-forty-four?"

My brother studies me for a beat, maybe making sure I'm not pulling a fast one. "You've got this mapped out down to the minute?"

"Pretty much."

* * *

At 5:39 on the dot, I'm suited up in pads, my jersey, skates and all. Ready and waiting at the authorized personnel entrance. Rowan already finished the VIP group I invited, and Leighton must have kept Sabrina occupied. Now all I have to do is handle the douche tour.

A minute later, Everly swings open the door, and a kernel of guilt wedges into my chest. I hope she doesn't hate me for what's about to go down. But a man's gotta do what a man's gotta do. Besides, these fuckers don't deserve to pay their way into our arena, no matter what the cost is.

For the first time I come face-to-face with the man Sabrina was going to marry. With slicked back blond hair and a smarmy smile, he's precisely what I pictured. He's wearing stone-washed jeans and a jersey for another team. The Las Vegas Sabers. And yeah, I don't feel an ounce of guilt.

He sticks out a hand. "Dude, I wish I could say I'm rooting for you tonight, but you gotta be loyal to the home team, right?"

I shake, crunching on his bones so hard he gulps. "You know it," I say, letting go before I break something.

I swing my gaze to her father, like I'm assessing an opponent on the ice. He wears pressed khakis and a button-down. His dark hair is peppered with gray and his shave is smooth. I loathe him with every fiber of my being, and I don't bother doing a thing but staring at him with knives in my eyes.

He flinches, and recognition flickers in his irises for a beat. I wonder if he's going to mention his daughter to me, but instead he flicks a piece of unseen lint off his shoulder.

That's fine by me. I'm up for the element of surprise too.

"And here is your group, Tyler," Everly says to me, then to the pack of dude bros with them—because holy fuck—Chad and Sabrina's Dad brought out a six-pack of asshats. I can tell their breed by the overwhelming aroma of body spray and the heads of gelled hair. Plus, all these guys have that dude bro look to them. So, fuck them.

"This is Tyler Falcon, number forty-four, one of our top defensemen," Everly says. "He'll be conducting your tour."

"Thanks, Everly," I say, then gesture down the hall. "Let me show you gentlemen around." Even though that title is a lie.

They're all sales-y types, showboat-y, snapping pics of themselves against posters of the Sea Dogs in the hall, cracking jokes about how lucky the Sea Dogs are to have them as VIP fans, and maybe they can pick up women at the game like the players must, then trying to peer into the locker room, even though it's off-limits.

"But we could just pretend we're on the team, right?" Chad says, and I want to wipe the smug smile off his face.

But all in due time.

"Probably not," I say, with my most charming fucking voice possible. "Or we might have to get the whole team to escort you out."

He blinks. "You'd do that?"

"You have no idea what I'd do," I say coldly, meaning it completely, then adding a *just kidding* smile. Since it's not quite time yet.

Almost, but not quite.

I guide them down the hall toward the tunnel. "And this is the tunnel. We go through here before we hit the ice. And yep, you can walk on the floor with skates."

"Impressive," Sabrina's father says, eyeing the sturdy floor, tapping it with his wingtips as he finally speaks for the first time. "Truly impressive everything that goes into the operation. Isn't it, gentlemen?"

And...he's even worse than I'd imagined. He truly only cares about appearances. About impressing people— whoever these frat boys are snapping endless pics of their annoying faces.

There's no remorse in me for what I'm about to do. Right on time, I clear my throat. "Thanks again for coming. There are just a few things I wanted to share before the game tonight," I say, and the men stop cracking jokes and turn to me right as I hear footsteps grow louder. Sneakers for sure. Along with boots, I think. Sabrina would still be in her warm-up clothes, so I'm praying the sneakers are hers, and that Leighton's wearing the boots.

"What's that, man?" Chad asks, all convivial as he plays leader of the pack.

I want to march right up to him and wring his neck. But there's a time for words and a time for deeds. This is a time for words.

I step closer, raise my forefinger. "You are the biggest fool I've ever met. You had the most incredible, wonderful, amazing woman ever, and by some twist of luck or fate, she agreed to marry your lying, cheating ass. And then you had the gall to treat her like she was an accessory. A means to an end. A path to a fucking bonus. You don't deserve VIP seats. You don't deserve nice things ever. And she always deserved better than you. I'm so damn glad she figured that out before she wasted another second on you."

"Dude, burn!" one of the other guys says, the one drenched in Ocean Forest Mist Dragon Sword Slayer spray.

What a great friend.

Chad just sputters, his eyes bugging out. "Who are you to talk to me like that?"

I take one step closer and I tower over him. "I'm the guy who knows how to treat a woman."

"Well, you certainly don't know how to treat a VIP or my daughter." That's her father, his voice strong, menacing as he cuts in.

But I'm ready for him. I've always been ready for assholes like him. I turn away from Chad Huntington, facing David Snow—the real enemy. Chad is just a figurehead. David Snow is the king on the throne of awful parenting.

No idea if Sabrina's here or not to witness her fantasy. But it's now or never. "You don't get to act like you were some supportive father. You ripped your daughter apart every chance you had, including on her wedding day. And including the *other* day," I say, stalking even closer so he can feel threatened, like he made his daughter feel every damn day growing up. "Do not ever come to *our* house again," I say, going out on a limb with the *ours* because I want my home to be hers as well. "Do not ever set foot on *our* property. And do not ever act like you have a single say in her life. You made her feel like she wasn't good enough," I say, then take a breath, gearing up to give him the full piece of my mind.

But the prick cuts in, hissing: "Who do you think you are to talk to me that way? I paid good money for these seats and to treat our clients. You can't get away with this."

"But I can, and I will. And I will cover the cost of your seats and donate it to charity. You don't scare me. I know men like you. I was raised by a man like you. And you lost out on an amazing, kind, caring woman as your daughter. It's your fault. *Yours.* You don't deserve to be a father. But thanks to you, if she'll have me, I will never stop making sure Sabrina Snow knows how much she is worth—and that's everything."

I take a breath, expecting him to try to butt in once more.

But the next voice I hear is feminine. And as strong as ice. "I believe it's time for you to leave. And don't ever come back."

I spin around as Sabrina delivers the send-off message, like she's heave-ho-ing this pair of assholes and their moron henchmen off the plank.

And maybe I wasn't making it up earlier about the team escorts, since Rowan, and Ford, and Miles and Max, and Wesley and Asher are all right behind me, standing guard, just in case.

"We'll see them out," Miles says in that no-nonsense captain voice of his.

Like a hockey mafia, my teammates—who are pretty much family one way or another—escort them to the exit, while Leighton disappears down the hall, giving us space.

I'm alone with Sabrina in the tunnel before the game. Her lips are parted. Her eyes are shining. She's...speechless, and I fucking love it.

"Did you hear everything?" I ask, my heart beating so fast.

"Every word," she says, like she's drunk on them.

Good. I think I am too. "I meant it all," I say, including the three words I should have said a while ago, but no time like the present.

But the moment shatters before it starts when Everly races down the hall, beelining for me, her shoes clicking loudly. "Did you just kick out our VIPs?"

I can see *my player just caused a PR disaster* in her big brown eyes.

I shrug. "I did, but one of them was a cheating asshole and the other was king of the assholes. So I don't feel bad."

"He was standing up for me," Sabrina says, like she's thrilled to back me up. Like we're a team. "They were honestly pretty awful, and he did the right thing by getting rid of them."

She sounds enchanted, and that's what I was going for.

Everly winces, but then takes a deliberate long breath, as if calming herself. "It'll be fine. I'll spin it. I'll say there was some history. I'll explain that heated words were said, but no one was hurt. That sometimes emotions run high before games. I'll handle it," she says, cool and calm, taking over the potential PR mess.

"Thank you," I say, genuinely grateful because I didn't make it easy for her. "Because I need to handle something else—"

"Time for warmups, boys. Let's hit the ice."

I groan at the sound of Coach's voice and the herd of hockey players thundering behind me. My brother waggles my stick and helmet my way, a look in his eyes that says *time to hit the ice now.*

I grab my gear from him, but turn back to Sabrina, still standing, pressed against the wall in the tunnel. Eyes still sparking with...possibility.

The same possibility I feel down to my marrow.

I'd planned to wait till later, but sometimes you have to shoot your shot when it comes your way.

"I love you, Sabrina Snow," I say, then I hit the ice.

49

A NAIL-BITER

Sabrina

When the second period ends, I'm ready. But in a whole new way. I've never taken the ice with someone backing me up like that.

Someone throwing down for me so clearly, so deliberately.

And so deliciously.

It's a brand-new feeling, this buzzing in my bones, this bubbling through my bloodstream.

When the team's emcee heads onto the rink with her mic, I take a deep breath from my spot in the darkened tunnel. "We're thrilled to have former women's figure-skating national champion and beloved local skating coach Sabrina Snow join us during our intermission."

My heart climbs up my throat at the word *beloved*. Tears threaten to fill my eyes, but I swallow them down, smiling from the center of my soul as I take the ice.

I'm wearing...my Halloween costume.

The one-shouldered, crystal-blue skating dress that made Tyler's jaw drop when he saw it.

I skate to the center of the arena with a stupid smile on my face. I stop, lower my face, and wait for the music to start.

It's a pop song by Amelia Stone. Something the whole crowd knows. But a song Tyler knows too. One we've listened to together in the kitchen. "Only You." The song I wanted to walk down the aisle to. A song that brings me joy.

And as it plays, I fly around the rink, arms spread, ice scraping, cool air rushing past me.

My parents tried. Oh hell, did they try. But they were never able to take my love of this sport away from me.

Now, I'm chasing the moon out on the ice with the strength of an army, it seems, behind me.

And I land every toe loop, every flip, every axel better than I ever have before. I feel like I'm both incredibly strong and utterly weightless.

When I circle the rink, my gaze catches on a row of people behind the boards. *My people.* Isla and Trevyn and Skylar, with Maeve and Josie right behind them. Then Jasmine and her parents. Tiffany and her mom. The head of the rescue, the heating repair woman, and...my fairy godmother.

Ah, what the hell. I give a quick wave to the row of them as I skate backward, faster and faster still. Crossing over, I move around the oval, and when I do, my gaze lands on three more people.

Elle, and the two little people I've fallen in love with. I can't help it—I make a heart just for Luna and Parker.

And they give me one right back.

I skate to the center of the ice as the music swells, then

glide on one leg, spinning in circles. After several, I then tuck my arms in and my knee, lifting my torso straight, whirling faster into a wild blur of a finale.

When I finish, I'm breathless. Electric. Overjoyed. Especially when Number Forty-Four tosses a bouquet of roses from the tunnel, right onto the ice.

I laugh, from happiness, from the thrill of a job well done, and from knowing that even though I didn't see him, he clearly sneaked out of the locker room to watch me.

Like he did that first time.

I feel like I'm glowing from the inside out. Because this man has always wanted to let me shine.

* * *

But there's still another period to play, and hockey games are hard-fought. When the Sabers tie it up, I groan from my spot in the corridor where I'm watching on monitors.

"Seriously?" I say to the screen, wrapping my arms tight around my chest. I'm still in my costume since Everly wanted me to skate at the end of the game if they win and toss crocheted dogs—modeled after the Sea Dogs mascot Scuppers—into the stands along with the team.

They've got to win though.

"C'mon," I mutter as a Sabers forward races toward the net, flicking the puck to a teammate who passes it right back to him a few seconds later, then lines up for a wrister.

In the crease, Max dives for it, stretching across the net, and slapping it out, right to Tyler's waiting stick as he takes the rebound down the ice, flipping it to his brother.

Who barrels toward the Sabers net, as if he's hell-bent on breaking the tie in the final minute.

But the Sabers goalie stops him, and a minute later, the game flips into overtime.

I hold my breath a little longer.

* * *

The puck changes hands so many times in the first four minutes that I consider biting my nails for the first time ever. They're gel, so it'll be tough. But I'm tempted to try. Especially since there's only one minute left till this game goes to a shootout.

I watch by the tunnel, biting my lip, urging on the Sea Dogs as Asher, Wesley, and Rowan battle it out on the ice against the Vegas team, a three-on-three style play. Asher fights for the puck in the corners, passing it to Wesley, but the Sabers goalie blocks the shot. Thirty seconds left, and Miles, Ford, and Tyler hop over the boards, with Tyler tearing down the ice like a cheetah on blades, and in two seconds, he picks it off from the Sabers forward, ferries it down the ice like a man possessed, and flicks it to Ford, who's set up near the goal.

He lifts his stick and wastes no time—the puck whips past the goalie's outstretched arm and lands right in the twine.

Game over!

"Yes!" I shout, and I'm jumping on my skates, cheering so hard as the guys swarm each other in the biggest embrace with Tyler, Miles, and Ford at the center of it all.

And the second—no, the nanosecond—Tyler breaks free, I stop thinking.

I move. Like lightning, pushing past the gate to the ice, rushing out there, racing to my man.

And it's not for the crocheted dogs. It's for Number Forty-Four.

I fly across the arena, right into his waiting arms, and I jump up into them.

"I love you too, Tyler Falcon."

He whips off his helmet. He's sweaty, breathing hard, and he crushes his lips to mine. Him in his jersey, me in my sparkly sequined costume, kissing in front of the whole entire crowd.

I swear I can hear all my friends, and a little boy and a little girl I love cheering for us as we start over.

I never thought I'd have this—a love that's real, a love that's safe, one that's bold and unafraid. But now I do, in the center of the rink, under all the lights, with this man kissing me like I'm his world.

When he breaks the kiss, he says, "You know what this means? You're coming home with me. *Upstairs*. And that's where you'll stay."

"Good. Because I love you," I say again, because I can, because I mean it, and because he's the one for me.

"And I love you so much."

Then he gives me another overtime kiss.

50

SHINE ON

Tyler

With one hand wrapped around her gift, I reach for her palm and we walk back into the rink. All the crowds have filtered out, the crocheted dogs have been thrown, and my kids have gone home with their mom. My teammates and most of the crew have taken off for the night. But before we can truly start over, we need some real talk.

Best to have it here—by the place where we both feel most at home. The ice. It's also where this big love started for me. We walk through the tunnel, past the players' bench, and into the second row, where we sit down.

"We need to talk," I say as I set down the bag with the present.

"We do," she says softly.

I tuck a strand of shiny blonde hair behind her ear. "Have I told you I love you?"

She smiles. "Only a few times."

"Get ready for me to say it over and over again," I say,

but then I clear my throat. "I should have said this sooner —that I love you. I should have said something the other night. Instead, I choked. I shut down because I thought you were shutting down. And I didn't want to be another person who hurt you. I was a dumbass and thought I was being noble. News flash: I wasn't noble. I was a chicken. But I am so sorry I hurt you. I never want to hurt you."

She gives a soft, forgiving smile. "I know that. I think I knew it all along. I just tried to deny it because..." Her smile vanishes. "Everything hurt after my dad showed up."

"Of course it did, baby," I say, stroking her cheek.

"But I should have told you the details, Tyler. I should have told you what was going on. I should have insisted we talk that night. I was just so leveled out from the confrontation that I went into perfectionist mode, and that's not fair to you."

I squeeze her hand. "And I read everything wrong. I thought I was too much for you. With the kids and—"

She squeezes my hand even harder. "You dumbass, I love your kids."

My throat tightens. I roll my lips together, fighting off the swell of emotions. "You do?" Am I dreaming? Is she really saying that?

"Of course I do," she says, her eyes swimming with tears. "They're wonderful little humans. Luna is so outgoing and enthusiastic, so bright and happy, so tough and strong. She's you and Elle. And Parker is serious and surprisingly funny. He's inquisitive and more loving than I'd ever imagined. He's like a cat. And Luna's like a dog. And you know I love animals, and I just love them so much. I love all of you."

I didn't think a moment could be more perfect. But I

was wrong. This is. And I fight like hell to stop the goddamn tears that are threatening to roll down my cheeks. But this woman? She loves my kids. I'm so far gone.

I kiss her so I don't cry. When I find the will to end the kiss, I say, in a hoarse voice, "I'm not letting you go. I want you in my life. I want to build a life with you. Like I told you, I'm nothing but serious, and that's exactly how I feel about you."

"You sure about that?" she asks, playful but also protective. I get it—she's been through a lot. She'd want to be certain.

This is the moment. Where I let her know just how all in I am. "I don't want you to just be my girlfriend. You're my partner—if you'll have me. And, well, Luna and Parker too. We're a package deal, and we all want you in our lives. For real." Then I take a beat, my chest filling with hope but nerves too. Because I know this is a lot. *I'm* a lot. "If you're ready for that."

"You're really not a casual guy, are you, Falcon?"

I laugh, but not for long. "I'm not."

She doesn't make me wait a second more. "I'm yours. And, well, I'm theirs too."

And I kiss her again, with a new sense of...calm coursing through me. For so long, I've honed my focus on my kids, just my kids, figuring big love was for another time in my life. Then Sabrina came along and upended everything I'd thought I could have. Now, I know I can have my family and a love that knocks me to my knees.

I pick up the bag, hand it to her, and say, "Open it."

With curious eyes and a quirk in her pretty lips, she dips a hand in the bag, then gasps. "Tyler, you didn't."

"I did."

With uncommon glee, she takes out her gift—a sparkly tiara.

She hands it to me. "Put it on me."

"With so much pleasure," I say, then set the glittery little crown on her head, adjusting it just so. "Beautiful."

She bobs a shoulder. "I do like shiny things."

"You'll get many, many more," I say, holding her gaze so she gets the full meaning.

"Keep them coming." Then she nods to the exit. "Let's go. Your *partner* is going to have to start working on a whole new list real soon. Like, say, tonight."

I'm up and out of there so fast.

When I reach the corridor I remember something—I snagged a ride here with Miles. "I don't have my car. Do you?"

"I got a ride with Leighton. But don't worry—I've got this."

Fifteen minutes later, Rhonda rolls up in her Prius, pokes her head out the window, and eyes me up and down. "Looks like you're riding that hot daddy."

"Yes, I am," Sabrina says.

And whatever Sabrina wants, she gets.

We hop into her fairy godmother's carriage and ride off into the night.

51

JOB OFFER

Sabrina

"I love...this headboard...so much," I say, as I hold on tight to the cushioned headboard in his bedroom while I ride Tyler's face.

He growls against me, his fingers digging into the flesh of my ass as I grind against him, his whiskery beard scratching my thighs, his tongue rocking my world, his lips devouring me.

No surprise he insisted on eating first. My man is hungry, and I like to make sure he's well fed.

My fingers curl tighter. I rock faster. He plunges deeper. "Oh god," I gasp as pleasure curls inside me, pulsing bright and hot through my cells.

It's like neon's flashing in my mind. Fireworks bursting in my chest. Champagne rushing through my veins.

I have never felt better, and soon I feel so much better still as my vision blurs and I cry out, then shatter into a million beautiful pieces.

Before I can even come down from this blissful high, he slides me down his body, his big hands gripping me hard. "Get on my dick," he commands.

"Yes, sir," I say, then position him right where I want and sink down.

And oh my fucking god. It feels so good. The way he fills me. How he fucks me. And when he grunts and moans. When he shakes and shudders.

And when he sits up, grabs my face, and hauls me close. "I fucking love you," he says, like he's compelled. Like he has to say it.

He punctuates it with a hard, deep thrust, and I lose my mind. Soon, I'm coming again as I ride him passionately, savoring every second, every moment.

Including the second when he tips over with a guttural groan and a long, passionate *yessss*.

I collapse onto him, my breasts pressed to his strong chest, our bodies aligned. He runs a hand down my back. "Like your new bed, baby?"

Which raises a good question. After we clean up and get back in bed, I roll to my side and prop my head in my hand. "So, in the immortal words of *Hamilton*, what comes next?"

He laughs. Probably because he knows the song too. I love that he knows it, even though it's not pop or a kids movie. But then, maybe it *is* a kids musical—almost every young person I know has seen it.

"You," he says simply.

I furrow my brow. "Me?"

He slides a hand down my side to my waist and curls it around me. "I plan on making you come again, baby. Many, *many* times."

I swat his sturdy chest. "That's not what I mean."

He drops a kiss to my nose. "I know," he says softly. Then he pulls back. "I guess we'll need to hire your replacement. Stat."

"What?" My stomach bottoms out. He said he wasn't firing me. But...did he change his mind?

My muscles tighten, but he tugs me closer, his voice instantly reassuring. "Baby, at the start of this year, I paid you through the end of the season. Why don't we find someone to help us out? So you're free to grow your coaching business whenever you want to. So you're not taking on all the parenting. So you..." He presses another kiss to my lips. "Can keep shining." Then he draws a deep breath. "And we can keep taking care of the kids... together. As a family."

Damn him. I swipe a finger under my eyes. They're all wet. "I've always wanted to have a family."

He props himself up higher. "That raises a good question," he says, his tone intensely serious. "Do you want children?"

Oh. Well. We're moving quickly, aren't we? Faster than I'd expected. I push up too, thinking about how to answer him.

But before I do, he holds my gaze with earnest eyes and says, "I'm good with whatever your answer is. Just know that. It's not a test."

My heart stutters. My chest fills with warmth. Acceptance too. "I didn't feel tested," I say, then I pause, gathering my thoughts, wanting to be honest. I tell him the truth. "If I did want more children, I'd want to adopt." Another pause, and I shake my head. "But I think I'm good...just like this. Fostering pets." I sit bolt upright, my chest tightening. "Olive!"

And, because I can, I hustle downstairs naked and grab the foster kitten. A few minutes later, she curls up on Tyler's bed and settles in.

I do the same.

EPILOGUE
THE SUNNYSIDE

Tyler

"So you're what exactly? Partners? That word is so boring," Luna says as she sorts through Lego pieces on the living room table after school on Monday.

Parker furrows his brow as he plucks a tawny piece and slides it on top of another, finishing off a goat. Asher gave him a farm animal sanctuary Lego set recently, and Luna's helping him—it's a rare moment when she likes to do the same things he does. Well, they like to make presentations, I suppose.

He looks up from the goat. "It sounds like you run a bank together," Parker says.

I snort. "We definitely don't run a bank together."

"Partners," Luna says again, with a heavy sigh. She really doesn't like this word. "You don't like boyfriend or girlfriend?"

"I'm not a boy," I point out. "I'm an adult."

"And I'm not a girl," Sabrina adds. "I'm an adult too."

Parker looks up, arching a brow. "Adult friend? Man friend?"

Sabrina cracks up. "We're definitely not doing man friend, woman friend, or adult friend."

"Yeah, those are even weirder, Parker," Luna says, thumping him playfully on the head with a chicken.

He backs off. "Hey, watch it. You're no sister friend."

"Sometimes you're not a brother friend," she points out.

Out of nowhere, a tiny calico jumps onto the table and skids across the pile of Lego bricks, sending pieces scattering across the metal, some tumbling to the floor.

"Olive!" Parker shouts, but then he cracks up when the kitten, in a most cat-like fashion, stops abruptly and proceeds to wash Lego dust off her paw in the middle of the animal sanctuary.

"She understood the assignment," Luna says. Then she looks at the two of us again, holding hands on the couch, telling them we're together and that we're serious about each other. She studies us thoughtfully, then gives a happy shrug. "I guess I approve. It's good enough. Parker?"

He looks up from sorting the pieces. "Yeah. Works for me too."

"Good," Sabrina says with a smile, then leans forward. "There's one more thing I have to tell you."

"We're keeping Olive?" Parker asks hopefully.

"That's not it."

"Fine," he harrumphs.

"Don't you want to save more cats, dodo?" Luna says to him.

"Obviously."

Sabrina waits for them to return their focus to her, then says, "I love you two."

They both snap up their gazes. "You do?" Luna's voice pitches up.

"Really?" Parker's rises too.

"I really do," she says.

And they launch themselves at her on the couch, knocking me toward the arm so they can cuddle up to my...partner. Maybe it is a little dry.

"I love you too," Parker says, hugging Sabrina.

"I love you," Luna seconds, resting her head on Sabrina's shoulder.

When they let go, I'm still noodling on the word. Maybe significant other?

"Are you going to live up here now?" Luna asks as she returns to building a small barn. "Are we getting a new nanny? Who's taking us to school? Will you still coach?"

And I couldn't have asked for a better response—the quick shift from gooey love to practical matters.

We answer the questions, then I circle back to the house one. I glance around the living room. "I was thinking...since this is a rental, why don't we all go home shopping after my next road trip? We can all pick out a house together—for the four of us?"

They all say yes. Then I turn to the brilliant woman by my side. "What about...my better half?"

Sabrina laughs, then shakes her head and kisses my nose. "Call me whatever you want—it's all the same. We're together."

And really, that's all that matters.

* * *

A few weeks later, we venture into our 529th home

viewing. Or something like that. Balancing the opinions of four people is no joke.

Parker wants room for a science lab and a foster kitten room. Luna keeps upping the ante, asking not only for a room big enough for a couple of disco balls, but also for a bigger yard to foster dogs too. I wouldn't mind a weight room, to be honest. A big living room is a must for everyone. We have a huge couch, and we need the space for it and our movie nights, face mask parties, and, well, the mornings when I wake up with cardboard signs on my chest or raccoon eyes on my face. I'd like a big primary bedroom suite, with a huge shower and plenty of room for the emperor bed and the tiny sex diary with our brand-new list. Spoiler alert: I gave her the thing she told me she wanted that day on my couch. She gives it to me too. Our list keeps growing, and that's the way we like it.

Sabrina's the easiest, though, when it comes to houses. She likes, well, almost everything.

But that's her. She's not picky or particular about things. She learned how to make do with her own resilience, her notebooks, and her skates.

That's why I want to find a place where she can do yoga—or where we can do it together—and where she has room for a desk and computer so she can edit her skating videos and run her skyrocketing coaching business.

The video of her at Cozy Valley? It took off and word spread. Her business has picked up even more at the perfect time since she's expanding it to include girls' nights out, couples' lessons, and lessons for adults of any age who want to learn to skate for the first time. *Skate With Joy* is her new tagline, and it's perfect.

When we walk into this home with a sky-blue door in

Hayes Valley, in the heart of the city, not far from the Sea Dogs arena, she shoots me a sly smile.

"Your favorite color," she says.

"Your eyes," I say, then drop a kiss on her cheek.

And my shoulders relax. No more hiding—no more jerking apart. We're free to kiss and hold hands, and that is its own type of lightning.

Once inside, Sabrina takes in the wide-open space like she's drinking it in—the light filtering through, the gleaming surfaces, the blond hardwood floors. Her smile spreads like the morning sun.

Yes, I want everyone to be happy, but most of all, I want this woman to be happy. Because that's what she's done for me.

I hold my breath as the kids race through, then Parker declares it perfect, and Luna, never to be outdone, says it's more than perfect. "There's enough room for our new foster kittens," she says, since we just picked up a pair of tabbies named Frick and Frack.

"Sabrina?"

"I love it," she says, then clasps my hand. "It feels like ours."

"It will be then," I say, and I turn to the realtor and add, "we'll take it."

* * *

"I don't have much for a down payment," Sabrina says to me that night after the kids are in bed. "But I saved most of the money from the ring I sold. I never had to use it to live on. And I invested it—accounting degree and all. So I can contribute."

I tug her close and drop a kiss on her forehead. "I love that you want to."

"I do. I mean it," she insists.

And part of being a good partner, significant other, or what-have-you, is knowing when it's important to say yes.

"Okay then."

But I have a plan too.

A month or so later, Sabrina and I head into the closing for our new home. Yes, we used her down payment, but I told her I'd paid cash for the rest of it. After all, a man's gotta do what a man's gotta do.

When the escrow officer sets down the paperwork, Sabrina's eyes shine, and she whispers, "It's our home now."

"It is," I say, loving that word, so I say it again. "Ours."

But then the escrow officer hands her another set of papers, this one with just her name on it.

"Is this for the same home?" Sabrina asks, confused.

The officer shakes her head, barely able to hold in the secret. "It's not."

Sabrina frowns, turning to me. "What's this for, then?"

"I'll show you," I say.

Twenty minutes later, I lead a blindfolded Sabrina across the parking lot and to the entrance of Sunnyside Rink, the place where she holds all her skating lessons.

When we reach the door, I lift a hand and undo the blindfold. Sabrina looks up with curious eyes.

"Tyler?" she asks, blinking in confusion. "What's going on?"

I don't bother fighting off a smile. "Hank and Marla were ready to retire, so I bought their rink. For you. It's yours, baby. All yours."

Her jaw drops. Her hand flies to her mouth, then falls

just as quickly. "Are you serious?" Her voice is so high-pitched she sounds like Minnie Mouse.

"Sure am," I say, then take out a key from my back pocket—a bright, shiny one with the words *Skate With Joy* engraved on it.

She's always had a key to this rink. But she's never had one with her name on it as the owner.

"Try the key. It's a brand-new one. Just for you."

She looks at the key, then at the paperwork with this address and her name across the top.

She rolls her lips together, her shoulders trembling, but she steadies herself. She opens the door and steps inside, her eyes wide, glassy with emotion.

"It's really mine."

"It's really yours," I say.

And then she throws her arms around me and whispers, "Thank you so much. I love you so, so much."

A beat later, she pulls back, grinning. "Do you want to have that skills competition now?"

"It's a date."

And I take her there that weekend—and many, many more.

Binge the entire Love and Hockey series today!

Want to see how generous, filthy-mouthed hockey star Wesley falls hard for his teammate's little sister? **Grab The Boyfriend Goal Here!**

Max and Everly's enemies-to-lovers, forbidden romance is told in **The Romance Line!**

Asher and Maeve's brother's best friend/marriage of convenience romance is here in **The Proposal Play!**

Miles's forbidden romance with the coach's daughter is here in **The Girlfriend Zone!**

Sign up for my newsletter and follow me on Amazon to be notified when Ford and Skylar's fake dating romance comes out in The Flirting Game. You will also get notified whenever I have a new release!

For more Tyler and Sabrina, click here for an extended epilogue or scan the QR code!

EXCERPT: MERRY LITTLE KISSMAS

Chapter One: Nutcracker Ban

Rowan

Two words that should not go together – nut and cracker. But every November they do and somehow this year I let my teammates drag me to the Nutcracker Auction.

Two other words that don't go together? Christmas and me.

I don't deck the halls, I don't dash through the snow, and I definitely don't rock around trees, Christmas or otherwise. Trees are for oxygen, full stop.

Unfortunately, I can't stop the calendar, or the guys I work with from making me go to this event tonight. But you bet your holiday ass I assured Tyler and Miles I'd watch the clock the whole time. I also promised them I'd have zero fun, but they still insisted I attend. Why have enemies when you can have teammates?

The world's most infernal holiday song blasts over the speakers outside the Resort Hotel, clanging like a warning bell as it signals the start of an endless month of feral festive-ness. I only wish the season were twelve days long.

"What kind of gift even is a partridge in a pear tree?" I ask Tyler and Miles as the tune hits the same line over and over and fucking over again while we head up the garland-lined steps of the hotel in the heart of San Francisco. "And why would anyone want a pear tree? I hate pears."

With an eye roll, Tyler adjusts his Santa hat. "Of course you do."

"Do you hate partridges too?" Miles asks, getting his dig in and adjusting his red tie with illustrations of dogs sporting jingle bells on their collars. "That's on brand for you disliking an innocent little bird."

"No," I grumble. "Birds are cool. It's just pears I take issue with."

"Just pears," Miles repeats with a chuckle. "If you only hated just pears. But I suspect your burn book is as long as Santa's naughty list."

I yank on the brass door. "Is this the beginning of your seasonal wordplay?"

"It's the beginning of Grinch season, isn't it?" Tyler says to Miles — his brother — all while shooting me the side-eye as we head inside.

"Yeah, well if you'd had the Christmases I'd had, you'd be glad I'm only a Grinch."

The reminder of my ghost of Christmas past earns me a sympathetic nod from each of my teammates, but the sympathy only lasts so long.

"That's why you're here with us now, man," Miles says, in an upbeat tone that's par for the course for the guy. He's all about seeing the bright side.

But his comment doesn't add up. "How is that why?" I

ask. "Because you believe in torturing a teammate who'd much rather be home playing board games with his kid than going to a swanky auction where he needs to rub elbows with fancy-ass people?"

"Those fancy-ass people are also known as the sponsors of our team," Tyler points out, unhelpfully.

"Don't remind me. My financial advisor has done that enough," I say.

"And we're here to remind you that Christmas doesn't have to suck," Miles adds.

Ah, so that's their master plan tonight. Too bad I'm all out of holiday fucks to buy what they're selling.

We stride through the disgustingly decorated lobby festooned with wreaths, garlands and twinkling lights, and scented with pine. I bet there's even mistletoe hanging all over the place, just waiting to trick people into thinking romance and Christmas go together. I've got the scars to prove they absolutely do not. "It looks like Christmas threw up in here."

Miles turns to Tyler, exchanging what looks suspiciously like, well, like a knowing look. But neither brother says a word.

"Well it does," I add, needing to make my point with a highlighter, and a Sharpie too.

Tyler sighs heavily. "Rowan, are you really still trying to get us out of taking you to this thing? Because the deed is done."

"Yes! Yes, I am. Want me to read back the transcript of our walk? Allow me to refresh your memory. I'd rather be—"

They cut in and say in unison: "Doing anything else."

I roll the tape in my mind for a few seconds as we pass a waterfall sculpture spewing green and red colored water.

"I don't think I said that exactly, but I believe that encapsulates my feelings."

"Yeah, we got the message loud and clear," Miles says, then turns to his younger brother. "Didn't we, Ty?"

"We sure did," Tyler seconds as we reach the entrance to the auction, a white door with snowflakes etched into the glass. The shiny brass plate next to the door tells me the name of it is actually the Snowflake Room. I stifle a groan.

"But listen, you should bid on something," Miles points out. "The money all goes to charity, and didn't Jason say that was another benefit of you coming here?"

That's Jason Marlowe, my agent, but more so, my best friend since college. Trust him with my career, and, well, my life. "I know. Trust me, I know. But I could donate without attending," I say.

An attendant hands each of us our numbered paddles. I tuck mine into my back pocket.

Time to face the dragon's lair of a holiday party.

I take a fortifying breath. This is no different than fending off savage forwards on opposing teams on the ice. Hell, I prep all day, every day to jostle and elbow and, okay fine, check as many guys into the boards in a game as I possibly can. I can handle my personal hell—three hours of holiday-themed auction items with Christmas music playing the whole time.

Miles pats me on the shoulder. "You've got this, man. I have faith in you."

I furrow my brow. "Niceness will get you nowhere."

Miles rolls his eyes, then darts out a hand, grabbing a candy cane from a silver bowl by the door. "Here you go. Something you like. Plus, it'll shut you up."

Dammit. Candy canes are my kryptonite. I can't resist.

"Fine. I'll take it," I say, then open it and toss the crinkly wrapper into a trash can.

"Good man. Now don't start any fights or throttle any trees. We need to go say hi to our women," Miles says.

"You check out the auction list. We'll catch up with you soon," Tyler adds before they leave.

I wave them off. I've got candy cane company and that'll do for now. I scan the sparkling room, even more glittery than the lobby and decorated with nutcrackers on every surface, even the edge of the stage.

I beeline for the hors d'oeuvres since the one thing I can stand about the holidays is food. I've got zero problem with treats or sweets, and I'm pretty sure there are some of those snowball cookies calling my name.

But I like to window shop first, so I stroll along the table, draped with a white tablecloth with mistletoe illustrations. All manner of sweet and savory treats are spread out here, from chocolate orange ganache cookies to bruschetta with arugula and sundried tomatoes. As I suck on the minty goodness, I ignore the toast points with brie and cranberries, zeroing in on the raspberry thumbprint cookies right next to the punch bowl.

As I make my way to the end of the table, my attention snags on the cardboard folded signs on the table listing the auction items.

A holiday lights tour, chauffeured in a horse-drawn carriage. Pass. No way the horses like that.

Mistletoe installation service to ensure no spot in your home is without holiday romance. Please. I'd rather take a puck to the eye.

Signed memorabilia from the Sea Dogs, including pucks and jerseys from yours truly, the team's most badass defenseman. That's a great gift for anyone, but I can't bid on that and deny a fan.

A VIP suite for a women's pro hockey game. Now, that's cool and maybe worth my bidding on. They play their hearts out in every game.

I squint at the next item. *Find Your Mistletoe Love.*

I snort, then step closer to the placard next to the punch bowl, reading the entry.

Looking for the perfect gift this holiday season? Treat yourself—or someone special—to an exclusive matchmaking package with Cupid's Confidante. With a proven history of creating real connections, Cupid's Confidante will help you find the one who makes your holiday sparkle. Because nothing pairs better than romance and holiday cheer!

I roll my eyes so far that I can probably see the door behind me, then mutter around the candy cane in my mouth, "This is the most pointless thing I've ever seen. Who'd bid on fucking romance?"

A throat clears. A pretty voice, like bells, says, "I would."

I freeze, those two words still hanging in the air like a puck mid-slap shot. I didn't even know anyone was there, let alone someone with a voice that sounds *dangerously* familiar.

I look up, and yep—oh shit, indeed. It's Isla Marlowe. Jason's sister. Waves of lush chestnut hair. Bright blue eyes. Pretty red lips, all glossy and sparkly. A red sweater with a snowflake right across her chest. And the absolute *last* person I expected to see here. The one person I've maybe, possibly, had an irritating, annoying, infuriating crush on for longer than I'd like to admit. Fine, I'll say it – I used to listen to her dating podcast religiously while I worked out, until I realized I was addicted to the sound of her voice, and forced myself to stop a year ago.

I open my mouth to say *hey,* something casual, maybe even cocky, but I forget the candy cane is still there. It launches out with a spectacular *twang* and lands dead-center in the punch bowl.

It floats there, bobbing like a tiny striped shepherd's hook in a sea of Christmas-red punch.

There's a long moment of silent horror as we stare at the bowl, defiled by an unwanted visitor. "Five-second rule, right? I think we're in the window," I ask rhetorically, then grab the ladle lightning-fast, scooping the candy cane out and hunting for a glass to drop it into.

Pretty sure no one saw me, so no harm no foul.

But a slim hand wraps around my wrist. From across the table, Isla tilts her head, stopping me. "Oh no, Rowan! You can't do that. The punch is already ruined."

Before I can think twice, I say, "My mouth doesn't ruin anything, sweetheart."

For a second, her gaze swings to my mouth, but then she snaps her focus back to my eyes, like she's caught herself. She says nothing for a beat as the silence stretches between us. Not sure what she's thinking, but I damn well know what I'm thinking.

And it's a problem.

Since you can't do a damn thing about a crush on your best friend's sister.

Preorder Merry Little Kissmas here!

Want to be the first to know of sales, new releases, special deals and giveaways? Sign up for my newsletter today!

ACKNOWLEDGMENTS

I am incredibly grateful to many amazing people! Big thanks to Lo for holding my hand even when I darted and dodged. You kept me centered and focused and you always do. Thank you to KP for listening and understanding and GETTING IT. Big thanks to Kristy for all your guidance and insight. The story is better because of you. Sharon, you're my hockey goddess and you're stuck with me! Thank you to Rae for your insight into sugar and ice! Huge thanks to Rachel! Wow. You came in at the last minute and you delivered! I could not have finished this without you.

Thank you to Kim for keeping track of it all and making sure the story sang. Thank you to Sandra, Kara, Claudia, Kara and many others!

Thank you Kayti for brainstorming. With deep gratitude to my editors Lauren and Rosemary who make stories shine! Big love to my author friends who I rely on daily — Corinne, Laura, AL, Natasha, Lili, Laurelin, CD, K, Helena, and Nadia, among others.

Thank you to my family for making it all worthwhile.

Most of all, I am so amazingly grateful to you — the readers — for picking this up! I've loved writing this series and I'm thrilled you're enjoying it!

BE A LOVELY

Want to be the first to know of sales, new releases, special deals and giveaways? Sign up for my newsletter today!

Want to be part of a fun, feel-good place to talk about books and romance, and get sneak peeks of covers and advance copies of my books? Be a Lovely!

I've written more than 100 books! **All of these titles below are FREE in Kindle Unlimited!**

The Love and Hockey Series

<u>The Boyfriend Goal</u>

A roommates-to-lovers, teammate's little sister hockey romance!

<u>The Romance Line</u>

An enemies-to-lovers, player and the publicist, forbidden romance!

<u>The Proposal Play</u>

A brother's best friend/marriage of convenience romance!

The Girlfriend Zone

A coach's daughter romance!

The Overtime Kiss!

A single dad/nanny romance!

The Flirting Game!

A neighbors to lovers, fake dating romance!

<u>My Favorite Holidate</u>

A spinoff from this series! Fake dating the billionaire boss!

The My Hockey Romance Series

Hockey, spice, shenanigans and cute dogs in this series of standalones! Because when you get screwed over, make it a double or even a triple!

Karma is two hockey boyfriends and sometimes three!

Double Pucked

A sexy, outrageous MFM hockey romantic comedy!

Puck Yes

A fake marriage, spicy MFM hockey rom com!

Thoroughly Pucked!

A brother's best friends +runaway bride, spicy MFM hockey rom com!

Well and Truly Pucked

A friends-to-lovers forced proximity why-choose hockey rom com!

The Virgin Society Series

Meet the Virgin Society – great friends who'd do anything for each other. Indulge in these forbidden, emotionally-charged, and wildly sexy age-gap romances!

The RSVP

The Tryst

The Tease

The Dating Games Series

A fun, sexy romantic comedy series about friends in the city and their dating mishaps!

The Virgin Next Door

Two A Day

The Good Guy Challenge

How To Date Series (New and ongoing)

Friends who are like family. Chances to learn how to date again. Standalone romantic comedies full of love, sex and meet-cute shenanigans.

My So-Called Love Life

Plays Well With Others

The Almost Romantic

The Accidental Dating Experiment

A romantic comedy adventure standalone

A Real Good Bad Thing

Boyfriend Material

Four fabulous heroines. Four outrageous proposals. Four chances at love in this sexy rom-com series!

Asking For a Friend

Sex and Other Shiny Objects

One Night Stand-In

Overnight Service

Big Rock Series

My #1 New York Times Bestselling sexy as sin, irreverent, male-POV romantic comedy!

Big Rock

Mister O

Well Hung

Full Package

Joy Ride

Hard Wood

Happy Endings Series

Romance starts with a bang in this series of standalones following a group of friends seeking and avoiding love!

Come Again

Shut Up and Kiss Me

Kismet

My Single-Versary

Ballers And Babes

Sexy sports romance standalones guaranteed to make you hot!

Most Valuable Playboy

Most Likely to Score

A Wild Card Kiss

Rules of Love Series

Athlete, virgins and weddings!

The Virgin Rule Book

The Virgin Game Plan

The Virgin Replay

The Virgin Scorecard

The Extravagant Series

Bodyguards, billionaires and hoteliers in this sexy, high-stakes
series of standalones!

One Night Only

One Exquisite Touch

My One-Week Husband

The Guys Who Got Away Series

Friends in New York City and California fall in love in this fun
and hot rom-com series!

Birthday Suit

Dear Sexy Ex-Boyfriend

The What If Guy

Thanks for Last Night

The Dream Guy Next Door

Always Satisfied Series

A group of friends in New York City find love and laughter in this series of sexy standalones!

Satisfaction Guaranteed

Never Have I Ever

Instant Gratification

PS It's Always Been You

The Gift Series

An after dark series of standalones! Explore your fantasies!

The Engagement Gift

The Virgin Gift

The Decadent Gift

The Heartbreakers Series

Three brothers. Three rockers. Three standalone sexy romantic comedies.

Once Upon a Real Good Time

Once Upon a Sure Thing

Once Upon a Wild Fling

Sinful Men

A high-stakes, high-octane, sexy-as-sin romantic suspense series!

My Sinful Nights

My Sinful Desire

My Sinful Longing

My Sinful Love

My Sinful Temptation

From Paris With Love

Swoony, sweeping romances set in Paris!

Wanderlust

Part-Time Lover

One Love Series

A group of friends in New York falls in love one by one in this sexy rom-com series!

The Sexy One

The Hot One

The Knocked Up Plan

Come As You Are

Lucky In Love Series

A small town romance full of heat and blue collar heroes and sexy heroines!

Best Laid Plans

The Feel Good Factor

Nobody Does It Better

Unzipped

No Regrets

An angsty, sexy, emotional, new adult trilogy about one young couple fighting to break free of their pasts!

The Start of Us

The Thrill of It

Every Second With You

The Caught Up in Love Series

A group of friends finds love!

The Pretending Plot

The Dating Proposal

The Second Chance Plan

The Private Rehearsal

Seductive Nights Series

A high heat series full of danger and spice!

Night After Night

After This Night

One More Night

A Wildly Seductive Night

Joy Delivered Duet

A high-heat, wickedly sexy series of standalones that will set your sheets on fire!

Nights With Him

Forbidden Nights

Unbreak My Heart

A standalone second chance emotional roller coaster of a romance

The Muse

A magical realism romance set in Paris

Good Love Series of sexy rom-coms co-written with Lili Valente!

I also write MM romance under the name L. Blakely!

Hopelessly Bromantic Duet (MM)

Roomies to lovers to enemies to fake boyfriends

Hopelessly Bromantic

Here Comes My Man

Men of Summer Series (MM)

Two baseball players on the same team fall in love in a
forbidden romance spanning five epic years

Scoring With Him

Winning With Him

All In With Him

MM Standalone Novels

A Guy Walks Into My Bar

The Bromance Zone

One Time Only

The Best Men (Co-written with Sarina Bowen)

Winner Takes All Series (MM)

A series of emotionally-charged and irresistibly sexy standalone
MM sports romances!

The Boyfriend Comeback

Turn Me On

A Very Filthy Game

Limited Edition Husband

Manhandled

If you want a personalized recommendation, email me at
laurenblakelybooks@gmail.com!

CONTACT

I love hearing from readers! You can sign up for my newsletter today! Find me on Instagram at LaurenBlakelyBooks, Facebook at LaurenBlakelyBooks, or online at LaurenBlakely.com. You can also email me at laurenblakelybooks@gmail.com